Alexander Bothgate

Picturesque Dunedin

Dunedin and its Neighbourhood in 1890

Alexander Bothgate

Picturesque Dunedin
Dunedin and its Neighbourhood in 1890

ISBN/EAN: 9783337366674

Printed in Europe, USA, Canada, Australia, Japan

Cover: Foto ©Andreas Hilbeck / pixelio.de

More available books at **www.hansebooks.com**

PICTURESQUE

DUNEDIN

OR

DUNEDIN AND ITS NEIGHBOURHOOD

IN 1890

*With a Short Historical Account of the City and its
Principal Institutions*

EDITED BY

ALEX. BATHGATE

WITH ILLUSTRATIONS

DUNEDIN
MILLS, DICK AND CO., PRINTERS AND PUBLISHERS, OCTAGON
1890

TO
HIS EXCELLENCY
THE RIGHT HONOURABLE,

THE EARL OF ONSLOW,

GOVERNOR OF AND COMMANDER-IN-CHIEF OF
THE COLONY OF NEW ZEALAND, AND VICE-ADMIRAL
OF THE SAME,
THIS WORK
IS (BY PERMISSION) RESPECTFULLY
DEDICATED
BY THE PUBLISHERS.

CONTENTS.

LIST OF ILLUSTRATIONS.

EDITORIAL NOTE.

The editor desires to place on record his indebtedness to Mr. Hanson Turton, District Land Registrar, Dunedin, for his kindness in obtaining, at no little personal trouble, the information regarding what may be called pre-historic Dunedin, embodied in the introductory chapter. Mr. Turton's well-known ability as a Maori scholar, and the pains which the editor is aware he took in obtaining, and verifying by interviews with many of the older natives of the locality who still survive, the facts there recorded, are a guarantee that the interesting particulars given regarding the original inhabitants of Dunedin are thoroughly accurate and historically correct.

PUBLISHERS' NOTICE.

The Publishers desire to return their most sincere and hearty thanks to Mr Alexander Bathgate for the valuable assistance he has gratuitously rendered in editing this work, and also to Messrs. G. M. Thomson, F.L.S.; G. J. Binns, F.G.S.; N. Y. A. Wales; Professor Salmond, LL.D.; J. Hislop, LL.D.; J. A. Torrance, and G. H. Turton, all of whom have likewise, without remuneration, kindly furnished their respective contributions.

Whilst the scope of the work has been unavoidably altered to some extent since the title " Picturesque Dunedin " was first chosen, and the picturesque aspects of our city and its surroundings have not received the prominence originally contemplated, the publishers feel confident that the work will prove of interest to both the passing visitor and the permanent resident, to the latter of whom it should form a pleasing memento of our Exhibition year.

Dunedin, January, 1890.

INTRODUCTORY.

PICTURESQUE DUNEDIN! Even in this land of the picturesque the fair city of Dunedin may well claim the title. Few cities are more richly endowed with beauty in their natural surroundings. Whether it be viewed from the heights above the town, whence the scene embraces a wide panorama of partially wooded hills of pleasingly diversified contour encircling the land-locked bay, whose blue waters lave its wharves, or from the opposite shore of the harbour, whence are seen the varied buildings closely packed on the lower ground, with the white houses straggling up the hill sides amid embowering trees, it equally charms the eye, and forms a picture of the rarest beauty. Close though the hills stand to the town, and its lake-like harbour, no oppressive sense of seclusion is awakened in the mind of the spectator, for away to the southward the wide breach in their circling ramparts affords a prospect over the heaving waters of the mighty Pacific. Fair though the surroundings of Dunedin be, and always must be, they owe little of their beauty to the hand of man, who has rather hitherto played the part of a destroyer. Five and twenty years ago the hills surrounding the harbour were densely clothed from their summits to the water's edge, by an almost unbroken forest, which has largely disappeared before the axe of the hardy settler. Yet, while the bay has thus necessarily lost beauties which can never be restored, it has gained others from the green pastures and smiling homesteads with which these hills are now studded. The situation of Dunedin is so romantically picturesque, that each of its inhabitants might well bestow upon it the endearing epithet which the residents of the Dunedin of the northern hemisphere never tire of quoting, and call it

"Mine Own Romantic Town."

Yet, though this new Edinburgh is rich in natural attractions, it has as yet none of the romance which adds such a charm to the beauties of the mother town. But who could look for romantic associations in a city whose years do not yet number half a century? Of the history of Dunedin and its neighbourhood before the advent of the white man very little is known. No doubt the giant moa roamed over the flax-clad hills to the southward in days long past, for their remains have been found in close proximity to the present site of the town, and in all probability the huge Harpagornis, a bird of prey which rivalled the fabulous roc of Sinbad, cast the shadow of its mighty wings over the scene as it sailed in circles in the air, watching for some hapless moa chick which had strayed from the protecting care of the mother bird.

Doubtless, also, when the Maori appeared on the scene, these peaceful hills and dales have witnessed many a scene of blood and savage cruelty, relieved, perhaps, by deeds of valour. Little information, however, can now be obtained of those days, but the Maoris tell that the site of Dunedin, or at least its water frontage, was occupied by the Ngatiruahikihiki, the Ngaitaonga, and the Ngatikawariri hapus of the larger sub-tribes of Ngatikuri and Ngatiwairua, which were offshoots from the tribes known as the Naitahu and the Ngatimamoe, and also by the Ngaitepahi, a hapu descended from the same tribes. The native settlement on the site of Dunedin proper, which does not appear to have been very extensive, extended from about where the Post Office now stands, a spot called by the natives Otepoti (beyond which you cannot go), to the Water of Leith (Owheo) embracing in its limits Nga Moana e rua, now the gaol site, and Mataukareao, which was the name for a plot of land lying between the foot of Hanover-street and the Water of Leith. A prominent chief of the district, who lived about one hundred and fifty years ago, was Poho, a chief of the Ngatiwairua, from whom the creek flowing into Pelichet Bay, by the present rifle range, took its name Opoho, which has since been transferred to the neighbouring district. According to the Maor traditions, however, there must have lived at some distant date in the immediate neighbourhood of Dunedin no inconsiderable number of natives, for they speak of a large pah at Anderson's Bay called Puketai, and of a battle fought at Taputakinoi (near the locality now called Half Way Bush), ages ago, as the Maori narrator phrased it. It is a matter of regret that some of the earliest settlers did not obtain and leave on record some of the Maori traditions connected with Dunedin and its neighbourhood, which might have been procured in the early days of the settlement from the older chiefs, for few of those now alive can give much information, while the younger natives, like young colonials generally, seem to have little love or veneration for antiquity. Beyond the facts already given, only a few of the native names are now obtainable, and it may prove interesting to some readers to know some of them. The Maoris appear to have been great geographers, in that they bestowed names on every locality, even though its natural features would in our eyes be of but trivial importance. For example, a small creek near Musselburgh they named Kaikarai; the site of the gasworks, where a swampy creek debouched on the bay, was Kaituna; Hillside had the high-sounding name Ko ranga a runga te rangi; Logan's Point was Taurangapipipi; while Mount Cargill or one of the adjacent hills was Whakaari. The latter name has been preserved in Wakari, which is still applied to the further side of the Kaikorai Valley, though it is often mis-spelt Waikari. This mis-spelling of native names, which is far from uncommon where these have been preserved in our neighbourhood, must often occasion anguish to the soul of the Maori scholar; but even in their garbled form they are generally more euphonious than many of the names bestowed by the European settlers. For instance, Waitati, which should be Waitete, is a prettier name than Blueskin, though the latter name is not devoid of association, for it owes its origin to the fact that the chief of the district, Te Hikutu, who was a chief of the Ngatiwairua and Ngaiterangaamoa hapus, was at the advent of the whalers, an old man very much tatooed, which does not appear to have been at all a universal custom amongst the natives of this district, and from this circumstance the British whalers irreverently dubbed the old gentleman old Blueskin, and the name was subsequently transferred to the locality.

No traditions of any incidents which occurred in the immediate neighbourhood of Dunedin are now obtainable, but as showing what manner of men were the original inhabitants of the site of this now fair city, the story of the fight of Purakanui may be cited, and we may feel assured that similar scenes were enacted where many a peaceful home now stands. Very trivial grounds were sufficient to give rise to a bloody fight, and though the Maori proverb says that "land and women are the causes of all evil," yet even childish differences at times gave rise to bloodshed. This was the case at Katiki (now called Kartigi), near Moeraki, where a bloody battle arose from a boy belonging to one hapu being bullied at play by a boy belonging to another family. Neither were these feuds confined to those who were aliens and natural enemies to one another; for at Purakanui the contestants were brothers, in the Maori language, which probably signified cousins more or less remote. Sir John Lubbock, in his "Origin of Civilization," tells us that it was no uncommon thing for savage races to have no distinctive word for the relationship we now call cousin, and he says that, " Among Aryan races the Romans and Germans alone developed a term for cousin, and we ourselves have, even now, no word for a cousin's son." However, the connection was not ignored, but those standing in such relationship to one another were called brothers. This was the case with the Maoris, so that close investigation must often be necessary before the exact relationship between different individuals can be satisfactorily eluci-dated.

The victor of Purakanui, a chief named Taonga, came from the north on a friendly visit to his younger brothers, Te Wera and Patuki, who may really have been older men than their visitor, for among the Maoris the issue of elder sons were deemed the elder brothers of the children of a younger son, even though they were younger in years. Be this as it may, in the present instance, Taonga adopted a very domineering tone towards his relatives, whose pride was therefore offended to such an extent that Te Wera killed a woman belonging to Taonga's party. After having murdered his victim, Te Wera put to sea with a number of his tribe, and paddling close to the shore whereon Taonga was camped, he showed the latter the body, and after taunting him in Maori fashion, shaped his course to Oamaru, where many of Taonga's people lay. There Te Wera landed, and falling suddenly on Taonga's tribe, took them by surprise, and after slaughtering several of them he returned to Purakanui. Taonga retired to his home, resolved on vengeance, and shortly after he returned to Purakanui at the head of à large party, all eager to wipe out the insult in the blood of the foe. Near Purakanui Bay a small peninsula juts into the sea, beneath the overhanging cliffs round which the railway now winds to Blueskin. At this time the peninsula, which now looks merely picturesque and peaceful was occupied by a strongly fortified pah, called Mapoutahi. Thither Te Wera and Patuki had retired with their followers, no doubt dreaming themselves secure behind the strong palisading which crossed the neck of the peninsula. The attacking party lay a short distance away, and some days passed without active hostilities, for the pa was carefully guarded from within, and its position rendered it well nigh impregnable. But the man of vengeance waited, and his opportunity came. The season was winter, and one wild night, when the snow was falling. Taonga sent one of his men to reconnoitre the movements of the enemy. The scout returned with the report that notwithstanding the inclement weather, the palisade was still guarded, and that he had seen the sentry on the watch moving backwards and forwards. Taonga was so greatly surprised at the intelligence that he proceeded to verify it for himself. As he cautiously approached the pa he at first thought his scout's report was really a correct one, but still he crept closer, and watching keenly he at length perceived that the supposed sentry was nothing but a lay figure made up for the occasion, suspended from a support, so that the wind swayed it to and fro, whereby the appearance of life and movement was imparted. Hastily summoning his men, Taonga led them to the palisade, which they quickly and quietly scaled, and thus gained the interior of the fortress of their foe. A few moments and they were distributed throughout the pa, and the alarm given. Te Wera's party rushed from their huts dazed by sleep and darkness, and fell an easy prey to Taonga and his warriors, who ruthlessly slaughtered nearly every inhabitant of the ill-fated pa, only a few escaping in the confusion by leaping into the sea. When morning broke, the slain, among whom was numbered Te Wera, lay around in heaps, and the victors bestowed the name of Purakanui (heaped up) on the locality, in memory of their

glorious victory.   This bloody event must have happened about
one hundred and fifty or two hundred years ago, for its hero,
Taonga, was the direct ancestor of Te Onetopi (Toby), the chief
of Ruapuki, who is still alive, an old man of about eighty years
of age, and the narrator named four chiefs between Taonga and
Te Onetopi, which places the occurrence six generations back.
What was the number of the slain cannot now be determined,
though the tradition indicates a large one, but it was probably
a hundred or two at the most.

The Maoris appear to have been somewhat of a migratory
habit, wandering over the country as the search for food supplies
or the lust of bloodshed led them.   Tribe after tribe came from
the north looking for fresh fields of conquest, and the last of
these were the Ngitahu, from whom with a small admixture of
the Ngatimamoa, their immediate predecessors, the present
remnant of the natives of Otago are descended.   As to what led
to the withdrawal of the original inhabitants of the site of
Dunedin from its neighbourhood tradition is silent.   But that
they did so is undoubted, for the old whalers tell us that there
were no natives living here when they first visited the Otago
Heads.   It is possible that the advent of the whalers themselves
upon the scene may have led to the withdrawal of the last of the
Maori residents of Dunedin, by attracting them to the various
points along the coast where whaling stations were located.
The allurements of the many luxuries brought by the pakehas
in the shape of iron tools, blankets, and tobacco, must have
proved a strong magnet to draw the vagrant Maori, and one of
sufficient potency to lead them even to sink their intertribal
differences.   According to Mr. Haberfield, a hale and intelligent
old man, now resident at Moeraki, whose reminiscences would
doubtless form an interesting chapter of our early history, there
was a population of between two and three thousand natives at
Otago Heads in the early part of 1836, when he first arrived there,
but there were none of them who resided up the harbour.   Round
the coast at Purakanui there was another settlement, numbering
some 500 souls; and Mr. Haberfield says he has seen as many
as a dozen large double canoes at one time off Otago
Heads.   Contact with the white man quickly proved disastrous
to the Maori, who succumbed to the influences of incipient

civilization and the diseases which followed in its train. Measles proved the most deadly scourge, and carried off the natives by hundreds. It must have been a stirring life that of these old whalers, full of excitement and adventure. A mere handful of white men surrounded by a large population of such stalwart and warlike savages as the Maoris then were, must have had plenty of food for anxiety, if at all of an anxious turn of mind. But no doubt this latent danger, as well as the actual perils of their calling, merely added a zest to the enjoyment of life by those young sea-dogs. It was not the chance of making money that was the attraction, for even with a good take their money remuneration would not amount to a large sum in a season. The "lay" might appear a fair one, but as it was calculated on the value of the oil at the station, and not on the market value at Sydney, the owners fared much better in the distribution of the proceeds than did the whalers who risked their lives in their procurement of them. In order to lessen their dangers from the natives, who might have been tempted to kill the goose for the sake of its golden egg, and rifle the storehouse of its treasures, it was the practice to enlist a number of the most important young men in their enterprise; at least three out of each boat's crew, who put off in pursuit of the giant cetacean were Moaris of blue blood. The young chiefs took kindly to the exciting sport, and proved expert boatmen in the chase of the sea monsters, and were, without their knowledge, hostages for the good conduct of their kindred on shore. For the cooper and carpenter, and those of the pakehas who were left ashore, could communicate with their comrades at sea by hoisting a signal of distress on their flagstaff, if any indication appeared of an intention on the part of the natives ashore to take advantage of the absence of the majority of the whites to resort to violence.

Mr. Haberfield says that at the time of his residence at Otago Heads, the only residents at the head of the bay, where Dunedin now stands, were wild pigs, descendants from those turned loose by the illustrious navigator Captain Cook. But shortly before the advent of the pilgrim fathers of the Province of Otago at Dunedin, whose doings and history are recounted later on, one or two white settlers were attracted to the scene from other parts of the Colony by reports of the proposed settlement, but they were so few and their occupation of the locality before the arrival of the first shipment of old identities was so brief, that one may say that these sturdy pioneers really formed their homes in an unpeopled wilderness. High though the hopes of these early settlers were, not one of them can have been so sanguine as to imagine that little more than forty years would reveal such a city as the Dunedin of to-day. The history of the settlement, and also an account of some of the most interesting features of Dunedin and its neighbourhood, will be found in the following pages; but it may not be out of place to take a cursory glance at the fair city which has arisen in the few short years which have elapsed since the foundation of the settlement. When one looks along the well formed streets, with their substantial buildings, filled with shops replete with all the requirements and luxuries of civilized life, and notes the evidences on every side of the energy of the Anglo-Saxon race, it is hard to realise that its site has so recently been wrested from the wilderness. The telephone wires forming a network overhead, the cable trams conveying their loaded cars up the steepest gradients, and other recent triumphs of human ingenuity, all speak of the activity and capacity of its inhabitants. Nor are there lacking evidences of other than material progress. Churches abound, of all denominations, some of them of no mean order of beauty. We see from the spacious district schools dotted over the city, the picturesquely situated Boys' High School and substantial University buildings, that education is not neglected. Our Art Society, with its annual exhibitions, our Flower Shows, our Athenæum, our musical societies, and our scientific and literary institute, all tell that opportunities of culture and refinement are not wholly lacking. Facilities for mutual assistance and friendly intercourse abound in our Masonic lodges, Friendly Societies, and other institutions. In short, we possess all that could be looked for in a community of some 40,000 souls, situated much nearer to the world's great centres of life and civilization, and Dunedinites have no need to be ashamed of their town, or to apologise for its youth, while of its beauty of situation they may justly be proud. In conclusion, we would ask if so much has been accomplished in less than fifty

years, what may not be expected when Dunedin attains its
hundredth anniversary? If the next generation of Dunedinites
inherit the spirit of our fathers, we may safely answer, a city as
great as it is now beautiful.

HISTORICAL.

THE idea of the promoters and founders of the settlement of Otago was to make it as far as practicable representative in its character. Its inhabitants, institutions, localities, and towns were mainly to be derived from and identified with Scotland. To a large extent this was carried out down to a recent period; hence Otago is often called a Scotch settlement. The name of its chief town or city is itself indicative of this—Dunedin, a word of Gaelic origin, signifying "the face of the hill," or "a knoll on the hillside," which in former times was frequently applied to the Scottish metropolis. Hogg, the Ettrick Shepherd, was particularly fond of using the name in his poems.

> Dunedin, thy skirts are unhallowed and lone,
> And dark are the rocks that encircle thy throne;
> The dwelling of beings unbodied is there,
> There are spirits abroad, let the traveller beware!

This in many respects is descriptive of the early condition of the subject of this sketch.

Several names were suggested for the capital of Otago, such as New Edinburgh, Edina, and Chalmers, in honour of the great divine who occupied the foremost position in the Free Church of Scotland. Fortunately, the choice fell on the name it now bears, it being more descriptive of the physical appearance, as well as in itself suggestive. Instructions were also given to the chief surveyor to name the streets pretty closely after those in Edinburgh, which accounts for the similarity obtaining within the original boundaries, though this arrangement has been completely abandoned in the extensive additions recently made by reclamation. The present appearance of the city, as regards limits and conformation, gives but a slender indication of what the town was about thirty years ago.

Taking first a view of the limits. The total area of the town as first surveyed was nine hundred acres.

On the landward sides there have been no alterations in the boundary, as the Town Belt completely prevents such a thing taking place in that direction. Seaward, or properly speaking, along the foreshore, the changes and extensions are very marked and extensive. Starting from the southern point, at the junction of Anderson's Bay Road with Princes-street, the water of the bay naturally stretched inward, covering the Market Reserve until restricted by Market-street and Manor-place, till Princes-street was again reached. From this point the shore-line continued in a pretty straight course to Jetty-street, then inclining inwards to where the Colonial Bank and Custom House now stand. Practically, it may be said that Princes-street from High-street southward constituted the eastern boundary; all the sections fronting the water having been reserved for wharfage purposes. Then trending along the base of Bell Hill round the Jail and Stuart-street, the tide again made an inroad, its waves lapping the line of Great King-street, and sometimes even George-street, receding again round Athol-place. The line of Pelichet Bay may almost yet be traced by the Wharves' and Quays' Reserve on to the furthest extremity at St. Abb's-place, little changes having been as yet effected in this direction.

Take now a view of the surface. From Moray-place northward and down to the water's edge was a flat piece of land, in some places swampy and dotted all over with flax, fern, tutu, and lawyers. It was a good forenoon's work to struggle along the surveyor's line to the Leith and again return to High-street. Popularly, this flat was known as the Swamp, although there were redeeming features, as along the banks of the Leith and for several chains on the town side of it there was a splendid forest of timber, which made that portion a coveted spot, and the sections were soon bought up.

In the front of the town stood Church Hill, afterwards known as Bell Hill, because on it the first alarm tower was erected, flanked by an old ship gun. Although only attaining a height of 113 feet above high water mark, Nature intended it to adorn and beautify the town; but other objects were in view, so its reduction was decreed. How much more useful and ornamental would that eminence have been to the city in its original condition than it now is!

The streets were as far as practicable laid off at right angles. Of course in some instances, from the steep and broken nature of the ground, this rule had to be departed from. The number of streets laid off was about sixty, several being over a mile long, and the length of the whole close on thirty miles, each street being a chain wide. About the centre of the town an octagonal piece was laid off as a reserve to be kept for increasing the attractions of the place, and not to be built on. Notwithstanding the precautions taken to keep this piece of land sacred for public uses, an insidious attempt was made by Land Commissioner Mantell to alienate it from its original purpose and hand it over to the Bishop of New Zealand for the exclusive use of the Anglican Church. So soon as the secretly-devised scheme was discovered, a meeting was held, and a representation made to the Governor of this flagrant attempt at a breach of faith on the part of his subordinate, and fortunately the protest was made in time, as initiatory steps had been taken to have the necessary documents prepared to validate the illegal gift. The return mail brought the satisfactory reply that all proceedings had been stopped. To show that it was not from animosity or ill-feeling the interdict was applied for, the prime movers offered to contribute liberally so as to purchase sections in an approved locality for the use of the Church. This Land Commissioner on other occasions showed by his conduct a spirit very inimical to to the settlers and injurious to the settlement.

Other smaller reserves for special purposes were also set aside, but the non-building restriction was not applied to them.

Reference has been made to the Town Belt, the landward boundary of the city, and by far the most important recreation ground. To those unacquainted with the colony it will be necessary to explain that the "Belt" was a wise provision made, not only as regards Dunedin, but also in the cases of several of the towns of the colony, whereby a wide strip of land, as far as practicable circumambient, was laid off and reserved inalienably as a public park or recreation ground for the use of the inhabitants. In the case of Dunedin, as has already been shown, the Belt did not encircle the town, because the waters of the bay intervened; but the Belt as it existed has ever been carefully watched over by the residents, and so tenaciously have their rights been adhered to and maintained, that even when two small portions, consisting of not over an acre in each case, were temporarily appropriated, one for an Observatory and the other for a Fever Hospital, not a stone was left unturned until both were removed and the sites thrown open to the public. An attempt was also made at one time by the City Council, when Corporation finances were at a low ebb, to lease the Belt in sections for the purposes of revenue and improvement, but so strong was the feeling of the populace adverse to the proposal, that although the leases had been offered and sold by auction, the contracting parties were obliged to abandon the transaction under threat of legal proceedings. It is true all the cemeteries for the town and city have been taken from the Belt, and exceptional excuses may be pleaded for this concession; but when it was proposed a short time ago to increase the size of the Northern Cemetery by including another piece of the Belt adjoining, and of no present value, the opposition was so great that the Legislature refused to sanction the alienation.

The Belt contains 500 acres, and added full one-half to the area of the town, and is now under the control and management of the City Council, although it does not absolutely belong to the citizens, but is the property of purchasers or owners of land within the original Otago Block. From a hygienic point of view, the value of this Belt to Dunedin cannot yet be appreciated, as there is always an abundance of pure air around; but so soon as the smoke from thousands of workshops arises from the lower parts of the city, (and the time is not far distant), the residents will bless the day such a wise provision was made for the health and enjoyment of the population.

Flagstaff, with its associate Silver Peaks that heave their darkling heads aloft, and oft-times

Wear their caps of snow,
In very presence of the regal sun,

form a fine background, environing the city so as to render it impregnable to an invading force. These grand ramparts, Saddle Hill, Chain Hills, Silver Peaks, Flagstaff, Pine Hill,

Cargill, Signal, and Goat Hills, form a bulwark which renders Dunedin unassailable by a land force, and the approaches by water could be easily guarded. Formerly, an old honeycombed gun from on board a stranded ship, having been placed on top of Bell Hill, was sufficient to repel any whale-boat or ship's boat attempting to invade the security of the inhabitants, and, in addition to this formidable weapon, all the male inhabitants were sworn and banded together to defend their hearths and homes against any intruder. Half-a-dozen sailors from an American whaler knew this to their cost when they attempted to disturb the serenity of the locality by boisterously singing songs and otherwise misconducting themselves, in 1848, who were forced ignominiously to retreat before the special constabulary.

The view which the site of Dunedin and its surroundings presented to the beholder from the bay before the theodolite touched the soil, was truly magnificent. Nature displayed herself in her most gorgeous attire. The attraction lay not alone in the wild mountainous scenery already alluded to. There was something more exquisite still to admire. From the shore brink up to and over the lower ranges inland, and stretching east and west as far as the eye could encompass, was one great ocean of forest, over whose vast expanse not one break could be seen. The contour of the land was plainly traceable, now rising up to the ridge top, again descending to the valley below, with interminable undulations, but nowhere could the most experienced eye or powerful telescope descry a glade from which an observation could be obtained. This enormous vegetable carpet did not, however, weary the eye with a continuation of sombre shades and dismal hues; it sparkled with colour, bright, distinct, blended. Shades and tints were everywhere noticeable. The tall-growing pines, towering here and there above their fellows, looked like raised work on the otherwise smooth surface, whilst the vestal purity of the flowers of the clematis peering forth from the uppermost growths of the lesser trees, looked like coy maidens glorying in life's sunshine. There, arrayed in colours equal to those of the rainbow in number, the foliage of the enormous varieties of trees and shrubs formed a groundwork which to the appreciative eye was a source of joy, which now to realize would require a visit to some primeval virgin forest of New Zealand.

It was no easy task to penetrate the shades which these pristine tenants threw over the solid earth, for here, there, and everywhere, entwined and entangled, were supplejacks and lawyers, barring all progress, without the assistance of a tomahawk or by paying the penalty of leaving a piece of raiment or skin as a forfeit. "How far have you got to-day?" was wont to be a question. "Nearly a mile," was the satisfactory reply; and he was a very good bushman who in those days would blaze a track of one mile in eight hours.

Underneath this dense and ponderous foliage there were other vegetable products, lower in the scale, but amply repaying any labour, inconvenience, or suffering needful to learn their history. First lay prone some of the forest monarchs whose heads aspired during their lifetime far above their fellows. Totara, red, black, and white pines, had ·in their dotage sought the shelter of mother earth, and now their trunks, dead enough in themselves, are clothed with a new life, a wonderful vegetable existence, living in shadow, dying in light. And as attendant mourners over their departed greatness, shrubs small in stature but striking in their growth, foliage or blossom, combining with the tree ferns in all their characteristic elegance, cast a feeling over the mind of the reflective beholder, that while death is a pervading element, other life follows close or accompanies it.

In those wooded dells, along whose depths the burnie flowed, gathering volume and strength from each rill which trickled down the hillsides at frequent intervals, and particularly lurking in and about some rocky crannie, on the margins of these streams, a world of wondrous variety of ferns, lycopods, and mosses were to be obtained, which amply repaid any toil or difficulty in securing them. Perhaps no space in New Zealand of equal size contained such a profusion of vegetable products, from the stateliest timber tree, always excepting the giant kauri, down through all the grades to the minute filmy fern and moss, as did that contained within the site of Dunedin and its immediate vicinity.

The denizens of the forest were not numerous. The wild pig, an intruder, was the only animal of value, and early

Dunedinites had rare fun in hunting him up Maclaggan-street and towards the Leith. The native rat, as voracious and destructive as his successor, the Norwegian, and the poor little harmless lizard, now nearly extinct, were the only quadrupeds.

The birds were plentiful and various in species and families, from the little Wax Eye, Tauhou (Zosterops), the sprightly Wren (Xenicus), the homely Robin (Petroeca), the fantastic Fantail, Piwakawaka (Rhipidura), the gregarious Ground Lark, Pihoihoi (Anthus), the familiar Kingfisher, Kotare (Halcyon); then the Parson Bird, Tui (Prosthemadera) with its white feather bands dangling from its throat, the best of our mimics, but very averse to being confined; along with the Bell Bird, Moki (Anthornis) pealing forth its rich notes through the woody depths, responded to by the faint "coo" of the Wood Pigeon, Kuku (Carpophaga), which in greatest wonderment at the noise, made no attempt to fly any distance to be out of range of the fowler; the Paradise Duck, Putangitanga (Casarca), the drake adopting curious stratagems to direct attention from his brood of young; the Grey Duck, Parera (Anas), the most appreciated of native birds for the table, flocked plentifully around; the Wattled Crow, Kokako (Glaucopis), which selected Mount Cargill as a favourite residence; and relieving the watches of the night the Laughing Owl, Whekau (Athene), which has altogether disappeared along with its principal staff of support, the native rat, and its smaller relative the Morepork, Ruru, with which every early settler was so familiar from its peculiar cry which conferred on it its name, as well as from its occasional habit of sharing his residence; the since proved destructive Parakeet, Kakariki (Platycercus), and Kaka (Nestor) had not then the grain or fruit which civilization introduced to feed on and destroy, revelled on the insects· and blossom designed for them by Nature; a lone Heron, Kokuku (Ardea) in its snow-white plumage might be seen diligently fishing for eels or other small fish on the sedgy streams, whilst the Woodhen, Weka (Ocydromus) with its thievish propensities willingly appropriated whatever attracted its notice, and earned for itself the reputation of being the connecting link between the bird and the mammal, a rudely formed notion having arisen that there were no male birds, the hens dropping sucklings; and then of more honest disposition the Swamp Turkey, Pukeko

(Porphyrio), with its red shanks and bill, occupied another position; and bringing the list to a close, another connecting link, not certainly so wide, was found in the Ground Parrot, Kakapo (Stringops), which scientists hold to connect the Owl and the Parrot, was wont to be plentiful; and these also roamed at freedom the almost wingless Kiwi (Apteryx), which runs like an ostrich, and by striking the ground with its foot brought up the worm on which it desired to feed. And last and greatest of all was the Moa (Dinornis), who stalked around in imperial majesty; and although having ages ago quitted this sublunary sphere, anticipating incredulity as to presence, laid himself peacefully to rest on the banks of the burn which trickled down from the hill and flowed through the South Recreation Ground, and when his bones were in 1864 unearthed, and carefully collected by Alex. Begg, then curator for the Botanic Gardens; now in proof the·complete skeleton is exhibited in our museum.

On the 27th November, 1847, the ship John Wickliff sailed from London with Captain Cargill, the official agent, and 90 immigrants, and on the same day the ship Phillip Laing sailed. from Greenock with the Rev. Mr Burns and 236 immigrants; the Wickliff arriving at Otakou on 23rd March, 1848, and the Phillip Laing on the 15th April following. The weather was extremely fine, and the surroundings being enchanting, the great majority of the new arrivals were highly satisfied with the place and with their prospects. The male portion were first conveyed to town principally by boats, but a few of the more adventurous preferred to try their skill in penetrating the dense bush that intervened between Koputai or Port Chalmers and their future home. All arrived safely and soon busied themselves in making preparations to accommodate the women and children, either in barracks or in roughly built huts, and in about three weeks this was satisfactorily accomplished, and the nucleus of the future community thus formed. A spirit of indomitable resolution pervaded the whole company, and each vied with the other in their efforts to promote the settlement.

Arrangements were soon completed for enabling those entitled to select their sections, and the first choice made was that corner of Princes and Rattray streets, on which the Bank of New Zealand now stands. Following this, selections were made in different directions from Manor-place to the Leith, just as the taste or judgment of the party indicated. Immediately all available labour was directed to building, clearing, and fencing. The work of street formation, being in the hands of the Resident Agent, was from various causes not carried on so energetically as was desired, and this became a subject of common complaint. As a proof of the energy and enterprise exhibited, the church and school were erected and opened on the first day of September. As further evidence of the vitality of the small community, a newspaper, the "Otago News," made its first appearance 13th December of this year, having at its start a fortnightly issue, subsequently coming out as a weekly, and surviving until the 20th December, 1850, when the ninety-first number announced itself as "the last of its race," and bade its readers a "sad farewell." The little paper was characterized by a vigorous outspoken style. Holding views differing from those of the large majority of the settlers, it did not hesitate to express them, in one or two instances thereby causing deadly offence. So strong was the dislike to the opinions of the little paper, and so great was the fear that its so-called misrepresentations would do incalculable injury to the growth of the settlement by retarding or diverting the influx of immigrants from the old country, that it was determined to withdraw all support and start an opposition journal. The main points which constituted the offence were the persistent attacks made on the distinctive principle of a class settlement, and the repeated assertions that the soil and particularly the climate were such as to prevent all hope of ever being able profitably to grow cereals, particularly wheat, so that the energies of the people would require to be directed to stock raising and wool-producing, which would not employ a large population. Serious enough was this estimate of the capabilities of the settlement, long since disproved, but whether deserving of such severe punishment may be open to question. There can be no doubt the proprietor, editor, printer, and publisher of the "News," for he held all these positions in his own person, had at the starting of his paper a very high estimate as to the land of his adoption, judging by the motto which he selected for his paper : "There is pippins and cheese to come."

For the period ending 31st December, 1848, the public revenue, exclusive of land sales, was £909 10s 7d, the expenditure being £659 4s 9d; and according to the census taken on the 31st March, 1849, twelve months from the first arrivals, the population of Dunedin consisted of 240 males and 204 females, a total of 444; the births having been 25, the deaths 9, marriages 8. The buildings erected were 46 in clay, battens, fern-tree, and poles, 41 in wood, 5 of grass and poles, 5 of poles and logs, 2 of bricks, and none in stone; the total being 99, and the estimated cost of the whole £6102. The householders numbered 102, there being several joint-holders. Facilities for commerce were limited to a wooden jetty abutting on a stone pier at Jetty-street, equipped with a crane equal to three tons weight; and Princes-street for a distance of about 400 yards from the foot of High-street was metalled, so as to connect with the jetty. There was also a metalled footpath, 110 yards long, leading from Princes-street to the church and school.

There were also at this date two hotels for the accommodation of travellers, a branch of the Hand and Heart Lodge of Odd-fellows, a Building Society, and Cricket Club. The first anniversary was celebrated by a regatta, horse races and rural sports; whilst the more staid and sedate commemorated the event by services in the church both fore and afternoon.

A quotation from a writer of the period will be appropriate.

"As pioneers and founders of a new colony, the world has "a right to demand the benefit of our first year's experience; "more particularly those intending to be settlers who are anxiously "waiting for disinterested information from parties already "settled. . . . The principal part of the houses at present are "built between two small hills in Princes-street, which runs in a "continuous line from north to south of the town. The unevenness "of the ground, although it may render it more picturesque, "unfits it in some respects for business purposes, and no doubt "as the number of inhabitants increases, the main body of the "town will lie towards Pelichet Bay and North East Valley, on "what at this time presents the appearance of a swamp; but a "few good drains would carry off all surface water and leave fine "level sites for building purposes. The small hills at the back "will form delightful spots for crescents and villa residences,

"affording a prospect of the bay and the town, with a peep at
"the ocean beyond.

"Below may be seen the edifice set apart for a church and
"school, a plain wooden building with a library attached, the
"manse, and Capt. Cargill's residence, neat mansions of wood
"towards the south end of the town, with small gardens; Mr
"Valpy's house forming a conspicuous object, but not a very
"pleasing one in point of architecture; the principal surveyor's
"house, on a small rising ground, with its fanciful verandah,
"a confused cluster of houses round the Commercial Inn and the
"Royal Hotel; these are some of the most prominent objects in
"the picture of the town. Here and there, too, dotted among the
"houses, may be seen the painted tops of gipsy-like tents, or
"the more rustic dwellings of clay and grass, peeping from amid
"a bower of trees. There is a police magistrate, two physicians,
"one solicitor, three merchants, two butchers, two bakers, five
"shoemakers, one tailor, and several storekeepers, carpenters,
"and sawyers."

Passing from the more material features of the infant town
to those of a more intellectual character, as was to have been
expected from the foundation of the settlement, provision for
religious instruction was at once attended to. Working plans,
windows, doors, and other fittings for a church were brought out
in the "Philip Laing," and no time was lost in getting the building erected. The most imposing position in the town, where the
First Church now stands, was the site first selected; but the
church was not, however, placed there, but close down to the
water's edge, at the rear of the Standard Insurance buildings.

On the first Sunday after his landing, the Rev. Mr Burns
preached to the assemblage in the forenoon, and the Rev. Mr
Creed, Wesleyan missionary for the district, discharged the same
duty in the afternoon, an excellent friendly feeling subsisting
between the two parsons. Although Otago was essentially a Free
Church settlement, sectarian bigotry was not practised, and as there
was a good number of members of the Episcopal Church within its
bounds, it was natural to expect that provision would soon be
made for holding service according to their particular form.
Accordingly, on the last Sunday of January 1849, the first congregation of that body met and service was held in the jail, and

intimation was given that public service would commence at the same place each Sunday at 11 a.m. The associations connecting the building and its designed purpose with that to which it was thus appropriated, do not appear very congruous, but in those early days people were obliged to put up with strange bedfellows and not be over nice in many particulars. The building was tenantless as a prison.

The library too was prosperous. The books, although not numerous, were select, each one worthy of a place, and so as to facilitate their distribution, the plan was adopted of sending monthly selections to the more remote settlers, who were thus saved the toil and expense of a weekly journey into town. Popular lectures were also instituted, most of the shining lights contributing their quota to the general diffusion of knowledge. And in addition to local talent, more experienced colonists (among others Mr, now Sir William, Fox and Mr J. E. Wakefield) were introduced from the north to illume somewhat the obscurity of the future.

For the proper arranging of these lectures, it was necessary that some particular body should be liable, and naturally and properly it fell to the lot of the Mechanics' Institute to come to the front. This Institution, which had an early start in the community, was steadily growing in importance and influence, and was able, by voluntary subscriptions, to erect a hall where the Cargill Monument now stands, which in its day did good service in different directions. The building itself had wooden walls and shingle roof, and in design was of Doric architecture, the size being forty feet square, and its holding capacity about two hundred. Used at first as a lecture and reading-room, it was subsequently utilized for holding the meetings of the Provincial Council, Law Courts, public meetings, and Town Board. Afterwards used as the location of the branch of the Oriental Bank; then as the chambers of a firm of solicitors, both members of which now occupy seats on the Bench in our supreme judicature; next transformed into a meat market; it was at length swept away to make room for other requirements.

Lighter entertainments were also provided to relieve the tedium and monotomy of existence. Occasionally concerts were got up, and in the absence of professional performers, volunteers were not awanting, and as a matter of course their efforts were rewarded with rapturous applause. Less seldom, too, a ball or dance was quietly organised, which tended largely to assunge the longings of the youth for more excitement and amusement.

More serious affairs, however, were not overlooked. Taking a foremost position was the regulations for hours of labour. To the settlers in Dunedin is the credit and renown due of being the first community in the British dominions where eight hours was acknowledged and established as a fair and adequate time during which the labourer and artisan should work for his hire. A few of the more niggardly employers were opposed to the rule, and in this they were supported by the General Agent of the New Zealand Company at Wellington, who, when asked to make the system operative among his employés, replied that their brethren in Wellington worked longer hours. In spite of this opposition the indomitable pluck displayed by the true friends of the workman prevailed, and before the first year of the existence of the settlement had passed over their heads, the eight hours system of labour was an established fact. Less fortunate was the attempt to limit the lowest rate of wages for labour to three shillings a day. The price was ridiculous. No man in the colony for eight hours' work should receive less than twice this amount, but at the time the rulers were squeezing down to half-a-crown! a feat they did not accomplish, for with an expansion of trade and increasing numbers, the honourable employers took up all honest labour at much higher figures.

Possibly the question may be asked, From whence did the early settlers obtain their supplies of life's necessaries? In the first place the ships brought out extra supplies supposed to last for twelve months, and then from the neighbouring settlements of Nelson and Wellington, flour and potatoes could be obtained until the land enabled them to supply themselves. Then as to fresh beef and mutton, Mr John Jones's station at Waikouaiti was within easy communication, and there were some "auld Scotchmen" in possession of the place before the settlers arrived, who had a few sheep and bullocks to sell; and moreover the harbour was well stocked with fish.

A few of the early settlers spoke and wrote rather doubtfully as to the wisdom of placing Dunedin where it stood. Some thought the chief town ought to have been at Port Chalmers; another small coterie asserted that the distinction should have been conferred on the Clutha district; the majority, however, heartily approved the choice. Unfavourable comments were also made by the newspapers in the neighbouring settlements as to the character of the community. Nelson and Wellington were particularly pointed and venomous in their remarks. "The inhabitants" were represented as being "poor, characterized by "inertness or laziness in their proceedings; that having seen the "harbour with its bar, its squally gusts, its steep precipitous "shores, the town with its surrounding wilderness of hills, and "the Taieri with its formidable swamp, the judgment which "would inevitably be pronounced as to the capabilities of the "place would be unfavourable in the extreme."

Against these malign remarks the more sanguine in their expectations pointed with satisfaction to the utterances of the Bishop of New Zealand and Governor Grey, both of whom said that a man must see every settlement in the colony before he could know and appreciate the advantages of Otago, and also to the fact that the new arrivals had of course the option of choosing where they liked, and yet all of their own accord, with two exceptions, selected their quarter-acre sections in Dunedin. Again, the settlers on the rural land, all but four, had gone to the Taieri instead of the Clutha, not because it was better land, but as it was nearer a town and market. Nay, even one landed proprietor who went to the Clutha district, returned, finding life there but a Robinson Crusoe affair after all.

At the outset the settlers were rather dismayed by seeing the announcement in a Wellington paper of April, 1848, to the following effect :—

"Mr Strode proceeds to the Otago settlement for the "purpose of swearing in three or four gentlemen as Justices of "the Peace, and Sergeant Barry with four privates of the "mounted police are likewise under orders for the same "destination."

This was, indeed, a projected farce, which happily for the reputation of the "authorities" was never carried out, as Mr Strode arrived as chief of the police, with a half-caste Maori as his only assistant. The idea of sending an organised semi-military force to maintain the peace where disturbance was unlikely to be known, was only equalled in its absurdity by some of the later performances. A vaunting display of officialism seems to have been the pervading idea of the "authorities" in Wellington, and in subsequent details instances of this will be given. The chief constable had very soon afterwards an addition made to his dignity by his appointment as Resident Magistrate and sub-treasurer, and the genus Justices of the Peace so grew apace, that in a short time it consisted of one J.P. for every twenty of the whole male inhabitants.

To solace the remaining portion of the residents, and to give a stamp of authority to the action of the officials, in February, 1850, the "authorities" in Wellington generously proclaimed Dunedin entitled to the name of town. A town certainly, with plenty officers to administer laws, regarding which the people were in total darkness, and of which the magistrates themselves were profoundly ignorant. As a crowning favour, the Governor himself paid an official visit to the newly created town, held a levee, and was informed by one of the presentees that "the place was hard up for leather; they had plenty of everything else." His Excellency appreciated the sentiment. However, he did not consider it went far enough. So in an address to the public he somewhat astounded his audience by saying that it was his intention to recommend the Home Government to sanction his proclamation of a Lieutenant-Governor with attached staff, at a cost of a few thousands a year, to supervise and control the actions of a handful of people whose united earnings would scarcely amount in gross to the sum required to pay the royal representative. This grand idea, however, did not eventuate; but another, equally absurd, was splendidly carried out.

The Dunedinites were slow to perceive the great boon to be derived from a host of rulers and administrators of laws and ordinances, which the people themselves had no say or representation in either framing or passing. It was consequently the duty of the distant "authorities" to force on a recusant community, and against their emphatic protest, the presence of a Resident Judge of the Supreme Court of the colony of New Zealand. Was it not a fact that for the two years that had elapsed since the settlement was formed, one criminal case, and that trivial in its character, had occurred? True, but what might happen in the future was better known in Wellington.

So Mr Justice Stephen arrived in Dunedin in due course, and was awarded a reception befitting the high office which he occupied, and all sought to do him honour. As it was known that in official affairs very little attention would be required, something, consequently, must be found for him to do. The Horticultural Society readily came with its aid, and appointed him president. The Society for the Diffusion of Useful Knowledge solicited his aid in opening up some dark features in science or history, which he promised to do, but failed to perform. Twelve months after his appointment he was subjected to the direful necessity of opening the first session of the Supreme Court; but there was neither criminal nor civil business to transact.

A second session of the Court was held three months after the first; but no business was on hand. A third sitting followed, with a similar result, and now matters had come to a terrible pass. Something must be done. So, as His Honor could not get any cases to try, might he not himself become a subject for trial before the inferior judicatory? And of verity he effected it; for in January, 1852, he was arraigned before a bench of magistrates for assault, and was acquitted by a majority of one only, the minority administering to him a severe rebuke, to which His Honor replied, "Could I wait for the tedious and tardy process of the law?" The assaulted was about half the size and weight of the judge; but as a wind-up of the affair, one of the J.P.s, a well-known M.D., challenged His Honor to a duel, as the knight-errant of the lady who had been insulted. In March, 1852, Mr Justice Stephen and family left Dunedin. In May a proclamation was issued at Wellington abolishing the Supreme Court at Dunedin; yet strange to relate, for the first day of June following a sitting of the Court was announced, to which thirty-six unpaid jurymen were summoned, and attended to find there was no business to transact, and no judge to preside had there been any.

Before quitting for the present the department of the law, it may be stated that the building first used as a Court House in 1848 was the Survey office, near where the Colonial Bank now stands, but it was so small that four men could hardly move in it after the space allotted for the justices and clerks was reserved, the interested public standing outside. "The first special Court "House was situated near the present jail, was a common unlined "weather board erection about 12ft. by 12ft., with a 'door and "two windows all in the front,' the court room being entered "right from the street. A rough deal table in the centre of the "room formed the bench, at which sat side by side the police "magistrate and the clerk. In a small recess off the court-room "the magistrate had his bed, where he spent his nights." This detailed description is from the pen of one who knew. Other little episodes, similar to those of the Supreme Court judge, occurred among the rulers of the people, whether following example or for diversion's sake, cannot well be determined. Perhaps too many authorised authorities in a community is a greater misfortune than no authority at all; but the majority of the people pursued the even tenor of their way, and brought their town rapidly into prominence. An endless task it would be to detail in order the processes by which this was done. Those old pioneers had a specific object in view, and attain it they would, let who like repine. Nor would they tamely submit to a dictation in commercial affairs, which, unfortunately, they had to accept in more public life. Gifted with and guided by the spirit of self-reliance, these resolute men of old put their shoulders to the wheel, and in a short time raised many monuments of progress. Property Investment Societies, to assist in putting up buildings, were soon in full swing, and proved of immense advantage. Flour mills, driven by water-power, were a first requirement. Hitherto the grain was ground by steel hand-mills, and for this work the women were generally told off.

There were certain circumstances existing, however, which greatly crippled the march of progress, and hindered the residents from advancing as rapidly as they could have wished. In the first place the surplus of the public revenue, after the expense of collecting was defrayed, was sent off to Wellington to be applied for purposes there, whereas it should have been retained and expended in the district in works of public utility, such as road-making, bridges, jetties, &c. It leaked out that the sub-treasurer had on hand £900, which he was forwarding to the north under charge of Captain Stokes, of H.M.S. Acheron, which had arrived in port after completing the coast survey. A public meeting was at once convened, at which strongly condemnatory resolutions were passed, and a demand made that the money should be sent back, the "Acheron" having sailed in the interval. The firm attitude taken up by the settlers had the desired effect, and the money was forthwith returned and expended on works.

Another drawback was the absence of banks or other institutions by which monetary transactions could be facilitated.

To supply this much felt want, it was proposed to establish a Joint Stock Company to start "The Bank of Otago," to be conducted on Scotch banking principles. The necessary capital was subscribed, the requisite arrangements completed, and the notes ready for issue; all that was wanted was a charter from the Government to legalise the institution. This was, however, not granted, so the venture was reluctantly abandoned, much to the chagrin and regret of all concerned.

There was no regular intercommunication, postal or otherwise, between Dunedin and the other settlements, everything depended on small coasting vessels, on the regularity of whose visits no dependence could be placed. In fact there was no post office at all in Dunedin, nor Custom House either, both of these important institutions being located at Port Chalmers.

A steady progress continued to be made against all adverse circumstances, so that at the end of 1852 the total population of Dunedin amounted to 628—not a very great increase, certainly, yet it bore a fair comparison to the increase which had taken place in the settlement generally, as at the same date the total population was 1,752. The Editor of the "Witness" newspaper, which had come into existence on the departure of the "News," in concise, comprehensive and conclusive language recorded that during the year "births were incessant, marriages numerous, deaths few." Truly happy was the state of a community such as this.

Our narrative has now arrived at the close of the first epoch —a period during which the people had not a word to say as to their own government, their head centre was a far off, vague, ill-to-be-realised idea, which exercised a power, legitimate or otherwise, quite unknown to those most interested. Now, however, the end of this indefinable existence was at hand, and a new era was approaching which would in its realization prove that a people, however few and far remote from other constituencies, can be far better governed by their own conclusions than by the obtruded opinions of others.

The early part of 1853 was taken up in making preparations for the three different representative elections, which were to take place under the new order of things. Every one was interested, and a considerable amount of feeling was roused between the two contending parties. The first two questions to be decided were the claims sent in by the settlers under which they sought to have their names placed on the electoral rolls; and were the Maori inhabitants entitled to a vote? The party most urgent in pressing the claims of the Maoris to be registered, was composed of those who from the first were opposed to the distinctive feature of the settlement and were distinguished as the "Little Enemy," their number being comparatively small. What was lacking in numbers was, however, made up by the pertinacity with which they urged and stuck to their points. It was of no use, however. The opinion of the law officers of the Crown was obtained on the question, and they ruled that the natives were not qualified to be registered. The bench accordingly refused the applications, and the rolls were thereafter completed. Unaccountable delay, however, occurred in Wellington in having the New Constitution brought into full operation, but this removed, the elections soon took place; that of the Superintendent of the Province was carried by acclamation. Dunedin returned by a unanimous vote one member to be representative in the General Assembly; and by a poll selected three members for the Provincial Council.

It may be mentioned here in passing that for both the Assembly and the Council elections the Province of Otago was divided into two electoral districts only, viz.—town of Dunedin, and country. These districts were very soon afterwards increased in number by the subdivision of the country into several districts, so as to meet the wants of the settlers, and give the different localities a fair share in the representation.

The town was now to have the benefit of some kind of local responsible authority.

The Provincial Council having met, after arranging their own internal economy, was prompt in acknowledging the requirements of the town; and at its first session in January, 1854, passed an ordinance entitled the "Dunedin Public Lands," under which a Board of Commissioners was appointed, consisting of all the members of the Provincial Council itself, and in addition "six other persons to be elected by those qualified to vote in any of the electoral districts of the province." The special duties of this Board were defined to be: "To deal with the lands reserved for public purposes in and about the town of Dunedin." It will thus be seen that the Dunedin reserves originally made, were not exclusively, or in any way particularly for the residents in the town, but were set apart, reserved and destined for such public purposes as were detailed.

The public purposes for which the lands were reserved were, "such as fortifications, public buildings, sites for places of public worship and instruction, baths, wharves, quays, cemeteries, squares, a park, and other places for health and recreation in and about the town of Dunedin." The municipal estate was a speciality for the town alone.

The powers vested in the Commissioners were to let on lease for any period not exceeding nineteen years any part of the said lands for any purpose not inconsistent with the purposes for which they were destined and reserved. Particular stipulations were also made regarding "that part of the lands called the Town Belt," by which every precaution was to be taken for preserving "the trees and shrubs therein, or such parts of them as it might be desirable to preserve, with a view to the order and amenity of the ground, and also for draining and improving it, and ultimately laying it down in grass, with walks and carriage drives, as a public park or place of public recreation, provided that no buildings or other erections other than the necessary fencing be erected on the said lands."

It is needless to say that no leases were made nor rents collected for any of those reserves, in fact, in spite and in face of the Ordinance and the Commissioners, a large amount of squatting took place, houses and wharves of the usual description and of the material most easily obtained, were planted on almost every place, save and except the Octagon.

Summonses were issued and evictions decreed; but these were seldom carried out, being generally disregarded by almost all concerned.

The only exemption to this was in the case of the jetty, for which a special ordinance was passed, authorizing and empowering the Commissioners to levy tolls, dues, and wharfages on a scale set forth in a schedule attached, and from which a fair revenue was derived.

The powers of the Commissioners were thus limited to merely the reserves in and about Dunedin. It was necessary, therefore, that a more extended authority should be created. For this purpose an empowering ordinance was passed, vesting in the Superintendent certain powers heretofore exercised by the Governor or Lieutenant-Governor of New Zealand and by the Resident Magistrate of Otago. Among these were powers providing for deeds and vital registration, licensing publicans and auctioneers, debts' recovery and roll courts, militia and constabulary, sheriff and coroner, prison regulations, asylums, slaughtering, savings' banks, education, census, rates and tolls, dogs; on all of which the Superintendent could legislate with the advice and consent of the Provincial Council.

As the town had now become a district, and even a separate part of the Province, it became necessary that some distinct and separate powers should be conferred on the inhabitants. Accordingly, in the second session of the Provincial Council, 1855, an ordinance was passed, " constituting a Public Board for the town of Dunedin, to be incorporated under the name of the Town Board, to have the administration and management of various matters and things concerning the town, which might be from time to time beneficially devolved on such a Board elected by the inhabitants." The Board was to consist of nine members, who would accept and hold for the benefit of the town and its inhabitants all lands, buildings, goods, and other property, have and use a common seal, and borrow money for the execution of any undertaking entrusted to them by ordinance of the Provincial Council.

This enactment was followed by another ordinance to regulate the management and control of streets and other things

within the town of Dunedin, and in, through, or upon the lands
commonly called the Town Belt, which were thereby declared to
be the limits of the town; and for liquidating the expense of all
works authorized and resolved on by the Board, it could levy a rate
upon all properties within the limits not specially exempted by
the Act. Two years later, power was also conferred on the
Board for revenue purposes to tax all vehicles using the streets
for traffic, and to issue licenses authorising them to ply for
hire.

The whole powers and machinery having been created, the
registered electors for the town district in August 1855, made
choice of the members of the first Town Board, who, having been
duly installed in office, proceeded to take immediate steps to
improve the condition of the town and promote the comfort of
the residents.

Like other communities where liberty of judgment and free
expression of opinion is allowed, there were battles, bloodless
battles, to be fought. In Dunedin it was the battle of the
streets, and it had three phases. First, every man who bought a
section, even in the least accessible spot, loudly demanded that
good access should at once be provided for him. These malcontents
being discredited, their attack on the Board was of the lighter sort.
The next was more formidable, and was over the levels and
drainage. No systematic plan had been laid down as to
permanent levels, for very valid reasons; there was no available
talent to work out a suitable plan, and if there had been, no cash
in the exchequer to pay the labourer for his hire. Hence, some
houses which had in the dim past been built on piles, or were,
as a wag of the day described them, "dwellings on stilts,"
had now the door-steps level with the street, and others that had
in the same misty bygone times been built level with the
surface, had now the "croon o' the causeway" topping their
eaves. Darkness had been made light in some places, in others
light had been made darkness. The diversion of the streams
had made some sections desert which formerly were well
watered, and old dry places of the earth were now morasses.
Actions were on all sides threatened, and what could the Board
do but remain dormant? Such would have been the case,
on the principle that "keepin' a quiet sough things would settle

doon," had not the most formidable of the opponents come into prominence. Now, it was not the internal economy of the town which was attacked, but how to get out of the "plagued place" away to the south. The Board was its own enemy, and the warfare was hot and furious. Three exits from the town were proposed. From priority of selection and its final accomplishment, the "South Gate" receives first notice. On the original plan the main road to the south followed the present tram-line to Kensington, thence over an impracticable hill past the cemetery down to Caversham, or alternately the route of the tram as now carried out. In the latter case it was simply making a road through a bog. The Board had nothing to do with the route after leaving its boundary; but before reaching this point there was the swamp from Manor-place to consolidate, which would absorb all and more than all revenues. Beyond the margin of the town its authorities could not interfere, and this remark applies to each proposed diversion. However, the Superintendent had selected his residence on the south line, which, according to popular opinion, constituted another vote in its favour. The "Middle Gate" next claims attention. This followed up Stafford-street, crossed the Belt, and detoured on to the district road and followed down Cargill Hill. The objection here was the steepness of Stafford-street, and that it was to serve private interests. The latter fault was extenuated, it might be said condoned, by the fact that the implicated proprietors had at their own cost proved that a practicable road could be made, and then asked the Board to contribute towards its further development. Later on, when their hopes from official support were blasted, an appeal was made to the country settlers to come forward and help them. The "West Gate" was advocated, supported, and attempted by the majority of the Board. This road was up and through Maclaggan-street, described at the time by a candidate for a seat at the Board as a dark subterranean passage through a labyrinth of trees and rocks. The majority, however, called for tenders for its construction, and had the work carried on until all the funds had been expended, when its advocates wisely abandoned the scheme, almost concluding it to be impracticable. The greatest difficulties would, however, have arisen after the limit of the Board's territory had been arrived at. Fortunately for all, the solution was arrived at by the Provincial Government undertaking not only to fill up the south end swamp, but also to form and maintain the whole length of street from the entrance to the town at Cargill Hill, to the exit at the Water of Leith, thus treating it as a portion of the main trunk road running from north to south of the province. Although thus relieved of a great responsibility, the Board had still serious difficulties to contend with. Every street presented a formidable undertaking to make it fit for traffic, and constant appeals had to be made to the Provincial Council for assistance, which generally were very graciously granted.

There was also the difficult question of sanitary drainage, which was raised by a few alarmists. The culvert across Princes-street from High-street was the source of a large amount of contention. As in other cases, so in this, every one had his own idea of how best to put the evil down. At length, after a long period of incubation, the happy idea of building a stone culvert across the main street was resolved on, and having been contracted for and honestly completed, this fountain of complaint was finally dried up. Minor questions arose as to other localities, which were looked on by those immediately interested as of first importance, but time, that soothes down all things, so acted as to relieve the Board of responsibility.

It being deemed advisable to close the original cemetery at the top of Rattray-street on the grounds of its inconvenient position, and the risk of drainage therefrom proving injurious to the health of the inhabitants, the Board first selected for a burial ground a portion of the Town Belt at the southern end (28 acres), which was known at the time as "Little Paisley," having been so named by a native of that ancient town who had squatted there, who afterwards obtained the renown of being the first weaver of woollen cloth in the Province. A second site was afterwards chosen (also part of the Belt, 31 acres) at the entrance to the North East Valley, close to the Water of Leith, and now the Botanical Gardens. But this one was eventually abandoned, both because it was considered unsuitable, and because it was objected to by a number of the settlers.

Very general dissatisfaction prevailed in Dunedin at the absence of any means for ascertaining the correct time. True, there was a bell and a bell-ringer, but it appeared that the bell-ringer was displeased with the amount of the contributions received by him from the public for his year's services in ringing the bell three times a day, and consequently declined further operations. The complaint was made that a public index of the time was of too much importance to be left to the caprice of an individual depending on the voluntary contributions of the public for his pay, and the Board was urged to take up the matter and provide a public clock, or adopt any other practicable means by which the good people of Dunedin might know "the time of day." Financial difficulties, however, presented themselves, so that the worthy Board-men could not comply with the request.

At this particular juncture the members of the Board were not a very happy family, and some difficulty was experienced in keeping up the requisite number of members; and it so happened that on one occasion when an advertisement, signed by the Superintendent, appeared calling on the ratepayers to assemble within the Mechanics' Hall to elect one person to be member in room of one who had resigned, the general meeting consisted of two ratepayers, and a fit and proper person having been duly proposed and seconded, the presiding officer declared him elected without a dissentient voice, and the important proceedings having been brought to a close, the meeting shook hands at the door and separated in a most orderly manner. Indifference like this was exceptional, as two of the members resigned immediately afterwards, and on the announcement for their successors to be elected being made, quite a little stir arose among the ratepayers, resulting in four candidates being nominated, necessitating a poll, which was appointed for the following day. On the understanding that the poll would be open from 9 a.m. till 4 p.m., the ratepayers were not anxious to hurry up, but judge of their surprise when arriving at the building about eleven in the forenoon the constable in attendance announced to the astonished electors that the whole affair was over, as the returning officer at 10 a.m. had declared the two candidates who had the largest show of hands at the nomination duly elected. An emphatic protest against such an arbitrary proceeding was lodged in the hands of the

Superintendent, signed by 17 ratepayers, and calling on His Honor to declare the so-called election null and void.

Tho satisfaction received in return was a very poor one, to wit, that tho ordinance empowered the Returning Officer to hold the poll closed if no votes had been recorded before 10 o'clock.

To secure a revenue was a first duty of the Board. Without this nothing could be done by way of improvement. Accordingly, a committee was appointed to report as to ways and means. In due fulfilment of their duty, they stated that in their opinion the Provincial Government having sold a large number of town sections, should be applied to for aid in making and improving the streets, and thus by affording more convenient access further sales would be promoted; and suggested that the Government should be asked for a vote of £1000 for the streets generally, a further sum of £1000 by way of loan for general improvements, and another £1000 for completing and metalling the main lines; in all £3000.

Income was expected from two other sources, first the Municipal Lands and next the reserves, which were estimated to produce £300 per annum—an amount which would rapidly increase. A third source was suggested, but one which involved an important step, applying for power to levy a rate on sections sold, but not occupied or fenced, which could not be reached under tho existing law. These numbered some 350, and a tax of 10/- each would, deducting expenses, yield another £150. The question of toll-bars was also mooted, but laid aside as premature.

It was universally admitted that it would be a scandal and disgrace to Dunedin if another summer were allowed to pass without something being done towards making footpaths, and rendering passable the main thoroughfares. But the question arising was, how far the Town Board was the most competent body to carry out these improvements with efficiency and economy? The administrative capacity of the Board was by many doubted, and as a specimen Jetty-street, which was in a disgraceful condition—in fact a perfect bog during the previous winter, was pointed to.

A general consensus of opinion, however, prevailed not only as to the propriety, but the necessity for taxing unoccupied sections. A large influx of population had commenced under the new immigration scheme, two ships from London arriving within three days of each other with 220 passengers, and no house accommodation could be found for them; and although scores of sections were unoccupied, not a foot of land could be obtained on which suitable houses could be erected. Grasping speculators had the land locked up for their own special interest, and to the detriment of the town itself.

The opinion of the Provincial Solicitor having been obtained on the point of levying an extra rate on unoccupied sections, the Board in May, 1858, passed the following motion: "That the resolution imposing a uniform rate of one shilling and sixpence in the pound be rescinded, and be substituted by a rate of one shilling in the pound on improved and occupied lands and buildings, and a rate of two shillings and sixpence in the pound on waste sections, the property of individuals." On this basis the assessment for the year amounted to £486 4s. However, the Board, much to the chagrin of its members, ultimately found that the exceptional rate they had resolved on could not be enforced, and they were reluctantly compelled to abandon it, although to their credit be it said several of the proprietors of vacant sections expressed their readiness to pay the amount charged.

The general trade of the town was confined to supplying the residents of the Province with their few simple necessities and requirements to enable them to prosecute the operations on farm and station. The mutual dependence on each other was felt and readily acknowledged by both. As the country progressed, the town benefited, and trades multiplied, expanded, and improved. The strides were not great nor rapid; they were sure, albeit a little slow. Fluctuations in value then as now caused a little depression, and as the value of cereals had considerably fallen from what had for some years ruled, the impression was that this fact " was likely to be productive of some inconvenience, if not temporary embarrassment among agriculturists. On the other hand the increased value of wool would go far to neutralize the deficiency in the value of grain." On the whole, however, the commercial prospects were good. The amount of real wealth had increased rapidly; the great complaint was the want of money or something to represent the real property of the country.

The sales of sections within the town, which took place by auction, were rapidly proceeded with. Competition was strong, and prices realized considered very satisfactory, in some instances exceeding fifty pounds a-piece, although not in the most attractive situations.

The Dunedin Harbour, too, at times presented an unusually gratifying appearance. In one week there were six sea-going vessels at anchor off the town. The barque "Dunedin," of 400 tons, direct from London, lay within a mile and a half of the jetty, having sailed up and discharged a portion of her cargo, was beginning to take on board a freight of oats for Melbourne. The "Gil Blas," brig, had discharged her inward cargo and had almost concluded her loading with oats, also for Melbourne, her cargo, when completed, being valued at £3000. The captain of this vessel had the credit of bringing the "Gil Blas," the first vessel of any considerable tonnage, up to the Dunedin Harbour, and the hope was entertained that soon the jetty and its tramway would be sufficiently extended to enable the "Gil Blas" to load and unload alongside. The schooner "Ellen" was also discharging kauri timber from Auckland, and the "Emerald Isle" a general cargo from Wellington. There were strong advocates for placing a small steamer in the harbour, which it was predicted would prove an excellent speculation by making one or two trips a day to and from the port, carrying passengers and mails, and as occasion required, towing vessels.

The idea of a steamer monopolized public attention. Besides the increased facilities it would afford to trade, and the augmented traffic it would create, the greater opportunities it would afford the Dunedinites of a little rational and healthful enjoyment was a consideration of importance, and not to be overlooked in connection with what would be its real and greatest value, its auxiliary aid in the trade of the harbour. To institute or assist such a service was beyond the power of the Board; but it was hoped that the Provincial Council might get it accomplished.

One writer, speaking of this period (1857), says:—"With "regard to the capital of the province, Dunedin, there are now "evident symptoms of enlargment. For some years the place "had been almost stationary; now, however, one who has been

" absent for twelve months cannot fail to perceive great changes.
" The place bids fair to be something like a town. We know of
" few more picturesque positions, containing commodious sites
" for commercial purposes as well as for villas and private
" residences. Before another year passes there will be some
" public buildings worthy of the place; at present there is
" nothing deserving of the name.

 " The population of Dunedin is composed chiefly of officials
" of Government, merchants, storekeepers, and tradesmen. It is
" the seat of the Provincial Government and Courts of Justice,
" and the channel through which the whole exports and imports
" of the province pass. The amount of business done is much larger
" than the appearance of the place would indicate. The Union
" Bank of Australia has an establishment here. There are four
" hotels in the town, two printing offices, three places of worship,
" a high school with its rector, one male, and one female teacher,
" supported by the Government, besides a private academy.
" There are two breweries in the neighbourhood, which promise
" to make the place celebrated for its ale, the climate being
" peculiarly adapted for brewing. There is one flour-mill in
" operation, and another flour and oatmeal company have
" commenced to build on the Kaikorai stream, there being a
" third in the Tokomairiro, all driven by water power. A candle
" manufactory has recently been started, which turns out very
" superior candles, and works up all the material to be found in
" the province. It is intended shortly to start a tanyard on a small
" scale. A good deal of money used to be sent away for candles,
" which is now retained, and the same thing will occur in regard
" to leather. An attempt has been successfully made by the
" enterprising landlord of one of the hotels to produce gas, and
" his intention is to extend his operations considerably farther.
" A bleach-field has been started near at hand, to which house-
" wives can send their yarn and clothing to be put through
" the necessary operations. A photographic establishment has
" been opened in Prinçes-street for some time past, and is well
" patronised by the public. Watchmakers, chemists, and other
" similar branches of trade are all having representatives, and
" the printing offices vie with each other in turning out their
" almanacs and weekly newspapers, in which poetry and prose,

"facts and fiction, politics and polemics, are wondrously
"combined and displayed.

"Of the 2000 qnarter-acre sections which comprise the town
"of Dunedin, 979 have up to date been selected At the upset
"price of £12 10s, very few are now disposed of. So keen is the
"competition that £20 and up to £50 is often obtained. The
"business part of the town has of course all been selected, and
"no better idea could be given of the advance in the value of
"land, which but ten years ago was a valueless wilderness, than by
"stating the fact that sections which originally cost ten shillings
"were now worth £500 to £1000. Of course this refers to the
"business part only."

Vessels drawing fourteen feet of water could come within
two miles of Dunedin jetty; the probability being that as the
place progressed vessels of much larger tonnage would be
brought up, a very small outlay only being needed to increase
the depth to eighteen feet. The shipping interest of the town
consisted of three fairly large brigs and half-a-dozen sea-
going schooners, besides several smaller crafts. When several
of them were at anchor in the bay, the appearance of the water
presented an air of importance very gratifying to those who were
the pioneers of the settlement.

In regard to the foregoing remark as to the status of the
population being composed chiefly of "officials of Government,"
it may be explained that the Provincial Government soon after
its advent had the Post Office and Custom House both removed
from Port Chalmers, their original location, and established in
Dunedin, where all the business was transacted. For the
accommodation of the different branches of the service, the Provincial authorities erected a long stretch of one-storied buildings
from the corner of Jetty-street down to what is now Liverpool-
street, which were occupied by the Superintendent and Provincial
Treasury, the Custom House, Post Office and Constabulary; but
the sum total of the whole crowd of these officers did not tot up
to the number of Justices of the Peace in the Province.

During the four years from 1853 to 1857, several other
interesting events occurred in addition to those already en-
numerated. A fair and market were established, or rather
attempted; the fair intended to be half-yearly and the market

weekly. From the want of suitable buildings and sufficient population, both soon collapsed. The first vessel of any size, the schooner "Star," of wondrous celebrity, was built and launched. Regular mail service was established between the town and Waitaki in the north, and Invercargill in the south. The loyal sympathies of the people were excited by the terrible accounts of the European War, which was then raging in the Crimea, and in response to an order from His Excellency the Governor, a solemn fast for peace in Europe was proclaimed and observed by every one, so far as cessation from business was concerned ; and not only this, but a subscription to assist the Patriotic Relief Fund was opened, and the handsome sum, for so small a community, of £485 5s was transmitted to London. In ecclesiastical matters, too, progress was being made. The Presbytery of the Church of Otago was constituted, and the Anglican portion of the residents resolved on the erection of St. Paul's Episcopal Church, the services of this body having been conducted in a small building on the east side of Bell Hill for some time past.

On 31st December, 1857, the population of Dunedin was : males, 444 ; females, 446 ; total 890. The value of imports, £65,401 ; exports, £22,908 ; Customs Revenue, £8218 ; the valuation of the town property, £4400, for rating purposes and the rates at 1/- in the pound, £220, every penny of which was collected.

The year 1858 may justly be characterised as the period of a fresh departure in the voyage of life, not only to the Dunedinites themselves, but also to all the Province. Even if nothing more definite and striking in interest and importance were pointed to than bringing the Province within the circle of steam navigation, this of itself was sufficient to put a distinguishing stamp on its history. Hitherto shut up almost within themselves, having no reliable means of transport or of communication with the outer world, they were now furnished with an interprovincial and intercolonial service. And in addition a direct export trade was started to London, which it was foreseen would prove of immense advantage.

Again, by the impetus given to immigration by the special agency opened up in Glasgow and Edinburgh, as well as from other sources, the number of vessels which had arrived at the

Port during the year, outside and beyond coasters, amounted to 52, of which nine were steamers; and the departures were 47, bound for Britain, America, India, China, and the adjacent colonies. Some of the immigrant ships arriving brought complements of from 263 to 375 passengers each; the total for the year coming close up to 3000. The larger portion of these found their way to friends in the country, still a good many tradesmen remained in Dunedin. Although there was, during a portion of the winter, a number of these out of employment in Dunedin, for whom work was provided on the roads by the Government, by far the larger number were readily absorbed by the developing resources of the community.

Dunedin had greatly improved during the year. A large number of houses had been built, every day new ones were being commenced, and an improvement as regards size and stability was also noticeable. In Princes-street a two-storied stone store was in course of erection, and a two-storied stone dwelling house was in progress at Elm Row, and stands there still, being the oldest stone building in Dunedin. The Club House, too, in Maclaggan-street, which, although of wood, is still to be seen in proximity to the Police Station, will give an idea of the more advanced style of architecture of the period. The state of the streets was the great cause of complaint, particularly during the winter; nothing could be finer than the climate overhead, but on the ground under foot progress was hardly possible from the state of the streets.

The shipping trade demands particular notice.

The first direct ship from Dunedin to London.—On the 22nd May 1858, the ship " Strathallan " cleared the Customs, and two days after got to sea. The cargo consisted of 780 bales of wool, valued at £19,010. It was much regretted that for want of co-operation among exporters, the ship had been detained much longer than expected, and did not carry a full cargo, thereby entailing a very heavy loss to the enterprising charterers, Macandrew and Co. Trade jealousy was at the bottom of the affair, engendered and kept aflame by petty spleen on the part of one or two offended politicians. Had the merchants been actuated by a desire to further the interests of the province,

there would have been a direct ship two years before, as had been
the case in Canterbury.

Shortly after the sailing of the "Strathallan," the "Strath-
fieldsay" was laid on by the same charterers to load for
Melbourne, and sailed on the 16th June with 2757 bags of oats
and 59 bales of wool. In this case, also, the charterers were
unsupported and unfortunate, as on arrival at Melbourne prices
for grain had fallen below the prices paid in Dunedin, so the
cargo was stored on shipper's account.

Another wonder was, however, in store for the Dunedinites,
through the enterprise of the same mercantile firm. On the 28th
August, the screw steamer "Queen," of 182 tons, was seen
gracefully steaming up the harbour and anchoring about half a
mile from the jetty. The town was taken by surprise at finding
a steamer of such dimensions coming up the bay so far, the
possibility of which would have been ridiculed a short time
before. Few occurrences since the formation of the settlement
called for such hearty demonstrations of rejoicings. On heaving
in sight of the town she was greeted with a salute of 21 guns
from the cannon on Church Hill. This was responded to by a
display of fireworks from the steamer. Of course everyone
visited the steamer, and the universal testimony was that she was
a perfect model, divided into four water-tight compartments, and
fitted up with every comfort and convenience for the accomoda-
tion of a considerable number of passengers. The residents were
in ecstacies, and claimed that no other Province in New Zealand
could boast of such a vessel, and each congratulated his neigh-
bour on the great addition to the shipping of the town, sincerely
wishing that Mr Macandrew, to whom the Province was
indebted in this matter as in others, would meet with such
encouragement as would enable him to continue the vessel in
the trade for which she was intended. It was expected that her
ordinary passage from Melbourne to Otago via Foveaux Strait
would be accomplished in six days, and the intention of her
owner was to run her once every two months to Melbourne, the
intervening time being occupied on the New Zealand coast from
Auckland to the Bluff.

The success which attended the first venture in locally
owned steam, together with the great favour shown by the

residents all over the Province towards the enterprise, and the resolution shown to support it, together with the more assuring, because tangible fact that the Provincial Government, after considerable delay and evasion, at length agreed to subsidise the service, induced the owner of the "Queen" to add to his fleet another larger and more powerful vessel, the "Pirate," of 285 tons, which had originally been built for the Glasgow and Liverpool trade, but afterwards sent out to Melbourne, was purchased and placed in the trade between that port and New Zealand.

A further addition was made to the steam fleet by Mr John Jones, who purchased the P.S. "Geelong," 108 tons, in Melbourne, and placed her on the trade between Dunedin and the coast to the north; and the Government in this case also supported the trade by a subsidy for a period of two years.

And it was not long ere the remaining gap was filled, as early in May the little screw steamer "New Era," formerly "Pride of the Yarra," came up to Dunedin Jetty, and by special invitation quite a small crowd took advantage of the favourable day to visit Port Chalmers and inaugurate the trade. Favours often come double, so within a few days another small screw steamer, the "Victoria," also arrived from Melbourne, the question arising was whether there was sufficient trade for both.

The census returns for 1858 give the population of the town on 31st December as: males, 863; females, 849; total 1712. The imports for the year valued £96,620; the exports, £47,029; custom revenue, £11,173.

The aspect of the town continued steadily to improve. Many existing buildings were added to, renovated, and raised to the altered levels of the streets, and new ones of more attractive and superior character were being proceeded with. "One municipal section which, in the very centre of the town, had formerly been an unsightly nuisance, was now covered on both frontages with stylish shops." This was rather a high-flying character to give the buildings at the corner of High and Princes-streets, recently pulled down to make way for the Insurance building. As a verity, the only private building which had up till the end of 1861 been erected with any pretensions to stability or design, is that now owned by the New Zealand Government Insurance, at the corner of Rattray and Princes-streets. Although the buildings were increasing in number, and their character was improving, no architectural display worthy of notice had taken place. The Union Bank was contented with a small shanty at the corner of Manse and High-streets; the Oriental Bank held the Mechanics' Institution. The Government offices for Post Office, Customs, Treasury, and Police, were a range of wooden, iron, and stone structures, one story in height, stretching from Jetty-street to Liverpool-street. The Hospital and Lunatic Asylum occupied the sections on which the Corporation buildings now stand, and the Immigration Barracks, two stories in height, fronted Walker-street. The whole of these were almost entirely in wood, the cooking and heating apparatus not having received any particular care in plan or execution; yet, strange to say, no case of fire occurred.

The Town Board erected a special habitation for itself, and for a fire engine which had been imported at the cost of the then only Insurance Company. This dwelling was set up on the beach near where the present Custom House stands, and the appliances for extinguishing fires being safely housed therein, the inhabitants considered themselves secure, even although there was no water supply except from the bay.

The Board, however, was not the only occupant of this choice site. It sat there on sufferance. The Provincial Government were the supposed owners, and to make provision for the Maoris, whose territory had been invaded and land acquired at a nominal value, the Council voted a sum for the erection of a comfortable residence for the natives adjoining the Town Chambers, which was called the Maori Hostelry, in which the aborigines kept up their usual rites, disposed of their wares, entertained their visitors, and finally laughed at the Pakehas for their credulity. It turned out afterwards that this piece of ground was a Maori reserve, and the Provincial authority had to pay a very large compensation.

The Supreme Court sittings were resumed in Dunedin, and at the first meeting, although there were a few irregularities, one case of a serious nature was tried, but the charge was reduced to a lower scale. At next Sessions His Honor explained it was his intention to have holden a Session some months ago, but the absence of His Excellency prevented; however, in future he proposed to hold a Session in Dunedin twice a year, and would endeavour to arrange his arrival and sojourn to meet the convenience of the public. His Honor, however, deplored that Dunedin was behind all other parts of the colony. There was no accommodation for the Court, which was of first importance in administering justice; there were the total absence of restraint and discipline in the building courteously denominated a jail; and worst of all, there were no prisoners in it. A few paltry and inadequate additions were being made for the accommodation of prisoners when they could be got, but there was no fence around the building to prevent escape, and no turnkey to keep control. In fact, when there was a prisoner he was habitually sent to town for his own rations without any guard; nay more, from the system of indulgence adopted, the prisoners remained the *guests* of the gaoler, because forsooth their so-called prison house was made to them a comfortable house of accommodation of which they were glad to avail themselves. Such a state of things did away with the wholesome terror of the law, and brought its administration into ridicule and contempt; nay more, it induced the gaoler to commit a crime, the punishment for which might be the same as for treason or murder. He trusted the Grand Jury would find it their duty to use their influence to the utmost point to put an end to a system so demoralising to the population and so disgraceful to the Government.

It was not only of the prisons the learned Judge had to complain. He was grieved to find that equal apathy prevailed as to finding accommodation for the Supreme Court. It was with considerable difficulty, and after more than one refusal by the committee, that the use of the building in which he sat was obtained, and at one time he seriously thought of adjourning the Court until proper accommodation was secured.

The Dunedin gaoler was celebrated for the tact he displayed in managing his prisoners under very disadvantageous circumstances. The first prison was erected on the section at the corner of Stuart and Cumberland-streets, adjoining the present gaol, and contained two large cells, with a day room, and was surrounded with a substantial wooden fence 7ft. high, which gave it the appearance of security. From some untoward cause it caught fire in 1855, at the time containing only one prisoner, who worked very hard to save his domicile, on the justifiable principle that he had been very comfortable in his lodgings therein, and was afraid in the future he would not be so well off; however, notwithstanding his exertions, total loss ensued. The Provincial Council had been alive to the necessity of making increased accommodation for the number of prisoners, unfortunately bound to increase by the increase of population, and so a new building was at once pushed on to completion on the site of the present erection. The gaoler, Mr Monson, who had held office since June 1851, got arrangements completed, and at once transferred himself and his single guest to the new quarters. The building was very inconvenient, and had nothing like room for its forced occupants, on some occasions numbering 26 and 27 —mostly runaway sailors. Nor had the keeper any regular assistant. He had the moral support of the chief constable, and sometimes the presence of an unarmed warder, on whom no great reliance could be placed. The law of kindness was adopted, since that of severity could not be enforced. The prisoners were in the habit of coming up to town for their rations once or twice weekly, and being generally good-tempered tars, were often treated by the people; but when the hour for closing up arrived, a homeward-bound tack was at once followed, so as not to get the old man into trouble by locking them out. That many escapes were made is undoubtedly true, but the settlers generally aided and abetted the escapee, as the majority of sailors were not only very handy about a place, but also ever ready to put their hands to work. It was like a social gathering to visit the gaoler's garden (where Findlay & Co.'s yards now are) and find the prisoners busy among the vegetables being grown for their own use, and have the master himself pointing with pride to his strawberry beds, which, when the fruit was ripe, would be given to those of his boys who behaved themselves.

The new gaol was not by any means a place for the safekeeping of its inmates. By the simplest means the tenants could effect their escape by door or window, and even though a seven foot palisade surrounded the building, that was easily scaled by an ordinary mortal, and much more easily by an expert. It was a usual custom, too, for outside friends to pass in to the recluses presents of any description, and such transfers were frequently made, as witnessed by the fact of occasional rows taking place, and of the gaoler frequently bringing bottles of grog to light.

"A sum of £5000 had been voted by the Council for a new gaol, and plans had been prepared and submitted for the approval of the General Government more than nine months before, and the delay in proceeding with the new building was attributable to the indecision of the General Government. Considering the means at command of the gaoler, the gaol was in a highly creditable state as regards cleanliness and order." These remarks of the Grand Jury were elicited by the opening statement by His Honor, who added that ere long their gaol would cease to be, what it had hitherto been, an object of derision to beholders, and a reproach to the flourishing Province. Furthermore His Honor said he would forward the presentment of the Jury to the proper quarter.

Another Court called the District Court was also established early in 1859, and a day appointed for the first sitting; but as the Government had neither appointed a Crown Solicitor nor forwarded instructions, Judge Harris had to adjourn the sitting until word was received from Auckland, which had now become the seat of Government. Some months afterwards the appointment was made and business was commenced.

The suggestion was thrown out at a soiree held in the church that it would be much for the benefit of the townspeople were an Athenæum established in the town, that being a better name than Mechanics' Institute. To carry out the idea a meeting was subsequently held, which resolved to form such an Institute, and a committee was appointed to wait on the Board as to obtaining a site for the proposed building. Accordingly, at the next meeting a resolution was passed agreeing to lease to the Athenæum managers the section at the corner of Manse and High-streets at the nominal rent of five shillings a year. The preliminaries being arranged the committee drafted a constitution with a view of submitting the same to the proprietors of the Mechanics' Institute, in the hope that an amalgamation would be affected. However, a strange difficulty occurred. So little interest appears to have been taken in the affairs of the Institute, that for several years no committee had been elected, and when a general meeting of members was called, it was found there was actually only a single individual entitled to claim the privilege—Mr Macandrew, as he alone had paid the amount to constitute life-membership, none of the others having paid their annual subscriptions. The only practical course was adopted, publishing a statement of the finances and inviting the public to enrol, so as to revive the society. From the statement it was shown that a balance of £130 5s 9d belonged to the Institute, which sum was deposited in the Union Bank; the whole having been realised from rents. After considerable delay sufficient interest was awakened to resuscitate the Institute, and at a meeting of the newly-enrolled members it was among other things resolved, in order to place the Institution on a satisfactory practical footing, to confer with the Athenæum committee, the opinion being that the existing building was quite inadequate for combined uses, and that a more suitable edifice could be erected. The Government being on the look-out for a post office site, it was thought they might, on account of its eligibility, select that belonging to the Institute, and pay handsomely for it.

Satisfactory proceedings ensued. Both committees met, and the interview was cordial and harmonious. The design and objects of both being the same, it was resolved to amalgamate and jointly provide for intellectual recreation and advancement in science, art, and literature, by means of a public library, reading-room, museum, and public lectures.

The plans for the new building for the Atheneum and Mechanics' Institution having been approved by the members, tenders were called for and one accepted for close on £5,500, the whole to be completed within six months from the signing of the contract. The business of nominating trustees and otherwise arranging for carrying into practical effect the objects of the Institution were also decided on, "the committee relying on the hearty co-operation and support of the entire public, the object being the founding and carrying out to a successful completion of an Institution in which the community in general was interested, which would serve a great moral purpose, furnish the means of intellectual enjoyment, be a convenient resort alike for town and country settler, and all in an erection which would be the pride and ornament of Dunedin." A call was to be made on the inhabitants to provide sufficient funds, as all then available was £3,000, which left £2,500 to be collected.

The proposal was received with enthusiasm, but the appeal for subscriptions was not so successful, so after considerable delay a wooden building of more modest design was erected, which still remains at the corner of High and Manse streets.

Horticultural excellence was one of the earliest aspirations of the Dunedin settlers. A society for the furtherance of this was part of the programme laid down for the community at its very first existence; it was not, however, until the town was in its eleventh year that an attempt at a Floral and Fruit Show was made. On Anniversary day, 1859, the first show was held in the schoolroom, and of course the room was beautifully decorated and the exhibits far beyond expectation in number, quality, and variety. A special feature of this first show was that professional gardeners (and there were a goodly number of first-class hands) abstained from entering into competition, leaving the contest altogether to amateurs. The appreciation by the general public of this useful institution was shown by the fact that over 400 visitors paid for admission during the afternoon. The number of competitors was 11, and exhibitors 24. Grapes, peaches, melons, pears, apples, gooseberries, vegetables, native ferns, besides flowers in bloom, cut and in pots, in collections and in devices, were staged in splendid order. A second show, held on the Queen's Birthday was equally successful, speaking volumes in favour of the quality of the soil and the mildness of the climate ; the depth of winter presenting but few checks to vegetation. The schoolroom was found far too small for the exhibits and visitors, and it was resolved to apply for a piece of the Botanic Garden reserve for the use of the society, on which by erecting a large tent, or some other device, to make a place suitable for the exhibition, whereby a very desirable impetus would be given to the operations of the society.

In both the following years this society continued in active existence, holding their public shows and more private meetings, at which specimens of native and introduced plants were exhibited and their merits discussed, and useful horticultural know ledge disseminated. A very large amount of enthusiasm existed, and it was all needed, because the attention of people was more closely devoted to provide the necessaries of life than to indulge in what may be called its adornments.

A flute band was also another sign of the march of progression. The streets, especially of a dark evening, wore a most lugubrious aspect, and the musical devotees who set agoing this movement were heartily to be thanked for their generous effort at whistling the populace into something like good humour and spirits. Starting with the flutes and drum as the nucleus of a full instrumental band, an appeal was made to the public to provide the means to obtain the necessary instruments. The very thought of old familiar tunes being pealed over Dunedin from Bell Hill was enough to relax the purse strings of the most parsimonious. With accustomed liberality Dunedin responded willingly to the appeal, so that ere long a fully equipped band was under instruction, ready with its martial strains to lead on to fame and glory those who aspired to such celebrity.

Simultaneously almost with this new departure a movement was set on foot to form a volunteer rifle corps, and at a meeting convened by the Superintendent in July 1860, a large committee was formed to make the necessary arrangements, His Honor undertaking to write to the General Government for a supply of rifles. A considerable number of the males from youth to middle age very soon enrolled themselves, and at the first muster on Bell Hill a respectable squad of seventy-five men put in an appearance, and in the presence of a wondering crowd took their first lesson in military drill. Very regularly the company assembled and mastered the movements under the able tuition of Adjutant Junor and Captain McCallum. Rifles were long of coming to hand, as the Colonial Secretary sent notice that there were none in stock, but that in due time a supply would arrive and so enable him to administer to the wants of this loyal and deserving muster. Assured by this hope the question of dress was next discussed, and almost by universal assent the Highland garb was adopted. Unfortunately there was not enough tartan to supply all who ordered, so a little delay took place in turning out in full parade order. A sound from a distance was in the meantime heard, not certainly the tocsin of war, but the more grateful one of auriferous discoveries, so that ere a sword had been drawn or a rifle handled, that first regiment of Dunedin volunteers dissolved into nothingness, and the majority of the units took to the more congenial task of using a long handled shovel and a tin dish, their uniforms being a blue jumper and water-tight boots.

But not to anticipate. The "Harbingers of the Town" were still further developing as regards accepted refinement. The old original style of transit was by bullocks on sledges. Wheels were of no use comparatively, for the sledge could slide along, where the dray would sink to the axle. The time for a new departure was, however, at hand. The bullock team, dray, and sledge must give way to the more useful horse; accordingly horses and carts made their appearance on the street in 1858, somewhat of a wonder to most, but the innovation was cordially welcomed. A greater surprise, however, was in store for the townspeople when Alex. Mollison landed on the jetty a real coach, having the tremendous words "Royal Mail" in large characters emblazoned on each side. And this too for the conveyance of passengers and mails as far as the Clutha. James McIntosh, who had ridden the south mails for some time previous, was the plucky introducer of the coaching business, and handled his whip so deftly and well that this "coach" proved safe at all times. Jimmie is now located at Lawrence carrying on a wider extent of business.

And not only was the inland traffic accelerated and much more comfortable, the seaward became even more rapid, as the paddle steamers "Prince Albert" and the smaller "Ada" were added to the fleet, and trading to the southern ports. The "Storm Bird," a screw steamer, was also added, and a new intercolonial steam service with Melbourne was inaugurated, the "Omeo" being the first of the line. Not to be behind the times, joint stock companies came prominently to the front. The "Brethren of the Mystic Tie" were asked to become subscribers for the erection of a Masonic Hall, and shortly after a company was being formed to work the coal fields at Green Island and Tokomairiro.

Private enterprise was also being steadily developed. In order to meet the increasing demand for victuals, in August 1859, Duncan's flour mill at the Water of Leith was started. This mill was of much higher character than any of its predecessors, the owner having introduced the most modern machinery as well as erected his building on the most approved principle. This portion of the building, as well as the water-wheel, are still in constant work, although now largely added to.

Mason and Wilson's iron foundry and steam saw-mills were opened in January, 1860, and His Honour the Superintendent presiding at the opening ceremony, expressed his pleasure at finding Dunedin so far advanced as to give encouragement to such an enterprise; and although it was but a small beginning, the time was not far distant when numerous works would be started by ship-builders and boiler-makers, busily employing many hands in making iron vessels, steam-engines, and also railway engines and carriages.

Taking advantage of the steam-power, a coffee and spice grinding establishment was shortly after erected contiguous to the sawmill. A second candle and soap works also sprang into existence in King-street, under the name of the Albion. And to give greater monetary facilities for the increasing trade and commerce, a branch of the Oriental Bank was opened in July 1860, but in August 1861 retired in favour of the Bank of New South Wales.

Although there had from the earliest days been a goodly number of Masonic brethren in the town, no successful effort had been made to bring the members together until August 1860, when the first Lodge was formed. Oddfellowship had been, as formerly noticed, early established, and had now a very comfortable little building in Princes-street, near the Bank of New South Wales. At about the same time a Teetotal Society was also formed, and that wonderful display, a Church bazaar was also held on the last day of 1860. During the period the liberality of the inhabitants was frequently called upon and liberally responded to, the claims from Britain connected with the Crimea and India receiving liberal acknowledgement; whilst from nearer home the straits to which the settlers at Taranaki were reduced by the Maori rising, kindled the liveliest sympathy, and every effort was put forth to render prompt and effective assistance. Fortunately for the place, very little want or destitution existed. Incurables were attended to at the hospital, and private unostentatious benevolence met all other requirements.

A few discursive remarks in closing this sketch of the first or "Old Identity" period may be allowed. It may, however, be fairly stated that the whole treatise shows too much diffusiveness; but the object has not been to preserve strict continuity or to exhaust each subject, simply to deal with each event as closely as possible in the order of occurrence.

Considerable friction occurred regarding the street levels. The Provincial Engineer had the fixing of the levels of the main streets through the town, but these he would not furnish to the Board, possibly having got his back up because the Board would not allow him to cut a straight line across the Octagon to connect Princes and George-streets as they now are. This divided authority in the town was of considerable hindrance to the Board, as no levels for the streets abutting on the main line could be determined under the circumstances, so that intending builders were at a disadvantage. The Board itself had no funds to pay for a thorough survey, so that under threats and denunciations it knew not what to do. Consequently the idea of throwing the whole onus on the shoulders of the Government was suggested. The streets certainly had not been much improved even under the Engineer, so that it was well remarked that in going along the main road through the Cutting it was common for travellers to sink knee-deep, and females often got helplessly stuck, and had to be dragged out by force of arms.

This condition of affairs had something to do with the attempt to carry out an old suggestion—that of making the Pelichet Bay flat the business part of the town. One or two large proprietors of town sections about Albany-street had sufficient influence to induce the Provincial Council to vote a considerable sum to build a jetty at Pelichet Bay ; but this was the whole length to which the proposed change was carried into effect. The trade of the town had become fixed, with High-street as its centre, and to move it would be an arduous task. A considerable portion of the municipal estate was in that locality, and the most of it had already been leased for business sites. So great was the desire to get possession of these, that while at the first sale in 1856 prices ranged from 8/- to 12/- a foot, in 1859 some of these which had been forfeited were re-sold at £1 13s to £2 a foot per annum.

The new Court House, too, had been built alongside the gaol, and almost every other condition was opposed to the scheme.

In the month of October, 1859, a very strong gale of north-west wind sprang up, and unfortunately some fires had been burning in the bush on the road up to Woodhaugh, by which the grand old forest trees were set ablaze, destroying all the magnificent timber, going along the course of the Leith till shore was reached.   None of the houses were burned, but many narrow escapes were made.

The allusion may be pardoned, but to those who belong to the "Old Identity" period, the statement will perhaps be received with some astonishment, that of all the firms who were in business in Dunedin before the Golden Era, only two now remain under the same name, marking the time that has gone past, and these are William Couston (Rattray-street), and William Wright (Gt. King-street).

The valuation and revenue of the town are not at present available, but a few other statistics by way of example may be excusable.   On 31st December, 1860, the population was : males, 1230 ; females, 1032 ; total 2262.   The births during the year were 290, marriages 74, deaths 51.   On 16th December, 1861, the census showed : males, 3630 ; females, 2326 ; total 5956.   In this number were embraced 106 officers and men of the 70th Regiment.

	Imports.	Exports.	Customs Revenue.
1859.	£243,871	£87,720	£18,742
1860.	£325,162	£80,268	£31,769
1861.	£859,733	£844,149	£93,199

The exports for 1861 include gold.

The opinion, almost amounting to conviction, had been entertained from the earliest years that Otago would become celebrated as a great gold-producing country.   This feeling received confirmation and strengthening as time rolled on.   Sometimes the rumours and reports were practical jokes, at others a substantial basis was shown for the statement. A "lump" was first reported to have been found in the North East Valley creek, and all Dunedin went thither to find themselves only befooled.   Then more officially gold was reported, as found in quartz, at Goodwood.   The surveyors were finding traces at the Mataura, the

Makerewa, the Waiau, the Dunstan, and at Moeraki, but for some time nothing importance was discovered. In 1860 a knowing old digger showed a sample of rough gold, which he said he had unearthed down the Peninsula, and tried to sell his secret for a reasonable sum, so much down before divining the spot. A couple of explorers started in search, and having, with the help of Proudfoot, the surveyor, examined a good portion of the bush, at length discovered two or three prospecting holes, but not a trace of the metal; so his little game did not come off. In May 1861, discoveries of gold at the Lindis were announced, assured to be a certainty, and thereto was a hurried concourse of eager steps directed. The field, however, proved not sufficiently rich to maintain a population eager for wealth, The Micawberism of the people was not to be much longer put to the test; nor much delay to be experienced until the strained anxiety and expectancy which had been of so long duration was fully satisfied. Whilst yet the disappointed Lindis troop had barely time to return to Dunedin, many of them sadly cast down and forlorn, hungry and weary from their tiresome journey, the full blaze of success appeared in an opposite direction. Suddenly the fact was realised that within comparatively easy distance of the town gold in almost fabulous quantity had been discovered, to obtain which required nothing more than ordinary manual labour with a shovel, a tin-dish, and a cradle. Specimens or samples, the result of an hour or two of inexpert work, amounting to three ounces of gold exhibited in a shop window, set Dunedin all ablaze.

Past existence had been a monotonous, pleasant experience. A slow steady development had been taking place, the population was like a large family annually growing, knowing and trusting each other to a large extent, but in the event of one individual attempting to shoot ahead being manifested, jealousy and disparaging prophecies were certain attendants. Now, however, an extraordinary overturn was to take place. What had been calm and placid suddenly became excited and restless. Even the grave seniors lost their equanimity and with a wise head-shake would say, we knew years ago there was plenty gold hid in the soil of Otago, and only waited the sturdiness of youth to find it out, but now we will go and get a share of it; so that although it was midwinter, Dunedin with its comfortable housing and certain supplies was deserted for the upland houseless region of Tuapeka with its lack of any provision for domestic comfort, save a little manuka scrub for a fire and a chance wild pig or stray sheep, to catch which entailed no little difficulty.

On the 24th June, 1861, the Tuapeka goldfields were proclaimed by the Provincial Government. The news was spread abroad over New Zealand, Australia, and onward to Britain. If Dunedin was deserted by its "old identity" male inhabitants, it was not long before their places were filled up a hundredfold. So rapidly did the news spread, and so attractive and reliable was it considered, that within three months from the date of the proclamation diggers were landing in Dunedin from the neighbouring colonies, sometimes at the rate of over one thousand a day. These came principally from the Victorian goldfields.

The conditions of the town were quite out of joint with the altered times. Dwellings, stores, offices, wharves, magistrates, police, light, water, fuel, provender, carriage, all were in short supply, with a daily increasing demand, and from whence was the demand to be supplied?

Habitations for the crowds did not exist. Sleeping room on a hotel floor without a mattress, at half-a-crown a night, was counted a luxury. The floors of the churches were proposed to be utilized, but the great relief was under calico. The tents with which the diggers came provided were soon set up on vacant sections, street lines, reserves, at the rear of premises, anywhere and everywhere were they pitched, and a new and varied population was in possession waiting for opportunities for themselves and their belongings to be conveyed to their destinations, or until their other plans were matured. To the credit of the crowds be it stated that their conduct throughout was worthy of the honesty and intelligence a genuine gold digger is known to possess. With a nominal police protection the life and property of the deserted females were as safe as in more settled times.

The more noteworthy events which occurred in the early digging days having special reference to Dunedin, may be briefly enumerated before alluding to civic affairs.

Commercial matters had now assumed considerable proportions, and the number of merchants was largely increased. It was therefore considered necessary that a Chamber of Commerce should be formed, which was accordingly done on the 23rd August, 1861. There was urgent need for such a recognised authority to give directions and decisions on mercantile affairs. This will appear more manifest when the fact is stated that no fewer than three wrecks of steamers had taken place on the coast between the first day of the year and the date of the inauguration of the Chamber. These were the "Ada" at the Molyneux, the "Victory" at Wickliff Bay, and the "Oberon" in Bluff Harbour. And these were within the year followed by the "Oscar," at New River. Various questions connected with such calamities as well as from fires, were likely to crop up, on which the combined opinion of such a body would prove invaluable. The steamers and sailing vessels trading coastwise and beyond the colony had greatly increased, and serious conflagrations were sure to be numerous, as almost all the new buildings which were being rushed up were built of timber.

Warehouses, bonded and free stores, hotels and accommodation houses, were being erected in scores, as fast as tradesmen could be got to put them together. Dwelling-houses, too, in wonderful diversity of shape, and of any available material, were showing in all directions. Empty cases, tin and zinc lining, old iron, bags and bagging, were all in requisition to provide domiciles. A few remnants of these *outré* buildings are still to be seen in Walker, Stafford, and Maclaggan streets, but the great majority have been effaced.

Means of transit to the goldfields were speedily being provided. Lots of horses and waggons for goods were imported, and the ubiquitous Cobb and Co. started their first coach to Gabriels early in October, and in January, 1863, the Company's coach made the trip through from the Dunstan in one day. Of course the roads were in a fearful state, and the strain on the poor horses was very great. The traffic was, however, carried on with wonderful regularity and freedom from accident, and a month later the first cab made its appearance on Dunedin streets, to be speedily followed by many others in different designs. In November, the *Daily Times* newspaper made its appearance, the offices being in Princes street, but before it had been a fortnight in existence, the first serious fire occurred, causing a loss of £10,000, which included the whole plant of the newspaper. However, by dint of great perseverance, and the favour of other printers, it appeared as usual the next morning. The same month the Bank of New Zealand opened its office in Rattray street, where its business was carried on for several years, accompanied almost simultaneously by the Bank of Australasia. Being in the same connection, it may be noticed here that in December 1863, the Bank of Otago was opened in Princes street, and after undergoing several vicissitudes, the name disappeared, to be resuscitated as the National of New Zealand. Within a week of this Bank of Otago, a rival institution, the New Zealand Banking Corporation, opened its doors in Manse street. Soon finding that the name was cumbrous, and apt to confuse with another Bank, the name was changed to the Commercial Bank. Its career was not, however, very successful, and after a few years its existence terminated. Kindred in character, but less pretentious, the Dunedin Savings Bank was opened in September, 1864, the depositors numbering 127, and the deposits £717. Under the careful supervision of the manager this institution continues flourishing up to the present date, although when the Government system of Savings Banks was years afterwards introduced, the desire was to absorb the local institution, an attempt which was stoutly and successfully resisted.

As usually happens, the crowding of buildings of such a highly inflammable nature as wood, and containing goods of a dangerous class—spirits, oils, &c.—led to fires which became very numerous and destructive, in one or two instances attended with loss of life. A meeting to organise a fire brigade was held in August, 1862. The estimate has been made that the loss by fire to the end of 1865 amounted to £150,000. Several Fire Insurance Agencies had been opened, representing colonial and foreign offices, and in the end of 1863 a local Fire and Marine office was projected, and although started did not long survive. Early in 1862 a Gas and Coke Company was formed, and the lighting was in the hands of private enterprise until purchased by the Corporation in 1875 for £43,000. The first gas was lit in May, 1863. In September,

1864, the Water Works Company was formed, to introduce the water from Ross Creek, and continued in possession till their works were also bought by the City for £120,000 in 1874.

As was to be expected, with the increase of population came also an increase of infirmity and want. To provide for these attendant evils a movement was made to establish the Benevolent Institute, to which liberal subscriptions were given, and a bazaar held September 1864 realised £1,100 for the same object. As in former years to outside calls a deaf ear was not turned, the Lancashire Relief Fund having had about £1,000 transmitted, and the English and Scottish District Relief Fund close on £3,000. One very sad calamity occurred during this period. By a collision in the harbour on the 4th July, 1863, the Rev. H. Campbell, first rector of the High School, with his five children and two servants, who had only the previous day arrived from London, were all drowned.

The business requirements of the town demanded greater facilities of communication with the Port than existed. Everything must be done not only with the least possible delay, but with the utmost despatch. The road to Port Chalmers was like all the others in wet weather, execrable, so the first telegraph post was placed in position in May 1862, and the whole was completed and in working order in a very short time. The Government system to Invercargill and Christchurch was opened in 1865. Not to be behind in providing amusements for the people—and also for profit—the Princess Theatre was opened on 4th March, 1862, followed by the Theatre Royal on 12th July afterwards. Billiard matches and cricket, to which the most noted players that could be obtained were invited and tempted by high rewards for exhibition of their skill. Caledonian sports were held in the Horse Bazaar on 1st January, 1862, the Society was forthwith formed, and on the first day of 1863 the first gathering took place, which has interruptedly been held since on each New Year's Day. Horse racing had in the olden time been carried on by fits and starts, it was now to be confirmed as an institution. A Jockey Club was formed, and the first race-meeting took place on the 24th March, 1862 ; on 4th March, 1863, a champion cup of £1,000, with sweeps, was run for under its auspices at Silverstream, and won by Ladybird. All these things were the outcome of private enterprise, and give but a faint idea of the stir and bustle of the earlier years of the golden age.

The Provincial Government had heavy responsibilities cast on them by the new state of affairs. The maintenance of order and suppression of crime were theirs. A thoroughly efficient police force must be at once obtained, and in response to a request to the Victorian Government a commissioner and number of men were at once sent across from Melbourne, of whom any country in the world might be proud. St. John Brannigan and his officers and men had arduous and daring duties to perform in a country with which they were unacquainted, in a climate far more severe than that to which they had been accustomed, and in houseless, trackless mountainous regions, hardly fit at the time for human habitation. These duties were gallantly performed even to the sacrifice of the lives of several of their number. And the greater honour is due to the memories of some of them from the fact that they perished when out searching for some poor digger who had lost himself in the angry piercing snow storms which so often occur in the mountainous regions.

Owing greatly to the vigilance of the police, the record of crime of a serious character was a very light one. A case or two of sticking up, and one case of murder—which never was traced—another of poisoning, for which the culprit forfeited his life,—the first execution in Otago—were the only blots on Dunedin history. Not satisfied, however, with the police, the Government obtained a detachment of officers and men of the 70th Regiment, to be ready for any emergency. It was a needless precaution, however, so after about eighteen months' stay this only representation of the British army which had ever set foot on Otago shore, or is ever likely to do so, took its departure.

To provide wharf accommodation was also incumbent on the Government, so the wharf at Jetty-street was greatly extended, widened, and strengthened; new ones were also speedily run out at Rattray and Stuart-streets, and every effort made to give facilities for the landing of goods. In carrying out these new works, the first steps were also taken in harbour reclamation. The work of reducing Bell Hill began in October 1862, the excuse being that the stuff was needed to fill in the foreshore, and form Bond and Jetty-streets.

The Provincial Government deserve also credit for their liberal efforts to add permanent structures in the adornment of the town. To this period is due the erection of the Custom House, the present Post Office and Court House, and the Provincial buildings and Council Hall, the Colonial Bank (built for the Post Office), all of which, although not finished, were in hand. Then in memory of the first Superintendent the Cargill Monument was erected in the centre of the Octagon, but afterwards removed to its present site, so that the straight line of the street might be obtained. Perhaps the most plucky venture of all was the Dunedin Exhibition, the foundation stone of the building being laid masonically on 17th February, 1864. The idea was at first considered quite beyond the means of the province and premature. The result proved differently, as it was a complete success. The building is now used as the Hospital.

This may well be called the transition period of the town. The sudden emergence from almost rural simplicity and quietness into unwonted energy and bustle, occasioned many anomalies. The most of the business establishments were temporary in character, and have since been almost all swept away, and others of a more permanent nature occupy their place ; in many instances, too, the characteristics of the locality have been changed. Formerly Stafford-street and Walker-street were the busiest of the busy ; now they are greatly deserted.

How has the Town Board been progressing during this time? Certainly not satisfactorily, for on 13th April, 1865, an ordinance was passed by the Provincial Council dissolving it.

The authority which created it now pronounced its doom. And why ? Either the members were not fit for the position, or perhaps the body had not a sufficiently honourable title for the Dunedin of the period !

The Town Board may also have accomplished its temporary purpose, and was erased to make room for a new order. Let it be here recorded that in eleven short years afterwards the Provincial Government followed to the same bourne, as in 1876 it was abolished by the Act of the Assembly. This uncalled-for Act has been disastrous, as the Council was verily a true nursing father to Dunedin.

Extravagance and incapacity were imputed to the Board. In their favour something may be advanced. To form the streets, after reducing or filling up to the permanent levels, was a herculean task, and looking back now the wonder is how it was so well accomplished in the abnormal circumstances. The Provincial Government were certainly liberal in their assistance. For in addition to the continued maintenance of the main line, a loan of £30,000 was made, which was afterwards converted into a gift. The engineer, Millar, F.S.A., was one of the new introductions, and so were most of the members of the Board before its dissolution. One great blame cast on the Engineer was designing extravagant lamp-posts with the motto "secundo curo" (I prosper, I take care) impressed thereon, and which he had also added to and engraved on the public seal of the Board, which had borne hitherto neither device nor motto, but only the plain shield, and name.

There were differences of opinion among the public as to the wisdom of the Government action, one meeting having been held at which, the Provincial Council was denounced for executing the Board, by old identities particularly, who had a fondness for the title.

To fill the interregnum between the old state of affairs and the intended new order, a Board of three Commissioners was appointed to take charge of town affairs, and for the first time in its existence by this dissolution ordinance, Dunedin was called a city. It cannot be said that the dignity was due to any ecclesiastical position, as the first bishop was not designated for months afterwards. And it is furthermore a strange fact that in all the acts passed by the Supreme Legislature of the colony dealing with municipal corporations, Dunedin for long was the only one called a city, all the others ranking as towns or boroughs.

- The ordinance having been passed by the Provincial Council, the citizens were called on to elect their first mayor, which was done on 21st July, 1865, when there were five candidates. The city was divided into four wards, for councillors, each having two members, who were chosen on 1st August. The election of mayor is annual, and is made by the ratepayers of the city. The number of councillors was some years subsequently increased to twelve. Aldermanic days have not yet, however, arrived.

The different City Councils, since their initiation, have each and all done the best they could to improve the streets and render things more comfortable for the inhabitants. Mistakes have undoubtedly been made, but these are inseparable from all sublunary undertakings. Some of these have been gross blunders, and entailed large expenses, but with the buoyancy of a new life they were soon condoned.

The city thoroughfares had the primary claim, so every effort was made to get the proper levels and formation, which, being done, footpaths and kerbing speedily followed ; so that in the words of an old identity in 1870, who had for a short time been an absentee, "you can walk frae ae end o' the town tae the ither without filing yer shoon." A considerable amount has still to be done before the plans are completed, and many section-owners will be put to large cost to reduce their property to the street level. It would be tedious to give details of the costs of city works up to this period ; enough will be said when it is stated that the City Surveyor in 1878 estimated, in reply to a resolution of the Council asking for the cost of "works that ought to be undertaken in each ward, in order to complete the formatiom of streets and footpaths, and to provide for surface drainage," also for "the extension of underground sewerage for each ward, in order to complete a thorough system of drainage for the city,"— that "to complete the works required under the first paragraph of the resolution will require a total expenditure of £97,837, and the expenditure for underground sewers, of £44,000 ; being a total of £141,873." This, be it remembered, was additional to the large sums previously expended. However, the work of formation has now been carried out nearly to a successful completion.

The Gas Works threatened for a time to be a white elephant in the hands of the Corporation, and a source of lasting regret to the inhabitants that ever they had fallen into the hands of the municipality. Recriminations bitter and biting were made in the Council Chambers and in the Press. A solution was eventually discovered, when, by the substitution of Mr Graham as manager, the price has been reduced, the quality improved, the works renovated, and after all done, a handsome surplus accrues to the Corporation funds as profit revenue.

The Water Works bear a different complexion. The scheme, as originally designed, and for the purchase of which the city was mulcted in a large amount, was quite unsuitable for the requirements, and a constant source of ill-founded fears of danger. Several schemes were proposed to augment the supply, and acrimony in its worst features was displayed in the Council Chamber in discussing the various plans. Ultimately and wisely the Silver Stream project was adopted and carried out in a raw and undigested method, but which, by the expenditure of a few thousands additional, could be made renumerative and exempt from claims for damage. The cost of this additional water supply to the Corporation was £81,758.

There was nothing else of a public character worth noticing in which the Corporation had been engaged, excepting the erection of the Municipal buildings and the management of the city reserves.

These Municipal buildings were founded in 1874 and opened in 1875, at a cost of £22,000, the names of the mayors of both dates being inscribed on the portals. [As these and the other edifices of the city are particularly elsewhere herein described, further reference is unnecessary.]

The condition of the reserves is a public disgrace. Each and all of them intended to adorn and beautify the town, are instead a blotch on its fair features. Not but money has been thereon and therein expended. It appears to have been too easily obtained to have been so speedily squandered. Take any or all of them, the same remark applies to each. The Octagon (as the oldest) is disgraceful, the Triangle (as the youngest) is not one whit better. Any amount of expense has been gone to in providing, planting and protecting trees, but this having once been done, no further care has been taken, so that the Octagon has become a mark of reproach, and the trees in the Triangle broken down by thoughtless football players. Visit the Botanic Gardens, which, a few years ago, were unfortunately transferred to the City Council as conservators, and instead of having improved under the new custodians, have become a byeword among the people. The old native growths, which afforded grand botanic specimens, have been ruthlessly destroyed, never to be restored, and a few of the most common pines of Europe occupy their place. Let no one expect in visiting these Gardens to find any plant either native, rare, curious, or attractive, worthy of notice. The Leith stream is also now an eyesore, and it would repay those interested to open a new channel through the hill at the Botanic Gardens, and fill up the present bed. The manure depôt at the University entrance is abominable.

The same calamity seems to attend the action of the Council in providing baths for the people. The ridiculous efforts made by the continued wisdom of the councillors in making provision in this behalf, culminated in the baths at Logan's Point, the waters of which are credited with containing a good admixture of city drainage. The matter is not, however, settled, and in its wisdom the Council may see fit to spend a few more thousands of the city taxes.

It is an easy matter to criticise and find fault with the action of others, at the same time the question may pertinently be put, By whom will it be better done ?

The great enterprises which have been developed in the city, whether industrial, as connected with metals and produce of all descriptions, together with our shipping, banking, insurance and other interests, will be found more fully detailed in the portion devoted to them specially.

The harbour improvements alone need therefore be alluded to. These must in a great measure speak for themselves. Reclamation was commenced by the Provincial Government as formerly noticed, and in 1874 Otago Harbour Board was constituted, to which the further prosecution of this work, along with others associated, was fully committed. Although the name gives it the wider range of Otago, still strictly speaking the principal part of the work done, and to be done, is connected with the city. In earlier days there were two channels leading up from Port. The long and deep one round by Macandrew's Bay was that principally used, the shorter and present one was only available for lighter-draughted vessels, and even then only at high water. Considerable discussion ensued as to which was the better to be made the permanent one, and with a wise discretion Mr D. L. Simpson, the Engineer, a man eminently fitted for the position, decided on the short one, and otherwise designed all the harbour improvements. Had the Engineer received fair play from his Board, he would have continued in his position, and the works would have been much further forward. However, an amount of personal feeling was introduced, and caused his retirement.

The Board from time to time has been allowed to borrow £700,000, more than half of which has been expended on the upper harbour and on the jetties, with the success that now ships drawing close on to 20 feet can be safely brought up to the city to discharge and load. The extent of the proposed reclamation will add to the city area about 420 acres; this does not include all the harbour endowment, a portion being attached to neighbouring boroughs. The revenues arriving from this reclaimed land is annually increasing. Like all the other portions of our commonwealth, the Harbour Trust has had to undergo a period of 'trial, but with returning prosperity it enjoys an increasing revenue, and will, no doubt, soon be able to resume those operations which scarcity of funds has caused for the present to be suspended.

With wise and enlightened policy the Board has made the new streets, which are by its work added to the city, in some cases one and a half chains wide, and in the case of Cumberland street has so increased its length as to make it about two and a half miles long. This street throughout its added length will be built on only one side, as eastward it is used by the Railway. The advantages which have accrued to the citizens generally, by the deepening of the harbour, cannot be over-estimated. That it has been detrimental to Port Chalmers cannot be questioned, and that it will soon be more so is self-evident, as the channel must be so much further deepened as to allow all vessels crossing the bar to stear up to the city wharves.

A word may be said in regard to the suburban boroughs. The first new township proposed was at the end of 1860, when Richmond Hill—a portion of what is now Mornington—was placed in the market, and meeting a fairly ready sale, was followed by Balaclava, another portion of the same borough. The township of St. Kilda next followed suit, laid out with some pretensions to be a resemblance to a town. The boroughs, in the order of their charter of erection, stand: South Dunedin, St. Kilda, Caversham, Mornington, Roslyn, Maori Hill, North East Valley, and North

East Harbour. Some of these names are rather lengthy, requiring more time and ink in their frequent inscription than the borough rates can afford. Old associations were wrapt up in them, however, and with becoming dignity the originators adopted the motto, " Wha daur meddle wi them ? " which feeling is aptly illustrated by the case of the " Sawyer's Bay " railway station, when the Government tried to change its name to the more euphonious title of " Glendermid." The people would not have it, and the voice of the gods prevailed over the fiat of the crown.

Fluctuations in prosperity have been often experienced ; sometimes matters getting so bad as almost to induce despair anon brightening, raising hopes to enthusiasm. These alternations can neither be predicted nor averted. They come almost as if in the usual course. Influences from without are the most powerful. Our country can produce far more than its population can consume. And if a responsive market cannot be found, we must stagnate. On the prosperity of our agriculturists mainly depends that of the town. Wool-growers show larger values in yields and exports ; but for every hand the squatter employs the farmer represents ten. And on the larger number the mechanics and handicraftsmen of the city mainly depend.

If it had been the design in this imperfect history to provoke a smile, arouse indignation, elicit a surprise, or cause a tear, it could easily have been done. Did not the first City Council among its first acts issue an ukase that thenceforward no bells would be allowed to be rung on the public streets, which still holds good ? This cruel edict silenced for ever the sound of Sandy Low's warning voice, and evoked the awful blast of Joe Manton's trumpet. Did it not fall to be the duty of the first Mayors' Court to try the sheriff of the Province for larceny as a baillee, and allow him an easy way of escape ? Was it not a fact that at dead of night the cannon's roar was heard along all the affrighted shore, and yet when the brave defenders turned out in battle array they found themselves the subjects of a laughable hoax ? Did not the dew drops "fa' frae the ee" when the city representatives returned from Wellington and were received with a shower of "sulphuretted hydrogen," and the stirring strains of the rogue's march in sweetest cadences on kerosene tins? And did not the people hold a Fast for disasters by sea and land? Did not a scion of Royalty visit our plebeian town and dance with the Mayoress? Yes, of a truth, there is sufficient data.

In 1871 the University of Otago was formally opened; in 1872 the Port Chalmers Railway was partially opened, and a month thereafter the first cablegram arrived from London in eight days, congratulating the Province on the event. The construction of the Government Railways was also after 1870 undertaken, and eventually opened both north and south. No one rejoiced more than the able financier who had conceived and brought to maturity this Public Works scheme, which, in the detached state of interests formerly existing, must have been for some time postponed but for his ability and energy. In 1874 the ship " Surat" was cast away at Catlins River with a large complement of Government immigrants on board, though happily no lives were lost. This circumstance is mentioned because the " Surat" was the first passenger ship coming to Otago from Britain to which any serious casualty had occurred. There had hitherto been an almost total exemption from accident during the six-and-twenty-years that had passed.

Remarks general must now be brought to a focus, and as figures convey better ideas than words, a line or two may profitably be devoted to statistical references.

The amount of the rates, rents, and licenses, forming the city revenue, was in 1878 £27,932, in 1884 it had increased to £41,000, in 1889 it had receded by something like £10,000, thus showing the depreciation in the value of city property. The city alone was not the only sufferer; every interest and department had to undergo a trial, of which sufficient for the day was the evil thereof. Up and away again is the principle on which colonial life is actuated, and herein was no exception. In this year of grace, 1889, with the material increase in the quantity, variety, and value of our products and exports, the dawn of returning prosperity has fairly set in, and with greater prudence, learned from experience, it will steadily increase until the lost in the past is regained in the future.

By the last census, taken 28th March, 1886, the population of Dunedin proper was 23,243, or with the contiguous boroughs of Caversham, 4,448; South Dunedin, 3,902; Roslyn, 3,609; Mornington, 3,334; North East Valley, 3,221; Maori Hill, 1,388; West Harbour, 1,295; St. Kilda, 1,078; Ship board, 93; the gross population amounted to 45,611; Auckland with its suburbs alone, among the towns of the colony, exceeding this number with a total population of 46,654. The population for subsequent years cannot be given with anything like accuracy, the excess of births and arrivals over deaths and departures being the only basis on which to estimate. There can be no doubt in any unbiassed mind but that the population generally has been reduced during the past two years.

The vital statistics for Dunedin are :—

	Births.	Marriages.	Deaths.
1886	1589	354	621
1887	1497	391	582
1888	1430	383	600
7 months, 1889	794	240	345

The declared value of imports and exports, and the revenue collected at Custom House for Otago during

1886	Imports	1,875,396	Exports	1,737,899
1887	,,	1,721,840	,,	1,901,661
1888	,,	1,706,295	,,	1,792,984

The values are not correctly stated in the Customs returns, as the last port of departure and possibly first of arrival gets credit for the whole value of the cargo, although the largest part properly belongs to other ports. The direct steamers are the cause of this discrepancy, of which the frozen meat trade returns afford a striking instance.

The Customs revenue collected at Dunedin for—

1886	was	£319,499
1887	,,	£309,584
1888	,,	£350,913

The quantity and value of gold exported from Dunedin from 1861 to 1888 is 4,656,126 oz., value £18,374,522.

The latest development of progress, and one which deserves special attention, is the New Zealand and South Seas Exhibition. Twenty-four years have passed since the first Exhibition was held in Dunedin on the lines of the Great World's Fair at London in 1862. A satisfactory result ensued from the attempt.

It is true that the Provincial Government, with the Provincial revenues at its disposal, was the mainspring and greatest supporter of the whole affair. By it the building was erected as a permanent structure, and as formerly noted, serves now another purpose.

The present Exhibition is a spontaneous outcome from the citizens themselves. All ranks and degrees have taken a share in the risk. From the highest Commercial Institutions subcribing their hundreds, on to the workers in shops and factories contributing their shillings; each is earnest in the effort, and where so much enthusiasm internally prevails, it is bound to spread and elicit a hearty response from an extensive circle. Everything promises well. Even the weather, which in former years was wont to deluge the country during the winter months, has this season restricted its outpourings, and the people congratulate themselves on having the driest period ever before experienced. If the large amount of support promised comes at all in its fulfilment up to the mark, there will be one of the most extensive and interesting displays of the past and present mechanical tastes and abilities of the aboriginal South Sea Islanders, in contrast and comparison with the best efforts of civilization, which has ever been presented to the world. Local jealousies, which at the initiation of the project showed themselves, are now becoming hid or extinguished, and for the sake of the colony it is to be hoped that Dunedin, having single-handed undertaken the whole cost and responsibility—except a small contribution from the Government—of this somewhat expensive undertaking, will find that loyally the other cities and provinces will rally around, and by combined effort make this exposition of the colony's industries a stepping-stone from which every interest in the colony will make a rapid and steady advance.

The Commissioners are doing their very best, and under the guidance of the chairman, Mr John Roberts, whose cautious, yet earnest and clear foresight has opened the way, are making rough places plain, little doubt can exist; but that this effort will result in proving that these distant colonies of Britain are able to compete in many departments of trade with the mother country.

Instead of quoting " Seé Europe Once," a transposition might be made, and we might say—

Dunedin, late "a mighty wild, science and art unknown "; and contrast that comprehensive description with what now obtains. The fathers have lived to see their infant settlement growing in growth and strengthening in strength day by day, and ere yet the last of these old worthies has vanished from this changeful stage, the scene is presented of the primeval wild transformed to a state of high civilization. A large and handsome city occupies the site, where, within memory's reach, not a house existed, and a godlike image was not. Where the umbrageous shades of myriads of stately trees and witching fronds afforded shelter to those numberless denizens of lowly nature, to whom this retreat had been given as their special birthright; and where afterwards a type of humanity, void of culture, obtained a footing and revelled in atrocious deeds; are now palaces and towers, teeming warehouses and emporiums, streets and terraces, tramways, palace cars, busses, cabs, and carriages—every approved means of locomotion; the arts and sciences; education in its every grade; religions numbering in their divisions nearly a score, amusements, games, and the thousand and odd accompaniments of modern civilization, which have all taken root, and flourish amazingly in this juvenile Dunedin. A precocity in growth does not always indicate weakness or premature senility.

JAMES MACINDOE.

GEOLOGY OF DUNEDIN.

BY GEORGE J. BINNS,

F.G.S. (Lond.); Mem. of Council, G.S.A.; Ord. Mem. North of
England Inst. of Mining and Mechanical Engineers; Government Inspector of Mines, and Lecturer on General Geology
at the Otago University.

IN writing the following paper, the author has taken
full advantage of the various publications dealing with
the subject, and desires to mention the progress reports of the New Zealand Geological Survey (Sir Jas.
Hector, K.C.M.G., F.R.S., Director); the "Geology
of Otago," by Profs. Hutton and Ulrich, and several
papers in the Transactions of the New Zealand Institute.

For convenience of reference, the subject is divided as
follows :—

    I. Introduction and sketch of geological structure.

    II. Economic geology.

        1. Soil.

        2. Coal and oil shales.

        3. Sand.

        4. Clays.

        5. Building and ornamental stones, including cements.

        6. Gold.

    III. Minerals.

    IV. Appendix.

I.—INTRODUCTION AND SKETCH OF GEOLOGICAL STRUCTURE.

It is possible that while to the casual observer the geology of
the neighbourhood of Dunedin might not prove so interesting as
that of many other portions of the colony, still, for the general
student, there are many instances of geological phenomena which
would rivet the attention, and furnish ample food for reflection.

At the same time, there are various points capable of affording matter for investigation and discussion.

It would, perhaps, be best in giving a general sketch of the structural features of a locality to ascend in a balloon, and while suspended in mid-air, to take a bird's-eye view of the surface of the country, noting the configuration and character of the land, and observing how each formation has left its impress on the present features of the soil. An opportunity of this nature seldom, however, offers itself, and failing such easy means of ascent, the next best thing is perhaps to climb, by a very easy path, it is true, to the summit of Flagstaff—a basaltic hill 2192 feet in height, and situated to the north-east of the city. To the admirers of scenery alone, their reward is immediate and ample Fain would the writer linger a moment in description of the grandeur and scope of the view, but regretfully he is compelled, for fear of trespassing, to leave any description of it to his colleagues in the congenial task of describing the surroundings of the capital of Otago.

Looking away to the west we see the peaks and pinnacles of the interior of the Province, part of the great mica-schist country through which the Central Railway is now slowly fighting its way to the inland plain of the Maniototo, the Ida Valley, and the fertile banks and river flats of the Taieri, the Clutha, and the Manuherikia. Turning round more to the south, the dark and rounded form of Maungatua forms a landmark, from which the eye follows the horizon down to Quoin Point and beyond to a distant glimpse of the Nuggets. Between Maungatua and Saddle Hill, which is another basaltic peak, come the fertile plains of the Taieri, laid out in true chess-board pattern, and marking an ancient lake, into which the river of that name flowed, no doubt as a muddy stream, and whence it pursued its limpid course towards the ocean, until in the fulness of time the lake became a swamp, and the swamp, under the fostering care and industry of man, grew into a fertile tract of land, dotted with homesteads and clustering clumps of trees. To the immediate east of Saddle Hill, we see the Kaikorai River, which marks about the centre of the Green Island coal-field, the soft rocks composing which have been hollowed out and eroded until the sea flows at high tide far up the flat. Slightly to the east of the river mouth—which is gradually filled up in fine weather with a sandy barrier, through which the water finds its way, and which is destroyed by the first flood—we again meet with the basalt, this time descending to sea-level, and forming what is known as the Green Island Bluff—a picturesque headland, with fine examples of columnar structure, and forming a protection to the soft sandstone cliffs further on, of which, however, we can, from our present position, see nothing. Could we look over the top of the cliff, we should see very striking evidences of marine erosion, pinnacles and caves—one of the latter of considerable dimensions—with natural arches through which the green seas rush and swirl in their hungry efforts to devour the land. This elevated stretch of country is terminated at the Forbury Head by a sharp descent to sea-level, the base of the hill forming a charming site for the sheltered health-resort named St. Clair; and from this point the eye follows the ocean level along a line of sandhills to another basaltic promontory known as Lawyer's Head, which forms the commencement of the Otago Peninsula. It has been proposed, at this point, where the distance between the open sea and the waters of the harbour is but small, to cut a channel through the isthmus, and form a shorter and better entrance to the Dunedin wharves. At present the idea is not in great favour, but like other extensive public projects, it will no doubt return to popularity, and perhaps eventually be carried out. The Peninsula is a tract of land about 15 miles in length, formed principally of basaltic and trachytic rocks, and indented with several deep and sheltered bays. As our line of sight is necessarily straight across the harbour, looking due east, the nearer elevation of Signal Hill intervenes between our stand-point and Harbour Cone; but it is only when the greater height of Mount Cargill shuts out the distance, that we lose sight of the Peninsula. Still turning round, we pass the isolated peak of Mihiwaka, and following the coast, the character of which is indicated by several basaltic hills, we come again to the mica-schist hills of the interior. Merely stopping a moment to say good-bye to the beautiful panorama around us, we must descend to the flat, and resume our observations in a more detailed manner.

On this occasion it is best to commence some distance from the town, so with the reader's permission, we will take him to

Waihola Railway Station, 26 miles away on the main South line, where, on the borders of the lake, and well exposed in the cutting, we find a deposit consisting of moderately coarse beds of sand and silt, containing large angular blocks, and dipping to the south-east at somewhat low angles up to 30 deg. Within the township these sands have been invaded by volcanic rocks, which appear as massive dykes from four to fifteen feet across, considerably altering and indurating the sands and clays, and within the upper township breaking through the lower beds of the coarser upper part of the formation. This deposit, which is supposed to be of glacial origin, extends from Waihola in a north-easterly direction to Brighton, a distance of about twelve miles, and is in its upper part, composed of exceedingly angular material, the blocks in places being from five to ten and even twelve feet in diameter, loosely compacted together, the fragments being often surrounded with fine material. Passing the Taieri River, which drains a considerable area of the north-eastern portion of Otago, and at the mouth of which, as also further down the coast, there are valuable deposits of manganese; we skirt the Taieri Plain, leaving an outline of the Green Island coalfield on our right, where the basaltic peak of Saddle Hill caps the coal measures, and plunge into the bowels of the earth at the Chain Hill tunnel, which is excavated through a formation of fine-grained laminated mica-schists or phyllites. These form a ridge of hills which run out to the sea-coast at Brighton, and soon after leaving the heavy cutting, we are on the borders of the coal measures, which lie unconformably on the schists, and deserve more than a passing notice. The rocks here consist of sandstones, shales and clays, with seams of coal; these dip in an easterly direction at one in ten under the Caversham sandstone, which is a tertiary marine formation, and is again overlaid by the volcanic rocks of the Dunedin basin. The coal-seams extend along the western boundary in a line running from the mouth of the Otakia Creek for about nine miles to the valley of the Water of Leith. Starting at Brighton, the south-western limit of the field, we find, not far above sea level, a seam of coal 14 feet in thickness, dipping to the east at six deg., and worked on a small scale by an adit. The natural cover of the seam has been in places denuded, and a recent

river-gravel takes its place.   " The grits, sands and clays forming
" the proper coal measures are here overlaid by limonitic
" sandstones and a gritty calcareous rock full of shell fragments
" that almost without exception belong to a species of oyster
" that cannot be distinguished from the black oyster of the
" Malvern Hills, Canterbury.   In the same beds occur
" numerous fusiform bodies, respecting the zoological affinities
" of which there has long been a difference of opinion, viz.,
" whether they should be referred to the belemnitidæ or simply
" considered cidaris spines changed to aragonite, and thus
" acquiring a fibrous, radiated structure.   Fortunately, among
" a considerable series of these fossils collected by Mr McKay on
" this occasion, there prove to be at least two specimens showing
" distinct traces of an alveolar cavity (no phragmacone being
" present); and there is also another specimen preserving the
" upper portion of the guard sufficiently well to show that
" originally there was a ventral groove or fissure, the lower part
" of which can be traced in the shell structure.   This would
" indicate that the fossil is a species of belemnitella, and not a
" true belemnite."   (Geological Survey report 1886-87, p. xxix.)
As the actual determination of this organism is obviously a
matter of great importance in determining the age of the coals,
it has been thought better to quote Sir James Hector's remarks
in full.

Above the locality here referred to, to the south-west, the
hill rises to a height of 1560 feet, and is capped by the dolerites
and basalts of Saddle Hill.   Round the edges of the schists, the
coal-measures follow the former land area, to an out-crop at the
Halfway Bush, but the coal there has the character of a
bituminous shale, and contains a large proportion of ash.   In
the Water of Leith, fragments of coal have been found, which
indicate that the seams in that direction have been altered by
the igneous rocks ; one specimen, stated to have been found in
the Botanic Garden Reserve, had the property of caking, which
is quite exceptional, even among the altered brown coals.

It is now necessary to return to the point where we left the
schists, and resume our course over the coal-measures, noting
how the working of the seams at Green Island has caused
numerous fractures of the surface.   Shortly before arriving at

Caversham station, we enter a tunnel which is 950 yards in length, and excavated entirely in the sandstone, here remarkably compact, containing only five or six cracks in its total length. It is a soft calcareous sandstone, generally bluish-grey, or yellow, and unfortunately not well adapted for building purposes ; had it not been for a protecting cover of basalt, no doubt erosion and weathering would have obviated any necessity for taking the railway below ground. Before arriving at Dunedin we skirt the hills on our left, leaving the South Dunedin flat on our right, bounded by the sandhills in the distance, and at the Kensington Crossing a fine exposure of spheroidally weathered basalt presents itself.

From the Dunedin station the railway follows generally the outline of the harbour, and as we pass, attention is naturally directed to the great excavations in the volcanic rocks, from which enormous quantities of road metal have been extracted. Further on volcanic tuff and trachytic rocks appear, until at Sawyer's Bay sandstone is again met with. This extends right across the harbour to Broad Bay, below Mr Larnach's mansion, which forms a landmark for many miles, and on that side of the harbour the formation yields an excellent building stone. At Port Chalmers there is a large quarry of trachyte breccia, of which the graving-dock at that town is built, as are also partially many of the large public buildings in Dunedin. Over the Mihiwaka tunnel lie volcanic tuff rocks, in which thin seams of coal have been found. In June 1886, while prospecting operations were being carried on, the writer had an opportunity of examining these deposits, and observed a two-foot seam of carbonaceous shale, with thin seams of jetty coal, dipping S. 15 deg. E. at 9 deg. It was stated that in a short distance the thickness increased to 4ft. 6ins. Further down the hill the seam dips at 35 deg. to the south-west, and is much faulted and broken ; it was here only 2 or 3 inches thick. Shortly after leaving the last tunnel, we creep along the Purakanui cliffs, looking down from a giddy height upon the green waters of the Pacific Ocean, lazily lapping the base of the rocks below, or surging and boiling with the fury of the storm. From the other side of the elevated portion of the railway, Blueskin Bay is exposed to view, at high tide a lovely bay, encircled by bush-clad hills, and almost enclosed by a sand-

bank, which runs out from the northern side. At low tide, when
the inlet is principally mud-flat, the prospect is much less allur-
ing. At Waitati Station we are again at sea-level, and to our
left, up the valley, calcareous sandstones are seen, while further
up [the creek are oil shales and a seam of coal. From the native
village of Puketeraki, we see the harbour of Waikouaiti, the
northern headland of which is formed of the Ototara sandstone;
this is sometimes pointed out as *the* natural harbour of eastern
Otago, and had fate willed otherwise than it has, there is no
doubt that the rolling downs behind the town would have made
a charming site for a city. On our left is now the great mica-
schist formation, with the coal-beds and greensands lying upon
its flanks, and here and there a solitary basaltic peak, the
renmant of a once continuous sheet, which, in Miocene or post-
Miocene times, was poured over the whole district.

Just before entering the town of Palmerston, we pass through
greensands, which are economically important, as they contain
considerable quantities of valuable iron ore. A sample taken
from the deep cutting opposite Mount Royal Station, though
apparently consisting of little else than greensand, yielded, on
analysis in the Colonial Laboratory, 37 per cent. of spathic iron
ore. Large masses of this stone exist, and no doubt some day
it will be utilised for the manufacture of iron.

From the foregoing sketch it will be seen that in this portion
of Otago, the following formations are present :—

1. *Quaternary.*—Recent Alluvium, æolian, and moa-beds.
2. *Cainozoic.*—Caversham sandstone, volcanic series.
3. *Cretaceo-tertiary.*—Coal-beds.
4. *Palæozoic.*—Schists.

I. *Recent.*—The recent deposits in the neighbourhood of
Dunedin comprise the river-beds, harbour deposits, and the
extensive Æolian deposits on the coast. The last-mentioned are
of considerable area and importance. They commence beyond
Green Island, at Brighton, near the belt of schist, which here
reaches to the sea, and forms the picturesque headland upon
which the township is situated. Further to the east they increase
in magnitude, and, as has been mentioned, the sand forms, at the
mouth of the Kaikorai stream, a bar, which is swept away in
times of floods, only to re-form as the volume of water becomes

gradually less. This forms a very good example of the opposing fluviatile and marine geological agencies. This point was evidently a favourite camping ground for the Maoris, for many good examples of their stone implements have been found in the locality. On approaching the Green Island Bluff, the sand has encroached very considerably on the land, and caused a good deal of damage; but from this point for about 3 miles we find no dunes, as the coast is formed of cliffs composed of the Caversham sandstone, which is easily worn away by the beating of the waves, assisted in stormy weather by an irresistible volley of basaltic boulders derived from the easily fractured columns at the Green Island Bluff. At St. Clair we again meet with sandy deposits, which rise into hillocks of moderate height, and are especially interesting because among them are found, in great profusion, beautiful examples of sand-worn stones having that peculiar triangular section which is so familiar and striking. About this point a short portion of the beach has been attempted to be reclaimed, and on it a marine esplanade has been laid out, but recently unusually severe storms have washed away the retaining wall, and greatly damaged the appearance of the locality. From the western extremity to Lawyer's Head, a distance of two miles, are wonderful natural facilities for the construction of one of the most magnificent promenades that could be desired; but the sandhills are at present by no means pleasant to walk upon, and the space between high and low water-marks is alone available.

Opposite the tram terminus, the isthmus connecting the Peninsula with the mainland, is only about three-quarters of a mile in width, and Maori tradition relates that in old days this was covered at high water, and the tides met. Now, however, the high-water mark on the seaward side is very much further back than even a few years ago, and several lagoons have been formed. For a long way round the Peninsula, after leaving the Tomahawk lagoon, high cliffs have prevented any Æolian formation, and it is not until near the Sandymount district that deposits of this nature are again met with. The loose, drifting material is here carried up to an extraordinary height, and has given its name to the locality. In other places round the coast, large deposits of a similar nature are encountered, but only one of these, at the Maori Kaik, requires mention, and that on account of the fact, that the rare phenomenon of sonorous or musical sand is stated to be occasionally heard.

The Moa deposits in the neighbourhood of Dunedin are not extensive ; crop-stones are occasionally met with, and only recently a tolerably perfect skeleton of dinornis casuarinus was ploughed up at Green Island. Mr J. Buchanan, F.L.S., one of the early settlers, has informed the writer that very numerous bones existed on the surface of the ground on Maungatua, but that the first fires destroyed them.

II. *Pleistocene, Newer Glacier Deposits.*—Formerly it was believed that glacially striated stones, with boulder clay and grooved rocks, were to be observed in, or near Dunedin, but on closer examination it was found that the former were merely spheroidal masses of basalt, in which decomposition had revealed a previously hidden structure, resembling striation. The grooved rocks also were found to be caused by water running over calcareous sandstones, in which it had formed narrow gutters.

Older Pliocene (?)—The large glacier deposit described on p. 79, and extending from Brighton southward, is referred by Prof. Hutton to this period, but Sir Jas. Hector considers it to be either Miocene or Eocene, at any rate prior to the latest manifestation of volcanic agency within the Otago district.

III. *Cretaceo-Tertiary.*—This formation has been determined by Sir James Hector, on account of the impossibility of making a distinct division between the Tertiary and Secondary periods. It comprises a large series of strata, which are stratigraphically associated, and contain many fossils in common throughout ; " while at the same time, though none are existing species, many " present a strong Tertiary facies from both the highest and lowest " parts of the formation, but even in the upper part, a few are " decidedly Secondary forms." (Hector " Guide to Geol. Exhibits, Ind. and Col. Exhibition," p. 55.) In the vicinity of Dunedin, the formation is commercially important, as in it are the coal deposits. As its area and character are described elsewhere, it need not be further referred to. In the appendix will be found some details of the more distant portions at Shag Point, and in the Clutha District.

IV. *Palæozoic. Silurian or Lower Carboniferous* (?)—The schists, which approach Dunedin to the south and south-west, and

through which the Chain Hills tunnel passes, belong to the Kakanui series, and consist of fine-grained laminated mica-schists and phyllites, passing insensibly into the coarser schists of the underlying Wanaka formation, which is possibly of Devonian age. As no fossils have been found in these rocks, their age can be merely a matter of stratigraphical conjecture To the north they disappear under the basalts of Flagstaff Hill.

Eruptive Rocks.—The eruptive rocks may justly claim a large share of attention in the consideration of the geological structure of the district we are discussing, as, but for their presence, the features of the country would have been entirely different. It is of the greatest importance, especially in a new country, to have materials for the construction of roads, and for this purpose, the compact basalts are eminently fitted. As settlement progresses, and the prosperity of the inhabitants increases, more substantial building materials are required than the timber which succeeded the wattle-and-dab order of architecture of the early settlers. Hardly any material can surpass as ornamental and durable building stones, the trachytes, breccias, and basalts of our immediate neighbourhood, which may be observed in tasteful combination with various sandstones in most of the public edifices of Dunedin. In the future, when massive stone piers and wharves are required to replace the present wooden structures, as our fine public buildings have replaced the timber and sheet-iron shanties of a few years ago ; these natural advantages will enable them to be erected with a maximium of durability and a minimum of cost.

Geologically speaking, the volcanic rocks of the Dunedin basin are of great interest and importance. The main mass of hills between Blueskin and Port Chalmers is composed of trachyte tuff and breccia, intersected with basaltic dykes. The structure of the east end of the Peninsula is very complicated, basalts and trachytes being mixed in the most confusing manner, while apparently underlying both, there is, at Portobello, an extensive development of a rather coarse-textured propylite, composed of greyish-green felspar with crystals of hornblende, etc. Underlying the volcanic series in the locality of Broad Bay, are, as has been already mentioned, sandstones and limestones, belonging to the coal series. The relation of the propylites to the sedimentary rocks is not very clear, but the former are supposed to underlie the latter, having probably the character of an intrusive volcanic outburst.

All around the centre of trachytic rocks, from Taiaroa Head, Cape Saunders, Tomahawk Bay, to Forbury Head, through Lookout Point above the Caversham tunnel to Flagstaff by Abbot's Hill, near Green Island, and past Swampy Hill to Blueskin Bay and Purehurihu, is an including belt of basalts. In other places there are only outlying patches, as at Saddle Hill, Stoney Hill, East Taieri, and North Taieri. The southern limit of the trachyte appears to be at Anderson's Bay on the east, and Pine Hill on the west. As has been stated, small coal seams are interstratified among the tufaceous volcanic rocks. but these have not, so far, been proved to be of a profitable character, nor is it likely that they will be. Attention has been drawn to the resemblance between this district and the Thames goldfields, where valuable mineral veins intersect the dioritic rocks, and the propylites of Portobello resemble those of the northern locality, but are much more crystalline, and at the Thames there is not such a strong development of the surrounding basalts. As we shall subsequently see, the parallel is not only in lithological and geological conditions, for at Harbour Cone, in the crystalline diorite rock, there has been found sufficient gold, if not to create a prosperous goldfield, at least to cause a hope that such a desirable consummation may some day be attained.

In places the basalts exhibit very beautiful columnar structure, notably at Forbury Head, Green Island Bluff, on Mts. Cargill and Mihiwaka, and on Stoney Hill near Brighton. In many instances incipient columnar structure is developed, and spheroidal concretions are very distinct in the rocks upon which the First Church is built. In some localities the bold cliffs formed by these hard rocks give rise to very fine scenery, the Forbury Head, upon which stands Mr. Cargill's mansion, and more notably on the Peninsula, a little to the eastward of Lawyer's Head, where there are vertical cliffs 800 feet in height.

At the Glen quarry and in the Woodhaugh Valley beautiful zeolitic minerals are found, with crystals of calcite and aragonite, and good specimens of hyalite may be obtained at the former of these localities, as also at the Forbury cliffs. In the Kaikorai

Valley is quartzite, no doubt altered from the Caversham sandstones, and in many places halloysite and chloropal, with other
decomposition products.

II. Economic Geology.

We cannot, in the immediate vicinity of Dunedin, boast of
any great natural mineral riches; still the geological features of
the district are not of an unfavourable character for the development of a city. There are, it is true, no deposits of true coal,
but close to our doors is the excellent fuel from Green Island,
known as brown coal, and existing in very large quantities; and
on either side the Kaitangata and Shag Point coalfields (see
appendix) are ready to supply us with pitch-coal of the highest
quality. The coal at Green Island is hydrous brown coal,
containing, as will be seen by the following analysis, about
16 per cent. of water:—

Fixed Carbon	44·87
Hydro-carbon	35·21
Water	16·47
Ash	3·46
	100·01

(Mean of analyses of Green Island coal recently made in
Colonial Laboratory for Railway Department.)

It occurs in a seam 19ft. thick, and has when first got a
lustrous appearance and dark brown colour, but on account of the
large proportion of water contained, dessicates and crumbles on
exposure to the air. It burns freely, with a slightly unpleasant
smell, and leaves a bulky incandescent ash; as a fuel for
locomotion it does moderately well; and the slack and small coal
are largely used for stationary engines. When left below ground
the slack is very liable to spontaneous combustion, and many
mines have been lost from this cause.

In the coal measures are first-class clays and fire-clays;
indeed in the matter of materials for making bricks, the locality
is thoroughly well supplied.

An excellent sand for building exists in large quantities in
the neighbourhood.

The soil of Dunedin and the environs may be said to be
generally of an excellent quality; with the exception of the coal-

measures, and some few parts where the trachytic rocks have unfavourably influenced it, we have usually a rich decomposed basaltic soil, mingled in some places with the débris of limestone, and thus forming a most excellent material for dairy produce. The swampy flats, now drained, of the lower parts of Dunedin, and of the Taieri plains, are wonderfully fertile : the latter being formed in great part of decomposed schist rock, brought down from the interior of the Province, and enriched by the decay of many generations of plants.

The building stones surrounding Dunedin are principally in the volcanic rocks; certainly the Caversham sandstone has been used for this purpose, but without success, as it is incapable of resisting the action of the weather. The following analysis indicates its composition, which is mainly carbonates of lime and magnesia, with a small proportion of silica :—

Silica	24.4
Carbonates of lime and magnesia..	53·0
Alumina ..	17·6
Soluble clay	1·5
Oxide of iron	1·4
Water and loss	2·1
	100·00

On the Peninsula, near the camp, is a very good siliceous sandstone, which has been utilised by the Hon. Mr Larnach in building portions of his residence. From the volcanic series can be obtained not only the hard bluestone or basalt, but also trachytic breccias of considerable beauty and great durability; both are largely used in the public buildings of the city. For purposes of cement manufacture, very good limestones exist in several parts of Otago; and there is a large deposit of valuable hydraulic limestone in a line extending from Seal Point on the southern side of the Peninsula to Dowling Bay on the northern shore of the lower harbour. This yields an excellent material, but, unfortunately, the cost of cartage is too great to allow of its being extensively utilised.

The necessary mud for the manufacture of Portland cement is obtained from the Dunedin harbour

Although gold-bearing rocks exist in more than one locality near Dunedin, there has never been that conspicuous success in working them, which the investor has a right to expect.

As has been stated, an instance of an exceedingly interesting auriferous rock occurs at Harbour Cone, near Portobello, on the Peninsula. Although frequently spoken of as a quartz reef, this is in reality a dioritic rock, richly impregnated with iron pyrites, and apparently occurring in very large quantities. Several attempts have been made to work it, but all have, so far, proved ineffectual. Some years ago trial crushings were made in Victoria, which yielded 7½ dwts. to half an ounce per ton, and other samples from a portion of the deposit a little lower down the hill gave 8 dwts., 1 oz., 2 dwts., and 6 dwts. per ton respectively. Some doubt was felt as to the probability of finding gold in such a matrix, and other samples were tried in Dunedin, all of which yielded the precious metal. In late years, about 1886, another attempt was made to develope the field, but without success. Professor Ulrich, who has examined the locality, describes the deposit as a peculiar, hard, diorite-like rock, the structure being holo-crystalline and medium coarse-grained; the composition triclinic felspar, hornblende, and some quartz with iron-pyrites finely and uniformly impregnated, more especially through the hornblende part. He considers that a whitish mass overlying the crystalline rock is either a decomposition product or more probably a decomposed rock of genuine trachytic type, which has flowed over the other. This is indicated, he states, by the fact that on its line of continuation, only a few feet distant from the shaft, there exists on the hill-side a massive outcrop of a hard rock, which, according to all appearance, is of trachytic character, consisting of a very fine-grained greyish or yellowish-white base, with impregnated crystals of sanidine-like felspar, hornblende not being observable.

Presuming that the rock exists in quantity, and contains a general average of gold, such as has been mentioned, it seems a matter for regret that steps are not taken to thoroughly determine its value; the prospect of finding rich veins of auriferous quartz, such as are usual in the Thames district, would lend an

ditional inducement. In addition to the above instance, there is at Green Island a series of quartz reefs, known as the Saddle

Hill Reefs. The stone is of considerable thickness, up to 14 feet, and strikes S. 76 deg. E. It dips northward at an angle of 55deg., and is enclosed in soft phyllite. Several of the reefs carry gold, and some attempts have been made to work, but so far no success has attended the efforts, and the place is now let to a party of miners who are working surface stone.

III.—MINERALS.

Stibnite, Dunedin and Green Island.
Limonite.
Chloropal.
Siderite.
Sphœrosiderite.
Iron-ochre.
Iron-pyrites.
Marcasite.
Vivianite.
Melanterite.
Magnetite.
Galena.
Gold.
Mercury, native.
Cinnabar.
Coal (hydrous).
  Brown coal.
  Pitch coal.
Carbonaceous shale.
Ambrite (retinite).
Barytes.
Calcite (stalactitic and crystallised).
Aragonite (? with strontianite).
Alum.
Quartz—
  Jasper.
  Quartzite.
  Flint.
  Cornelian.
  Hyalite.
  Opal jasper.
Olivine.

Augite.
Hornblende.
Scolecite (?)
Gismondite.
Prehnite.
Natrolite.
Chabasite.
Gmelinite.
Nepheline
Clay.
Halloysite.
Muscovite.
Orthoclase Sanidine.
Labradorite.
Oligoclase.

IV.—APPENDIX.

No account of the geology of this portion of Otago would be complete without a reference to the adjacent coal-fields of Kaitangata and Shag Point.

The former is situated north of the Clutha River, about 40 miles to the south-west of Dunedin, and covers an area of about 40 square miles. The coal measures may be traced to 9 miles north of the Tokomairiro river, where the schist again appears.

The formation consists of conglomerates, sandstones, clays and shales, with coal seams, forming hills 700 feet high in the neighbourhood of Kaitangata, and of less altitude to the north, where they rise against the flanks of Mount Misery, which is upper schist rock. Very good sections would be exposed on the coast, were it not that faults have somewhat obscured the sequence. The seam worked in the Kaitangata Railway and Coal Company's mine, which is at present the only important undertaking on the field, varies in thickness up to over 30 feet. It is, however, somewhat dislocated, and the dip varies from a moderate inclination up to 45 degrees. The coal is a lustrous, black, compact fuel, with a conchoidal fracture. It ignites readily, and forms a first-class household and locomotive coal; but on account of the contained water, which causes it to ultimately break up on exposure, it is not fitted for long sea voyages. The roof is hard coarse conglomerate, 70 feet in thickness, and auriferous, but not sufficiently rich to be workable. The floor is hard clay.

Until quite recently only three workable seams have been known to exist in the field; the uppermost 3ft. 6in. in thickness, and the main seam, 500 feet below, which has been already mentioned. About intermediate between the two is a 9ft. seam, which has not been worked. Within the last few months, however, a seam 19 feet in thickness has been discovered 150 feet below the main seam.

The average analysis of the Kaitangata coals is as follows :—

Fixed carbon	..	..	..	43·03
Hydrocarbons	..	..	..	35·55
Water	..	..	..	15·48
Ash	..	..	..	5·59

The total output from this field to the end of 1888, was 542,123 tons.

The Shag Point coal-field lies to the north, at a distance of about 35 miles, and has been worked for a number of years. The coal seams dip E.S.E. at 10deg. below the sea, where they have been worked to a small extent, and where in all probability a very large deposit exists. Three seams have been worked, the maximum thickness having been about 12 feet, but they vary considerably both in thickness and in relative position. Quite recently a valuable seam is stated to have been met with, in a borehole, which was put down below what was the lowest known seam. The measures rise into the hills bordering the coast, and form an anticlinal arch, which is terminated to the westward by a syncline, from the base of which they again rise at high angles to Puke Iwitai. Out to landward side of the hills is a recently-established coalmine, from which the excellent fuel usual in the locality is obtained. According to late investigations by the Geological Survey ¡Department, the field should extend to a considerable distance southward. Recently a number of samples of Shag Point coal have been analysed in the Colonial Laboratory Wellington, with the following results :—

			A.	B.
Fixed carbon	..	..	51·38	55·00
Volatile hydrocarbon		..	22·78	24·83
Water	..	..	19·92	13·89
Ash ..	..	..	5·69	6·28

A. Analysed as received.

B. Analysed after exposure.

The total output from this field is 201,184 tons, to the end of 1888.

THE OTAGO UNIVERSITY MUSEUM.

BY F. B. ALLEN.

THE following is an extract from a guide-book to the Museum, printed in 1878 :—" The collection was commenced by Dr. Hector, for the Dunedin Exhibition of 1865. When this was over, the specimens were packed in boxes and stowed away. Subsequently in 1868, some rooms were allotted to it in the old buildings of the University in Princes street; but as only £100 a year was voted for keeping it up, no great improvement could be expected. In 1878, however, the Provincial Council made an annual grant of £500 for its support, and this was increased in 1875 to £600 a year. It was also resolved to place the now growing collection in a separate building. A site was selected in Great King street, and the foundation was laid in December, 1874. In July, 1877, the building and fittings were completed at a cost of about £12,500, and it was opened to the public on August 11th, 1877. In 1877 also, a Bill was passed by the General Assembly, handing the management and control over to the Council of the University of Otago.

" The building is arranged so that a wing may be added at any time on either side. The south wing is intended for the New Zealand collection, with an aquarium in the basement; the north wing for a Technological Museum of Arts, Manufactures and Ethnology, with the Geological and Mineralogical collections in the basement. This will leave the present hall for foreign Natural History collections."

The Museum is fitted up with class-rooms and Laboratory, and has a valuable library, supplied with most of the important scientific magazines of the day. Although nothing has been done since 1877, towards the completion of the building, the collections have been steadily increasing, and are now demanding more room.

In a museum, instruction as well as amusement should be aimed at, and museums on a comparatively small scale, by taking up some special branch, and illustrating it by a fairly complete and representative group of objects, may provide much useful information in a very agreeable form. The exhibits should be so arranged that the visitor glancing over them, should, as it were, be forced to unconsciously acquire some general, although perhaps not very profound, knowledge of objects exhibited. This is secured by orderly arrangement, without which the relation of any one object to another is obscured, the connecting links are lost, and the Museum is liable to degenerate into a mere collection of curios, which however interesting they may be individually, are, as a whole, well-nigh meaningless.

The Otago Museum, exhibiting the principal types of the animal kingdom, is essentially a zoological museum, and as such, and for neat and scientific arrangement, it probably takes the premier position in New Zealand. The method here adopted consists in arranging the members of the animal kingdom in order of their complexity and differentiation from an original structureless mass. The arrangement is according to nature; animals which are similar in structure are grouped together, and groups representative of successive degrees of development are placed in order as far as practicable.

To follow out this arrangement a start should be made on the desk cases of the upper gallery, commencing at the eastern side. Here will be found specimens of the lowest forms of animal life. The very lowest, being microscopic, are necessarily unrepresented by real exhibits; but instead, there are numerous enlarged models, which show, in an admirable manner, what complex and diverse forms these unicellular organisms assume. Many of the models represent foraminiferæ, which by the accumulation of ages have formed the large chalk deposits now existing in England and elsewhere. But though these are by no means uninteresting, a far prettier sight is afforded by Venus's Flower Basket, its interwoven fibres forming an extremely delicate network, which at one end terminates in long shreds. This pure white closed tube is nothing but a skeleton, and though apparently very frail, its finely woven meshes, being formed of silica, are strong and firm to an astonishing degree, and well-nigh indestructible.

Close to this is another skeleton formed of long strips of silica—the glass-rope. One end of the bundle is the resting-place of the organism whose skeleton it is, while the other is embedded in the mud at the bottom of the sea ; but the Japanese used to fix it in a piece of rock and affirm that the glass-rope grew there, reminding one forcibly of the story which declared that the birds of paradise were destitute of legs. These organisms are sponges, which name, however, is apt to convey to the uninformed an erroneous impression. The ordinary bath-sponge, for instance, is simply the calcareous skeleton of a colony of animals called sponges, from which all the soft parts have disappeared, and the fact is often forgotten that it was formerly a portion of a living animal. There are spirit specimens of sponges, with the soft parts preserved, and it is interesting to notice the great difference in appearance between these and the simple skeletons sold in shops.

Many of the sponges picked up on the beaches about Dunedin, are hard and not at all elastic. This is owing to their skeletons being composed of a horny substance containing silica, and, consequently, they are unfit for ordinary use.

Next come the jelly-fish, which, besides their attractive appearance, are noteworthy, in being about the first organisms in the animal kingdom, which have nerves by which to regulate their movements. Experiments have been performed, which show conclusively, that the muscular contractions of the swimming-bell by which the jelly-fish is propelled are due to nerves, for when these nerves, or the structures said to be such, are cut away, the animal is totally unable to originate or direct its movements. Jelly-fish also possess the rudiments of eyes and ears.

Closely allied to the jelly-fish is the Portuguese man-of-war, found occasionally on the sea-shore about Dunedin. Underneath its large hollow float are very numerous tentacles, of all colours, and capable of inflicting a sharp sting on anyone who inadvertently comes in contact with them. Owing to the perishable nature of this animal and the jelly-fish, which are chiefly water, they are represented in the museum by models and spirit specimens only.

The next cases contain the star-fish, sea-urchins, and kindred species, as well as a series of models representing the various stages in the development of a star-fish, from the primordial egg, with its circular bands of cilia, and large brush-like appendage at one end, up to the final stage where a portion of the larva becomes differentiated to form a five-rayed star-fish. In the last model, the young star-fish, attached to the now useless remaining portion of the larva, is shown just ready to float away.

In the sea-urchin, the spines which give it such a forbidding appearance are more for defence than offence. Being attached by a ball-and-socket joint, they are movable and may be readily stripped off, the sea-urchin then presenting to view a hard calcareous case, dotted with five double rows of holes, through which in life, the tube-feet project. The habitation of this animal is chiefly in crevices of rocks, the spines projecting on every side, prevent it from falling, and when the sea-urchin wishes to move forward, the tube-feet are thrust out between the spines and fastened to the rock, then by contracting they draw the shell along.

Star-fish and sea-urchins appear to be quite dissimilar in structure, but a little examination and a comparison with allied species will show that there exists between them a close connection. The ordinary star-fish has the grooves along which its tube-feet project entirely on the under surface, but there are other star-fish, shown in the museum, in which the arms are very much shortened, and have a tendency to turn upwards, showing the grooves on a side view as well as underneath. This is carried one degree further in the sea-urchin, which by the way is roughly pentagonal, and therefore represents the five rays of the star. The grooves, represented by five distinct dotted lines, are continued across the upper surface so as nearly to meet at the top. The external structure of the two animals is also very similar.

The class " Worms " follows next, and includes many well-known varieties, and among the rest some very good illustrations of parasitism.

As a general rule, parasitic animals are degenerated types, and simple in structure. Many of them have no mouth, or alimentary organs of any description, but simply absorb through the tissues of their bodies the partly digested food of their hosts.

There is in the museum a good spirit specimen of the bladder-worm of the rabbit, which, like many parasites requires two hosts in which to complete its life-history.

It occurs as a bladder about the size of an egg, and although perhaps never directly producing death, it certainly causes the rabbit great inconvenience. Attached to the inside walls of the specimen forming the exhibit are small white structures which, viewed under the microscope, are seen to be provided with suckers and a circle of hooks at their free extremity. When a rabbit having this disease is eaten by a dog, these little structures fasten on to the walls of the intestine, and develop into a tape-worm, which in time deposits its eggs. The rabbits running about eating the grass here and there, get these eggs into their system, where they develop into bladder-worms. Were it not for the dog no tape-worms would be produced, and the bladder-worms could not possibly get into the system of any rabbit not infected with them.

After worms come Crustacea, and to trace the · connection between these two groups is not so difficult as it would appear. The segmentation of the body, which first occurs in the higher worms, is the most obvious point of resemblance between them, and this is the first step towards the formation of such appendages as legs found in marine-worms. Crustacea have these appendages developed into fully formed limbs.

Crustacea are very well represented by specimens of all kinds, many of the crabs so simulating the surroundings in which they live as to be easily mistaken for stones or pieces of sea-weed. The king-crab, however, is one of the strangest forms. A strong, hemispherical dorsal shield covers the head, and to it is articulated a smaller abdominal plate, with a long caudal spine. The king-crab is an old water-breathing type, which, from the presence of a compound eye, and numerous smaller ones, together with various other characteristics, such as breathing by gills which resemble a series of parallel plates arranged like the leaves of a book, is probably more nearly allied to scorpions and spiders than to crabs and crustacea in general. Close to the crabs is the peculiar, caterpillar-like Peripatus, exhibiting scarcely any external signs of segmentation, and possessing some twenty pairs of imperfectly-jointed limbs, to each of which two claws are attached. Resembling worms in some respects, it has several features peculiarly characteristic of insects. Such are the respiratory organs, consisting of branched air-canals called trachea, ramifying through the whole extent of its body, and a pair of salivary glands for digestive purposes. It has, moreover, a pair of slime-glands, secreting a sticky substance resembling bird-lime. Thus Peripatus is the first animal in the ascending scale which has organs specially adapted for breathing air, and it stands midway between worms and insects. It is found at the Cape of Good Hope, Sumatra, Australia, and New Zealand, so that its distribution is widespread, but it is nevertheless local, or in other words the animal is confined to a small area in each of these places. In all probability it was originally widely distributed, but just as at the present day the native rat of New Zealand is being driven out by the common household rat, so Peripatus became supplanted by some stronger form, and was left in the isolated patches in which it is now found. Such distribution as this is generally found in the case of old generalized types, which represent the ancestors of existing species, and do not with any degree of nicety fit into the higher types of the present day.

Attention may here be drawn to the small maps placed near each group of animals, which give, clearly and effectively, by means of coloured patches, the regions occupied by the different species.

After Peripatus, follow in order spiders, locusts, flies, bees, and butterflies, affording many excellent examples of adaptation to the surroundings both in colouring and in form. Witness the walking-stick spider, which, by the way, is really not a spider but an insect. Its body, like a dried yellowish stick, and its legs like six spiny branches, cause it to be scarcely distinguishable from the blackberry bushes and manuka scrub, in which in New Zealand it is commonly found.

Many insects are very brilliantly coloured, others scarcely at all, while some butterflies, for example, although strikingly marked, and in a museum presenting a conspicuous appearance, are coloured and marked so completely in harmony with the leaves on which they settle, as to be with difficulty recognisable among the surrounding foliage. An extreme case of this principle is seen in an Indian butterfly (Hallima). Besides the markings corresponding with those of the leaf, the wings themselves, when folded, trace out the exact contour of a leaf, the head of the butterfly forming the petiole attaching it to the branch. The protection to be derived from this imitation of surroundings is obvious. As an additional means of safety, in many species of butterflies the female has a more subdued colouring than the male, and, in some, so much so, that the male and female are mistaken for distinct species. More uncommon than the above imitation of surroundings, is the case where an insect affects a brilliant colouring for the sake of protection, a signal of danger, as it were, to birds and other enemies. An instance of this may be given. In South America there is a brilliantly coloured butterfly, which, probably on account of some poisonous or unpalatable quality is entirely safe from birds. Another butterfly, of quite a different species, apparently aware of this, has copied the gay colouring of the first butterfly so accurately as to deceive the birds themselves, and so is, in its turn, safe.

The remainder of this row of cases is occupied by the beetles, among which is conspicuous the destructive Colorado beetle, by the great variety of moths, and by specimens of lamp-shells, so-called from their resemblance to the old Roman lamps.

The next grade in the ascending series is furnished by the molluscs or soft-bodied animals, the greater number of which are known as shell-fish. Extending round the east and north sides of the lower gallery, and round a large portion of the west side, they form a large and valuable collection. Some of the shells are so small that the microscope has to lend its aid to discover the brilliant and intricate markings many of them possess. But leaving these to enthusiasts, a few of the larger ones may be noticed. The single valve of the Haliotis or mutton-fish, bright with almost every colour of the rainbow, a native of New Zealand, and common in all Maori pahs, needs no description. Perhaps the prettiest shell of all is that of the Paper Nautilus. It occurs in the female only, and differs in structure from the shell of all other molluscs in being secreted

SCENE IN NICOL'S C

from the inner surface of two greatly expanded arms which are reflected back across the body. This delicate shell is a pure pearly white and greatly convoluted.

Close to this is a glass model of the squid. Differing considerably from the snail, the typical mollusc, it possesses several peculiarities worth noticing. One portion of the original foot of the mollusc forms the long tentacle-like bodies, the arms, which are provided with suckers for fastening on to its prey. It is in the midst of these arms that the mouth is placed, so that the mouth may be said to be in the middle of the foot. Another portion of the foot forms the syphon, a tubular structure on the under side of the body; and from this the squid is able to project a quantity of inky black fluid, sufficient to cloud all the surrounding water, and cover the animal's retreat from more powerful enemies. Having no external skeleton, the living squid is soft and limp, but on dissection there is found extending along the back and just below the surface, a long thin horny substance, the pen. From the presence of this, and the inky fluid above mentioned, the squid is known as the "pen-and-ink" fish.

There is another curious internal skeleton here exhibited, belonging to a different species of sepia, found on Australian coasts, which is utilised for making tooth-powder. It is formed of a thick layer of soft calcareous matter, and being oval-shaped and somewhat in the form of an ordinary valve, this cuttle-bone is at times mistaken for the external skeleton of some unknown mollusc. Of essentially the same structure as the squid is the octopus, the dread of sea-bathers. In its skin are numerous pigment spots, by contracting and expanding which, it can change its colour in accordance with the region over which it passes. This, no doubt, is a means of safeguard against enemies, as well as affording a cover under which to attack its prey. A very large specimen of octopus, formerly in the Museum, was sent to the Indo-Colonial Exhibition, and thence to the Dublin Museum.

The visitor has now looked through the inner desk-cases of the upper and lower galleries. To continue, let him retrace his steps, this time, however, examining the wall-cases. First of all, he will see on the western side the New Zealand invertebrata, the foreign specimens of which he has already examined. Then follow on the northern side, the New Zealand fishes. Among the spirit specimens may be noticed the ribbon-fish, like a long and slender band of silver, and the originally transparent glass-fish, which has unfortunately become opaque in the spirit.

Attention should be directed to the fact that the skeleton in the skate and lower fishes is cartilaginous. The skeleton in fish, however, as we ascend the scale becomes a bony one, and as in all the higher animals, forms the main support of the body. In the shark will be seen the five gill-slits, with a small hole just behind the eye. In higher fishes, these become covered by a bony plate, the operculum, which hides from view the gills beneath it. Then again, a further development is seen in the respiratory organs, in the Australian mud-fish, which in winter breathes by gills in the ordinary way, but in summer when the rivers are low, breathes air by means of lungs.

In the wall-cases along the eastern side of this gallery are some good fossil remains of fish, showing the skeleton almost intact.

Besides the ordinary collection of animals, the Museum possesses an excellent assortment of skeletons, both natural and disarticulated. The disarticulated skeleton of the New Zealand ling illustrates what a difficult task it is to thus arrange and preserve all the separated bones in their correct relative positions.

Amphibia, represented by frogs, are the next advance on fishes, and living as their name implies, part of their life above, and part under water, have necessarily more fully-developed respiratory organs.

The next exhibits of special interest are sets of models showing the development of the chief types of animals, and of the eye and skull in vertebrata. Those illustrative of the frog, show first the undivided egg-cell, then as it appears divided into two, into four, into eight parts, and so on into an innumerable mass of cells. This mass next develops cavities, and gradually shapes itself into a tadpole with external gills. The tadpole is a water-breather, and exists chiefly on vegetable food. After living for a time in the water its external gills disappear, and respiration is carried on by internal gills; but then comes a further change, which is illustrated in the models. The operculum grows over the aperture of the gills, closing it, and the tadpole becomes a frog, breathing air by means of lungs. The tail, moreover, has disappeared and limbs are developed.

This is a new mode of progression, and excepting in the snake and whale, the hind limbs in all animals above fish, are employed as a means of locomotion. In the frog and the majority of the other vertebrates the fore limbs serve the same function, but in the whale they are modified to flippers, in birds to wings, and in man to arms.

Reptiles are represented at the southern end by alligators and crocodiles. Above these exhibits is a very instructive set of longitudinal sections of the skulls of different animals, showing the development of the brain. It will be seen that the brain, coming forward, causes the jaw-bones to be less prominent in man than in any other animal.

At the top of the staircase is a very rare specimen, the great ribbon-fish, an inhabitant of the deep sea, and like the frost-fish, only obtainable when by some extraordinary circumstance, it is cast up upon the shore. The skeleton has been removed from the body, and is shown above it in a good state of preservation. The skin has been stuffed, and its delicate markings and colouring have been renovated and rendered permanent. This was necessary, as fish which live deep down under a high pressure, are very liable, on coming to the surface, to fall to pieces, and lose their brilliancy in a remarkably short time.

In the upper gallery, the wall-cases are occupied by the very large class of birds, which undoubtedly form a fine display. Nests containing eggs are exhibited in many instances, and offer an additional attraction.

Birds are the best marked group of vertebrata ; they have no intimate connection with other groups, and are readily recognisable. The presence of feathers, together with the fact that by means of the large air-sacs in connection with the lungs, and the porous nature of the bones, the air in respiration finds easy access to all parts of the body, causes the blood supplied by a very large heart, to be maintained at a temperature higher than in any other animal. This, with the peculiar differentiation of the fore-limbs into wings, enables the bird to support itself in flight.

Along the western side of this gallery are the foreign birds, among which may be noticed that enemy of snakes, the secretary-bird, so-called from its pen-like tuft of feathers on each side of the head, the brilliant, if not very elegant, trogon of Central America, and the horn-bills. The huge bills of these birds, although composed of bone, are very light, owing to the presence of extensive air cavities.

Conspicuous among these foreign specimens are the little humming-birds of South America, which, sporting in the sunshine of their native land, rejoice in a hundred such fanciful yet suggestive names as "sunbeam," and "golden light."

At the end of this row of cases is a cast of the now extinct dodo, and near it, its nearest living ally, a pigeon found only in Samoa.

Then come the New Zealand birds. Strangers will be struck at the majestic appearance of the large albatrosses, and near these are some fine specimens of shags. One of them, the Imperial shag, is especially brilliant.

New Zealand possesses a surprisingly large number of birds capable of flight, but many of the ground-feeders, having no natural enemies from which to escape by flying, have lost this power, and hence such examples as the weka and the kakapo. Although the latter has large wings, it has scarcely any keel to the breast-bone. This shows the absence of large muscles capable of moving the wings and supporting the bird in flight. It is a matter of regret that many of the fine birds of New Zealand, handicapped by the loss of the power of flight, are in all probability doomed to early extinction, owing to the introduction of enemies from which they are unable to escape. A skeleton is shown of an extinct goose, which, judging from its small wings, and the absence of keel, must have been incapable of flight; and there is also a skeleton of an extinct duck found near Alexandra. Close by is, perhaps, the most interesting of this class of birds, the takahe, or notornis, which, if not quite extinct, is very nearly so. Only a few specimens of it have been obtained, and these at widely distant periods, and the skeleton shown, although imperfect, must be regarded as a treasure. This bird also could not fly. There are two paintings representing this bird's appearance in life, placed above the desk-cases.

Coming to the eastern side, the argus pheasant at once catches the eye, with its fine display of fan-like feathers. The markings on these, called ocelli, are very beautiful, and exactly resemble balls placed in cups. The head is concealed behind one of the wings, as if the bird were aware of what a remarkable contrast to its splendid plumage this unadorned member presents. Here, too, are the different varieties of the domestic fowl, which illustrate how different species may be formed from the same ancestors. The jungle-fowl of India, a bird something like a game-fowl, and a little bigger than a bantam, becoming domesticated has given rise to all the domestic fowls, and it is remarkable how some of these, for example, the Cochin-China, and the Polish, differ from each other.

Passing over the rest of the birds on the side of this gallery, the New Zealand species of the Ratitae, or true flightless birds are met with in the cases at the south end.

The Ratitae are the lowest among birds, and originally widely spread, are now disappearing, and with one exception—the ostrich—are confined to the southern hemisphere. One species of the ostrich is found in Africa and Arabia, another in South America, the emu in Australia, the cassowary in North Australia and New Guinea. Attached to these, and to many of the specimens throughout the museum are detailed descriptions, giving an interesting account of the chief characters and peculiarities.

New Zealand possesses the only other existing genus of Ratitae, the kiwi, the most remarkable among living birds. It has a most peculiar walk, its feathers are hair-like, its wings vestigial and apparently absent, its eggs are large out of all proportion, its habits are nocturnal, and it is the only bird which has its nostrils at the extremity of its beak. The kiwi is dying out, and of the four known species, one, Haast's kiwi, is represented by only two skins (in the Christchurch museum), and a solitary but very perfect skeleton in the Otago museum. Penguins, showing the enormous mass of down on the young birds, are well represented. Although not able to fly, they do not belong to Ratitae. Being sea-birds, their wings have become modified to form powerful swimming paddles, on which the small scale-like feathers lie remarkably close. At the head of the stairs are remains of the now extinct moa, the largest and most curious of the Ratitae, or flightless birds. Some of the throat bones are in an excellent state of preservation; other bones are charred, showing that, in all probability, the moa was killed and used by the Maoris as food, and that, at any rate, it was contemporaneous with man.

In the same cases may be noticed the casts of the enormous eggs, a footprint, and several series of the bony rings of the trachea. Some of the exhibits illustrate peculiarities in the skeleton, about which doubt formerly existed. Some feathers and a leg and throat, to which skin and flesh still adhere, form unique and valuable specimens, but the fact that the flesh has not decayed and disappeared does not necessarily prove that this particular moa was of more recent date than those of which skeletons alone have been found. The skeletons of these gigantic birds are commonly found, several together, in swampy ground, and the bones are so intermingled that it is rarely that an "individual" and perfect skeleton is obtainable. On the ground floor are shown skeletons of seven out of the fourteen species of moa, and all but two of these have been made up.

In connection with birds and the position they occupy in the animal kingdom, the cast of the extinct bird, Archœopteryx, may be noticed. It is well known that although the tail feathers of birds are often very long, the tail itself is quite a short structure. In fact, it is composed of a short, compressed bone turned up, from the end of the back-bone. But the tail of Archœopteryx, is, like the lizard's, very long and tapering. It is composed of many separate vertebræ, from each end of which a pair of tail feathers arise. Then, again, in the lower gallery is a cast of an extinct reptile, Compsognathus, which in appearance must have been remarkably like a bird. Besides its long tail, it had a very long neck and a small head; its hind legs were strong, and similar in structure to those of a bird, while its fore-limbs were short; and it is probable that the reptile hopped along, in a semi-erect attitude, upon its hind-legs. It would thus appear that Huxley had grounds for saying "birds are glorified reptiles."

On the ground-floor, at the western side, are the duck-mole and the spiny ant-eater, the first representatives of mammals. They differ greatly from the rest of mammalia, and in many respects resemble reptiles. They lay eggs, and are destitute of teeth. In many ways they differ more from the next highest sub-class of mammals, the marsupials, than any other two do from each other.

In one of the cases at the north end, is a curious example of the canine tooth, or tusk of the pig. It has grown round and entered the cheek, piercing the lower jaw just below the teeth and even entering the tongue. Such instances of teeth with persistent pulps, growing to an abnormal length, are not infrequently seen in rats and rabbits, where the teeth in one jaw have been lost, and nothing is left to wear away those in the other.

Along the eastern side are lions, tigers, and such-like animals, after which come many varieties of monkeys. The series ends with two skeletons, the one of the powerful orang-utan, the other of a man, and these are worthy of comparison. The orang usually assumes a semi-erect position, and its long arms then rest with the knuckles upon the ground.

The great majority of mammals are land animals, the bat alone is aërial. A membrane stretched between its greatly elongated fingers enables it to fly, and another curious fact about it is, that when asleep it hangs by its two hind limbs, head downwards. The few mammals which live in the sea, are represented by seals, whales, and a few others. These are shown in the enclosures, and among them, the crested seal, and gigantic sea-elephant may be noticed. The lower jaw of a whale, in the same enclosure, contains teeth, whereas in other species of whales, as in the large one suspended from the top gallery, teeth are replaced by numerous plates of baleen or whalebone.

In the other enclosures are many typical skeletons, the New Zealand skeletons forming a distinct group.

At the south end is an interesting model called an index collection. It consists of an upright stem, from which rods branch off at different heights. Along the stem and branches are placed various animals representative of groups. Most of the rods tend upwards, while those pointing downwards denote degeneration in the animals upon them. The model endeavours to graphically represent the mutual relations of the several groups of the animal kingdom, and to give their degrees of development ; and to each specimen are attached labels stating the scientific classification, and giving the position in the museum where similar examples may be found.

Beneath the staircase are specimens of the New Zealand woods. Cut into blocks and polished, some of them show very pretty markings, and although it is unnecessary to go into the value of these woods, many of them make useful and durable building materials. The kauri, for example, is for many purposes one of the finest woods in the world.

Just here, too, are specimens illustrating the process of manufacture of the native flax, which also has proved itself a valuable product of the soil.

Along the wall-cases are many interesting Maori relics, which testify to the artistic taste of the natives of New Zealand. Many of the greenstone images and implements must have required an immense amount of time and labour to fashion.

The exhibits of the volcanic dust, deposited during the recent eruption in the North Island, should prove of interest, and near at hand are some twigs and the skin of a bird encrusted a silvery white, with silica.

The little glass cubes containing wash-dirt from the Otago goldfields, also attract attention, and are no doubt, of value in showing the nature of the ground in which gold is most likely to be found. Near this stand is another, on which are specimens of the chief building stones obtainable in the colony.

Coming to the minerals, a case containing specimens of the stone, and illustrating the mode of extraction of the tin at the Bischoff mines in Tasmania, is now of special interest in view of the late discoveries at Stewart Island.

The other cases contain examples of the principal groups of minerals, to fully describe which would occupy too much space ; suffice it to say, that many of the crystals are very pretty, and attractive to even those who know little of their scientific nature and value.

Thus it will be seen that, as far as possible, the exhibits in the museum have been arranged in their natural order, and pains have been taken to render the specimens more interesting and instructive by placing by the side of the most peculiar animals, descriptions and maps of distribution.

The reader is, however, recommended to visit the museum, and judge of these matters for himself.

BOTANY OF NEIGHBOURHOOD.
By G. M. THOMSON, F.L.S.

HERE are certain favoured spots in every country where the naturalist feels that while enjoying all the advantages of town life, he is yet in the immediate proximity of rich hunting grounds. Those who know Edinburgh and have ever wandered in search of wild flowers up Colinton Glen or over Arthur's Seat, and round the flag-margined swamps of Duddingstone, will recall with delight the floral wealth of that charming region, rich not alone in the gifts of nature, but in all of human interest that adds zest and piquancy to life. The new Edinburgh resembles her old and stately namesake in several respects, and pre-eminently in this, that she is placed in a region rich in natural wealth. In a compass of a few miles every variety and gradation of natural feature may be found, from the sand-dunes on the coast to the sub-alpine mountain-top. If any who have travelled over this colony will give the matter one moment's consideration, they will admit that no other city or town within these islands is so favourably situated for the study of natural history as is Dunedin. The coast line of bay and ocean; the alluvial flats of the Forbury, the Kaikorai, and the Taieri; the wide bush-covered areas ranging from sea-level up to 2200 ft. on Mount Cargill; and the open hill-sides stretching across the Belt to the Chain Hills, Flagstaff and Swampy Hills, 2400 feet high; these all provide within walking distance the finest collecting ground in New Zealand. Few persons have any idea what an immense variety of plant life is to be found within the limits of the Town Belt alone. Starting at its Southern end on the knolls and slopes about Montecillo, and following round in front of Mornington, Roslyn, and Maori Hill, then crossing down into the Leith Valley, up the hill above the Botanical Gardens, and round the further side of Pelichet Bay, the lover of flowers and ferns will meet with hundreds of species, many of them of striking beauty. The first thing perhaps in such a walk which would strike a visitor from the old country would be the English aspect of the grass and many of the flowers. And it is the case that over one hundred species of English plants have invaded and taken possession of the soil. The sward is largely composed now of cocksfoot, ryegrass, crested dogstail, soft Yorkshire fog, and sweet vernal grass, intermingled with gowans, ox-eye daisies, buttercups, the purple self-heal, white clover, and many other old and familiar friends. But the scrub, though occasionally touched up by blazes of yellow broom, and whitened by elder bushes, retains on the whole its primitive character. The trees appear somewhat sombre in general aspect, but their darker olive-green is relieved by the bright hues of the white mapau and the glossy foliage of broadleaf, black mapau, and panax. In spring, glorious festoons of white clematis abound, and later the carpodetus, so named from its ring-bound fruit, comes out a mass of fine whitish fragrant flowers. Over the slopes of Maori Hill the pretty houhere is found, a graceful little dark-foliaged tree, with white star-like blossoms often produced in great profusion. In December the white-flowered parsonsia, a common climber at the edge of the bush, trails its panicles of little waxen bells over many a less ornamental, but friendly support. Nor must we forget the vivid display made by the manuka scrub when in full bloom. Both species of manuka thrive and grow side by side in many parts of the Belt, and however common, and therefore to many persons uninteresting the plant may be, there are few prettier objects than a well-flowered spray. One of the most characteristic objects to be seen in the Belt, especially in the wooded portions, is the fine display of the very handsome flax-like Astelias. These are only a few of the commoner plants to be found in a walk round the Belt, but there are some botanical curiosities which are worth looking for. One of the rarest of these is—and we must here and there inflict a technical name for lack of any other—the yellow-flowered *Senecio sciadophilus* the only climbing senecio known. A little of it grows in the bush near Littlebourne, but except when in flower it is very difficult to distinguish, and even then very difficult to find. It flowers also very late in the season, about the first or second week in March. Hooker, in his "Handbook of the New Zealand Flora," gives it only as occurring in Banks Peninsula, but it is not uncommon on Otago Peninsula, though like the bush itself, it must be fast disappearing from that favoured spot of earth.

Down in the lower part of the Leith Valley, near Woodhaugh, some more rather rare plants are to be met with, but the wholesale destruction of the bush has already made many former denizens of this sheltered spot disappear, and those named here are fast following in their wake. Here are to be found at the foot of rocky precipices a few plants of the milk-tree (*Epicarpurus*), very often characterised here as elsewhere, by the diseased appearance of its male spikes. Nestling close to the damper rocks may also be found an occasional patch of a slender, glossy, dark green little herb, with most minute and inconspicuous flowers, known to science as *Australina pusilla*, which, as far as this part of New Zealand is concerned, is by no means a common plant. In this neighbourhood also, on the trunks of trees, has been occasionally found a patch of that curious little epiphytal orchid with the long name of *Sarcochilus adversus*. Perhaps, like other rather small plants, this species is commoner than its recorded occurrence seems to imply, being readily overlooked by any but trained eyes, for it has also been found at Sawyer's Bay. It is the only New Zealand orchid known to the writer in which the pollen-masses, after being pulled out of their anther-case, move downwards in such a way as to be in position to strike the stigma of the next flower they come in contact with.

While on the subject of orchids, it is noteworthy that the very curious greenish-grey or brown *Gastrodia* is not uncommon in the thicker and damper parts of the Belt; while the tree trunks, especially in the Leith Valley, are frequently matted with the pretty little epiphytal *Earinas*. Of these the narrowleaved one, *E. mucronata*, produces its delicate little panicles of yellowish flowers from November to January, while its stiffer and darker-leaved relative, *E. autumnalis*, bears its white trusses usually about February or March. The latter plant is very common on the rocks of the Quarantine Island, near Port Chalmers. Both species are very fragrant when in flower. The only other New Zealand epiphytal orchid besides those mentioned is *Dendrobium Cunninghamii*, a very insignificant species among dendrobes, but with pretty white flowers, bearing a crimson patch on the lip. This species was formerly common enough down the north side of the harbour; a patch of it, fortunately well preserved and jealously guarded, still grows on the big rocks just above Port Chalmers.

A little divergence from the Leith Valley up the Reservoir creek and then up to the left along the Wakari or School Creek —now, alas! with its waters sadly polluted—brings us to a spot where one or two more kinds of rather uncommon plants are to be met with. The hina-hina, or *Melicytus ramiflorus*, so named from having its little flowers arranged along its branches, is a common tree on the Belt. But up this wooded creek-bed two other species of *Melicytus* occur sparingly, viz.—*M. lanceolatus*, with long, narrow, dark-green leaves, and *M. macrophyllus*. The former species also occurs in the bush at West Taieri, while of the latter only one plant has been found at the locality named, and its exact position has since been lost.

The abundance of mistletoes in the bush on the Town Belt is remarkable. *Tupeia antarctica* and *Loranthus micranthus* are abundant, and are not unfrequently found parasitic on one another. But the two remarkable little species of *Viscum*, the genus to which the English mistletoe belongs, are both to be found, only like many other inconspicuous plants, they are easily overlooked. *V. salicornioides* can always be found in a patch of small-leaved manuka, a little way up Ross's Creek above the waterworks; while *V. Lindsayi* occurs on the coprosma bushes in the Botanical Gardens.

An interesting afternoon's ramble is over the hill from Anderson's Bay to the Tomahawk lagoon and the headland beyond. Fifteen years ago, as one went along the Anderson's Bay road, several plants were to be found which are now things of the past. The curious shrubby ribbon-wood, *Plagianthus divaricatus*, grew on the mud near the gas-works, but ammonia-liquor and coal-gas impurities have quite destroyed it. It is still to be found round Pelichet Bay, however, and it is worth while walking round there in October or November to see its curious little fragrant flowers. At the rocks near Mrs. Tolmie's house, there used to be, as indeed there formerly was all round

Dunedin, abundance of anise (*Angelica gingidium*). The plant is, however, such a favourite with cattle and sheep, that it is nearly exterminated in this neighbourhood. An interesting little patch of it occurs on a ledge of sandstone rock on the south road below Look-out Point. Cattle cannot get down to the ledge from above, and human beings can hardly reach it from below, and here survive a few plants of what used to be one of our commonest species. Along the same cliffs, near Musselburgh, but especially round on the sunny faces at the entrance of Anderson's Bay, grew patches of the little fern so characteristic of dry hill-sides, *Cheilanthus sieberi.*

The road across the Peninsula at Anderson's Bay is interesting on account of the glorious views it unfolds. Standing near the highest point from which one can see across to Dunedin, a magnificent panorama is presented, indeed, there are few finer points of vantage in the neighbourhood. A little further on and the whole coast-line opens out away down to the beach near Kaitangata. The road takes a sharp bend at the little cemetery a calm spot within sound of the unceasing break of old ocean, in which to rest after all the toil and tossing of life's restless sea. Down it goes to the edge of the sand hills, and crosses the lagoon at its mouth by an uninteresting bridge. The lagoon is not a pretty object now, it has rather a shabby stagnant look, and the cattle have trampled its banks and destroyed the scrub that used to grow about it. Yet it retains much of its interest to the naturalist. In the first place it is a surviving relic of the numerous little bays which formerly occurred in abundance along the east coast of Otago, but which by the upheaval of the coast-line, are now transformed into lagoons and mud-flats. Along the stones at the mouth of this lagoon occur numbers of a curious crustacean, like large wood-lice in form, called *Idotea lacustris.* This is the only locality known for it in New Zealand, while the only other place where it has been found at all is at Port Henry, in the Straits of Magellan! There is a question of geographical distribution for the naturalist.

Let us walk round the meadow by the south side of the lagoon, and see what is to be found. The close sod is largely made up of water crowfoots—*Ranunculus rivularis*—with numerous aquatic sedges and grasses. Besides many common marsh-plants, some interesting aquatics are to be found, such as the ubiquitous species *Zannichellia palustris* and *Ruppia maritima*. The latter has the curious property of sending its little flowers up to the surface of the water, on delicate stalks. Once they are floated up, they open and are no doubt fertilized by the wind. When this necessary act has been accomplished, and the seed-vessel begins to grow, the stalk twists gradually like a corkscrew and pulls the fruit down nearly to the bottom of the water, where it may ripen in comparative safety. Another ubiquitous water-plant found here is *Limosella aquatica*, along with which is to be met with the minute *Tillæa sinclairii*, one of the smallest of our flowering plants. A few scrubby *Coprosma* and *Melicope* bushes mark the position of what used to be a dense patch of scrub. We can hardly walk through this without getting a few stick-insects on our clothes ; at one time they occurred here in thousands. At the head of the lagoon, now quite destitute of trees, used to grow a bit of bush famous for its ferns, now things of the past ; while round the northern shore we come on patches of *Corokia cotoneaster* and *Cyathodes acerosa*. The former is a tortuously-branched little shrub with black bark, white under-sides to its leaves, and little golden yellow flowers, which are open in October and November, followed about January or February by red berries. Altogether an easily-distinguished, though sometimes rather a scrubby looking plant. *Cyathodes*, on the other hand, is a tall shrub, with very small, prickly leaves and miniatue heath-like flowers, bearing in autumn rather large snow-white berries. The north side of the lagoon generally has abundance of duck-weed and *Azolla*, and is one of the best spots near Dunedin for the microscopist, the water swarming with an immense variety of small life. The Tomahawk head forms a pleasant termination to this walk. Besides the usual littoral plants such as Euphorbia, white flax, large-flowered Veronica and Pimelea, which grow along the coast-line, one here meets with the small solitary-flowered forget-me-not, *Myosotis antarctica*. A large form of everlasting daisy (*Gnaphalium trinerve*) is common, together with the small stemless buttercups (*Ranunculus acaulis*). Peeping out of the sand are numerous fragile white flowers of *Claytonia*, and occasional patches of the pretty little purple-striped *Mimulus repens*. Altogether a good ground for a botanist, who, if he be fortunate enough to ramble up here in the month of November, will carry off as much in a couple of hours as will keep him occupied with study—if he be of a philosophical turn of mind—for a couple of months.

A much longer ramble, and one better taken later in the year, say in the month of January, is over Flagstaff Hill, and on to the top of Swampy Hill, coming down again into the Leith Valley by Morrison's Creek. Perhaps the best way is to go up through Ross's clearing, above the waterworks; the track leads out on the shoulder of Flagstaff, the trees gradually giving way to flax-bushes, intermingled with spear-grass. Many young cedars (*Libocedrus Bidwillii*) grow at the edge of this bush, together with abundance of native holly (*Olearia ilicifolia*). Here is the ground for *Alsophila colensoi*, a small tree-fern, which is very abundant on this hill-face. If the pedestrian prefers to come up the hill by way of Nichol's Creek, he may chance to light on a patch of *Gleichenia cunninghamii*, an uncommon fern in this neighbourhood. The hill-side is rich with snow-berries of several varieties. Early in the season it blazes yellow with the so-called Maori onion—*Anthericum hookeri*—which recalls the pretty yellow asphodel of a home bog. At this time of year it is white with everlasting daisies and celmisias, and dotted here and there with small orchids, such as *Caladenia lyallii, Chiloglottis traversii*, and the curious green *Pterostylis*. Yellow *Senecios* are also just breaking from bud. A few white and blue-striped violets may be found, and numerous little white or blue bells. Crossing the low saddle between the two hill-tops, if the day be still and warm, we rouse an immense amount of insect life, chiefly small, quiet-coloured but prettily-marked moths. The ground is almost fragrant in parts with the finely-divided leaves of *Ligusticum aromaticum*. Rising a few hundred feet on to Swampy Hill, we meet with a phenomenon not uncommon in this country, a peat-moss on the very highest bit of ground in the neighbourhood. As we ascend, the soft spongy nature of the ground shows that the grass is being replaced by *Sphagnum*, and in this spongy bed are a number of alpine plants, such as *Fostera sedifolia, Oreostylidium subulatum*, and others. On the very summit is a small lagoon; an attempt—only partially successful—has been made to drain this. Coming down the hill again by a natural drainage channel, which is the beginning of Morrison's Creek, we come on an interesting mass of tutu bushes. Many botanists consider that there are three species of *Coriaria* or tutu in New Zealand; here they are growing all together, with so many intermediate forms, that the most inveterate species-maker would be puzzled to place some of them correctly. A pretty rough scramble it is down the creek-bed, the steep banks of which are densely fern-clad, where the Goths and Vandals with their axes have not yet penetrated. How long they can be kept away is another question.

What profusion of growth is here. The stones and the tree-trunks are covered with delicate mosses and liverworts; here is the pretty little bright green *Nertera* with its crimson, coral-like drupes. On the spray-sprinkled rocks are mats of the white-flowered wood-sorrel (*Oxalis magellanica*) interspersed with the singular little *Corysanthes*. These are remarkable orchids; each plant has only one kidney-shaped leaf, and bears in early spring a single purple flower, the long-tailed sepals and petals of which give it the appearance of a gigantic spider sitting in wait for its prey. We do not know how it is fertilized, but often when a flower is opened an unfortunate little fly is found inside, glued by its head to the sticky gland of the column. The top of Swampy Hill is about six or seven miles from the Post Office, but it is rather a severe walk for an afternoon, on account of the height to be climbed, and a whole day should be devoted to it.

If the botanist has time and can devote a day to it, he will be well repaid by a trip to Outram, from which a good walk and climb of 3000 feet will land him on the top of Maungatua. This remarkable hill is the most interesting ground in the east of Otago. Its vegetation is very varied and singular in character, and more alpine in appearance than perhaps an other other spot at so low a level, north of Stewart Island.

Altogether over 400 species of indigenous and about 120 species of introduced flowering plants have been catalogued as occurring in the neighbourhood of Dunedin, a very considerable number, when we reflect that only some 1200 species are known for the whole of New Zealand.

The district was formerly very celebrated for its ferns; one had only to walk to the north end of George-street to be into

magnificent ground. But now, owing to wholesale cutting down
of timber, and extensive burning, the collector has to go much
further afield than formerly was the case. Including club-
mosses, about 70 species can be gathered in the neighbourhood.
Some of these have been already referred to. The common tree-
ferns are *Hemitelia smithii, Dicksonia squarrosa*, and the silver-
leaved *Cyathea dealbata*, the latter especially near the sea.
About 15 kinds of filmy ferns have been gathered in the Leith
Valley, or the thickly-wooded parts of Pine Hill and Mount
Cargill, but some of these, as *Hymenophyllum javanicum* and
subtilissimum are now rare. *H. malingii* is still to be met with
occasionally on Mount Cargill, but its former haunts on Pine
Hill and Flagstaff Hill have been invaded by axe and fire.
Another rarity sometimes met with in the Leith Valley is
Trichomanes Colensoi, one of the most delicate of these little gems.
Todea superba, variously known as crape fern and Prince of
Wales' feather, is still a sufficiently common fern in localities
near the Leith Valley. The only maiden-hair which occurs in
this neighbourhood is *Adiantum affine* (called *A. cunninghamii* in
Hooker's Handbook). This is not uncommon on Otago Peninsula, as well as the North side of the Harbour, and is met with
in suitable localities all along the coast. Species of *Lomaria,
Asplenium, Aspidium, Nephrodium*, and *Polypodium* abound everywhere, and give the undergrowth of the bush its characteristic
appearance. We must not overlook two little plants usually
classed with ferns, and both of which are represented here. The
little adder's-tongue *(Ophioglossum)* springs up in grassy
meadows, especially when the sward is kept closely cropped
down. When in spore from November to February it is distinguishable, but at any other time its simple little frond is
passed over as a short blade of grass or other plant. The Moon-
wort *(Botrychium lunaria)* is a species which appears in all sorts
of unexpected places, disappearing again for whole seasons.
This is in part due to the fact that its fronds take some four
years to mature, spending three of these under the surface. It
has been frequently gathered in the Town Belt, and in various
localities round Dunedin.

The foregoing little sketch will give an idea of the botanical
wealth of this neighbourhood. It must be remembered that

brilliant-flowered plants are the exception in New Zealand. Nor do any poetical or historical associations cluster round our plants such as give a halo of romance to the familiar flowers of the mother country. But an interest apart from these, attaches to every plant which the true naturalist meets with. Each species has a history, which can be unearthed only by patient research and observation. Each has become suddenly subject to new conditions, which in many cases lead to its extermination. Each has a peculiar relation to the insects and the birds which formerly abounded here, but which are now being replaced by new arrivals. And as this change goes on before our eyes, we see the relation of these indigenous plants being altered and subverted, and can see a new struggle for existence taking place around us. No doubt in time a sentiment of regard will arise for the old forms which are fast disappearing, and steps will be taken to arrest the wholesale destruction which is at present going on. And fast as this has progressed about Dunedin, there are still left here more of the natural features of bush and brake than occur in any other town of considerable size in New Zealand, and here therefore we can welcome the botanist and assure him of a good harvest and much of interest.

THE UNIVERSITY.

By Rev. Prof. SALMOND, D.D.

HE University of Otago was founded in 1869 by an ordinance of the Provincial Council, "with the intent to promote sound learning in the province of Otago." It now possesses endowments to the extent of 221,000 acres of pastoral land. The original grant was 100,000 acres; but this was supplemented by an equal amount in 1872, further increased by 10,000 acres in 1874, and again by 11,000 in 1877. In addition to the revenue derived from its leases, the University also receives £1800 per annum as its portion of the Educational revenue of the Presbyterian Church, whereby it pays the salaries of three Professors. In course of time, and as settlement advances, the University is likely to become a wealthy corporation, and a growingly influential factor in the life of the community.

When first founded, the Otago University was empowered by the constituting ordinance to grant Degrees in Arts, Medicine, and Law, and had made application for a Royal Charter for the same purpose in order to increase the value of its Degrees; but the privilege was surrendered and the affiliation withdrawn in 1874, on the establishment of the New Zealand University; and although, from force of custom it is still called the University, it ought now properly to be designated University-College. Along with the Canterbury College, and University-College, Auckland, the University of Otago is exclusively a teaching body: and all three are affiliated to the New Zealand University, which alone confers degrees in the Colony. Some regrets are felt that the University of Otago surrendered its privileges, and only recently an unsuccessful attempt was made to recover them: but it is improbable that existing arrangements will be interfered with. The University

system of the Colony may be regarded as completed for several generations, when we shall have teaching colleges in Dunedin, Christchurch, Wellington, and Auckland affiliated to one degree-conferring University.

The University was opened in 1871, with a modest staff of three Professors—in Classics, Mathematics, and Mental Science, under charge, respectively, of Professors Sale, Shand, and McGregor. In addition, there are now Professors of English Language and Literature, of Natural Philosophy, of Chemistry, of Biology, of Mining and Mineralogy, and of Anatomy and Physiology. There is also a Lecturer in Law, two Lecturers in Modern Languages, numerous Lecturers in the most important branches of Medicine, and three Lecturers in branches attached to the School of Mines. Altogether there are nine Professors and fourteen Lecturers. The three Professorships, endowed from the revenues held in trust by the Presbyterian Church, on behalf of the country, are those of Mental Science, English Language and Literature, and Natural Philosophy. The University is, however, altogether unsectarian, no theological tests being tolerated, and no Church having any internal control of its affairs.

Originally, the University held its seat in the heart of the city, and occupied the building now converted into the Colonial Bank. Having sold its possession to the Bank for the sum of £27,000 (as many think, far beneath its proper value), the present buildings, with the adjoining Professors' houses, were erected in 1878, on a spot more quiet and Academic, on the banks of the Leith. The structure remains unfinished, although it has already absorbed a sum of £40,000; and there are various opinions in regard to its architectural beauty, and the fitness and sufficiency of its internal arrangements.

The Classes in the University are open to all who choose to take advantage of them, and are, for the most part, held in the evening, in order to consult the convenience of such as are engaged in business or in teaching during the day; and such constitute a considerable section of the students in attendance. In the earlier years there used to be a large attendance of young men engaged in business; the number has diminished, with experience that technical studies cannot be prosecuted in *amateur* fashion ; while the number of professional teachers attending continues to increase. Although the Classes are open to all, such as intend to graduate, must, before attending Classes have passed the Matriculation or Entrance Examination of the New Zealand University, which prescribes to all Candidates an Examination in English, Arithmetic, and one Language, ancient or modern, the remaining subjects being optional. If the Candidate have chosen Latin or Greek as his language, he must pass in three additional optional subjects; otherwise, he must pass in four. The voluntary subjects are such as History, Geography, Elementary Mechanics, Physics, Chemistry, Biology, &c. Ordinarily, a student obtains his Degree of B.A. after keeping three years terms : and a year's term is kept by attending each session at least two Classes, and passing the Class Examination in each. The higher Degree of M.A. is obtained by passing a more severe Examination subsequently in one of the branches of study taken up for the B.A. Degree. The value of the Degrees has been enhanced by the fact that the examiners are appointed in England : and it is believed that as a test of scholarship they will bear comparison with any similar Degrees in the United Kingdom.

The cost of education at the University is not great. There is a fee of £3 3s. charged for each Class per session of six months. The student also pays £1 1s. college fee. The main cost is the student's maintenance while engaged in study. Fairly comfortable board and lodging are obtainable from 18/- per week upwards; as good as could be reasonably desired for 25/-.

The salary of each Professor is £600 per annum; and a house is provided also for each of the four senior Professors. The Professors also receive, each one, the fees of the students attending his Classes; and these vary from a few pounds to £200 or more, some subjects being compulsory and others optional, some also naturally attracting a larger number of minds than others. The largest classes are generally those of Classics, Mathematics, and Chemistry.

The University of Otago, alone in the Colony, has full provision for the instruction and training of students intending to graduate in Medicine. A student of Medicine may prosecute his entire course in Dunedin, and receive from the New Zealand University a diploma which is valid and recognized throughout the United Kingdom: and the cost of the whole course, including class fees, and the fees charged by the New Zealand University, for the Professorial Examinations and for the Degree of Bachelor of Medicine is under £100. A large number of Medical students prefer graduating at a Home University, partly on account of the larger experience obtained by prosecuting their studies in such places as Edinburgh or Glasgow or London: and such are allowed to pass two years of their whole curriculum in Otago.

The School of Mines is not yet so fully organized and equipped: still, with provision already made for instruction in Mathematics, Theoretical and Applied Mechanics, Physics, Palæontology, Theoretical and Technological Chemistry, Qualitative and Quantitative Analysis, General Geology and Surveying, a good beginning has been made towards the creation of a School of Engineering. Under present arrangements, a student may obtain the distinction or title of "Associate of the School of Mines, Otago"; and receive certificates of "Mining Surveyor" and "Metallurgical Chemist and Assayer."

Beyond the appointment of a Lecturer, very little has yet been done in the matter of instruction in Law; but as recent changes have made it practically necessary for all Barristers to obtain the LL.B. Degree of the New Zealand University, it is probable that a fresh impetus may have been given to the development of a Law School.

The University is under the control and government of a Council, the members of which are nominated by the Government, and who hold office for life. The Chancellor and the Vice-Chancellor are elected by the members of the Council out of their own body, and hold their office for three years. The names of the Chancellors and Vice-Chancellors who have successively held office since the foundation of the University are, as follows:—

CHANCELLORS.

The Rev. Thomas Burns, D.D., elected Nov. 10, 1869.

The Hon. Major Richardson (afterwards Sir John L. C. Richardson), elected March 3, 1871; re-elected Feb. 26, 1874.

His Hon. Henry Samuel Chapman, elected Aug. 14, 1876.

The Rev. Donald McNaughton Stuart, D.D., elected Sept. 11, 1879; re-elected Sept. 19, 1882; Sept. 30, 1885; and Sept., 1888.

VICE-CHANCELLORS.

The Hon. Major Richardson, elected Nov. 10, 1869.

The Rev. Donald McNaughton Stuart, D.D., elected March 3, 1871; re-elected Feb. 20, 1874, and Aug. 29, 1877.

His Honor Mr. Justice Williams, elected Sept. 11, 1879; re-elected Sept. 19, 1882, and Oct. 6, 1885; and Sept., 1888.

The Council appoints the Professors and Lecturers, manages the finances of the Institution, and attends to all its external relations; but the conduct of the educational arrangements of the University, the discipline of the students, the courses and hours of study, the management of the Library, and such like, are entrusted to the Professorial Board.

In addition to their share in the Scholarships of the New Zealand University, several scholarships are available exclusively for students attending the Otago University. The Richardson Scholarship (founded in 1871 by the late Sir John Richardson, then Chancellor of the University) is of the annual value of £40, tenable for three years. It is won by the student who obtains the highest marks in an Examination in six subjects, selected from the following: English, Latin, Greek, French, German, Arithmetic and Algebra, Geometry and Trigonometry, Natural History, Chemistry, Geography and History.

The Scott Scholarship (founded in 1874, as a memorial of Sir Walter Scott), is of the annual value of £20; and its conditions are of a similar nature to those of the Richardson Scholarship.

The Gray Russell Scholarship was founded in 1882 by George Gray Russell, Esq., is of the annual value of £40, and is also ordinarily tenable for three years. The examination is of the same character and under the same conditions as to subjects and marks as that prescribed for the Junior Scholarships of the New Zealand University.

There are also Scholarships available for Pupil-teachers in connection with the Normal School.

In the year 1884, James Fulton, Esq., M.H.R., presented a hundred guineas to the University Council " to form the nucleus of a Scholarship Fund for boys and girls from the Taieri, who may desire to attend the Otago or any other University." The fund is now accumulating.

In the year 1885, J. Sperrey, Esq., Mrs. Burn, and Miss Dalrymple handed to the University Council the sum of £375 10s, collected by public subscription, to be devoted to a Scholarship for women, tenable at the Otago University. The fund is now accumulating, and will be applied to its purpose when the annual interest shall amount to £30.

Ever since the foundation of the University, the number of the students in attendance has steadily increased ; and, whereas, in the earlier years only one or two students graduated each year, the number now annually graduating has increased till last year it reached the number of twenty. In proportion to the population, the numbers are not only equal to, but in advance of the attendance at the English and Scotch Universities. The University is viewed with pride and admiration by the whole population, and is justly considered one of the most valuable institutions of the Colony.

ARCHITECTURE OF DUNEDIN.

BY N. Y. A. WALES.

THE Architectural features of Dunedin, unlike those of Victoria and the older and more populous Australian colonies, owe their origin more to private enterprize than to the Government of the colony. Here no Parliament houses, treasury buildings, printing offices, public library, handsome railway station, nor modernised hospital, such as the Alfred Hospital at Sydney, rear their classic columns or pointed gables to attract the attention of our neighbours, who may honour us with a visit to our National Exhibition. Nor have we any engineering monument like the Princes Bridge. Nor would it be becoming of us to boast of the Exhibition building, though we may cherish a latent pride in contemplating the proportions to which it has grown from small beginnings, if we may not enter into comparisons with the vastness and grandeur of the buildings erected for exhibition purposes by our Victorian and New South Wales neighbours.

The Dunedin Exhibition building has been designed more with a view to economy than appearance, more for utility than effect, more for large proportions to provide space for exhibits than for symmetry and beauty of design, and more with a view to subsequent utilization and substantial returns, than for present visual gratification. Yet it is not altogether without pretensions. Its façade, in comparison with other structures of the kind hitherto attempted in New Zealand, is indeed palatial and imposing, and bears the stamp of some originality, and has some commendable features.

Strangers and tourists in search of health or pleasure, or travellers on business bent—and a large number of both classes visit us for the sake of our salubrious climate, or to obtain a share of our trade—all speak highly of our city and of its buildings, and the architectural merit they display. Some even betray surprise at the rapid advancement of so young a province, and give expression to their feelings by applying such words as "magnificent," "beautiful," and "substantial," as descriptive of some of the buildings.

During the earlier years of the Province, the discovery of the gold fields and the consequent rapid influx of population, gave such an impetus to buildings, that the town grew mushroom-like to large proportions, and wooden buildings sprang up as if by magic on all sides, with here and there a bank or store of more ornate and substantial pretensions. But the mercantile requirements were of such a pressing nature, and the wants for domestic accommodation were so urgent, that the question of materials to be used was decided by the speed with which they could be manipulated and transformed into shape.

Notwithstanding the necessarily flimsy character of many of the buildings erected at that time, a foundation of prosperity was being laid that has enabled the pioneers to replace many of them with commodious and substantial and even handsome structures.

The site upon which the young and growing city stands is one of the most picturesque in the southern hemisphere. It is bounded on the east by the beautiful land-locked bay, and beyond by the Peninsula—famed for its fertile and productive soil, over which the rising sun sheds his fructifying rays, and lights up the church spires and the tall smoking factory chimneys. All round on the other side it is encompassed by numerous hills and glens, whose sides are covered with rich native bush, filled with ferns and flora peculiar to the district. A portion of these encircling hills form the Town Belt, which has this advantage—that no matter how embarrassed in pecuniary matters the civic authorities —who are the trustees—may find themselves, they cannot alienate any part of it; nor indeed would they be permitted to do so if they had the power, so jealously is the right to it, as common property guarded by the citizens. Would that the beautiful native shrubs and foliage were as rigidly preserved and protected from the vandalism that prevails. Hence town sections bordering on the "belt" are rated at higher values, and outside of this "tapu" boundary the suburbs spread out fan-like, with neat and trim-looking cottages, and well-kept gardens, studding the valleys and hill sides; while nearest to the "belt," both on the town and suburban sides, many of the more successful citizens have built themselves picturesque and commodious villas that add to the beauty and attractiveness of the landscape.

Anterior to the stirring times of the goldfield days, the progress was slow, though none the less sure and of a permanent character. During this period little or no attention was given to the architectural appearance of the buildings'; but this notice would be incomplete and lacking in a most essential part, without some reference to the buildings of the early settlement.

Some few framed houses were brought out with the early settlers. These were of the ordinary type of three or four roomed cottage architecture. Others of what the Australian would call the " wattle and daub " style, that is, the Ti-tree or Manuka scrub and puddle, were speedily improvised. While others again slightly more pretentious, had their walls constructed of fern trees, placed upright side by side, the inside being plastered with puddle-clay, which adhered firmly to the rough fern tree, and made comfortable and warm rooms, less draughty than many of the more modern and rough lined and papered houses. The writer lived in one of these earlier erections near Port Chalmers for a few years, and one of them still stands and can be seen in Roslyn at the " Half-Way-Bush," nestling in a grove of native bush, and forming one of the prettiest features in the district.

Another of these romantic-looking fern tree cottages stood at the corner of London and Pitt-streets, and was originally occupied for many years by Dr Purdie. Sir Francis Dillon Bell, at that time Mr Bell, afterwards became proprietor, and wishing to enlarge the residence, found the old structure in the way, and felt much disposed to raze it to the ground. But being imbued somewhat with archæological tendencies, at last decided to surround it with such accommodation as he required. The premises are now occupied by Dr Maunsell, and the old cottage still exists ensconced within a setting of more luxurious surroundings than the flax bushes and maori heads, which grew abundantly in George-street, during the earlier years of its occupation. Passing from these older associations and pleasing reminiscences of the past, which are tempting to dwell upon, to give some idea of the progress of architecture in Otago, it will be necessary to

THE FIRST CHURCH, DUNEDIN.

notice some of the more prominent buildings. Amongst the first of these are the churches.

The First Church was designed by Mr R. A. Lawson, architect. It is a handsome building of early Decorated Gothic, with a finely proportioned tower and spire rising to a height of 175 feet. It is built of Oamaru stone and with the Manse close by, occupies a most conspicuous site on Church Hill, overlooking the harbour.

Though named " The First Church," it is really the fourth building erected for the congregation. The first building was erected in 1848 where the Standard Insurance Company's building now stands. It was a wooden building of no pretensions, to which followed a stone structure of a primitive style, and that also had to be vacated for a larger though temporary building of wood, which was erected fronting Dowling-street, on the site occupied by the Lyceum, now called the City Hall. This third building was sold for removal, and was converted into tramway stables, and was ultimately burnt.

Of the first building, the Rev. Dr Burns, the first and able minister, who with Captain Cargill, was the pioneer founder of the Presbyterian settlement, very humorously and with consider-able feeling said : " The poor old church ! Never was there an " honester, a more faithful, or a more useful servant. I may say " that it was a good servant of all work. It could cleverly turn " its hand to anything. Its sacred—its proper work was on Sunday, " but from Monday to Saturday it held itself ready for any service. " It was a schoolroom ; it was a public lecture room ; it was the " humble servant of the Dunedin Land Investment Company ; " it lent itself to many a stormy political meeting ; it was the " willing servant of the Horticultural Society; with patriotic zeal, " it accommodated the Provincial Council; it lent itself to many a " concert, to many a musical party; and then it was without pride, " and it had no ambition ; from the highest to the lowest, it was " equally at the command of all.

"It was possessed of at least one great quality that should not " be left untold—it utterly disdained a mercenary spirit; it never " would work for wages—and it was this great quality that " hastened its fall. Adversity came, and so soon as its last trials " began, they came thick and fast.

"The first trial was indeed hard to bear—our congregation turned its back on it for ever. A handsome new church rose under its very nose ; and, last of all, it was itself let out for hire. For seventeen long years, it had occupied with the utmost credit to itself, the high and honourable position of the First Church of Otago. In one sad hour it fell from its high estate—the First Church of Otago was converted into a wool-shed—it sank down to the level of a common hired drudge of the lowest grade. The poor thing never recovered the blow—it died of a broken heart—it perished like a martyr at the stake ; it breathed its last in the midst of devouring fire. Peace be with the ashes of our poor old church."

Knox Church, designed by the same architect, is of the same style—perhaps less ornate externally, and yet as pleasing in appearance. The inside is an improvement on the First Church. The galleries are continued round the sides, and meeting over the pulpit, form the organ loft there.

The first building erected by the Episcopalians was also temporary. It stood fronting Cumberland-street, nearly opposite the gaol. It, too, had to make way for more commodious buildings ; and St. Paul's (pro-cathedral), fronting the Octagon and Stuart-street, was built in 1862, and has since been followed by St. Matthew's and All Saint's in the city, and by several smaller churches in the suburbs. Recently, the spire of St. Paul's has been taken down. The stone of which it was built was a loosely compacted limestone, and had disintegrated so much as to become dangerous.

The Wesleyans were early in the field, and erected a large church of wood fronting Dowling-street, which has since been taken down, and the stone building at the corner of Stuart-street and Moray-place is now occupied by the congregation. Numerous other smaller churches have been built in the city and suburbs by that body.

The St. Joseph's Cathedral, Roman Catholic, is an imposing building, and occupies a commanding site. The nave and two front flanking towers only, have been constructed so far ; the transepts and central tower are to be added as funds accumulate.

The design, by Mr F. W. Petre, is of the Gothic 15th century Decorated. The complete building will be cruciform in plan, and will have a tower and spire rising to a height of about 220 ft. The extreme length and breadth will be 222 ft. and 102 ft. respectively. The stained glass windows are from the Royal Factory at Munich, and are beautifully executed, and some of the stone carving inside is very rich, and peculiar to the style. Already, £22,000 has been expended on this building.

Of the scholastic institutions, the University building occupies the first place. Although unfinished, it looks a venerable pile. The style is Domestic Gothic, somewhat severe, being built of basalt, slightly relieved with Oamaru stone; and with the quaint-looking, Queen Anne style of dark-red brick houses for the Professors, adjoining, it looks altogether what it is intended for.

Were it not that criticism would be out of place in a semi-historical sketch like this, a hint might be given, that were a few trees planted about the site and the adjoining grounds to the south, which belong to the University, and a more becoming fence erected, with the approaches neatly laid out, its appearance would be vastly improved.

The Boys' High School, a semi-ecclesiastical building, pertaining more to the Domestic Tudor style of mediæval architecture, stands up prominently on the western outskirts, overlooking the harbour. Its interior arrangements consist of a large hall with galleries, surrounded with class-rooms providing accommodation for 450 scholars.

The other school buildings, known as Government schools, of which there are five in the city and several in the suburbs, very much resemble each other in outward appearance and in internal arrangements ; and were it not for the surroundings, a stranger who has just been examining one, and coming suddenly upon another in some other part of the town, would—as a recent traveller in Holland said in describing the monotony and sameness of the buildings there—imagine he had retraced his steps, so much alike are these buildings.

The public buildings, such as the Post Office and Court House, Telegraph Office, Custom House, and Public Works buildings, and the Railway Offices, affect no style; but may be classed utilitarian. Built with little or no pretension to art, they are suitable for the purposes to which they are devoted, except, perhaps, the Supreme Court House, which is tacked on to, or rather, is a part of the Post Office buildings, and was originally erected as a chamber for the Provincial Council meetings. Upon the abolition of the provinces it was transformed into a Supreme Court House; but its adaptation is not a success. These buildings are all within easy distance of each other, and occupy prominent positions in the centre of the city. The functions of the New Zealand Government evidently do not embrace the development or cultivation of æsthetics in architecture. If they did, the public institutions should bear the impress.

The Cargill Monument, which was erected to the memory of the late Captain Cargill—the founder of the Otago settlement—stands in the triangle between the Custom House and the Bank of New Zealand. It is one of the finest and neatest pieces of early Decorated English Gothic architecture to be met with anywhere. Though more ornate, it almost reminds the beholder of the Queen Eleanor Crosses, erected by Edward the First.

The Museum is an unfinished concrete building, being the central block only of what was intended for a large structure, and the blank panels in the upper part of the façade were designed for sculpture intended to be characteristic. It is now well filled, and under the able and enthusiastic management of Professor Parker, will soon require to be enlarged.

The Hospital, like many other buildings in Dunedin, notably the Colonial Bank and Supreme Court House, is used for a purpose for which it was neither designed nor suitable. It was built ostensibly for a public market; but a rumour was current at the time that the Colonial Legislature might be located in Dunedin, and that this building would become the central block, and be used for the departmental offices, while larger buildings would be erected on either side for the two Parliament Houses. Dame Rumour on that occasion was at fault, and "what might have been is not yet." The building is of the Italian style, designed by Mr William Mason, architect. The first use made of it was for the purposes of the First Dunedin Exhibition, held in 1865. Some of the annexes then erected still stand, and now form part of the Hospital. As a hospital it has served the purpose well, and can comfortably accommodate 'over 100 patients. Though not conveniently arranged, it is kept by the management in fairly good sanitary condition, and its low average death-rate may be attributed to the skill and unwearied attention of the medical staff. In connection with the Hospital there is a medical school and an operation theatre which accommodates over forty students.

The Lunatic Asylum is the largest public building in the colony. It was designed by Mr R. A. Lawson, after the Scotch Baronial style, and stands on a commanding, though insecure site, overlooking the Pacific Ocean about 20 miles north from Dunedin, presenting an imposing appearance to travellers by land or sea. It was built to accommodate 350 patients, and cost about £80,000.

The gaol—well, it is nothing to boast of. It was—compounded (perhaps is the better word, and more applicable than designed or constructed) of stone and corrugated iron. But it was one of the early buildings, and has been added to as occasion required. The idea of building a new one has been talked of, and perhaps the authorities will one day realize the necessity.

The banks until recently led the van in erecting ornate and handsome buildings ; but now their claim to the first position is disputed by the Insurance Companies and hotels.

The Colonial Bank of New Zealand has its headquarters in perhaps the largest, most conspicuous, and most centrally-situated building of the kind in this city. It was erected in the first instance in the height of the gold-digging days, " the good times," by the General Government for a General Post Office. The then Postmaster-General, in giving his instructions to the architect, after describing the requirements, told him to design the building " after the style of St. Martin's-le-Grand."

As a piece of classic architecture, it is an ornament to the city, and does credit to its founders, and to the architect. The building was never used as a Post Office. The Provincial Government, which was then in power, and the General Government, disagreed as to the terms of occupation in some way ; and the former erected the massive but plain red brick building adjoining, that now does duty as Post Office, accommodating the Survey and Registration departments, and the Supreme and Resident Magistrate Courts ; and what was intended for the Post Office was handed over to the newly-established University.

The University Council, after using it for a time for University purposes, and as a Museum, sold it to the Colonial Bank Corporation, and erected premises on what they considered a more suitable position, with the proceeds. This building, now the Colonial Bank of New Zealand headquarters, though of an imposing and stately character, is overshadowed by the Grand Hotel, and threatened by a more imposing building just opposite now being erected for the Colonial Mutual Insurance Association of Victoria. The Union Bank of Australia, built on the second block further south, also classic, with a handsome Corinthian portico in front, is in like manner thrown into the shade by the massiveness and towering altitude of Wain's five storied hotel, on the opposite side of the street. The Bank of New Zealand occupies a prominent position on the corner of Princes and Rattray-streets, across the triangle from the Colonial Bank. This is also a purely classic structure, designed with good taste, is boldly relieved, and presents an effective outside. The large Banking Hall is conveniently arranged, and chastely furnished with richly carved cedar fittings. The ceiling is pannelled and decorated with neatly modelled enrichments. It was the work of the late Mr Armson, Christchurch, and for purity and richness of design after its kind, as a piece of street architecture, stands unrivalled. The Bank of New South Wales, and the National Bank of New Zealand, built on the same block fronting Princes-street, though both presenting good and imposing façades, do not affect so pretentious a style.

But the large four-storied building recently erected on the Dowling-street corner of the same block by the Australian Mutual Provident Society, a boldly conceived Italian design, shares with the Bank of New Zealand, the honours of the situation. While exactly opposite the Bank of New Zealand, the New Zealand Government Life Insurance Company has purchased a site, upon which it is anticipated that a building will be erected which will excel all previous structures. The Bank of Australasia occupies one of the finest and most prominent sites in the city, but the building suffers in comparison with all other institutions of a similar semi-public kind, and is completely dwarfed by the New Zealand Insurance Company's buildings, recently erected on the opposite corner of Crawford and Rattray-streets.

The Bank of Australasia building was originally erected for the Otago Daily Times and Witness Company, and was vacated by that Company for larger premises, their business becoming too extended for the limited accommodation.

The wholesale soft goods warehouses deserve notice. Messrs Ross and Glendining's in Stafford-street, Brown, Ewing and Co.'s in Manse-street, Bing Harris and Co.'s, and Butterworth Bros. and Co.s' in High-street, and Sargood Son and Ewen's in lower High-street, are all large buildings, and present imposing façades. The last-named is perhaps the most conspicuous, from its prominent position opposite the Railway Station, and fronting the Triangle Reserve.

There are several other buildings in the city, of a more or less ornate character, possessing breadth of design and boldness of execution, such as the U. S. S. Company's offices, the Evening Star Newspaper premises, with its two frontages to Crawford and Bond-streets, the Universal Bond, and W. G. Neill's stores, Briscoe's Ironmongery Warehouse, and Stout and Mondy's (solicitors) offices ; but in the limited space allowed for this article, the details of each, and their architectural merits, cannot be separately discussed.

The several manufactories, too, the Roslyn Worsted and Woollen Mills, the Mosgiel Woollen Manufactory, A. and T. Burt's Copper and Brass Works, all famed for the quality of their productions, might also be noticed, but would be more in place perhaps, amongst the industries of the town ; and to describe the domestic architecture, the variety of styles adopted, and their quaint developments, would require a chapter. But before closing, the Town Hall must be visited. This is an unfinished building, the front part only comprising the departmental offices and the Council Chambers being completed. The façade is after the Italian style of architecture, boldly treated, and is surmounted with a bell-tower and look-out station, rising to a height of 165 feet, from which visitors can get an extensive view of the city. From there can be seen the numerous tall chimney stalks, emitting dense volumes of smoke, the "stately edifices" towering one over the other up the steep hill sides, upon which the residences of the inhabitants are mainly built, the neat and cleanly painted cottages, surrounded with the tastefully cultivated gardens, or with their flower-plots in front; and the bright and many varied hues of green foliage that covers the Town Belt; while away in the distance to the north and to the south, lie the cemeteries, each a " God's acre, with its narrow " green mounds and pale stone records; and further away still " rise the bleak mountain tops, about whose irresponsive peaks " amorous white clouds continually creep and cling and nestle in " misty adoration.

EDUCATION.

BY DR. HISLOP.

PROVISION FOR EDUCATION UNDER THE ORIGINAL OTAGO SETTLEMENT
SCHEME.

THE settlers of Otago manifested from the outset a determination to establish and maintain a liberal and comprehensive system of public school education. When the settlement was founded in 1847-48 by the Otago Association under an agreement with the New Zealand Company, the price of land in the Otago block was fixed at forty shillings per acre. Only one-fourth of the proceeds of the land sales was to be retained by the Company; the balance was to be expended on various public purposes in certain fixed proportions. It was part of the agreement that one-eighth of the entire proceeds should be set apart for "religious and educational uses," under the control of Trustees acting on behalf of the Presbyterian Church of Otago. Instead of this proportion of the proceeds being paid to the Church Trustees in cash, it was invested in the purchase of land within the settlement, so as to form an endowment for the maintenance of churches and schools. When the New Zealand Company's scheme came to an end in 1852, the Trustees had acquired in this way 22 properties of $60\frac{1}{4}$ acres each, viz., 22 quarter-acre town sections; 22 ten-acre suburban sections; and 22 rural sections of 50 acres each; making in all, $1325\frac{1}{2}$ acres. The original aggregate price of these properties was £2651. For some years the annual revenue from them was trifling, the average for the six years 1852-57 scarcely reaching £34. Of late years, however, the revenue has been considerable, the amount of rental received for the year 1887 having been returned at £4,892 13s 3d.

In the year 1852, the Imperial Parliament passed the New Zealand Constitution Act, by which the original Otago block was greatly enlarged, and was constituted one of the seven Provinces into which the colony was divided by the Act. The arrangement between the New Zealand Company and the Otago Association was consequently brought to a close, and no further additions could be made to the estate held by the Presbyterian Church Trustees "for religious and educational uses." The duty of providing the means of education within the newly-formed Province of Otago was left to the Provincial Government, in whom the administration of public affairs was now vested. This duty was taken up so heartily by the Government and the Provincial Council, that the Church authorities very wisely resolved to refrain from maintaining rival denominational schools.

No agreement had yet been come to regarding the proportion of the Presbyterian Church endowment that should be appropriated to educational, as distinct from ecclesiastical uses, and after full discussion of the question, a general willingness was expressed by ministers and members of the Church that some definite proportion should be devoted to educational purposes, from which not the Presbyterian Church alone, but the whole of the community, should derive benefit. It was agreed that the proportion should be one-third, and in 1866, the "Presbyterian Church Lands Act" was passed by the Colonial Parliament, providing that two-thirds of the clear annual revenue derived from the endowment, should be devoted by the Synod of the Presbyterian Church to ecclesiastical purposes in Otago and Southland,* and that the remaining third should be applied by the Church Trustees to the erection and endowment of a literary chair or chairs in any college or university that might be established in the Province of Otago. The funds thus placed at the disposal of the Trustees have enabled them to establish three professorial chairs in the University of Otago, viz.—Mental and Moral Philosophy, 1871 ; English Language

---

* The purposes specified by the Act are as follows: "Building or repairing of manses and churches in the Provinces of Otago and Southland, and endowing or aiding in the endowment of any Theological chair or chairs in connection with the Presbyterian Church of Otago in any College or University which may hereafter be erected in the Province of Otago, or any or either of such purposes according to regulations that may be prescribed from time to time by the Synod of Otago and Southland."

and Literature, 1881; and Natural Philosophy, 1884. As the
annual revenue from the trust has now probably reached its
highest limit, or nearly so, there is little or no prospect of any
addition being made for some considerable time to the number
of chairs already instituted. Very full information regarding the
Otago Presbyterian Church Fund is supplied by the Rev. W.
Gillies, of Timaru, in a "Historical Narrative" published by
him some years ago.

The following balance-sheet was submitted to the Synod at
its annual meeting in October, 1888:—

EDUCATION FUND.

For twelve months ending 30th September, 1888.

Dr.

December 31st, 1887.
To Cash paid—

Professors' salaries £1800	0	0	
Assessment, Synod expenses 100	0	0	
Insurance premiums 2	14	3	
Commission, 5 per cent. on £589 9s 1d .. 29	9	6	
	£1932	3	9
,, Balance	11,960	9	0
	£13,892	12	9

Cr.

December 31st, 1886.

By Balance	£11,738	5	6
December 31st, 1887.			
,, One-third net revenue £1564 18 2			
,, Interest on investments 589 9 1			
	2154	7	3
	£13,892	12	9

Memo. of Balance.

December 31st, 1887—

Loans on mortgage	£8767	10	0
Fixed deposit	2000	0	0
Debentures	300	0	0
Cash in Bank	892	19	0
	£11,960	9	0

THE FIRST SCHOOL AND TEACHER.

Among those who arrived in the ship "Philip Laing," in
April, 1848, along with the Rev. Thomas Burns and other immigrants, was Mr. James Blackie, whom the Otago Association had

appointed Schoolmaster of the settlement. He conducted a school with much acceptance in a portion of the original First Church building until September, 1850, when failing health compelled him to retire from active duty. He left for Sydney shortly afterwards for change of air, but he survived only a few months. When Mr. Blackie left Dunedin, his friend Mr. James Elder Brown, now of Milton, was prevailed upon to take temporary charge of the school, with a view to its being kept open. Mr. Brown can thus claim to be the oldest ex-teacher of an Otago public school now living.

MR. BLACKIE'S SUCCESSORS.

By arrangement made with the Church authorities, the school was taught successively by the following-named gentlemen : Mr. William Mackenzie, who was afterwards accidentally drowned while working the punt at Taieri Ferry ; Mr. Robert M'Dowell, who subsequently left the colony; and Mr. William Somerville, now Clerk to the Bench, Dunedin, who continued in charge until the arrival, in October, 1856, of the late Mr. Alex. Livingston, who had been appointed at Home to the Rectorship of the Dunedin School.

OTHER SCHOOLS IN DUNEDIN AND SUBURBS.

A small private school for girls was kept by Miss Peterson for a short time at the lower end of Walker-street. The late Mr. Gebbie, of Saddle Hill, conducted a school in a fern-tree whare with a clay floor, erected on Church land in the North-East Valley, near the Town Belt, until 1854, when he married Miss Peterson, and by agreement with the Kirk Session and settlers of East Taieri, opened a school in the church that had been erected there for the Rev. Mr. Will. Mr. Gebbie remained in charge of the East Taieri School until November, 1856, when he was succeeded by Mr. John Hislop. Mr. Robert Short succeeded Mr. Gebbie as teacher of the North-East Valley School ; and when that gentleman entered the Provincial Government service as an officer in the Land Department, Mr. Andrew Russell took charge of the School until the arrival and appointment of Mr. A. G. Allan in 1858. Shortly after the Provincial Government had been established, Mr. J. G. S. Grant arrived from Victoria, and for some time conducted a school which he named "The Dunedin Academy." About the same time, a school was taught in the church building at Green Island Bush by the Rev. Alex. Bethune. He left in 1856 to join the band of pioneers who sailed from Dunedin in that year to occupy the recently surveyed district of Invercargill and neighbourhood.

FIRST STEPS TAKEN BY THE NEWLY CONSTITUTED PROVINCIAL COUNCIL.

The Otago Provincial Council, during its first session, 1853-54, appointed, on the motion of the late Mr. James Macandrew, a Select Committee to consider and report upon the subject of Education, more particularly the establishment of a High School in Dunedin. There is no record of any report having been submitted by this Committee. The Superintendent, Captain Cargill, in the course of his address at the opening of the second session of the Provincial Council in 1854 said : "On the subject of a general system of Education, resolutions will be proposed to you declaratory of the mind and purpose of the Provincial Legislature thereon, and embracing a moderate appropriation for the initiatory step of bringing out three qualified teachers— one of them to be the teacher of a Normal or High School in Dunedin." The promised resolutions were subsequently brought forward by Mr. W. H. Reynolds, leader of the Executive Council, and were referred for revision to a Select Committee consisting of Mr. Reynolds, and the late Messrs. Macandrew, John Gillies, and Alex. Rennie. The Committee's report was adopted by the Provincial Council in December, 1854, and was to the following effect : (1) That provision should be made from the public funds of the Province, or by assessment, for providing a liberal education for all the children of the Province as far as practicable ; (2) That permanent provision for such education should be made by special ordinance or ordinances, setting forth clearly and distinctly the character of the education to be provided, and the mode in which such provision should be made ; (3) That as a first step towards effecting the desired object, a proper High School should be established in Dunedin, wherein could be taught all the branches of education necessary for qualifying the pupils for entering a University, and that in the meantime one qualified master for the school should be obtained ; (4) That a superior female teacher should be provided for Dunedin ; (5) That a well-qualified teacher for Port Chalmers, and, at the least,

three for other districts in the Province, should be procured ; (6)
That provision should be made in the appropriation ordinance
for paying the passage money of these teachers from the Home
Country, and for the purchase of the necessary school appliances ;
(7) That the annual salaries of the proposed teachers should be
as follows : The Rector of the High School, not less than £200,
nor more than £300 ; the schoolmistress and the other teachers,
£100 each ; and (8) That the appointments should be made by
the Home Agents on the recommendation of one of Her Majesty's
Inspectors of Schools for Scotland, and the Rectors of the Free
Church Normal Schools in Edinburgh and Glasgow.

APPOINTMENT AND ARRIVAL OF TEACHERS FROM THE HOME COUNTRY.

The Provincial Government and the Home Agents lost no
time in giving effect to the resolutions of the Council. The first
teachers who arrived were Miss Margaret Dodds and Mr. Alex.
Ayson. They were passengers by the ship " Southern Cross,"
which reached Port Chalmers, after calling at Northern ports, in
April, 1856. Miss Dodds was appointed to the Dunedin school,
and Mr. Ayson's services were secured by the settlers of
Tokomairiro. Three additional teachers arrived by the ship
"Strathmore" in October, 1856, viz. the late Mr. Alex. Livingston,
who had been selected by the Home Agents for the rectorship of
the Dunedin High School ; Mr. Colin Allan, who was engaged
by the Port Chalmers School Committee ; and Mr. John Hislop,
who was appointed to the East Taieri School. The services of
the late Mr. Adam Wright, a schoolmaster who had arrived by
the " Strathmore," were engaged for the Green Island school.

EDUCATION ORDINANCE, 1856.

The first Otago Education Ordinance (1856) had been passed
before the arrival of the teachers from the Home Country, and
under its provisions an Education Board and several school
districts with their respective school committees, had been
constituted. The Board was composed of the Superintendent of
the Province, his Executive Council, the Rector of the Dunedin
High School, and two representatives elected by each school
committee. The annual salary of the Rector of the High School
was fixed at not less than £250, and those of the district school
teachers at £100 each, with a residence consisting of at least

three apartments, and a piece of ground not exceeding ten acres, properly fenced. The school fees collected by each district school teacher were to be "imputed *pro tanto* of his salary," and it was upon such moderate terms that the earliest school teachers of Otago were engaged. It is worthy of mention, however, that the Provincial Council in successive years, as long as the Ordinance of 1856 was in operation, generously voted to each teacher, in addition to the fixed salary of £100, the amount of the fees levied by him, on the School Committee certifying that he had performed his duties successfully and satisfactorily.

The Education Ordinance provided that the teachers' salaries should be defrayed by a tax not exceeding 20/-, to be paid annually by every male person resident in the Province. So strong and widespread was the resistance to the levying of this poll-tax, that no attempt was made by the authorities to enforce payment; the entire cost of the schools was met out of the ordinary Provincial revenue and the school fees, supplemented in a few instances by local subscriptions.

The selection of the teacher was vested in the School Committee, subject to the following provision:—"Every candidate for the office of school-master in any public school shall produce a certificate signed by a minister of the denomination to which he belongs, attesting his religious and moral character, and shall be subjected to such examination as may be prescribed by the Board; and no person shall be inducted as such schoolmaster until he shall have passed such examination, and have obtained and produced to the School Committee a certificate by the Board approving of his appointment; and said examination shall be open to the School Committee, who may suggest such questions as they may think fit, except in the case of schoolmasters who shall have been selected and appointed in Great Britain, under the authority of the Board."

The following was the provision with regard to religious instruction in schools:—"Every School Committee under this Ordinance shall appoint certain stated hours for ordinary religious instruction by the schoolmaster, at which children shall not be bound to attend if their parents or guardians object. If a complaint shall be presented to the School Committee by any two heads of families, being parents or guardians of children who attend any public school under this Ordinance, accusing the master of such school of teaching religious opinions at variance with the doctrines of the Holy Scriptures, the School Committee shall, with the sanction of the Board, and with such assistance as the Board shall direct, inquire into such complaint; and if it shall be proved that the schoolmaster has taught such opinions, or has persevered in doing so after remonstrance, the School Committee may censure, suspend, or deprive the schoolmaster, as they may think fit: provided always that every such sentence shall be approved by the Board." The writer cannot recollect that any proceedings were ever taken uuder this provision of the Ordinance in the course of the five years during which it remained in force. Power was given to the Board, on receipt of a complaint from two heads of families, being parents or guardians of children attending the school, to censure, suspend, or dismiss a schoolmaster for "crime or moral deliuquency," after due inquiry and consideration of any statement in defence that the schoolmaster might make.

FIRST EDUCATION REPORT.

The late Mr John M'Glashan, who ever took a warm interest in the welfare of the schools, added to his duties of Provincial Solicitor and Provincial Treasurer those of Secretary and Treasurer to the Education Board, until the repeal of the Ordinance in 1861. When the Board submitted its first annual report (1856-57), there were five public schools in operation. The following summary of information is compiled from the report :—

SCHOOLS AND TEACHERS, SEPTEMBER, 1857.

Schools.		Teachers.	Salaries, including School Fees.			Average Attendance
Dunedin ..	..	A. Livingston	£250	0	0	} 101
,, ..	..	A. R. Livingston	100	0	0	
,, ..	..	Miss Dodds	124	0	0	14
Port Chalmers	..	C. Allan	135	0	0	31
Green Island	..	A. Wright	132	0	0	20
East Taieri	..	J. Hislop	140	10	8	36
Tokomairiro	..	A. Ayson	120	17	5	34
						236

The school fees for the Dunedin school, which amounted to £189 16s, are not included in the table, the teachers having been paid fixed salaries. Miss Dodds received £24 as rent allowance. The exact amount of fees collected in Port Chalmers schools is not given, but the sum mentioned is believed to be about the amount.

ARRIVAL OF FIVE ADDITIONAL TEACHERS FROM HOME.

At the date of the report, the localities of Portobello, Wakari (Half-Way-Bush), Anderson's Bay, West Taieri, Waihola, and Clutha, had been constituted school districts, but no schools had then been opened in them. In the course of the following year (1858), five additional teachers were sent out by the Home Agents, and were appointed as follows :—Mr Alex. G. Allan to N. E. Valley; Mr Adam D. Johnston to Wakari; Mr Andrew Russell to Anderson's Bay; Mr Alex. Gardner to West Taieri; and Mr Alex. Grigor to Inch Clutha. A side school in connection with the Port Chalmers school committee was opened in the same year at Portobello by Mrs Edwards, wife of a settler there. Mr Grigor, of Inch Clutha, is the only one of the original teachers now in the service of the Education Board.

The Education Ordinance, 1856, continued in operation until its repeal in June 1861 by another ordinance. At that date the number of schools had increased to 18, and the number of teachers to 20. The average attendance was about 560, inclusive of an attendance of 125 at the Dunedin school. The amount expended on the public schools by the Provincial Government for the 5½ years ending September 30th, 1861, was as follows:— Buildings, fencing, &c., £7240 5s 5d; teachers' salaries, £5313 11s 9d; total £12,553 17s 2d. The schools in operation in 1861, in addition to those already mentioned, were N. E. Harbour, North Taieri, Waihola, Otakia, South Clutha, Warepa, and Waikouaiti.

EDUCATION ORDINANCE, 1861.

On the passing of the Education Ordinance, 1861, Mr (now Dr) John Hislop, of the East Taieri school, was appointed to the joint offices of Secretary to the Education Board and Inspector of Schools; and he held these offices until January 1878, when he removed to Wellington to assume the duties of Secretary to the Colonial Education Department. But the ordinance of 1861 was disallowed by the Governor, on account of a technical error that occurred in some of its provisions for levying a school rate on heritable property within the several school districts. The Provincial Government was consequently under the necessity of carrying on the schools upon its own responsibility until another Ordinance should be passed by the Provincial Council.

EDUCATION ORDINANCES, 1862 AND 1864.

An amended Education Ordinance was passed in 1862, and it remained in force until it was superseded by the Ordinance of 1864, which regulated the administration of school affairs in Otago until the abolition of the Provinces in 1876. The main reason for the repeal of the Ordinance of 1862, was the strong dissatisfaction expressed more particularly in the gold fields districts with the provisions relating to religious instruction in the schools. These required that, in addition to the daily reading of the Bible, such religious instruction should be given as the School Committee might appoint, and that no religious instruction should be taught "at variance with what are commonly known as Evangelical Protestant doctrines," no child being bound, however, to attend on such instruction contrary to the wish of the parent or guardian. In the Ordinance of 1864, the following provision was substituted :—"In every school the Holy Scriptures shall be read daily, and such reading shall be either at the opening or close of the school, and no child whose parent or guardian shall object to such instruction shall be bound to attend at such times."

It was provided by the Ordinance of 1864 that the Education Board should consist of the Superintendent of the Province, his Executive Council, and the Speaker of the Provincial Council. A school committee for each district was to be elected annually by the owners and occupiers of land and the householders within the district. The teachers were to be elected by the school committees, no election being valid until the person elected produced a certificate of fitness from H.M. Committee of Privy Council on Education, or from the Board's Inspector of Schools. School fees were authorised to be levied from the scholars attending the several schools; but committees were authorised to remit them in cases of poverty. Authority was given to committees by the Ordinances of 1862 and of 1864 to defray a portion of the school expenses by the imposition,

when necessary, of a special rate upon heritable property
within the respective districts. The levying of this rate was
attended with so much difficulty and opposition that the
Provincial Council passed a resolution in 1865 to render the
continuance of the rate unnecessary, by increasing the annual
fixed salaries of teachers from £50 to £100 each, and by bearing
a larger share of the other expenses, the remainder being met by
the school committees out of the school fees, supplemented by
donations and subscriptions from the friends of the several
schools.

PUBLIC LIBRARIES AND READING-ROOMS.

The Ordinance of 1864 authorised the Education Board to
encourage the formation of public as well as school libraries by
expending on the purchase of books to be placed in any such
library, moneys equal in amount to any sum or sums raised by
public subscription or otherwise within the district. Advantage
was taken of this provision to a very considerable extent by the
settlers throughout the Province, and the Otago Public Library
scheme became somewhat widely and favourably known.*

The following extract relating to public libraries is taken
from the Board's report for 1875—the last report published
under the Provincial system:—"Books of the value of about
£1,700 have been distributed among the public libraries during
the past year. The amount expended by library committees on
the purchase of books, or paid into the treasury by them, was

---

* "I went round the town (Lawrence), and visited the Athenæum, or
reading-room. In all these towns there are libraries, and the books are
strongly bound and well thumbed. Carlyle, Macaulay, and Dickens are
certainly better known to small communities in New Zealand than they are
to similar congregations of men and women at Home. The schools, hospitals,
reading-rooms and University were all there, and all in useful operation,
so that life in the Province of Otago may be said to be a happy life, and one
in which men and women may, and do have food to eat and clothes to wear,
books to read, and education to enable them to read the books."—Anthony
Trollope's "Australia and New Zealand."

"The public library books are not only to be seen in the more comfortable
and accessible dwellings in the settled districts. It is not an uncommon
thing to find recently-published English books of a high class, bearing the
Board's stamp upon them, in the shepherd's solitary abode among the hills,
and in the digger's hut in gullies accessible only by mountain bridle-tracks."
Otago Education Report for 1872.

fully £800. The 88 public libraries now connected with the Board may be classified as follows :—17 public libraries, with reading-rooms connected with them ; 63 public district libraries, many of which are also available as school libraries, and 8 purely school libraries. Since the beginning of the library scheme, the following-named public institutions have received grants of books through the Education Board :—The hospitals at Lawrence, Clyde, Wakatipu, Invercargill, and Oamaru ; and the gaol at Invercargill. The managers of the following-mentioned libraries have been permitted to purchase at cost price a few books which were not particularly needed at the time for public libraries :— Dunedin Athenæum, Dunedin Police Library, Dunedin Gaol Library, Knox Church Library, St. Paul's Sunday School Library, and St. Joseph's Church and Sunday School Library." The Board was also authorised to encourage by grants of money or books, the formation of reading clubs or libraries in connection with teachers' associations that might be formed by the public school teachers in the Province.

The Ordinance also authorised the Education Board to establish scholarships, to be held in the High School, Dunedin, or in any university in Great Britain, Australia, or New Zealand, to be held by pupils of the public schools of Otago, such scholarships to be submitted to public competition.

APPOINTMENTS OF MESSRS. PETRIE AND TAYLOR AS INSPECTORS.

In consequence of the large increase in the number of schools, Mr. Donald Petrie, formerly senior classical master of the Scotch College, Melbourne, was appointed additional Inspector of Schools in January, 1873 ; Mr. William Taylor, who had been in the Board's service for ten years, was appointed Sub-Inspector in September, 1875.

SUMMARY.

The following summary of information regarding the public schools in Otago when the Provincial system was abolished (Dec. 31, 1875) is compiled from the last report submitted to the Provincial Government :—

Number of schools (Otago and Southland) 157
  ,,   schoolmasters   .. 161
  ,,   schoolmistresses .. 47
  ,,   teachers of sewing.. 14
  ,,   male pupil teachers 17
  ,,   female pupil teachers 49
                 —— Total teachers .. 288
  ,,   pupils who attended at all in 1875—
                 Boys, 8709; girls, 8488 .. 16,097
  ,,   ,, in average attendance during 1875 .. 9822
  ,,   ,, in attendance at the close of 1875 .. 12,096
  ,,   ,, learning the higher rules of Arithmetic 2420
  ,,   ,, ,, Mathematics 312
  ,,   ,, ,, Geography 9323
  ,,   ,, ,, History 1933
  ,,   ,, ,, English Grammar .. 8858
  ,,   ,, ,, Book-keeping 374
  ,,   ,, ,, Drawing or Mapping .. 3815
  ,,   ,, ,, Singing from Notes .. 5623
  ,,   ,, ,, Latin 287
  ,,   ,, ,, French 143
  ,,   ,, ,, Greek 6
  ,,   ,, ,, Sewing (girls) 4171

Moneys contributed by the Government towards—
Teachers' salaries £19,825 12 0
Rents, poor scholars, etc. .. 1164 11 3
                ———————— £20,990 3 3

Moneys contributed locally—
School fees £14,873 6 4
Subscriptions, etc. 2342 13 9
                ———————— £17,216 0 1

PUBLIC SCHOOLS IN DUNEDIN.

THE FIRST, NOW ARTHUR-STREET, SCHOOL.

Mr. Livingston continued in charge of the Dunedin School
until 1862, when he was appointed to the office of Provincial
Auditor, on the death of the late Mr. Charles Kettle. In view
of the establishment in Dunedin of an institution in which the
higher branches should be more exclusively taught, the Board
now resolved that the original Dunedin School should rank in

future as an ordinary district school. Mr. Thomas Halliwell, who had recently arrived in Dunedin from Victoria, was appointed headmaster. The school continued to be held in the old church until it was removed to a brick building erected on a site at the junction of Dowling-street and York Place, where it was known as the Middle District School. Owing to the lowering of Dowling-street by the City Council, the structure was rendered so unsafe that it had to be taken down in 1878, and the school was transferred to a new building erected in Arthur-street, on a site adjoining the old Asylum grounds, where the Boys' High School now stands. Mr. Halliwell resigned the headmastership in 1878, and was succeeded by Mr. Abraham Barrett, formerly of Tasmania, who still holds the appointment.

UNION-STREET SCHOOL.

In 1863, the Board established a second school in Dunedin for the accommodation of children resident in the northern parts of the town. A stone building was erected on a portion of what is now known as the Museum Reserve, and Mr. Alex. Stewart, the master of a private school at North Dunedin, was appointed to the headmastership, a position which he still retains. The original building was enlarged from time to time, but owing to the ever-increasing demand for accommodation, it was taken down in 1882, and the present large brick building, known as the Union-street School, was erected in its place.

SOUTH, NOW HIGH-STREET, SCHOOL.

In 1864, a third district school was provided for the accommodation of the children resident in the Southern parts of Dunedin. It was accommodated in a brick building erected on a site in William-street, where it was long known as the South District School. Mr. John B. Park, master of the State School at Bothwell, Tasmania, was elected headmaster, and he still holds the appointment. Additions were made to the building from time to time to provide for the ever-increasing attendance, until it was found necessary in 1887 to transfer the school to a more commodious building erected on a more suitable site at the corner of Alva-street and Upper High-street.

ALBANY-STREET SCHOOL.

The increasing demand for school accommodation in North Dunedin necessitated the establishment of a school at Pelichet Bay in 1875, on a site in Albany-street, near the Railway Station The first headmaster was Mr. Alex. Montgomery, formerly of Mount Cargill School; and on the appointment of that gentleman, in the following year, to the mastership of the Normal School Practising Department, he was succeeded by the present headmaster, Mr. John L. Ferguson, promoted from the first assistantship in the Middle District School.

NORMAL SCHOOL.

In 1875 a large brick building was erected on a reserve in Moray Place for the accommodation of a Teachers' Training Institution, a Practising School to serve the purposes of an ordinary district school, and a School of Art. The Training Institution and Practising School were opened in January 1876, and at the same time the School of Art was transferred from rooms in the University building in Princes-street to its present quarters. Mr William S. Fitzgerald, Rector of the Oamaru Grammar School, was appointed Rector of the Normal School; and Mr Montgomery, as already stated, was placed in charge of the Practising School. Mr Montgomery died in 1885, and he was succeeded by Mr David White, promoted by the Board from the first assistantship in the Union-street school.

GEORGE-STREET SCHOOL.

In 1880 a sixth public school was provided for Dunedin by the erection of a very large brick building in George-street north. It was placed in charge of Mr David A. McNicoll, transferred from the mastership of the Outram public school.

STATISTICS FOR YEAR 1888.

The Colonial Education Act, 1887, divided Otago into the two separate education districts of Otago and Southland. The following tables supply information respecting the public schools of the Otago Provincial District for the year 1888, under the following classification :—(1) Schools within the city of Dunedin; (2) schools in the suburbs of Dunedin; (3) schools in the remaining portions of the Otago education district; and (4) schools in the Southland education district.

DUNEDIN CITY SCHOOLS, 1888.

Schools.	Teachers	Pupil Teachers	Attendance.	
			Average Daily for Year.	At Close of the Year.
Arthur-street ..	7	8	622	663
Union-street	7	8	594	672
High-street	7	7	635	679
Albany-street ..	7	8	657	759
Normal School ..	7	8	635	684
George-street ..	9	9	783	858
Totals ..	44	48	3926	4315

DUNEDIN SUBURBAN SCHOOLS, 1888.

Schools.	Teachers	Pupil Teachers	Attendance.	
			Average Daily for Year.	At Close of the Year.
N. E. Valley	5	5	418	506
Anderson's Bay ..	2	1	108	123
Caversham	7	8	623	660
Mornington	6	6	511	566
Kaikorai	6	5	480	587
Ravensbourne ..	3	2	200	229
Kensington	5	4	363	413
Forbury	5	4	378	448
Macandrew Road ..	6	7	591	672
Suburban Totals ..	45	42	3672	4204

SCHOOLS IN OTAGO PROVINCIAL DISTRICT, 1888.

Districts.	Teachers	Pupil Teachers	Attendance.	
			Average Daily for Year.	At Close of the Year.
Dunedin City ..	44	48	3926	4315
Dunedin Suburbs ..	45	42	3672	4204
Outside the above ..	264	58	11,345	13,604
Otago Total ..	353	148	18,943	22,423
Southland Total ..	131	44	6083	7959
Provincial District Total	484	192	25,026	30,382

THE OTAGO HIGH SCHOOL FOR BOYS.

FIRST STEPS TAKEN BY THE PROVINCIAL COUNCIL.

It has already been stated that a proposal was made by the late Mr. James Macandrew, in the first session of the Provincial Council, having for its object the establishment of a High School in Dunedin, in which "the higher branches of a liberal education" should be taught. During the second session of the Council (1854) the establishment of a High School formed part of the scheme of public school education adopted by resolution of the Council, and the Home Agents were directed to engage in Britain a gentleman qualified to perform the duties of rector. In the fourth session of the Provincial Council "The Education Ordinance, 1856," was passed; the ninth section of the Act is as follows: "There shall be established in Dunedin, under a Rector or Head Master of superior attainments, and well-qualified assistants, as they are required, a public school, to be called the 'High School of Dunedin,' which shall be conducted on the principles in the art of teaching most approved and adopted in the best schools of Great Britain, it being designed that it shall serve as a model to other public schools to be established within the Province; and at the aforesaid school not only the usual branches of a good elementary English education shall be taught, but also those higher branches of knowledge, the acquirement of which constitutes a liberal education; and the said school shall be open to both male and female scholars, and arrangements shall be made for the advanced male and female classes being taught separately."

It is evident that the late Mr. John McGlashan, who drafted the measure, had in view the establishment of an institution in Dunedin similar in character t) that of the Burgh Schools of Scotland, in which there are departments for both primary and secondary education, and in which pupils of both sexes are taught together. As already stated, Mr. Livingston, who had been selected for the rectorship of the contemplated High School, was placed on his arrival in charge of the school that had met in the First Church building from the foundation of the settlement, but as might be expected the work had been altogether of an elementary character. At the outset of Mr. Livingston's six years' tenure of office, the school officially designated "The High School," was of necessity a primary one to a very considerable extent, scarcely any pupils being sufficiently advanced to enter on the study of the higher branches. But as time wore on, Mr. Livingston, who was an accomplished classical and mathematical scholar, and a most assiduous teacher, succeeded in imparting instruction in some of the more advanced subjects to several of his pupils who had attained the requisite proficiency. Some of his ex-pupils now occupy influential and responsible positions in the Colony, and they speak in terms of admiration of their old schoolmaster's character, and of gratitude for the benefits derived from his instructions.

As years passed on the opinion gained ground that in justice to Mr. Livingston, he should be placed in his right position as head of a High School proper, and that provision should be made for the establishment of one or more elementary schools in Dunedin. In the ninth session of the Provincial Council (1860), Mr Macandrew, who had been elected Superintendent on the decease of Captain Cargill, strongly urged the consideration of this question, and transmitted to the Council a copy of a resolution adopted by the Education Board largely through his own instrumentality. The resolution was to the effect that the time had now come for organising a High School in Dunedin for the benefit of the entire Province : that it should be under the direct management of the Board : that there should be boarding-houses in connection with the school for the reception of pupils from the country; and that there should be two elementary schools in Dunedin, distinct from the High School, each under the management of a school committee. Accompanying the resolution was a letter from Mr. Livingston, in which he stated that although (yielding to circumstances) he had hitherto consented to perform, in a large measure, the work of a primary school teacher, he considered the time had now arrived when he should be placed in his right position as head of a High School. The Provincial Council, however, negatived the Government proposal, and resolved to vote no more moneys for school buildings until the Government should bring in a measure for the alteration of the Education Ordinance.

In the next session of the Provincial Council (Dec. 1860), Mr. Macandrew's Government introduced an Education Bill making full provision for a High School; but owing to the brief duration of the session, it failed to pass. The next session (June 1861) was opened by Major (afterwards Sir John) Richardson, who had succeeded Mr. Macandrew as Superintendent of the Province. Mr. Macandrew's Bill was again introduced by the Provincial Solicitor, the late Mr. James Howorth, and was passed. It contained the following provision:—"There shall be established in Dunedin a High School to be called 'The High School of Otago," under a Rector or Head Master, and such number of qualified masters and assistants as the Board shall, from time to time consider necessary, in which shall be taught all the branches of a liberal education—the French and other modern languages, the Latin and Greek Classics, Mathematics, and such other branches of science as the advancement of the Colony and the increase of population may from time to time require; and the said High School shall be entirely under the superintendence and control of the Board, and shall be maintained and supported, and all salaries and expenses connected therewith paid, out of School Fees and moneys appropriated by the Superintendent and Provincial Council for that purpose, and any other available funds." The same provision was retained unaltered in the Education Ordinances of 1862 and 1864, and under them respectively the High School continued to be administered until the passing by the General Assembly of "The Otago Boys' and Girls' High Schools' Act 1877."

HIGH SCHOOL RE-CONSTITUTED.

Notwithstanding the eagerness shown by the authorities for the institution of a separate school for the higher subjects, considerable doubt was felt by many as to the possibility of securing a sufficient attendance of properly qualified scholars, owing to the extremely small population of the Province: but all doubt on this point was removed by the extraordinary influx of people in the latter portion of 1861, and in the following years, consequent upon the discovery and opening up of the Otago goldfields. Accordingly on Mr. Livingston's appointment to the office of Provincial Auditor in 1862, the Education Board and the Government decided to take immediate steps to establish a separate High School for Boys; the site in Dowling-street, now occupied by the Girls' High School was secured; and money was voted for the erection of a building. It was also resolved to authorise the Home Agents to engage three highly competent Masters for the school, the selection being placed in the hands of the Provost of Eton, the Rector of the Edinburgh High School, and the Rector of the Edinburgh Academy.

The following resolutions were adopted by the Board in connection with the organisation of the proposed school:—"(1.) One of the masters shall hold the appointment of Rector or Principal, and shall have the general oversight of all the classes within the institution, and shall be responsible for the good government, efficiency, and success of the same; but each master, as far as possible shall have the charge of a distinct department of instruction. (2.) Subject to such modifications as circumstances may from time to time render necessary and expedient, the departments of instruction shall be arranged somewhat as follows, viz. :—

1. *Principal's (or Classical Master's) Department.*—To include Latin, Greek, French, &c.; Ancient History, Geography, &c.
2. *English Department.*—To include Advanced English, Reading, Grammar, Composition, and other collateral branches, Geography, History, &c.

3. *Arithmetic and Mathematical Department.*—To include Arithmetic, and Mathematics in theory and practice, Book-keeping, &c.

(3.) Writing, Drawing, Religious Instruction, &c. shall be taught by the several masters, agreeably to such arrangements as may be hereafter made; and care shall be taken, if possible, that one or more of the masters shall be qualified to impart instruction in Natural Science to the more advanced pupils by means of lectures, experiments, &c. (4.) Provision shall be made for the formation and maintenance of a well-selected library for the use of the pupils of the institution, and also for the supply of suitable apparatus, including diagrams, maps, globes, models, specimens, &c. (5.) No boy shall be admitted a pupil of the institution until he shall have passed an *Entrance Examination* of such nature and extent as may be fixed by the Education Board; and (6.) Every facility shall be afforded to settlers at a distance to avail themselves of the advantages of the school."

In due time the Home agents reported that the following-named gentlemen had been appointed Masters of the High School, viz. :—

Principal and Classical Master.—The Rev. Thomas H. Campbell, M.A., late Head-master of the Wolverhampton Grammar School; Fellow of St. John's College, Oxford; and Assistant Master at the Charter House School.

English Master.—Mr. George P. Abram, M.A., late Senior Scholar and Prizeman of Clare College, Cambridge; and Second Master of Wolverhampton Grammar School.

Mathematical Master.—Mr. Daniel Brent, M.A., late Senior Scholar and Prizeman of Queen's College, Cambridge, and one of the Mathematical masters of Tonbridge School.

ARRIVAL OF THE FIRST MASTERS FROM HOME.

Those three gentlemen arrived at Port Chalmers by the "Matoaka" on July 14, 1863. On the same day they proceeded to Dunedin, and Mr. Campbell made arrangements for the accommodation of his family. He then returned to Port Chalmers, and while proceeding to Dunedin the same evening on board the very small harbour steamer "Pride of the Yarra," with his wife, children, and servants, the vessel came into

collision with the steamer "Favourite," and was instantaneously
sunk, with the calamitous and appalling result that Mr. and
Mrs. Campbell, their children and servants, were drowned,
only the passengers, who happened to be on deck, being
saved by getting on board the "Favourite." The Province
of Otago was thus deprived of the services of a gentleman
who appeared in many respects to be eminently qualified
for the important position to which he had been appointed.
It was resolved by the Board to request the three
gentlemen formerly nominated, again to select a Rector for the
High School, in the room of Mr. Campbell. Mr. Abram, at the
request of the Board, readily undertook the duties of
Head Master until the arrival of the Rector. The school was
opened by Mr. Abram on August 3rd, 1863, and was conducted
by him, Mr. Brent, and an assistant, with satisfactory
results. The pupils numbered about 80; ten of these came
from various parts of Otago and the neighbouring Provinces.
The large central hall was the only portion of the building then
completed, and was temporarily divided into three class-rooms.

REV. F. C. SIMMONS, B.A.

In due course the Rev. F. C. Simmons, B.A., of Lincoln College, Oxford, and Head-master of the Dundee Proprietary School,
was appointed Rector, and he entered on his duties in May, 1864.
About the same time the teaching power of the school was
greatly strengthened by the appointment of Mr. J. H. Pope as
an additional master. The accommodation was increased by the
addition of two wings to the original building, in one of which a
residence was provided for the rector and his family, and for a
few pupil boarders. The attendance at the school continued
to increase for several years. Mr. Simmons conducted the school
with much ability and success until June, 1868, when he resigned
the rectorship on his appointment to the Principalship of Nelson
College. Mr. Simmons possessed considerable force of character,
and was of a generous though somewhat impulsive disposition.
His official relations with the Education Board were throughout
of a friendly nature. He exercised great influence over the
pupils of the school, especially those more immediately under
his own tuition, by many of whom his memory is still held in
affectionate remembrance. The duties of acting rector were

satisfactorily performed by Mr. J. H. Pope, pending the appointment of a successor to Mr. Simmons.

MR. STUART HAWTHORNE, M.A.

The Education Board invited applications for the vacant rectorship from candidates in New Zealand and the neighbouring colonies, and the choice fell upon Mr. Stuart Hawthorne, M.A., of Sydney University, and Head-master of the Ipswich Grammar School, Queensland. He entered on his duties in February, 1869, when only 56 names were enrolled. The average attendance for the whole of 1869 was 70; in 1871 it had risen to 126. In the beginning of 1871 Mr. Hawthorne removed from the residence in the south wing of the High School building to make room for the Girls' · High School, which the Board had resolved, after much consideration, to place under the same roof with the Boys' School. With a view to provide suitable board and residence for boys from a distance attending the school, the Education Board erected the boarding institution known as the Rectory on a site adjoining the Town Belt, near the place where the present Boys' High School now stands. Mr. Hawthorne entered on the occupation of the Rectory in 1871, and in a short time a number of pupil boarders were placed with him. About the same time the teaching staff gained a valuable accession by the appointment of Mr. George M. Thomson, (now F.L.S.) who has since rendered good service to the school in several capacities, more especially as Science Master, and, for a number of years, as head of the Boys' Boarding Institution in conjunction with Mrs. Thomson.

In 1872-73 the school showed a falling off as regards attendance and the standard of work reached. In May, 1873, the Superintendent, in accordance with a resolution of the Provincial Council, appointed a Commission " to inquire into and report upon the present condition of the Boys' High School, and to make such general suggestions as to the advancement of the higher education of the Province, as may commend themselves to their consideration." The Commission consisted of the late Sir John Richardson, Professor Shand, Sir Robert Stout, and Dr. Hislop. In the course of his examination by the Commission, Mr. Hawthorne attributed the falling off in the attendance and the lower standard of study to a variety of causes enumerated by him, over which he could not possibly exercise any control. In its report the Commission expressed the opinion that "the various circumstances referred to by the rector must have combined to exercise a most dispiriting influence upon both masters and pupils, to keep back intending scholars, and to injure the status of the school." In accordance with one of the recommendations made by the Commission, the Government, in July, 1874, appointed Sir John Richardson, Sir Robert Stout, the Rev. Dr. Stuart, Professors Shand and Macgregor, and Messrs. E. B. Cargill and James Fulton "to be a Board of Advice for the High School, to recommend to the Education Board such measures in connection with the organisation and management of the school as might be deemed advisable." The result of a conference between the Board of Advice and the Education Board was the adoption by the latter of a number of Regulations based almost wholly upon the recommendations made by the High School Commission of 1873. It is very much in accordance with these regulations that the school is now organised.

Mr. Hawthorne was of a gentle and sensitive nature, and the public criticism, usually of an adverse character, to which his administration of the High School was subjected for some length of time, at last produced the results that might have been expected. His health began to fail; he completely lost heart; and in September, 1874, he resigned his appointment as rector, intending to carry on the work until the end of the year. But his illness proved of so serious a character that he was compelled to retire from active duty some time before the close of the session. Mr. Hawthorne's health was never again completely re-established, and he died at his residence in the neighbourhood of Dunedin on June 8, 1875. He was a gentleman of high principle and of an amiable disposition, and his loss was much regretted by a large circle of friends. It is known to the writer that a number of generous acts, sometimes involving pecuniary outlay, were performed by him in cases that came under his notice in connection with his official work. The duties of acting rector of the school, from the date of Mr. Hawthorne's retirement until the arrival of his successor, were successfully performed by Mr. Brent. Mr. Petrie, Inspector of Schools, also rendered good service as master of the classical department

About this time the staff of the school received a valuable accession to its strength by the appointment as English master, of Mr. Alex. Wilson, M.A., now Principal of the Girls' High School.

MR WILLIAM NORRIE, M.A.

The selection of a successor to Mr Hawthorne was entrusted to the late Mr John Auld, Home Agent of the Provincial Government, and his choice fell upon Mr William Norrie, M.A., Classical Master in Dr. A. H. Bryce's Edinburgh Collegiate School. Mr Norrie entered on his duties in April, 1875. A number of the changes that had been resolved upon by the Board were made during the first year of his term of office, and the staff was increased for the purpose of more thoroughly and satisfactorily working out these changes. The result was an increase of the school attendance ; while the boarding institution, under Mr and Mrs Norrie's management, seemed for a time to be serving satisfactorily the purposes for which it was designed. But in the course of 1877, difficulties with regard to the boarding arrangements began to be experienced, and at Mr Norrie's own request the Board in June of the same year relieved him of the charge of the Rectory. It was then resolved that the boarding institution should be placed in charge of Mr Geo. M. Thomson, one of the masters of the school. Mr and Mrs Thomson entered on the occupation of the Rectory in the beginning of 1878.

Owing to several causes, which it is now unnecessary to specify, the relations of Mr Norrie with the Board and some of its officers became somewhat strained in the course of 1877. These relations became more and more unsatisfactory, and the result was that in August of the same year Mr Norrie resigned the rectorship, giving six months' notice as required by the terms of his engagement. About the same time the Colonial Government, at the request of the Education Board, appointed a commission to inquire into the position of matters in regard to the two High Schools, and to investigate certain charges brought against the Board and its officers in connection with the schools. The commission consisted of the late Mr Tancred (of Christchurch), Mr W. H. Pearson (of Invercargill), and Mr W. Fraser (of Earnscleugh). In their report the commissioners made a number of recommendations regarding the organisation and management

of the High Schools. Except as regards one or two matters of
trivial importance, the charges made against the Board and its
officers were not sustained. Mr Norrie and his family returned
to the Home Country in 1878. For several years past he has
been resident in South Africa. Information has quite recently
reached Dunedin to the effect that Mr Norrie has been fulfilling
for some time the duties of head master of the Kimberly Unde-
nominational Schools with much acceptability and success.

MR. WILLIAM MACDONALD, M.A., LL.D.

In the beginning of 1878, "The Otago Boys' and Girls'
High Schools Act, 1877," came into operation, by virtue of which
the administration of the two High Schools in Dunedin were
transferred from the Otago Education Board to a Board of
Governors, constituted as follows :—The Mayor of Dunedin, *ex
officio;* two members annually appointed by the Governor; two
members elected annually by the Otago University Council; and
two members elected by the Otago Education Board. In anticipation of this change, the Education Board had deemed it unad-
visable to take any steps for the appointment of a successor to
Mr Norrie, and consequently one of the first duties of importance
devolving upon the Board of Governors was the appointment of
a rector. After full consideration, it was resolved that Mr Brent
should be asked to undertake the duties of *interim* rector, and
that the Agent General (Sir Julius Vogel), Dr. Abbott (head
master of the City of London School), and Dr. Morrison (rector
of the Glasgow Acadamy), should be requested to act as commissioners for the selection in the Home Country of a suitable
rector. The choice of the commissioners fell upon Mr William
Macdonald, M.A., classical master in the Edinburgh High
School. Before leaving, Mr Macdonald, in recognition of his
eminence in his profession, and of his distinguished services to
the cause of education, received the honorary degree of LL.D.
from the University of Edinburgh.

Dr. Macdonald entered on his duties as Rector in Nov. 1878,
and for several years, the Boys' High School prospered greatly.
But in June, 1884, Dr. Macdonald was laid aside from duty, by a
very serious illness ; he obtained leave of absence for a time, and
resumed work at the beginning of the session of 1885. During
the interval, Mr A. Wilson, English Master, acted as Rector of

the school. But in the course of a few months Dr. Macdonald's strength again failed him. He continued nominally in charge of the school for some time longer ; but at last it became painfully apparent to the governors, that there was little or no probability of his being again able to resume the duties of Rector, and with extreme regret they found themselves compelled to take steps to secure a successor. Dr. Macdonald's official connection with the school ceased on Sept. 30th, 1886. His retirement from the Rectorship, caused the profoundest grief and disappointment to the governors and the friends of the school, and indeed to all within the Otago district, who had the interests of the higher education at heart. He had, during his short career in Dunedin, given abundant proof of surpassing ability, as Head Master of the High School, as well as in various other capacities, while his personal qualities had endeared him to a large circle of friends.

OTHER CHANGES.

In February 1883, Mr. M. Watson, M.A., entered on his duties as classical assistant to the Rector. He was selected for the position by Dr. Morrison, of the Glasgow Academy. In March 1885, Mr. E. E. Morrison, M.A., who had been appointed by Sir F. D. Bell, and Dr. James Macdonald, of Glasgow, commenced his duties as English Master, in the room of Mr. A. Wilson, who had been appointed to the Rectorship of the Girl's High School, rendered vacant by the resignation of Mrs Burn. In the beginning of 1886, Mr E. E. Morrison and Mrs Dr W. Macdonald, were placed in charge of the Boarding-House, in the room of Mr. and Mrs. Thomson, who had asked to be relieved of the duty.

THE REV. DR. BELCHER M.A., LL.D.

The Board of Governors placed the selection of a successor to Dr. Macdonald in the hands of Sir F. D. Bell and Dr. James Macdonald, of Glasgow, and these gentlemen made choice of the Rev. Henry Belcher, M.A., LL.D., Fellow and late Chaplain and Classical Master in the school, King's College, London. That gentleman entered on his duties in March, 1886, and his ability and indefatigable efforts, aided by a staff of well-qualified masters, have maintained the school in a high state of efficiency. The general tone of the school is undoubtedly most satisfactory,

while the distinguished success of late years of a considerable
proportion of the pupils at the University classes and in the
University and other public examinations, bears ample testimony
to the suitableness and the value of the instruction given in the
several subjects comprised in the school course. There is every
reason also to believe that at the present time the Boys' High
School possesses in a very large measure, the confidence and
good-will of the parents of the pupils, and the general public.
During the year 1888, the total number of boys enrolled was
309. The highest number actually in attendance on a given day
was 281. It is worthy of mention, that including scholarship
holders, forty one pupils enjoyed the privilege of free education
at the school in 1888. The following is an extract from the
Inspector General's report, dated Nov. 15, 1886 :—" This is one
of our best schools, and it appears to me to be improving in tone
and discipline. The present administration is able and vigorous.
The instruction given in some branches of physical science is
very good." The Inspector General's report for 1887 is as
follows :—" September 21, This school has received a remarkably
large accession of numbers this year. The organisation appears
to be singularly complete and perfect." The report for 1888 has
not yet been issued.

MR D. BRENT, M.A.

In bringing this brief historical sketch of the Otago Boys'
High School to a close, the writer feels it incumbent on him to
refer to the services rendered to the school by Mr Brent, who is
the only one of the original masters now on the staff. During
his uninterrupted connection with the school for the long period
of twenty-six years, Mr Brent has invariably acquitted himself
with singular judgment and prudence, and has ever maintained
the most cordial relations with the Board and his colleagues,
while in times of difficulty, he has rendered most valuable
assistance to the school authorities, either by performing the
duties of Acting Rector in a highly satisfactory manner, or by
co-operating heartily with one or other of his colleagues, who
had undertaken the duties.

Notwithstanding the changes that have taken place in
connection with the rectorship during the past twenty-six years,
it can confidently be claimed for the school that it has all along

been doing very good work, and has sent out a very large number
of youths, who, in their various walks of life have done, and are
doing, infinite credit to themselves and to the school. This is
owing in no small degree to the zeal and loyalty of Mr Brent, and
the other able masters employed in the school.

INFORMATION REGARDING THE PRESENT ARRANGEMENTS OF THE BOYS'
HIGH SCHOOL. *

The Board of Governors consist of the Rev. Dr. Stuart,
(chairman); Professor Shand, M.A., LL.D., (Hon. Treasurer);
the Hon. W. H. Reynolds, M.L.C.; Rev. A. R. Fitchett, M.A.;
James Fulton, Esq., M.H.R.; William Brown, Esq., M.B., and
the Mayor of Dunedin, *ex-officio*. The secretary is Mr. Colin
Macandrew.

The present buildings were opened by His Excellency Sir
William Jervois, Governor of New Zealand, on February 11,
1885, and occupy a most suitable and commanding position
adjoining the Town Belt. The plan of the building is that of a
main central hall, round which are grouped the several class-
rooms. The central hall is 74 feet in length, by 43 feet in width,
and is 30 feet in height, with a gallery carried round both sides
and ends. The several class-rooms, both on the ground and
upper floors, are very spacious, lofty, carefully ventilated, and
fitted with all requisites and appliances to suit their various
purposes. The drawing school has been constructed on the most
approved system, and is fully furnished with models, plaster
casts, and other materials of the art. The science room is
supplied with requisites for the teaching of practical and
theoretical Chemistry and Metallurgy. It also contains accessories
to the teaching of Physiology. The mathematical school has
been excellently constructed for its purpose, both as regards light
and contrivances for demonstration. The gymnasium has been
furnished on the exact model of that at Aldershot, and ranks among
the best equipped in the colony. The grounds on which the
school buildings are erected cover an area of about 6½ acres. A
large space around the school has been asphalted, and is occupied
by two fives courts, tennis courts, &c. There is also a large
cricket field adjoining the school ground. The rector's residence

* In writing this paragraph the Rector's report and prospectus have
been freely made use of.

and the janitor's lodge are near the school. The public of Otago are indebted to the influence and untiring efforts of Sir Robert Stout for having secured to them so suitable and so valuable a site for the Boys' High School. The boarders' house, under the superintendence of Mr. Morrison, English Master, is situated about five minutes' walk from the school, and occupies one of the finest sites in Dunedin. It is surrounded with recreation grounds, covering an area of about seven acres, with commodious playsheds, an asphalt tennis court, &c. The building was designed expressly for the purpose of a boarding institution for the High School boys, and the equipments are very complete, and in every way suitable. The domestic arrangements are very efficiently conducted by Mrs Dr. Macdonald.

The staff consists of the rector and the following masters:— D. Brent, M.A., Mathematics ; E. E. Morrison, M.A., English ; M. Watson, M.A., Latin; W. B. Williams, B.A., Modern Languages ; A. Y. Smith, Commercial; J. McPherson, F.E.I.S., Arithmetic ; J. R. Montgomery, M.A., and A. S. M. Polson, Assistant Masters ; G. M. Thompson, F.L.S., Natural Science ; D. C. Hutton, and D. Hutton, Drawing ; and John Hanna, Gymnastics and Drill. There are an Upper and a Lower School. The Upper School prepares for the University, for the learned professions, and all public examinations. The course of instruction comprises Latin, French, German, English Language, Literature and History, Mathematics, Mechanics, Chemistry, Metallurgy, Writing, Book-Keeping, Drawing and Gymnastics. While close adherence to this course is maintained, the rector does his best to meet, according to circumstances, the special requirements of boys whose school-time is drawing to a close. Any boy wishing to study Greek receives every assistance towards the attainment of his object. To meet special requirements, a liberal education is imparted without the study of Latin, on the basis of the Modern Languages, Mathematics, Science, and the customary details of English. Every encouragement is given to the study of Mechanics. Drawing is taught to all classes below the Upper V. Class. Gymnastics, according to an approved course, form part of the regular school work. The course of instruction in the Lower School comprises Latin, French, English in all its usual details, Arithmetic, Writing, Book-keeping, Drawing and Gymnastics.

THE OTAGO GIRLS' HIGH SCHOOL.

PRELIMINARY PROCEEDINGS.

The Otago Boys' High School was opened on August 3rd, 1863. About a week afterwards (August 11th) an ably-written leading article on the subject appeared in the *Otago Daily Times*. After dealing with the subject of the Boys' School in a very appreciative manner, the writer proceeds as follows :—"The High School, however, wants a companion institution. There is one direction in which we have attempted little and done less to promote the best interests of education and of families. We mean in the provision made for the education of girls, especially after they have arrived at an age when it is untasteful to their friends and obviously unwise that they should remain in the mixed common school." Then follow some well-put arguments in support of the proposal to establish a Girls' High School, and the article concludes as follows :—"It is to be hoped that a High School for girls will be promptly organised in Dunedin." A day or two afterwards, a letter appeared in the *Daily Times* over the signature "Paterfamilias," thanking the editor for his sensible and well-timed article, and suggesting that pressure should be brought to bear upon the Government to take steps for the establishment of the proposed school with the least possible delay. This was the first occasion on which the proposal to establish a Girls' High School in Dunedin was publicly discussed, and it is only due to the *Otago Daily Times* that this fact should not be lost sight of. But before and after the publication of the article referred to, the subject received careful consideration from the education authorities, and it was fully resolved that a Girls' High School should be established as soon as the difficulties that interposed should be removed, the chief of these being inability to procure a suitable site and building for the purpose. In the Provincial Council on November 4th, 1864, Major Richardson moved the following resolution, of which notice had previously been given by Mr Reynolds—(1) "That it is expedient to give encouragement to the education of girls beyond that afforded by the ordinary district schools; and (2) that the Government be requested to submit to the House during the next session some scheme by which this result could be attained."

The subject continued to receive consideration from time to time, but nothing definite was done until June, 1869, when, on the motion of Mr J. L. Gillies, it was resolved by the Provincial Council—"That the Government be requested to appoint an honorary commission to determine the best site and scheme for a High School, and to consider whether it is expedient that provision should be made in the same building for the teaching of girls as well as boys." The commission consisted of the following members:—The Rev. Dr. Stuart (chairman), Mr Justice Ward, the Hon. F. D. Bell, and the following members of the Provincial Council:—Messrs Reynolds, Turnbull, McIndoe, McLean, Reid, Haggitt, Duncan, Gillies, and Mouat.

In addition to other documents, the commission had before it a letter and papers received from a committee of ladies in Otago, who greatly interested themselves in the proposed establishment of a Girls' High School. The late Mrs. E. B. Cargill was President of the committee, and Miss Dalrymple was its most indefatigable Secretary. The commission expressed its deep obligation to the ladies' committee and to Miss Dalrymple, and embodied in its report a number of the recommendations made by them. The commission recommended that the rector's residence and boarding establishment should be removed to another locality, and that the rooms to be vacated, together with such additional accommodation as might be found necessary, should be occupied as a Girls' High School, a residence for the Lady Principal, and a boarding-house for girls from a distance; and that the other portions of the building should be enlarged and adapted to the purposes of a Boys' High School.

THE OPENING OF THE SCHOOL UNDER MRS. BURN.

At the end of 1870 the several additions and improvements recommended by the Commission were completed, and the Education Board was placed in a position to open the Girls' School, and to organise it in accordance with the Commission's recommendations. Mrs. M. Gordon Burn, formerly Lady Superintendent of Geelong Girls' College, was appointed Lady Principal, and the following teachers were also engaged :—Miss Macdougall (now Mrs. Neish), first assistant; Mrs. Rhind, resident governess; Miss Huie (now Mrs. Borrows), resident music governess; and Miss Bell (now Mrs. McGlashan), and Mr. Lees, visiting music teachers. The services of Mr. D. C. Hutton as Drawing Master were secured, and these have been continued ever since. Mr. G. M. Thomson rendered valuable service for some years as conductor of the Class Singing Lessons. It was also arranged with the Rector that the masters of the Boys' School should give lessons in some of the higher subjects to classes in the Girls' School. The prospectus issued by the Board set forth that the object of the institution was to impart to girls a thoroughly useful and liberal education, combined with careful moral and religious instruction; that the ordinary course would embrace a thorough English education, viz. :—Reading, Grammar, Composition, Elocution, History, Natural Science, Geography, Writing and Arithmetic, and also Class-Singing, Drawing, French, and Industrial Work; and that competent teachers would be engaged for Music, Singing (private lessons), Dancing and Calisthenics, German, and other branches that might afterwards be found desirable.

The School was opened on February 6, 1871, with a roll of 78 pupils; by the end of the quarter there were 102 in attendance; and at the close of the year there were 130 names on the roll, including 16 boarders. It was now found necessary to enlarge the school buildings, both for day-school and boarding-house purposes. In 1872 the number enrolled was 125. In the beginning of 1873 it was found advisable to discontinue the arrangements under which some of the masters of the Boys' School gave lessons to the senior classes in the Girls' School, and to transfer the services of Mr. Pope wholly to the latter. The number on the school roll at the end of 1873 was 137, and the average for the year, 126. In 1874, the attendance had increased to 155, and the accommodation again became insufficient. The number of pupil-boarders had increased to 24, and want of room compelled Mrs Burn almost every week to decline receiving more girls. The Board was therefore under the necessity of again making considerable additions to the building.

Mrs. Burn had thrown so much energy and zeal into the performance of her onerous and responsible duties that she somewhat overtaxed her strength, and towards the end of 1874 the Board asked her to accept leave of absence for a few months. A temporary substitute was engaged, and the work of the School was satisfactorily carried on. In 1875, the average quarterly enrolment of pupils rose to 168. The number of girls receiving music lessons in connection with the school was 77. As the upper division of the school became more and more composed of pupils who had been trained in the lower classes, a higher standard of attainment began to be reached than was at first possible.

In course of time the work devolving upon the Lady Principal, consequent upon the increasing number of day scholars and pupil boarders became so onerous, that, in response to her own proposal, the Board resolved to relieve her of the care of the boarding establishment, so that her time and energies might be confined solely to the superintendence of the day-school. Mrs. Martin was accordingly placed in charge of the boarding-house in July 1876, Mrs. Burn giving up the occupation of the official residence. Mrs. Martin continued to preside over the boarding department until the beginning of 1878, when the Board of Governors, that had been appointed under the High Schools Act of 1877, reverted to the original arrangement, and placed Mrs. Burn in charge of the boarding institution as well as the day-school.

Under the Board of Governors the School continued to prosper as in former years, the only difficulty being the occasional inability of Mrs. Burn's strength to bear the strain imposed upon it by her energy and zeal in the performance of her weighty and responsible duties. With a view to reduce the strain, the Board of Governors in 1883 resolved to secure the services of a highly qualified Vice-Principal, who should also act as Mathematical teacher, and Sir. F. D. Bell and Professor Sidgwick of Trinity College, Cambridge, were requested to make a suitable selection in the Home Country. Their choice fell upon Miss J. J. McKean, who entered on her duties in November, 1883, and has ever since performed them in a highly satisfactory manner. In 1884 Mrs. Burn was compelled, by the state of her health, to resign the Lady Principalship. It is very generally admitted that from first to last Mrs. Burn performed the duties of her office with rare ability, and with a devotion and zeal that could not be surpassed, and that under her superintendence the Otago Girls' High School proved an uninterrupted success. The following is an extract from the Inspector General's Report on the School about the time of Mrs. Burn's retirement :—" December 1, 1884. The Otago Girls' High School, which I visited on 17th September, maintains its high character for efficiency. Mrs. Burn, who has conducted it for so many years with distinguished ability, is about to retire."

MR ALEX. WILSON, M.A.

On Mrs Burn's retirement, the Board of Governors invited Mr Alex. Wilson, M.A., to accept the rectorship of the Girls' High School. Mr Wilson had for many years greatly distinguished himself as English Master of the Boys' High School, and on the occasion of Dr. Macdonald's absence in 1884, had fulfilled the duties of Acting-rector of the Boys' School with much ability and success. Miss Bathgate was at the same time placed in charge of the Boarding Institution. Under Mr Wilson and his very efficient staff the Girls' High School has well maintained its high character in all respects. In November 1886 the Inspector General thus reports of the school :—"This is also one of our best schools. The study of the English language occupies a prominent place. Latin and mathematics are well taught. The instruction in gymnastics is excellent. There are some good earnest students among the elder girls." The same gentleman's report in 1887 is as follows :—"This school is altogether in a very satisfactory condition, and it is pleasant to observe that the elder girls have acquired thoroughly good habits of serious study." The report for last year is not yet issued. There can be no doubt that, under Mr. Wilson's very able administration, the Girls' School possesses the full confidence of the governors, the parents of the pupils, and the general public. Five scholarships, including two University Junior Scholarships, were won by the pupils in 1888 ; several of them gained university distinctions, and eight of them stood high in the Otago University class examinations.

The attendance of pupils has also been well maintained. The highest number enrolled in any quarter of 1888 was 187. During the same year 71 entered the school for the first time. The enrolments during the last quarter of the year were 180, with an average attendance of 171.   The highest number at one time on the roll in the history of the school is that of the present year (1889), the number being 199.   There were 25 resident boarders and two day boarders in 1888, being a marked increase on previous years.   Twelve junior and four senior scholars of the Education Board were in attendance during 1888.

BUILDINGS.

On the removal of the Boys' High School in February, 1885, to the new buildings in Arthur-street, the whole of the premises in Dowling-street were given up to the Girls' High School. The buildings are extensive and commodious, and are situated in a healthy and central locality, easily accessible from all parts of the city and suburbs.   The main building contains a spacious central hall, in connection with which are a number of class-rooms well-furnished and adapted to the purposes of the school.   Ample and suitable accommodation is provided for the lady manager of the boarding establishment, the resident governess, and a number of pupil boarders. The girls' bed-rooms are large, well lighted, and ventilated, and are exceedingly comfortable.   Each boarder occupies a separate bed-room.   There are six bath-rooms with shower baths, and hot and cold water laid on.   Every possible requirement for an institution of the kind seems to have been provided, and everything has been arranged with a view to the health and comfort of the boarders, who are at all times under strict control and superintendence. The Boarding Department is under the direction of Miss Bath-gate, a lady of high character and much experience.   The recreation grounds cover an area of fully two acres, very completely and securely fenced, within which there are tennis courts, a fives court, playsheds, a large and exceedingly well-equipped gymnasium, &c.

GENERAL SCHOOL ARRANGEMENTS.

The school in common with the Boys' High School is under the control of a Board of Governors.   The ordinary subjects of instruction include English, (Reading, Grammar, Composition, Geography, History, &c.,) Mathematics, (Arithmetic, Algebra, and Geometry,) Latin, French, German, Natural Science (Botany and Chemistry,) Writing, Drawing, Needlework, and Gymnastics.

Visiting teachers are engaged for instruction in music. The teaching of the several subjects is provided for as follows :— English, the Rector and Miss F. E. Grant ; French, the Rector and staff ; Latin and German, Dr. F. A. Bülau ; Mathematics, Miss J. J. McKean (Vice-Principal) ; Science, Mr G. M. Thomson, F.L.S. ; Assistants, Misses E. E. Little, and S. Douglas ; Drawing, Mr D. C. Hutton ; Gymnastics, Mr John Hanna. The following are visiting teachers : Music (piano), Mrs. T. White, Madam Müller, and Miss E. Pratt ; Singing, (private lessons) Mrs. T. White. It is worthy of mention that two very efficient members of the staff, Misses Grant and Little, were formerly pupils of the school, and that a number of other ex-pupils hold responsible positions in High Schools and other schools throughout the Colony.

There is an upper and a lower school. On first entering, pupils are classified according to their general proficiency in the subjects of instruction. Those who join the first form are expected to be able to read and spell fairly, and to know the four simple rules of Arithmetic. In connection with the Science Class, there is a fully furnished laboratory supplied with apparatus for practical Chemistry, as well as with microscopes for higher Botanical work. The pupils have two lessons weekly in Gymnastics in the large and well-equipped gymnasium attached to the school. Too much emphasis cannot be laid on the opportunity thus afforded to girls attending the school of receiving a systematic and complete physical education.

THE SCHOOL OF ART.

In January 1870, the Education Board instituted the Dunedin School of Art under the directorship of Mr. David C. Hutton, formerly Master of the Perth School of Art. Mr. Hutton was selected for the position by the late Mr. John Auld, Home Agent for Otago. Two rooms in the building now occupied by the Colonial Bank were set apart and suitably furnished as class-rooms. It was arranged that the following classes should be formed : (1) A class for girls and young women ; (2) A class for the High School pupils and other youths who might desire to attend ; (3) Classes for pupil teachers, schoolmasters, and schoolmistresses, whether engaged in public or private schools ; (4) Evening classes for apprentices and others. When the Girls'

High School was opened in 1871, Mr. Hutton's services were also secured for that institution. For a number of years Mr. Hutton and his assistants gave lessons in the District Schools of Dunedin and suburbs, and in some of the District High Schools, but this has been discontinued owing to so many schools being now in operation, and the consequent inability of the staff to overtake the work, except at a rate of expenditure beyond the means of the Education Board. In 1876, the School of Art was provided with an excellent suite of rooms on the upper floor of the Normal School building, consisting of a very large general drawing-class room, a painting room, a cast room, a modelling room, master's room, store room, lavatories, &c. In all these arrangements Mr. Hutton's views and wishes were consulted.

The original scheme of instruction has been adhered to almost without a change. From the very outset Mr. Hutton has devoted himself to his work with rare enthusiasm, ability, and diligence, and with distinguished success. The benefit conferred by Mr. Hutton's labours on the large numbers who have successively attended his classes is really incalculable. Probably no class of students has profited to a larger extent than that of the apprentices and other youths, who in considerable numbers have attended the evening classes. Not a few of them, owing to the taste and skill developed by such attendance, are now occupying positions of usefulness and responsibility, for which they would not otherwise have been qualified. Employers of skilled labour in Dunedin and elswhere have borne testimony to this result. Many of the High School pupils, and the students of the ladies' afternoon classes have attained very considerable proficiency in drawing and painting, and a number of them have gained no small distinction. Probably the most distinguished ex-students of the school are Miss Mary Park, Miss Sperrey (now Mrs. Mair), and Miss M. Hartley.

The evening classes meet from seven till nine o'clock. Mondays and Wednesdays are given to freehand and model drawing, shading and painting in monochrome from the antique, modelling in clay and casting, painting in oil and water colours. Tuesdays and Thursdays are devoted to the study of practical plane and solid geometry, and mechanical and architectural drawing. Fridays are given to drawing and painting from the living model, draped.

The Teachers' and Pupil Teachers' classes meet on Mondays, Tuesdays, Wednesdays, and Thursdays from 5.45 to 6.45 p.m., and on Saturdays for an hour in the forenoon. Country teachers attend on Saturdays. The Normal School students in training attend for an hour every forenoon except on Friday. All these classes are organised to suit the circumstances of the students, and their several stages of advancement. The day classes meet from 8 a.m. to 4 p.m. for the study of elementary and advanced drawing, practical plane and solid geometry, mechanical and architectural drawing, painting in water and oil colours (elementary and advanced), modelling, &c. The morning class is attended by students from the School of Mines, and by young ladies who are engaged during the day; the former are studying practical plane and solid geometry, and machine drawing; the latter, drawing and painting. These classes promise to become very popular. The afternoon class is attended chiefly by those who are studying art as a profession, or for the purpose of improvement. The High Schools are statedly visited by Mr. Hutton and his assistant, who impart instruction in drawing of a very valuable character to the pupils in nearly all the forms. Mr Hutton is aided by a well qualified assistant and a pupil teacher.

The following is the present attendance at the several classes in the School of Art:—

Evening classes—Mondays and Wednesdays .. 90	
,, ,, Tuesdays and Thursdays .. 44	
,, ,, Fridays 9	
	143
Teachers and pupil teachers 109	
Not connected with the Public Schools 14	
Normal School students 55	
	178
Day classes 52	
Total	373

About 400 High School pupils receive instruction in drawing from Mr. Hutton or his assistant. .

TECHNICAL CLASSES ASSOCIATION.

On November 15, 1888, a society, named "the Dunedin Technical Classes Association" was formed at a public meeting for the purpose of promoting the education of the youths of the city by means of evening classes. The following named office-bearers were elected: President, Mr. Alexander Burt; Hon. Secretary, Mr. G. M. Thomson, F.L.S.; Hon. Treasurer, Mr. George M. Barr, M.I.C.E.; Committee, Messrs W. S. Fitzgerald, R. Harding, D. McNicoll, C. McQueen, J. Robin, R. S. Sparrow, D. White M.A., and Alexander Wilson, M.A. The association numbers about 100 members, including life-members. The subjects proposed to be taught at the outset have been grouped as follows :—(A) Literary; (B) Scientific; and (C) Manual; classes (A) and (B) to be open only to candidates that have passed the "sixth standard" or its equivalent; the subjects in group (A) to include English, Latin, French, German, Shorthand, &c.; in group (B), mathematics, chemistry, physics, &c.; and in group (C), freehand and mechanical drawing, carpentry, modelling, wood and metal turning, &c. Any person may become a member of the association by an annual subscription of 5s; and a life member by a single payment of £5 or upwards. As a rule fees are charged to all the pupils. The classes are held in winter, from the beginning of May to the end of October.

The first session opened in May, 1889, and up to 22nd August, the number of students enrolled was 283. The Education Board has granted free of charge the use of class-rooms in the Normal School. Mr George M. Thomson is superintendent of the classes. The subjects taught during the first session, the number of students and the names of the several teachers, are as follows :—

	STUDENTS.
English :—Mr J. H. Chapman	33
English literature :—Rev. Rutherford Waddell, M.A.	64
Latin :—Rev. A. R. Fitchett, M.A.	20
Greek :—Rev. A. R. Fitchett, M.A.	1
Algebra and Euclid :—Mr Alex. McLean	26
Arithmetic :—Messrs J. R. Montgomery, M.A. and F. B. Allan, M.A...	59

Chemistry :—Mr G. M. Thomson, F.L.S. .. 35
Shorthand :—Messrs Crosby Smith and S. M. Park 78
Carpentry and Turning :—Mr W. H. Scott .. 14

Drawing :—this subject is provided for by Mr Hutton's evening classes, described in the preceding article, which are attended by 143 students.

DUNEDIN KINDERGARTEN ASSOCIATION.

This association was formed during the present year (1889), for the purpose of establishing free kindergartens for the children of the poorer classes. The association is purely unsectarian, and is supported by voluntary subscription. The annual subscription for members is one guinea (with right of nomination of a pupil), or half a guinea without such right. Honorary members pay 2/6, and children 1/-. Any one may become a life member (with right of nomination of a pupil) by a payment of £5. The following are the office-bearers : President, Mrs. W. H. Reynolds ; Vice Presidents, Mrs. Belcher, Mrs. A. S. Paterson and Miss Bathgate ; Treasurer, Miss Marsden Smith ; Secretary, Miss Kelsey ; Assistant Secretary, Miss F. Wimperis ; twelve members of Committee, and six members of Finance Committee. The association began operations some months ago, having obtained from St Andrews congregation the use of the Mission Hall in Walker Street free of charge. At present one well-qualified lady teacher and two assistants are employed. The school meets from 9.30 a.m. to 3.30 p.m., with an interval of two hours. There are about 40 names on the roll of pupils. The association is still in its infancy, but as its sphere of operations becomes enlarged, and the value of the work proposed to be accomplished by it is more widely known and appreciated, incalculable benefits will no doubt be conferred on many of the poorer families of the city.

It is worthy of mention that other valuable educational work is carried on in the Walker Street Mission Hall. On Monday evenings there are penny readings, and occasional scientific experiments of a simple and interesting character. These meetings are crowded by the poorer classes in and around Walker Street. On Wednesdays there is a Juvenile Singing Class, and on Thursdays a class for girls for the giving of instruction in household management, &c. It is in contemplation to begin a night school on another evening in the week, for teaching boys the elements of arithmetic, combined with technical instruction of some kind.

LEAVITT HOUSE.

Good educational work among the young people of the poorer classes around Pelichet Bay, is carried on in Leavitt House by Mrs. James Miller and Mrs. George MacKenzie, assisted by a band of volunteer workers. This large building near Pelichet Bay station, formerly an hotel, is maintained by the Women's Christian Temperance Union, and is fitted up with a large hall for meetings, class-rooms, a work-shop, &c, and is in use almost every day in the week for educational purposes. On Monday evening there are classes for the instruction of girls and young women in needle-work, knitting, and crochet-work, and also in ironing. These classes are attended by about 75 young persons. On the same evening there are boys' classes for Junior English, short-hand, leather-work, &c. On Tuesday evening, during the winter months, there is a cookery class from 7 to 9 o'clock for girls and young women, with an average attendance of about 30. There is also a youths' class on the same evening for Senior English. On Wednesday evening there are classes for Junior English and book-keeping. On the evening of Thursday Mr Rankine conducts a class for two hours for the instruction of girls and young women in "cutting out," according to what is known as the "Ladies' Scientific System," simple lessons being also given in dressmaking. On the same evening there are also classes for Senior English, and for carpenter work, attended by about 35 youths. Altogether there is an attendance of about 86 youths at the Industrial Work classes. On Friday there is a Temperance or Band of Hope meeting, which is usually attended by about 100 young people. On Saturday evening there is a well-attended Mutual Improvement class for lads.

CATHOLIC CHURCH SCHOOLS.

The Reverend Father Lynch, in the absence of the Bishop, has been good enough to supply the following information regarding the schools maintained by the Catholic Church authorities in Dunedin.

The Christian Brothers' School at St. Joseph's, Rattray-street, is taught by five members of the Society of Christian

Brothers, assisted by two pupil-teachers and one visiting master. The course of instruction embraces all the subjects usually taught in good primary schools, in addition to which the upper classes receive instruction in French, Latin, Euclid, Algebra, Natural Philosophy, and Book-keeping. Much attention is given to Short-hand. Boys who remain sufficiently long in the school are prepared for the Civil Service and Matriculation Examinations. The school thus serves both as a Primary and an Intermediate School. Free-hand Drawing and Vocal Music, on the tonic sol-fa method, are taught in all the classes. There is a special Athletic class attached to the school, receiving instruction from an experienced teacher.

There is a fine playground provided with a well-furnished Gymnasium for the use of all the scholars, and the out-offices are constructed on the newest and most approved principles. The number on the roll for the present year (1889) is close on 300, with a daily attendance of from 250 to 270. The scholars attending the school have the advantage of a lending library and a small museum. The school is supported by the voluntary contributions of the parents of the scholars. There is a class for the literary improvement of the young held at the school. There are also classes for the religious instruction of boys and youths on Sunday afternoon. These classes are attended by over 200 scholars. In addition to the above, a very useful and flourishing Catholic Literary Society holds its meetings at the school every Wednesday evening during the winter months.

A Girls' High School, attended by 108 pupils including boarders, is maintained at the Dominican Priory, Dowling-street. The curriculum embraces all the branches of a liberal education, special attention being devoted to Latin and the Higher Mathematics, with a view to the preparation for matriculation of those pupils who complete the course. Vocal and instrumental music, crayon drawing, and painting, are cultivated to a high degree. Many of the ex-pupils are now among the leading musicians in the colonies. The piano, the organ, and the harp are taught by the nuns, and the violin by visiting masters. The classes for German and Italian are not numerously attended, as the taste for foreign literature is not sufficiently developed. With a view to form this taste, the nuns require their pupils to speak the French language at all times not devoted to English studies. Young ladies of all denominations are admitted to the school. The nuns, whose lives are consecrated to the work, devote special care to the manners and moral training of their pupils. With a view to the further culture of those who had been under their care, the nuns have established a Musical and Dramatic Club. Their past pupils meet monthly in considerable numbers at the convent. At these meetings, readings, recitations, the discussion of literary subjects, and music, are engaged in, and much lively talent is displayed.

St. Joseph's Primary School for Girls, Rattray-street, adjoins the Convent grounds, and is partially supported by the voluntary contributions of Catholic friends. Here the standards of education are similar to those of the public schools of the Colony. Girls who remain sufficiently long at the school, enter on a course of higher studies, and should they display aptitude for teaching they are systematically trained for that profession. Free-hand drawing, and singing on the tonic sol-fa method are taught in all the classes. The average daily attendance is 180.

Classes for religious instruction are carried on every day. On Sundays not only the school children, but working girls and young women attend.

Another primary school is conducted by the Dominican Nuns at South Dunedin, which, like all their schools, is unsupported by Government aid.

DUNEDIN JEWISH SCHOOLS.

Mr. J. Benjamin, secretary to the Jewish congregation, has kindly furnished the following information. The Hebrew School is attended on Sundays and Thursdays by 30 pupils. The Head-master is the Rev. B. Lichtenstein, assisted by Misses Clara Davies, Bessie Lishtenstein, and Louisa Cohen. The Sabbath School meets on Saturdays with the same staff and scholars.

PRIVATE SCHOOLS.

There is a considerable number of private schools in operation in Dunedin. Some of them are well-attended, and are doing excellent work. It has not been found possible, however, to

ST. JOSEPH'S CATHEDRAL, DUNEDIN.

obtain full and reliable information regarding all of them, and it has therefore been deemed advisable not to select any for special mention.

PROTESTANT SUNDAY SCHOOLS.

Very considerable attention is given by the ministers and members of the Protestant churches in Dunedin and suburbs, and indeed throughout the Provincial District, to the religious instruction of the young by means of Sunday Schools. With scarcely an exception every congregation maintains one or more schools of this kind.

There is a Sunday School Teachers' Union in connection with the Church of England, the office-bearers being the Right Rev. Bishop Nevill, President; the Ven. Archdeacon Edwards, and the Revs. Messrs Fitchett and York, Vice-Presidents; Mr. W. A. W. Wathen, Hon. Secretary; Mr. H. Wilson, Hon. Treasurer; and a committee of seven members. The Union embraces the three city schools—St Pauls, All Saints, and St Matthews—and five suburban schools. Each clergyman takes a direct interest in the supervision of the school work of his parish. Circumstances have prevented information being obtained as to the number of teachers and scholars connected with each of these schools. The attendance at all of them is about 1500.

In April, 1888, the officers and teachers of the other Protestant denominations formed the Otago Sunday School Union, which has been affiliated with the London Sunday School Union. The office-bearers are : Mr John Reith, President ; the Revs. Messrs Baumber, Hilton, Porter, and Walker, and the Hon. Thomas Dick, Vice-Presidents ; Mr W. A. Paterson, Hon. Treasurer ; Messrs P. Barr, and D. R. Eunson, Hon. Auditors ; Mr. W. T. Todd, Hon. Secretary, and an Executive of ten members including the President, &c. There are about 42 schools in Otago connected with the Union. They may be classified according to locality as follows :—

	SCHOOLS.	TEACHERS.	SCHOLARS.
Dunedin City ..	.. 11	292	2528
Dunedin suburbs	.. 20	312	2745
Remoter localities	.. 11	154	1438
Total ..	.. 42	758	6711

There are schools in Dunedin, the suburbs, and remoter localities that are not associated with the Union. Circumstances have rendered it impossible to obtain full and reliable information regarding such schools. Returns received from ten of them in Dunedin and suburbs show 150 teachers and 1304 scholars.

PUBLIC INSTITUTIONS.

By J. A. Torrance.

OTAGO BENEVOLENT INSTITUTION.

HE old familiar averment, " The poor ye have always with you," has formed the basis of many appeals on behalf of the poor and needy, and the stern fact of which it takes cognizance—a fact that has asserted itself in every community throughout the civilized world—has led to the formation of those charitable institutions whose name is legion. In the very early days of the Province of Otago poverty in the strict acceptation of the term was unknown. The first immigrants were by no means in affluent circumstances; they were simply a body of respectable and industrious Scotch working people who had the hardihood to launch out from the crowded home of their fathers to make for themselves a home in the Britain of the South. After the first period of inconvenience arising from the complete change from the crowded cities and cultivated districts of Scotland to an uncultivated country still lying in its primitive wildness, the pioneers had at least a sufficiency of the necessaries of life. Their wants were few, their mode of life simple, and delicacies and " appearances," such as prevail in older communities, were not thought of by them. It is true that as time passed by, and the number of immigrants increased, the young settlement once or twice passed through a painful experience. The early settlers had no foe in the shape of a warlike savage to contend with, but they had their sorrows and difficulties and dangers nevertheless. On two or three occasions, owing to the non-arrival of vessels with supplies, the worst of all foes—starvation—cast its dark shadow over the place, some of the necessaries of life being absolutely unattainable. Salt could be, and was, extracted from the waters of the bay by the homely and slow process of boiling in an ordinary pot over an ordinary fire, but flour and oatmeal could not be so easily manufactured. One colonial, writing to a friend in the Home Country, made the doleful statement, "There is but one barrel of meal in the place, and it is sold to people in trouble or for children at fourpence per pound." We would expect to find that man breaking out into loud and harsh grumbling, or expressing himself in tones of abject despair. But no, for with glorious contentment he immediately adds, "But we are all very happy!" Things, however, assumed a serious aspect, and not a few were allowing the conviction to take hold of their minds that a terrible mistake had been made. Even then the voices of the unemployed, crying for work or for bread, were heard, and the Provincial Government were repeatedly under the necessity of placing men on relief works. One gentleman, who was a resident of Dunedin at that time, avers that more than once the office of the Super-intendent, Captain Cargill, was besieged by numbers of the wage-earning portion of the population; and a copy of the little newspaper of the day contains a paragraph calling for a meeting of the labouring classes to take into consideration a proposal that had been made to charter a schooner to convey them to some other settlement, where they might have a better prospect of obtaining an honest livelihood. But these occasions were exceptional, and are not indicative of the then normal state of affairs. Of course, cases of need arising from sickness or accident or death now and then occurred, but these were readily met by the kind of tacit brotherhood and the neighbourliness that then characterised the community.

Anomalous as the statement sounds, grim want, in the true meaning of the word, did not appear in Otago until the discovery of the goldfields. By that discovery in 1861 life in the province, and especially in its capital city, Dunedin, was entirely changed. Ship-loads of immigrants of all sorts arrived in rapid succession from the Home Country and from the Australasian colonies. Within the space of one year the population of the province leapt from 12,000 to 30,000; and as a large proportion of the new-comers settled in Dunedin, instances of poverty soon became so marked as to attract attention. As might be expected, some of the new arrivals—individuals and families—were penniless, and at once required assistance to save them from starvation; others were physically and otherwise unfitted for colonial life, especially digger life, with all its risks and hardships and exposure, and numbers of these required help; others, again, leaving their wives and children in Dunedin, set out for the goldfields, and some of these families were left destitute by the desertion or death of the bread-winners, and they also had to be cared for. These and other contingencies in connection with families and individuals, speedily arose, and simultaneous with the opening of the goldfields, and consequent tremendous influx of population, there were calls for the kindly assistance of those to whom the instances of distress became known.

The first public reference to the necessity for some general organization to meet the too rapidly growing poverty took the form of a letter in the *Daily Times* of January 6th, 1862, and signed "An Old Otago Colonist." As that letter was the first step towards the establishment of the Otago Benevolent Institution —as it was the little seed that developed into that philanthropic organisation—we think it deserves *in extenso* a place in this narrative. It is as follows:—

"Sir,—With the large accession to our population it will be evident to every one who considers the subject that there must be amongst us those who have arrived in the Province within the past few months a great many persons in distress from various causes—sickness being the principal. Now, Sir, I think the time has arrived when we, in prosperity, should do something to relieve the necessities of those in adversity, who in time of sickness ' cannot dig, and to beg they are ashamed.' It may be said that the hospital is available for such cases, but it is well known that that institution is of limited capacity, is always full to over-flowing, and a great many cases consequently are refused admittance. To come to the point, we want a Benevolent Society formed in Dunedin, having for its object the relief, after proper inquiry, of cases of distress. At present, supposing a rich merchant or fortunate digger desires to make an offering for charitable purposes, there is no authorised person to receive it or organized body to apply it. This, I think, is a matter in which the ladies of Dunedin and its neighbourhood could do really essential service; and, moreover, I am sure that if the case were properly put to them they would join heart and hand in the good cause. To make a practical suggestion, would it not be a good plan to have a fancy bazaar to start the proposed society ? I will venture to say that it would be well supported. I enclose my name, and beg to tender my humble services as a *working* hand to any who are willing to assist in the formation of a

' Dunedin Benevolent Society.'   Trusting that these few words will cause a move in the right direction, I am," &c.

(It may here be parenthetically remarked that several years after the publication of that letter, and when the committee and supporters of the Otago Benevolent Institution had a course of usefulness to look back upon, Mr. A. C. Strode, speaking from the chair at the annual meeting, and while giving a *resumé* of the history and work of the institution from its inception, incidentally alluded to a letter he had written urging the formation of such a society.   As the letter of " An Old Otago Colonist " seems to be the only one that ever appeared, it is only reasonable to ascribe its authorship to that gentleman, and to award to him the merit of having been primarily instrumental in bringing into existence that organisation which during the past 25 years has ministered to the wants of thousands of men, women, and children in adverse circumstances, and provided for many homeless orphans.)

That letter quickly bore fruit, and within a month of its appearance a number of Dunedin gentlemen met with the view of giving effect to "An Old Otago Colonist's" suggestion. The movement was warmly supported by the *Daily Times*, which, in its issue of February 8th, 1862, said :—"With a population hastily attracted to the spot to follow an uncertain pursuit rather than a steady occupation, many must be severe sufferers by non-success. At one time, when every one knew every one, it was felt to be a privilege, rather than otherwise, to offer assistance in time of misfortune. But now, when men are mostly strangers to their nearest neighbours—when each one endeavours to jostle the others in the race after fortune's favours—the game of life has lost its unexciting "live and let live" character ; it is played with absorbing interest—the wrapped earnestness of those who stake their all on the hazard of the die. We can speak from absolute knowledge of much actual individual distress existing, which such an institution as a Benevolent Asylum would assist in alleviating. Persons suffering from chronic diseases, not admissible patients to an hospital, convalescents recovering from lengthened illnesses, unfortunates deprived for a time of work and subjected to temporary distress, women deserted by their husbands and children by their parents—these are the cases which do occur, and without the aid of a Benevolent Asylum they must remain unattended to."

Two months later the movement started by " An Old Otago Colonist " took practical shape, and at a meeting held at the office of Mr. A. C. Strode on April 24th, 1862, the Otago Benevolent Institution was formed, and the interim committee then appointed at once issued an appeal to the people of the Province, and took the necessary steps to secure subscriptions and to obtain a measure of government support. The *Times* of the following day announced the fact, and stated that the new society was established on the most cosmopolitan principle, its objects being " to relieve the aged, infirm, disabled, or destitute of all creeds and nations, and to minister to them the comforts of religion :—

" 1. By relieving and maintaining in a suitable building such as may be most benefited by being inmates of the Asylum.

" 2. By giving out-door relief in kind to families and individuals in temporary distress.

" 3. By affording medical assistance and medicine through the establishment of a dispensary. [The necessity for this provision was obviated by the opening of the out-door consulting department of the Hospital.)

" 4. By affording facilities for religious instruction and consolation to the inmates of the Asylum."

The *Times* again warmly supported the movement, and expressing the opinion that " the most effective form of relief would be an institution subsidised by government, with an independent management, and with private subscriptions," and the belief that " the people of Otago are not hardened by prosperity into indifference to the sharp cry of misery and to the weak wail of helpless want," and would not " rest under the reproach that in a community of undoubted richness there was neglect shown to the claims of charity," the editorial conveying the foregoing information went on to say :—" The principle is a sound one of taxing the whole community for the benefit of the unfortunate amongst its number. Hence, in England, the Poor Law Rate. Here, with a revenue in excess of the requirements of the country, it would be folly to have recourse to special taxation; but no one could grumble that out of the revenue derived from, and the property of the whole country, a portion should be set aside for the relief of the unfortunate. . . . The institution provides for the relief of the widest divided forms of want and distress. The wife and children unable to procure fuel will not be allowed to perish with cold; the immigrant arriving penniless will be enabled to get a meal and a bed until employment is available to him; the workman temporarily disabled will be able to get temporary relief; the convalescent will not be suffered to remain adrift on the world, unable, from the effects of illness, to cope with its stern necessities; and, lastly, the sufferers from chronic incurable diseases will be enabled to pass their few remaining days on earth, their pains alleviated, as far as can be, instead of being increased by want and exposure, and their religious wants attended to." The writer then leaves the issue of the movement "to the dictation of the nobler instincts."

Other meetings followed in rapid succession, and at a meeting of subscribers, held on May 22nd, at the Athenæum—(then in Manse street), St. John Branigan, Commissioner of Police, in the chair, it was resolved that the Institution be governed by a President, Vice-President, Treasurer, and Committee of eight, to be elected annually. At this date the financial condition of the Institution stood thus :—

Collected by Rev. E. G. Edwards and Messrs Strode, Douglas, Oswin, and Hardcastle	..	£172	19	6
Proceeds of Entertainment by the Garrick Club, per B. L. Farjeon	..	64	7	6
Government Grant in Aid of Building ..	..	1000	0	0
Government Grant in Aid of Maintenance	..	250	0	0
Subscriptions promised	..	221	1	0
		£1,708	8	0

As yet such subscriptions as had been received were entirely from the citizens of Dunedin, but 66 lists had been issued to gentlemen in various parts of the Province.

In addition to the grants-in-aid of the building and for maintenance, the Government signified their willingness to grant a site, but ere that question was finally settled, there was vexatious delay and a considerable amount of parleying and of " hope deferred." The first offer of the Government comprised

1¾ acres of the Old Cemetery Reserve at the top of Rattray
street, but the Committee decided that, while a piece of land 10
acres in extent was desirable, not less than 5 acres would suffice.
On the strength of a promise from Mr. J. H. Harris, Deputy
Superintendent, that he would recommend to his Executive " the
placing of an amount on the estimates to enable the Committee
to purchase an eligible site," the Committee called for tenders for
5 or 10 acres, not exceeding a mile and a half from the Octagon,
but there was no response. The second government offer was the
right of purchase of 100 acres of the Pine Hill Reserve at £1 per
acre, in lieu of the 1¾ acres of the Old Cemetery Reserve. The
Pine Hill Reserve, however, was, after careful examination,
rejected as a site, owing to its distance from the city and the
difficulty of access to it, but it was ultimately secured as an
endowment. Owing to the seeming impossibility of securing a
more suitable site, the Committee then signified their willingness
to accept the 1¾ acres at the Old Cemetery Reserve, but only
again to abandon it.

While the erection of a permanent Asylum was thus delayed,
urgent cases of distress forced themselves on the attention of the
Committee, and they therefore determined to lease some suitable
place for a time. In this also they were disappointed, for no
proprietors could be found willing to let their buildings for such
a purpose. Out-door relief, however, was administered to a
steadily-increasing number of applicants, whose cases were
carefully inquired into by a sub-committee. At the first general
meeting of the subscribers, held in the rooms of the Institution in
Farley's Hall, Princes street, the weekly average number of
recipients of aid was stated to be 50, no fewer than 10 children
being boarded out, and the amount expended weekly in relief was
about £25. The report submitted at that meeting stated that
" since the formation of this Society relief has been widely
distributed, and in several cases your Committee has the satisfaction of reflecting that the existence of this Institution has been
the means of rescuing many unfortunate persons from the misery
and temptation to which their circumstances exposed them, of
turning deserted and orphan children from the paths of vice, and
assisting helpless women to maintain themselves in honesty."

After further efforts to secure a suitable site, the uncertainty as to the location of the Asylum, and the inconvenience caused by the non-existence of something of the nature of a home, were at length brought to an end by the purchase, from Mr. J. H. Clapcott, of 8¾ acres on the Caversham Road for the sum of £600 ; and in the third year of the Institution, a wing of the Asylum building, designed by Mr. A. R. Lawson, was completed at a cost (including purchase of ground) of £3,114 7s. 2d.   Of this sum £1,500 was furnished by the Provincial Government.   As the years went by that wing was added to, piece by piece, as funds were provided by the Government and by public subscriptions, and now the Province possesses a Refuge for its aged, infirm, and disabled homeless ones, and also for a large number of orphan children, of which it may well be proud.   The main building, a magnificent edifice, is built of bricks, consists of three stories, and when the western wing, now near completion, is finished, it will comprise 17 dormitories, capable of accommodating about 60 women; 5 dormitories containing about 60 beds for children ; large sitting and sewing rooms for the women ; dining-rooms for all the inmates, inclusive of the male adults (separate rooms for the sexes) ; hospital ward and two maternity wards; kitchen, &c. ; and master and matron's and servants' apartments.   The Old Men's Home is separate from the main building, and it comprises 6 wards, with 71 beds; 2 large sick wards, with 34 beds ; cottage of 4 rooms, with 12 beds ; cottage of 2 rooms, with 6 beds ; and cottage containing smoking and reading rooms and small separate apartments for 5 men.   There are, besides, the necessary out-houses, including large school-room (also used as chapel and lecture-hall), playshed, &c.   Altogether, the Asylum can give accommodation to 250 inmates.

It was not contemplated by the promoters of the Institution that it should combine a home for the aged and infirm and an Orphan Asylum as well, and far less that it should take charge of criminal children.   But force of circumstances compelled the Committee to receive orphans, and by the " Neglected and Criminal Children's Act, 1867, they were for a time made the legal guardians of such children as were committed under the Act.   In consequence of this, and because of the lack of the necessary accommodation, and much to the regret of the Committee, a good many destitute children had to be maintained outside. This inconvenience, however, was remodied by the opening of the Industrial School at Look-out Point, whereby the Benevolent Institution was freed from the onus of caring for young people committed by magistrates. In 1873 it was proposed by a number of ladies that a Foundling Department (presumably for illegitimates) should be formed in connection with the Institution, but the overture met with no favour, and was wisely rejected. Although the poor destitute and orphan children who found a home in the Institution were not embraced in the benevolent aims of its originators, the benefits conferred upon them were, and are, incalculable, and cannot be fully known. All needful provision was made for their proper training for lives of usefulness. In a thoroughly equipped school, with duly qualified teachers, under the supervision of, in the first instance, Mr. (now Dr.) Hislop, and latterly of the Otago Education Board's Inspectors, good secular instruction was imparted ; and as the children advanced in years, they were hired out to service, and until they reached manhood and womanhood a kindly control and care for their well-being in all respects were, as far as possible, maintained over them. In the fourteenth year of the Institution there were 25 lads and 13 girls out at service, while in addition, 9 boys and 12 girls had, in the same year, been adopted by respectable families. These numbers respectively have since then been largely added to.

At first, comparatively few persons required assistance from the Institution, but with marked variations their number rapidly grew, by far the largest proportion being children. The preponderance of children is, of course, explained by the fact that as a rule families left destitute, through the illness or death or desertion of the breadwinnners, were ministered to. In the third year the total number of individuals was 592 (27 men, 133 women, and 432 children), but in the sixth year it fell to 456, inclusive of inmates of the Asylum. In the following year the number (out-door and in-door) rose to 728, and increased to 1,171 in the ninth year. Two years later there was a fall to 788, but in the next year the number swelled enormously, to 1,730—more than double. In the fifteenth year there was another fall—to 1422—but in the year following the total rose to 1,551, and from that time there was a steady rise year by year until the year 1888, when the total stood at 4,002. The variations in these figures are indicative of the varying conditions of the Province from prosperity to depression, and *vice versa*, in common with the other parts of the Colony. Times of depression are always marked by dearth of employment, when there is a necessity for charitable assistance, more or less, to those in enforced idleness. But the extraordinary increase in the number of recipients of aid from the Institution indicated in the foregoing statement was, no doubt, in the first instance chiefly due to the importation from the Home Country of many unsuitable and undesirable immigrants during the operation of the Public Works and Immigration Scheme. Drunkenness and the desertion of wives and children were also prolific causes of family distress ; and during the whole history of the Institution scarcely a report was submitted to the subscribers without strong reference being made to the shameful conduct of dissolute husbands and fathers. Disabling and fatal accidents to labourers, while the railways were in course of formation, were also fruitful in adding to the number of the destitute. It is surprising to find that in the fifteenth year of the Institution there were no fewer than 80 widows and 266 fatherless children receiving relief, and that these numbers rose in the year 1883 to 167 and 448 respectively. In the second instance. however, the alarming increase in the number of recipients was the very natural consequence of the passing of the " Hospital and Charitable Institutions Act, 1885."

All things considered, the Institution has, from the first, well fulfilled its functions, and now, besides affording out-door relief (as per report for 1888, the latest published) to 4,050 persons, all told, it gives an Asylum to about 180 men and women disabled by age, disease, or accident, and some 60 homeless children, and, in addition, it provides all the benefits of a maternity hospital to women too poor to pay for medical attendance and nursing in their own homes.

Financially, the Institution from its inception had a somewhat hard struggle, and more than once, by reason of the bleak look out, owing to the many calls for assistance and the lack of funds, its conductors seriously entertained the thought of closing the door, but they nevertheless succeeded wonderfully, and far beyond their expectations. Speaking at the tenth annual meeting of the Institution, the Rev. Dr. Stuart cheerily referred to its straitened circumstances and said :—" However dark the prospect seemed, it had always happened that funds were ultimately forthcoming. In the future the Committee would, no doubt, have similar experiences, and meet with similar difficulties, but they would also, without doubt, achieve similar victories." And they did.

As already stated, the Provincial Government, in the first instance, granted £250 towards the maintenance of the Institution. In the third year the Council voted £1000 for the like purpose, with a further sum of £500 towards the support of orphan and destitute children ; the Government grant, thereafter, to be £2 for every £1 subscribed. In the sixth year, however, the subsidy was increased to £3 for every £1 subscribed, but the amount was afterwards reduced to £ for £. The public subscriptions (shillings and pence omitted) varied from £172 in the first year to £1,058 in the ninth year, and from £996 in the tenth year to £3,411 in the twenty-second year. In the twenty-third year they fell to £2,462, and in the year following, when the " Hospital and Charitable Institutions Act " came into operation, and did away with the absolute necessity for voluntary subscriptions, to £512, and two years later to £448. But as the yearly cost (all expenses told) far exceeded the subscriptions and Government subsidies, recourse to other ways of raising funds was necessary. These took the form of entertainments, bazaars, and carnivals. The first movement of the kind, in anticipation of, and to further, the formation of the Institution, and which yielded the sum of £64 9s. 6d, was the Garrick Club entertainment in 1862, under the direction of Mr. B. L. Farjeon. In 1864 a Committee of ladies successfully conducted a bazaar, which, with a concert and ball by Mr. Lyster, placed the sum of £1,717 in the hands of the Committee ; and in the following year a bazaar, held in the Universal Bond, realised £1,026. In 1876 the opening of Guthrie and Larnach's large buildings (since destroyed by fire) was celebrated by a Carnival in aid of the Institution, £3,000 (with Government subsidy) being the result. In 1878 a second Carnival, held in A. and T. Inglis' premises, yielded £3,448, inclusive of subsidy. By a third

Carnival, held in the Garrison Hall in 1880, the Institution secured £4,594, including subsidy. Two years later another Carnival, held in Mr. Donald Reid's Wool and Grain Store, resulted in the addition of £1,826 to the Institution's funds; and in 1884, the twenty-second year of the Institution, a Committee-in-Aid, directed by Mr. Vincent Pyke, carried to a successful issue a scheme, comprising concerts, lectures, dramatic entertainments, gift auction, &c. By that effort the Institution gained £1,661.

Though the letter of " An Old Otago Colonist " was fruitful in leading to the formation of the Institution, the suggestion thrown out by the writer to " rich merchants and successful diggers," who might desire " to make an offering for charitable purposes," has, as yet, been almost resultless. The only offering on a large scale was the anonymous but generous gift of £300 in the year 1881 from a citizen of Dunedin for the support of orphan children. Three years previously, however, the Institution received the large sum of £7,515 for investment, being a portion of the accumulated profits on deposits in the Dunedin Savings Bank. For this handsome donation the Committee were indebted to the Trustees of the Bank, and to the Honourables W. H. Reynolds and Mr. (now Sir) Robert Stout, who carried the measure through Parliament. That the gentlemen in whose hands in the course of the years the affairs of the Institution were placed have wisely fulfilled their trust is evidenced by the fact that, after affording relief to many thousands of persons, and a home to many hundreds, the value of the Institution's endowments, as at March 31st, 1889, was £20,515. These comprise the Caversham property (on which stands the Asylum, Old Men's Home, &c.), the Pine Hill and Saddle Hill properties, and investments to the amount of £11,910.

While a goodly number of the colonists gave fair support to the Institution as the years went by—some, indeed, more liberally than could justly be expected of them—many well-to-do settlers persistently manifested a disposition to ignore its claims. On this point severe reflections were repeatedly made in the annual reports. Such sentences as the following have a painful sound :—" There are some very wealthy people in this Province, in town and country, who have vast quantities of land, who do not contribute towards the funds of the Institution to the same extent as people of far less means." " While many have subscribed, and do subscribe liberally, there is a large class of the community who contribute nothing towards the help of the destitute, the sick, the afflicted, and the widows and orphans." " It is to be regretted that a large proportion of the wealthy classes of the Provincial District do not subscribe, as reference to the subscription list will at once show." These are samples of the complaints made. This discreditable apathy on the part of men who ranked as successful colonists, and their unwillingness voluntarily to share the general burden, no doubt had something to do with the passing of the " Hospital and Charitable Institutions Act, 1885," under which authority was given to counties, boroughs, and road boards, to levy rates for the support of such institutions. By that Act, while, as was predicted, it increased the number of applicants, the scope of the Benevolent Institution's operations was largely extended, and it now gives relief to the poor of eight counties, twenty-eight boroughs, and two road board districts, besides providing an hospital for incurables, a maternity hospital, and an Asylum for orphan and homeless children. In this connection a proposition, made at the twenty-second annual meeting of the Society by Mr. John Bathgate (now deceased), may be noted. Deploring the large increase in the number of applicants for relief, and consequent increased expenditure (as in the previous ten years), in the course of which the outlay, all expenses told, rose from £3,030 to £7,868), he moved :—" That a memorial be framed and forwarded to the Government by the Committee, on behalf of this meeting, strongly recommending that an Empowering Act be passed, under which Elective Boards for the administration of charitable aid may be formed and incorporated in districts of convenient size, as regards area and population ; that funds be provided by requisition on the local governing bodies within the area, who may be authorised to meet the same from the ordinary rates, or from special assessments ; that unpaid overseers and assistants be appointed by the Boards, by whom all investigations shall be made, and relief, where necessary, distributed, as has been successfully carried out in Elberfeld (in Germany), New York, and other cities which have adopted the plan." Speaking to the motion, Mr. Bathgate said that the result of the scheme, as regarded Elberfeld, was that in five years the number of paupers was reduced from 4,000 to 1,500, and the expenditure from £7,000 to £2,600. Sketching the system, he stated that—" The town (equal in size to that of Dunedin) was divided into districts, and each had a certain number of visitors, and each visitor had four paupers to look after. The best families were called upon to serve, and they did it with the happiest results. In Elberfeld everything was scrutinised to the utmost degree, while, at the same time, a feeling of kindness and sympathy prevailed betwixt those who received relief and those who gave it. Parties receiving relief found out in abuses were sent to gaol. The system had been tried in New York, Boston, and various other towns, with excellent effect." The motion was carried unanimously, and remitted to the Committee for consideration, but nothing further came of it.

As has been already stated, at the meeting of the Interim Committee in May, 1862, at which the Institution was formed, it was decided that it should be governed by a President, Vice-President, Treasurer, and Committee of eight (afterwards increased to nine), to be elected annually. In the third year Trustees were added. It goes without saying, therefore, that from first to last a large number of gentlemen co-operated in the philanthropic work for which the Institution was established. Of those who throughout a course of years took a prominent part in the work, Mr. A. C. Strode, Mr. E. B. Martin, Mr. James Fulton, and many others, are still to the fore; but others of revered memory have gone to their rest. The names of Sir John Richardson, St. John Branigan, J. H. Harris, James Wilkie, John Bathgate, and Alexander Rennie, will long be held in kindly and grateful remembrance. Formerly the Committee and office-bearers were all elected by the subscribers, but now, under the Charitable Aid Act, and under the name of Board of Trustees seven of the Committee are elected by the Charitable Aid Board, and two by the subscribers to the Institution, the Committee being left to appoint their own Chairman and Treasurer. The first office-bearers and Committee consisted of Major Richardson, President; Mr. J. H. Harris, Vice-President; Mr. Day, Treasurer; and Messrs A. C. Strode, St. John Branigan, Julius Vogel, Douglas, Rattray, C. H. Street, Casper, and Henry Cook.

KNOX CHURCH, DUNEDIN.

Messrs A. C. Strode, St. John Branigan, and R. B. Martin, were the first Trustees. Mr. Strode gave 17 years' service to the Institution as member of Committee, Vice-President, President, and Trustee ; Mr. Martin gave 20 years ; and Mr. A. Rennie, the last President under the original system, also 20 years. The office-bearers and Committee for this year (1889) are : Mr. A. Solomon, Chairman ; Mr. Charles Haynes, Treasurer ; and Messrs John Carroll, James Green, Michael Fagan, George Calder, W. D. Stewart, W. Isaac, and R. Chisholm. For five years Drs. T. M. Hocken and F. Richardson (the latter now deceased) jointly acted as medical officers, and thereafter Dr. Hocken held the position for 17 years, he being succeeded by Dr. W. M. Stenhouse. As the Asylum now embraces an hospital for incurables and a maternity hospital, the duties of the medical officers are necessarily much more onerous than in years past. For 16 years Mr A. Boot held the office of Hon. Dentist to the Institution, and Mr. Septimus Myers now acts in that capacity. From the first the religious interests of the inmates of the Asylum were attended to. In the first instance Bible instruction was imparted daily to the children by the school teachers, and for 17 years Mr. James McFie (now deceased) held the position of Chaplain. Upon that gentleman's retirement, through failing health, the work was taken up by the Caversham representatives of the Presbyterian, Anglican, and Wesleyan Churches. Miss Coxhead was the first Governess appointed, and since her retirement (in 1873) the office has been held in turn by Misses Wilson, Ferens, and Hilgendof, the last-named lady having only lately been appointed. Of those who have held the responsible position of Manager and Secretary, Mr. Richard Quinn (now deceased) is remembered with respect. The office of Secretary is now ably filled by Mr. A. Clulee, and under the careful management of Mr. and Mrs. Mee, Master and Matron, the Asylum progresses peacefully and satisfactorily.

THE INDUSTRIAL SCHOOL.

The name with which this sketch is headed is doubly suggestive. On the one hand, the existence of an Industrial School in any community is indicative of grievous demoralisation of a section of its people, and of their criminal disregard of

the sacred interests of the children of whom they are the parents
or custodians ; on the other hand, it bespeaks wise and humane
forethought and action on the part of the powers that be.   The
necessity for Industrial Schools is matter for regret ; but their
establishment evidences the noble purpose to rescue from a
career of crime, and to train for useful and respectable citizen-
ship, the little ones born and reared in haunts of pollution and
infamy.   Not only for the sake of the poor children so
unfortunately circumstanced, but also for the welfare of the
State, preventive measures are imperative.   It is an old and a
true saying that "prevention is better than cure"—and cheaper
too ; and even on the low and selfish ground of cost, and apart
from the consideration of the benefit accruing to the country from
the well-doing of those rescued, it is beyond question that—
confining ourselves to our own Industrial School from its inception
until now—the thousands of pounds expended in feeding and
clothing and educating its inmates have saved tens of thousands
that would otherwise have been spent in restraining and
punishing most of them, and that the care by the State of the
children of criminal parents has prevented the necessity for the
increase of gaol accommodation.   "They haven't a chance, sir !
—they haven't a chance ! " was the indignant exclamation of one
who listened to the sad tale of one of the young Arabs of old
Edinburgh, a boy of twelve, who had just been turned out of
prison, but had no abode to go to worthy of the name of home.
In this lesser and younger Edinburgh, after the opening of the
goldfields, and consequent influx of mixed population, children
that "hadn't a chance" attracted attention, and the State in
mercy and in self-defence stepped in to ensure to them the
birth-right denied them by their dissolute and criminal parents.
" We laugh at the Turk," says the late Rev. Dr. Guthrie in his
"City—Its Sins and Sorrows," " who builds hospitals for dogs,
but leaves his fellow-creatures to die uncured and uncared for.
And doing so, we forget that dogs and horses enjoy by act of
Parliament a protection from cruelty among ourselves, which is
denied to those whose bodies and whose souls we leave
savage parents to neglect and starve.   I lay it down as a
principle which cannot be controverted, and which lies, indeed,
at the very foundations of society, that no man shall be allowed

to rear his family a burden, and a nuisance, and a danger to the community. He has no more right to rear wild men and wild women, and let them loose among us, than to rear tigers and wolves, and send them abroad in our streets. What four-footed animal is so dangerous to the community as that animal which unites the uncultivated intellect of a man to the uncontrollable passions of a beast?" As there was no law of compulsion that could reach such parents, the Legislature passed a law which deprived them of the dangerous power they possessed; and hence the establishment of the Industrial School.

The first step towards meeting the necessities of the children of the very poor in Dunedin, was the passing of a vote by the Provincial Council in 1863, for the maintenance of Free Schools; but the honour of initiating such schools seems to be due to a lady named Mrs. O'Rafferty. Pitying the children she noticed running wild in the streets,' at her own cost, and on her own responsibility, she rented a small apartment in St. Andrew street, and engaged and paid a competent female teacher, Mrs. O'Rafferty herself holding the position of superintendent. She also visited the homes of the poor, and in a short time the necessity for some such provision was made manifest by the class-room, capable of accommodating between 50 and 60, being found to be too small for the number of applicants for admission and for the proper discipline of the children. Owing to the urgent need for a larger room, and the additional expense being beyond her resources, Mrs. O'Rafferty brought her scheme under the notice of the authorities, and Mr. (now Dr.) Hislop, secretary to the Education Board, having inspected her school, and reported of it very favourably, the Government granted from the amount voted by the Provincial Council a liberal allowance in aid of her philanthropic effort. Her movement also won the approval of a number of gentlemen, who formed themselves into a committee to co-operate with the Government and with her, and with other ladies disposed to join in the work; with the result that the Government leased a piece of ground in Bath street, and placed on it one of the large buildings that formed the military barracks, vacated by the withdrawal of the Imperial troops. The daily average attendance then rose to about 80. The marked success of that mission, and the call for similar measures in other parts of the town, led to the opening of a Free School in Stafford street by Mrs. Dr. T. Burns and other ladies, and to a like effort in Pelichet Bay. Independently of these schools, however, the Government made every possible endeavour to ensure the proper education of children whose parents were too poor to pay school fees—first, by empowering school committees to remit in such cases the whole or a portion of the fees; and secondly, by providing for the payment by the School Board of 10s. per annum for every child taught gratuitously at the District Schools.

But while the Free Schools were of incalculable advantage to the young people received into them, they did not meet the need of a growing class of children who had the misfortune to be under the control, and thereby subject to the vicious example, of drunken and profligate parents or so-called guardians. In 1866 there were known to be over 100 such children in Dunedin and suburbs, many of whose names had appeared in the criminal records of the province. Referring to this startling fact, Dr. Hislop, in his report to the Hon. T. Dick, chairman of the Education Board, said: "It has become a question of the greatest urgency and importance what steps are to be taken on behalf of these unfortunates. The Free Schools do not at all meet their case; for no real good can be expected from their attendance at an ordinary day school, however efficiently conducted, as long as they are exposed to the counteracting and degrading influences of wicked and criminal home or street example and associations. In fact, the presence of those children in our ordinary day schools is greatly to be deprecated, as it cannot fail to exert a most pernicious influence on the children of honest and respectable parents; and unless means are taken to separate them entirely from their profligate relatives, and to renovate and raise their moral nature, their mere instruction and progress in secular learning may be productive of evil rather than of good to the community in after years."

It was the condition of these poor children that suggested to Mr. St. John Branigan, Commissioner of Police, in consultation with Dr. Hislop and Mr. (now Sir) J. Vogel, at that time Provincial Treasurer, the necessity for an Industrial School "for the proper education and training of vagrant and neglected children, under entire seclusion from their profligate relatives

and other adverse influences." As prompt action was urgently
called for, a temporary erection on a portion of the Hospital
Reserve at the Octagon (on which the City Council Chambers and
Fire Brigade Station now stand) was at first thought of, to be
succeeded by a permanent institution in some country district,
where the boys might be taught farm work, and the girls
be trained to become useful servants and dairymaids. The late
Mr Macandrew and Sir J. Vogel entered heartily into the
project. The former gentleman, just then elected to the position
of Superintendent of the Province, in his opening address to the
Provincial Council, said: "There are various questions deeply
affecting the moral welfare of the community—indeed, I may say
its future safety—which it seems to me to be imperatively
necessary we should deal with at once. I would allude
especially to the serious evil which is growing and festering in
our midst—viz., the large number of children, the offspring of
profligate parents, who may be said to be homeless, and who are
being utterly neglected, or trained up to vicious habits. It
appears to me that the State must in self-defence take steps to
repress this evil. It will cost us much less to do so now than it
will by-and-bye. I believe an Industrial School, which might be
made to a large extent self-supporting, would be the most
effective remedy. There is an excellent site for such a purpose
at Look-out Point upon the thirty acres reserved for a lunatic
asylum some years ago." The Council favourably received the
proposition, and promptly passed a vote for the purpose, and also
an empowering ordinance prepared by Mr. Haggitt, Provincial
Solicitor. A slight hitch was caused, however, by the discovery
that the powers proposed to be given to magistrates could only
be conferred by an Act of the General Assembly; but no time
was lost, and through the efforts of Mr. Macandrew and Sir J.
Vogel, "The Neglected and Criminal Children's Act, 1867," was
passed by the Assembly.

The Provincial Government then proceeded with the work.
The site proposed by Mr. Macandrew at Look-out Point was
approved of, ten acres of it being appropriated for the School.
It was determined that the building should be of brick, but as the
amount voted was insufficient to complete it, only a portion
adequate to meet immediate requirements was erected. That

portion—a good land-mark, as seen from the lower-ground on either side—has never been added to. As the years went by, however, and the number of children increased, and especially during the years 1874-7, when through the Public Works and Immigration Scheme, occurred a tremendous influx from the Home Country of most undesirable immigrants, more accommodation had to be provided. Temporary wooden buildings were therefore supplied. First, the building previously used as the City Hospital (which had been transferred from the Octagon to the Exhibition building in Great King street), and in 1878 the Scarlet Fever Hospital on the Town Belt; all of which were removed to and re-erected on the school site.

In January, 1869, the Industrial School was quietly and informally opened by the reception into it of a few boys and girls from the Benevolent Institution, and from that day, and from all parts, a steady stream set in of children committed by magistrates. As already indicated, the great increase took place during the years 1874-7, and from the first until now, upwards of 1800 have been enrolled in the books of the institution. At the end of October of this year (1889) there were 486 on the books. Of these, 83 boys and 43 girls were in the school, 29 boys and 12 girls were with friends under license, 180 of the youngest boys and girls were boarded out, 136 (of whom about 60 were girls) were hired out to service, three were in other institutions, and one of them in the Blind Asylum, Melbourne. All children committed to the school are detained till they reach the age of fifteen; but, irrespective of age, they can be hired out when they pass the fourth standard; and in whatever part of the country they may be, a kindly supervision is maintained over them till they attain their majority. This, as regards the boys, is done through persons in responsible positions, and, as regards the girls, through lady inspectors, who report half-yearly. The master of the school is virtually the parent of the young people, and all their business transactions are managed by him. He makes terms with their employers on their behalf, receives the amount of their wages quarterly, and these are banked in their respective names, with the names of Mr. Titchener (the master) and Mr. H. Houghton as trustees. Employers also, when remitting payments to Mr.

Titchener, give quarterly returns as to health, state of clothing, and general conduct, the forms for which are supplied when accounts for wages are sent them. The writer has before him quite a pile of these returns. The topmost one, referring to a boy, runs thus:—"Health—Good, plucky, cheerful. State of clothing—Very good. General conduct—Always keeping the same—quiet, willing, honest, trustworthy, and tidy." The next in order, referring to a girl whose parentage is as bad as bad can be, states :—"Health—As usual, excellent. State of clothing—In good order, and she has a full supply of all she needs. General conduct—Very good, and she is growing up to be a happy girl, willing to learn all she can." These examples will suffice. Bearing in mind that more than one thousand five hundred boys and girls have thus been dealt with, it can readily be understood that their withdrawal from debasing home surroundings, or from a neglected life, confers incalculable benefit not only upon themselves, but also upon the colony at large. It is an interesting fact that at this time the Trustees have in their possession 200 bank books, with credit balances amounting in all to close upon £2000, belonging to lads and girls hired out, or who are still under 21 years of age. While they are in their minority the money is laid out for them according to their requirements, and when they become of age, enter the marriage state before they become of age, or embark in suitable business of some kind, the balance to their credit is paid over to them. Thus, during the year ending November 11th, 1889, close upon £700, in sums varying from £5 to £83, was paid to fifteen young men and women released from control ; and during the sixteen months ending November, 1889, over £500, in sums varying from £1 up to £45, was paid to, or laid out on behalf of, fifty lads and girls still on the books, but at service. As showing the habit of thrift engendered, and the confidence of those who have been subject to the discipline of the institution, it is worthy of mention that recently a young man (a former inmate, and now in the North Island) forwarded £100 to Mr. Titchener to be banked in the usual way for safe keeping.

As already stated, the children receive ordinary school teaching up to the fourth standard ; but when they are hired out, their further education is ensured as far as possible by arrangement with the employers; and when they are boarded out, their schooling is carefully looked to. Music is one prominent feature of the instruction imparted, and about thirty of the boys in the Home form a remarkably good brass band, and practice daily under the leadership of Mr. Hugh Titchener (son of the Master of the Institution). That this training is not lost upon them is shown by the fact that some time ago, when Mr. Titchener, the Master, was on a furlough to Victoria, he met with several of his former band boys. They had grown to manhood, and were in various places connected with bands, one of them actually holding the position of leader of a musical association. If, however, that constituted all the proof of the success of the institution in producing good and useful men and women, it would not be much to boast of. But there is much more important and reliable evidence. The half-yearly reports from male and female inspectors, and quarterly returns from the masters and mistresses of those hired out, have already been noted; but in addition to these, and apart from innumerable and valuable letters from the boys and girls themselves, there are thousands of communications from employers and others, all bearing testimony to progress in well-doing; and, further, from the first separate records of all the young people who have passed through the school, from time of committal until final release, have been kept. In this connection may be mentioned an incident in the life of the late Dr. Guthrie, to whom allusion has already been made in this sketch. At a public meeting, the children of his Edinburgh Ragged School were spoken contemptuously of as "scum," whereupon the Doctor, under a fiery impulse, snatched up a clean sheet of note paper from before the Duke of Manchester, the chairman, and exclaimed with ringing eloquence, "This was once 'scum'—once foul, dirty, wretched rags. What is it now? In it—now white as the snows of heaven—may be seen an emblem of the material we send out, and of the work our school has achieved and is achieving!" As in the case of the old Edinburgh Ragged School, so in that of the young Edinburgh Industrial School— the results have exceeded the most sanguine expectations of its promoters. The writer has at hand a large number of returns of children found in the most unfavourable circumstances in different parts of the country and committed to the school. A few taken at random may be cited :—Emma H., 9 years, and Stephen H., 7 years, committed in 1868. Found in an infamous home, while mother in gaol. The girl now married and doing well on the West Coast; the lad an industrious and respectable workman. 2. James P., 8 years, illegitimate and homeless, committed in 1868. Working steadily, and has at present £18 to his credit. 3. Louisa, Eliza, Ellen, Eva, and Ada W., aged respectively 9½, 8, 7, 5½, and 3½ years, committed in 1868. Deserted by father, and mother an abandoned woman and in gaol. All except the youngest now married, and all living worthy lives. 4. Jessie and George M., 9 and 10 years, committed in 1869. Found in an infamous house, in which they were brought up from infancy. Father a convicted thief, and mother an abandoned woman. Jessie now married to a respectable man in good business, and George pursuing his way most creditably. 5. Henry and Robert R., 8 and 4 years, committed in 1869. Mother a transported convict, and father also a convicted thief. Henry and Robert have grown to be good men. 6. Isabella, Eliza, James, and David W., 10, 9, 5, and 2 years, committed in 1870. Found homeless and neglected. Father an elderly and sickly man, and mother drunken and of abandoned life. Eliza is well married, James is also married, and all are living worthy lives and prospering. 7. Edmund W., 10 years, committed in 1869. Convicted of theft, and said to have been for three years trained systematically to thieving. Has £14 now to his credit; doing well. 8. Anne F., 12 years, committed in 1870. Convicted of theft and vagrancy. Married and received balance of her earnings, about £20; doing well. 9. Thomas G., 11 years, committed in 1874. Convicted of theft. Father a transported convict, and mother also a notorious thief. Is now a farmer in partnership with his brother, also a former inmate, and both living industriously and respectably. The balance of Thomas's earnings, amounting to £15, was handed to him when he took up the land. These illustrative cases, taken indiscriminately from a mass, show conclusively (to quote the words of Dr. Guthrie), " the work which our school has achieved and is achieving." It of course goes without saying that some of those who pass through the school fall into evil ways, and

when such an instance occurs, there are always people thoughtless
enough to see in it evidence of the futility of the institution as a
reforming power. If, however, a moment's consideration be
given to the vile surroundings from which the children are
plucked, the horribly immoral and drunken scenes daily and
nightly witnessed by them, the blasphemous and obscene
language that continually falls upon their ears, and which they
learn to utter, the unholy impressions made upon their minds,
and which can never through life be effaced from memory, and
the impure and criminal habits they are led to form from their
earliest years—when all this is considered, apart from the law of
heredity, the marvel is that instead of the number of lapsed cases
being under 10 per cent., it is not over 90 per cent.

The work of organising the truly philanthropic institution
thus so successfully conducted, was entrusted to Dr. Hislop and
Mr. St. John Branigan. The latter gentleman was also
appointed Inspector of the school, and upon him devolved the
duty of framing the regulations that have operated so beneficially
to the "inmates." Upon his removal to Wellington in 1870 he
was succeeded as Inspector by Dr. Hislop, who held the position
until he, too, was removed to the seat of Government in 1878.
Though Dr. Hislop then necessarilly retired from that office, his
connection with the school to the present time has been
uninterrupted. By the transference of all the Industrial Schools
of the colony from the Department of Justice to that of Education
the control of the Caversham institution devolved upon him, as
Secretary for Education; and since his return to Dunedin in
1886, he has with his former warmth discharged the duties of
Official Visitor. Mr. Branigan, also, upon his return from the
north, laboured with deep interest and sympathy on the school's
behalf until he was laid aside by his final illness. The "Times,"
of September 16th, 1873, speaking of his connection with it,
said:—"Mr. Branigan may be regarded as its founder. To him
belongs the honour of suggesting its necessity, of having
carefully nursed it in its infancy, and of having mainly
contributed towards bringing it to its present admittedly high
state of efficiency." It was his official return, given in his
capacity of Commissioner of Police, that "revealed in all its
hideousness and loathsomeness" the evil to be grappled with.

The school, up to the present time, has been fortunate in having as its Masters two gentlemen eminently possessing the special qualifications for the work. Mr Britton, chosen by Mr Branigan, was the first appointed, and until his death in 1876, after a short illness, the institution made steady progress under his management. In his obituary notice it was stated that he " found the place a bleak and barren waste, and left it a well sheltered, pleasant, and richly-cultivated garden. With him, as with other devoted men, the ruling passion was strong in death. During his short and painful illness, the concerns of the institution and the interests of its youthful inmates were ever in his mind, and it may be said that he died with their names on his lips." After seven years' service in that capacity he was succeeded by the present Master, Mr. Elija Titchener, who has shown himself to be a man of a kindred spirit, and under his superintendence the institution has expanded to its present dimensions. Mrs. Britton, the first mistress, was a true help-mate to her husband, and Mr. Titchener has also had earnest coadjutors in his wife, the second and present mistress, and in two of his sons, at different periods head teachers of the school. From the first, Dr. Burns of Dunedin has honourably held the responsible position of medical officer. Mr. Collie was the first teacher, and since his removal to Burnham, where he died, that office has been filled successively by Mr. Neish, Mr. James, Mr. John Titchener (who, while yet a young and promising man, died in harness), Miss Christie, and Mr. Hugh Titchener, who now does earnest duty, and also acts as Bandmaster.

H.M. GAOL.

A good many years ago an Otago up-country journal very warmly congratulated the district it represented on the evidences of progress afforded by the erection of two new buildings, one of them being—a gaol. It did not seem to strike the writer that the progress indicated by the addition to its structures of a place of incarceration for evil-doers was scarcely a matter for gratulation, but one rather to be deplored. Unfortunately, wherever civilised communities are formed, there in due course the " progressive " gaol becomes a necessity. In the first days of the Otago settlement there seems to have been no urgent call for a prison, but as the years went by and the population slowly increased, breakers of the law forced the question of the establishment of a place of penal confinement on the attention of the authorities. At first, however, the culprits were nothing worse than jolly runaway sailors, with a slight occasional sprinkling of petty offenders, mainly through drink. There appears to be no means of knowing what Dunedin's first gaol was like, but it is probable that the second was a *fac-simile* of the first, possibly slightly enlarged. At all events, the first prison could not have been more simple and primitive than the second. The first official reference takes the form of an intimation in the Provincial Government Gazette of February 4th, 1854, that £75 had been voted as gaoler's salary for the year, and £60 for prisoners' rations. On December 20th following, the appointment of Mr. Henry Monson to be gaoler was announced ; and on the 27th of the same month the Gazette stated that the gaoler's salary was raised to £50 for the ensuing half-year, with £65 as the appropriation for prisoners' rations and contingencies. That the first prison was constructed on the assumption that all prisoners would be as docile as lambs, is evidenced by the fact that nothing of the nature of strong rooms or solitary cells had been thought of. But the need for some such accommodation apparently made itself felt, and accordingly we find His Honor the Superintendent, Captain Cargill, forwarding the following message to Parliament :—"On the urgent requisition of the sheriff and the gaoler that two cells should be added, with some little extension of the accommodation for the gaoler, so as to include a lock-up (presumably for refractories), a press for his stores and rations, and a place for the wheelbarrows and tools when not in use, and deeming the same to be reasonable and necessary, I recommend a further appropriation for this purpose not exceeding £20." This gaol was short lived, as on October 22nd, 1855, it was destroyed by fire. One interesting circumstance connected with this event deserves mention. At that time there was but one prisoner, and, prisoner though he was, he made strenuous efforts to save the building. He did not succeed, but he was saved from further confinement, the remainder of his sentence being remitted in consideration of the service he rendered. The erection of a new gaol was at once set about, but pending its completion, a portion of the Immigration Barracks in Princes street south was used as a temporary prison.

Whatever appearance the first gaol presented, the one that succeeded it was not, as an architectural structure, of a character to awaken admiration ; nor, indeed, is the present one. It was a one-storied timber building about 24 feet long by 16 feet wide, with a row of narrow open bunks, immigrant-ship fashion, running down each side, and an open passage between the rows, entrance to the bunks being effected endways. Into this dormitory light was meagrely admitted from the Bay side through two or three small windows, with thin perpendicular iron bars, fixed on with screws. At the outer end of one of the rows of bunks were two closed-in solitary cells, or strong-rooms, if the word strong can in this connection be applied to ordinary planks of wood and to a wooden door. Seeing that, in many instances the world over, massive stone walls and iron doors have failed to prevent the escape of men of the Jack Shepherd class, it goes without saying that the matchboard cells of the old Dunedin Gaol were altogether inadequate to frustrate the efforts of even less desperate men bent on regaining their liberty. More than one broke out and escaped, only, however, to be recaptured ; and one man, known as "Hobartown Jack," to whom a fellow-prisoner had passed a tomahawk through between the window bars, was only prevented from chopping the frail thing to pieces by a superior force overcoming him. This tiny and slim erection, which was suggestive of the idea of a travelling wild beasts' menagerie, stood on the present gaol site. Adjoining it was a yard about 60 feet by 40 feet, and both the prison and the yard, with the gaoler's residence, another small wooden edifice facing Stuart street, were surrounded by a paling fence six feet high, and with the rails placed inside. Without the aid of the rails as steps, however, any man of ordinary stature who objected to the deprivation of his liberty, could easily have hoisted himself over such a wall. The gaol lengthways faced the bay, the water of which washed up to the foot of the fence. On the opposite side of the street was the gaol garden (the ground now occupied by Findlay and Co.'s saw mill), and there the few prisoners reared vegetables for their and the gaoler's use. Making all allowance for the annoyance caused by occasional disturbing characters, life in that prison seems to have been, like the place itself, simple and primitive in the extreme. It has been currently reported from the early days of the Province, that the inmates of the gaol, with their custodian, formed a very happy family, and that Mr. Monson was wont to freely send numbers of them into town on errands, and even sometimes to grant them permission to take a stroll, with the warning, however, that if they were not back by lock-up hour they would not be admitted. Such was Dunedin gaol as late as 1858. But it was not destined to continue,—that is, as the Dunedin prison—though for several years afterwards it still served the purpose of a dormitory. The increase in population, and in the proportionate number of prisoners, necessitated the erection in 1860 of a larger and stronger prison —the stone building that now forms the western portion of the present gaol; and shortly afterwards the debtors' prison, was built—the iron building that now forms the eastern end facing the bay. (In the year 1874, when the Abolition of Imprisonment for Debt Act was passed, this portion of the gaol ceased to be a debtors' prison, and it was then turned into a dormitory for female prisoners). The additional accommodation was not provided too soon, for in the following year (1861) the goldfields were discovered, and then hordes of all classes poured into the colony from near and far, and among the newcomers were too many of a decidedly criminal stamp. Then also was formed the large and efficient police force, under the superintendence of Commissioner St. John Branigan; and so well did Mr. Branigan's men cope with the evil-doers, that in the space of twelve months the new gaol, as well as the old building, was crowded to such an extent that the then commodious chapel had to be used as a sleeping place. The contrast between the gaol of 1855 and that of 1862 may here be emphasised. In the first-mentioned year, when the prison was destroyed by fire, it had only one prisoner; in 1862, with all the large additions, the accommodation was altogether too inadequate—seven years' "progress" with a vengeance. But the tide turned, and—also through the vigour and watchfulness of Mr. Branigan's force—many of the criminal newcomers found Otago to be an unfavourable field for their operations, and deeming discretion to be the better part of valour, they gradually, upon their release, betook themselves from the colony, to the relief of the colony and of the gaol.

The stone prison was too manifestly not built with a knowledge of what a prison should be. The ground floor is faulty enough in all conscience, and difficult to work, but as regards the upper storey, if the designer had intended to place all power in the hands of the prisoners, and to make their control a work of immense difficulty and continual source of danger to the officers, he could not have succeeded better in his purpose. It is a perfect labyrinth—cells within cells, and corridors within corridors. There are a few single cells, in four small groups, as widely apart from each other as the walls of the building will allow ; but for the most part the cells are absurdly large, and were made to accommodate as many as eight, ten, twelve, and in one instance even sixteen men, in double tiers of bunks (one above the other), placed lengthways against the four walls, and to get to the single cells it is (or was) necessary for the warders, in discharge of their nightly inspection, or in the case of the sickness or sham-sickness of a prisoner, to pass between the tiers with their occupants. It will thus be seen that the internal construction is such as to afford every facility for conspiracy and sudden attack, and to place the officers at a dreadful disadvantage. The marvel is that the institution has existed so long without any very serious thing occurring, especially in the desperate days of '61-3. But, of course, no gaoler in his senses would place known dangerous men, or even doubtful men, in circumstances so favourable to themselves. Of late years the danger has been very much reduced by the removal of the double tiers of bunks, and the erection of iron gratings with locks. Still, as a gaol the building is extremely defective and inconvenient; but no doubt it will ere long be superseded by a prison formed on sounder principles, and more worthy of the name.

In the years 1870 and 1879 large accessions were made to the inmates of Dunedin gaol by the arrival of two batches of Maori prisoners from the North Island, the first being Waikato warriors taken in the field, the second the disturbers of the peace who knocked down the settlers' fences at Parihaka. The Waikato men were a fine, noble body. They conducted themselves with amazing good humour, and joined heartily, as if in competitive spirit with the white men, on the works in various places. They were treated with great kindness and leniency, and everything possible was done to lessen the bitterness of their imprisonment and enforced absence from their homes. So soon, however, as it became evident that the deprivation of their liberty was telling on their health, the Government promptly released them, and conveyed them back to their native hills. It is a pleasing fact that subsequently these men refused to take up arms against the Government, and the Waikato tribe have remained friendly ever since. The Parihaka men, a mixture of pure Maoris and half-castes, and who partook much more of the mischievous larrikin than of the noble, patriotic warrior, were also treated with special leniency, and after a short incarceration, they, too, were liberated and sent to their homes.

For several years also a few lunatics were located in the gaol, where for want of proper facilities they were a source of annoyance; but when the Lunatic Asylum was opened, they were removed to more suitable quarters. One amusing incident connected with lunatic life in gaol may not be deemed out of place in this sketch. One insane man, ordinarily a happy-souled being, but who, like many other insane persons, could show method in his madness, was peremptorily told by an officer to clean his (the officer's) long boots, and to " do them well." The officer's tone seems to have grated on the man's spirit, but he quietly answered, " Yes, sir, I'll do them well." In due course the boots were returned, shining to brilliancy. Forthwith the officer inserted his right foot, and, after it was down half-way, and with his fingers in the straps, and drawing himself together for the grand effort, he sent the foot home with a jerk, when lo! the member went right through, and away went the sole flying to the other side of the yard, while the perpetrator of the vengeful practical joke, with arms akimbo, stood against the wall leeringly watching proceedings. Close examination revealed the fact that the sewing or wooden pegs of both boots had been artistically cut, only two or three slim threads being left to keep the soles in their places! As the brushing of officers' boots was not government work, the owner of the tops could do nothing but growl.

From first to last much valuable work has been done by the prisoners, under competent overseers. In point of importance and magnitude the removal of Bell Hill ranks first, and, barring a small portion on the south side let by contract, it was reduced by the prisoners. It is difficult to give to those who never saw the hill an idea of its size and appearance, but it may be stated that from the level of Lower High street, behind the First Church and Manse, it rose to the height of 76 feet; from where the Garrison Hall stands it rose about 60 feet; from the plateau of the First Church (which stands 33 feet high), it rose 43 feet; and from Dr. Hocken's property it rose 35 feet; and (roughly) its base extended from Stuart street in the north, to the City Hall (late Lyceum) in the south, and from the telegraph posts in lower High street in the east, to the further side of Princes street in the west, and in that direction a portion of the hill still stands. The mountain may be said to have been literally cast into the sea, as the larger portion of it was used in reclaiming land from the bay. It was of volcanic formation, and much of it consisted of bluestone boulders, which were split by the prisoners and sold at 6s. and 7s. per load. Of that stone the Garrison Hall and the Princess Theatre were partly built, and it was used in the erection of many other buildings in the city. The work of removal was a long and tedious one, extending over a period of about 18 years. It was also laborious, and fraught with much risk, not only to the workmen, but also to the buildings, by reason of the proximity of the hill to the city. Nothing of a serious nature, however, occurred. It may here be appropriately mentioned that in 1877 the merchants of Princes street north paid a high compliment to the Department by giving to one of its officers— Sergeant Outram, who for fifteen years superintended the hill works—a testimonial, in recognition of the care and tact displayed in so conducting the dangerous blasting operations that no injury whatever was done to their premises.

Next to the removal of Bell Hill, the chief works accomplished by the prisoners up to the present time, comprise the formation of the road across the northern part of the bay, and which connects Anderson's Bay main road with the Lower Peninsula road; the widening and stonewalling of the Peninsula

road all the way to Portobello, and for a considerable distance
beyond that township; the Port Chalmers and Deborah Bay
coast road; the road across the Bay from Forth street to Logan's
Point, and on through some heavy cuttings to Ravensbourne ;
the opening up of the southern end of Maitland street—another
hill literally cast into the sea, and resulting in a large portion of
land being reclaimed from the bay; removal of the Octagon Hill,
ten or twelve feet high; formation of large portions of
Cumberland and Castle streets, into both of which the water of the
bay in places penetrated ; levelling the Girls' High School ground;
and filling up and forming (with construction of large stone
sewer underneath) Upper Smith street, which connects Stuart
street with the Girls' High School—a large work because of the
great depth of the gully ; formation and drainage of the Hospital
grounds, and planting of the hedge and erection of the fence all
round the block of five acres ; formation of the Boys' High
School Rectory ground, and the road leading from the Queen's
Drive to the rectory; extensive works at Caversham and the
Industrial School ; formation of the Maori road, which connects
the higher portion of Dunedin with Mornington; formation of
the Jubilee Park, &c., &c.   The heavy and dangerous cutting in
Pitt street was also begun by the prisoners, and for twenty years
the Botanical Gardens have been kept in order by a party of men
being daily told off for the purpose.   The more recent important
works are the formation of the breakwater and the mole at
North Otago Head, and the erection of the fortresses at Lawyer's
Head and Tairoa Head—the latter, a large work, being still in
progress.   In a number of these works the Maori prisoners took
an active part, and the Maori road, leading to Mornington, was
entirely formed by them, as its name indicates.   Such extensive
and important operations required very efficient overseers.   Of
those who took a leading part and spent longer or shorter
periods in the service, the following may be mentioned :—Mr.
Joseph Young, now farmer, Portobello ; Mr. James M'Intosh,
now in the Customs Department ; Mr. John Outram, retired ;
Messrs Strong and Duncan, both deceased ; Mr. MacNamara,
retired ; Messrs Ferguson, Flannery, and Prictor, all now in the
Prisons Department in the North Island ; and Chief-warders
Poynton and Armstrong, now in charge of the large works at

Taiaroa Head, and the former of whom superintended the breakwater and mole at the North Head.

While the various undertakings engaged in are necessarily entrusted to competent men, the great responsibility attaching to the works rests upon the chief officer, the gaoler, under whose supervision operations are conducted, and this, with the management of the prison and its inmates, and, in addition, the duties entailed upon him as Probation Officer, and the vast correspondence connected with all the branches of his department, makes his office to be no sinecure. Mr. Henry Monson, the first gaoler, was followed in succession by Mr. John Stoddart, Mr. James Caldwell, and Mr. S. C. Phillip, who is now in command; and the trying position of matron has been successively held by Mrs. Stoddart, Miss Heard, and Mrs. Shirley — the last-named lady being now in harness. Until 1877 Dunedin gaol was under the wing of the Otago Provincial Government, but on the abolition of the Provinces it, in common with the other gaols of the colony, was transferred to the General Government; and upon the appointment of Captain Hume as Inspector of Prisons it was placed under the one general and uniform system then adopted. Besides the Chief Inspectorship, the gaol is under the supervision of visiting justices and two official visitors. Upon the former gentlemen various powers are conferred, and among them that of adjudicating in special cases of discipline; but the latter gentlemen—Messrs. J. Matthews and William Simpson—only visit the prison and freely converse with the prisoners when they see fit, and report to head-quarters from time to time. The inmates have thus, through the visiting justices and the official visitors, ample opportunities for making themselves heard when they deem they have cause for complaint. The visiting justices are: Mr. E. H. Carew, R. M.; Captains Baldwin and Thompson, Dr. Hislop, and Messrs E. B. Cargill, John Logan, W. L. Simpson, G. G. Russell, W. P. Street, G. Fenwick, W. Elder, and J. R Mason. Dr. Williams was the first visiting medical officer to the prison. He was succeeded in the capacity of Provincial Surgeon by the late Dr. Hulme, and since that gentleman's decease the duties of the office have been assiduously discharged by Dr. R. Burns. Mr. S. Smith, subsequently minister of the Congregational

Church, Port Chalmers, was the first Protestant chaplain to the Gaol, and he was succeeded by Mr J. A. Torrance, who has held the position for over twenty-one years.   The Rev. Mr Ronaldson also visits on behalf of Church of England inmates.   For many years also good old Father Moreau, who is held in respectful remembrance by all who knew him, discharged the duties of Roman Catholic chaplain, and when he retired, the work was taken up by reverend gentlemen connected with the Roman Catholic Church in Dunedin.

THE HOSPITAL.

Though Dunedin Hospital ranks first in importance and usefulness among the city and provincial philanthropic institutions, and while the number of persons who have passed through its wards and received the benefits it confers exceeds by far the many who have been connected with all the other institutions put together, yet little can be said of it, and its story is soon told.

The principles on which the Otago settlement was founded were a guarantee that the sick poor within the bounds of the Province would not be neglected. At first, when the settlers were few, and when there was no migratory population, there were none who could in the general acceptation of the term be designated "the sick poor."   Nevertheless, ere the Province was two years old, steps were taken towards the establishment of a hospital.   But the action was premature.   Possibly those who initiated the movement deemed it wise to make provision for any emergency of the nature of an epidemic.   At least one immigrant ship, the "Moultan," was ravaged on the way out by the fearful scourge of cholera ; and although in such cases the vessels and passengers were kept in quarantine until all traces of the disease had disappeared, some general accommodation for convalescents might be required.   But whatever were the circumstances that prompted the authorities, in 1850 the subject was formally brought under the notice of Governor Sir George Grey, while he was on a visit to the young settlement, and he granted the sum of £250 out of the Otago Customs duties for the erection of a small hospital in Dunedin.   As already remarked, the institution, so far as actual need was concerned, was in advance of the times, for more than two years passed before any physically sick patients occupied its beds. Towards the end of that period, however, the building was made the home of three insane persons, and subsequently it was divided between the physically sick and the insane—the former, of course, ultimately preponderating.

The first hospital, built in 1851, was located on the site on which the City Chambers stand, on the south-western corner of the Octagon. For several years all requirements were comfortably met by small extensions; but when the gold diggings broke out in 1861, and immigrants poured into Dunedin, the demand for much larger accommodation very soon became urgent. Towards the end of 1862 extensive additions were made, and while these were in course of completion a portion of the Immigration Barracks in Princes street south was used as a temporary hospital, under the charge of Mr Wm. Dryburgh, who is still in the service. Like all institutions that have grown from small to large compass, the buildings that formed the hospital at the Octagon were disjoined and irregular. In 1866 they consisted of a one-storied wooden building, containing 25 beds; another, containing 16 beds; one three-storied wooden building, with 72 beds; two two-storied buildings, with 32 beds each; a stone building, with 11 beds; a maternity ward of timber, with 12 beds; besides operating room, mortuary, entrance lodge, and superintendent's residence—all separate. All these buildings now do duty in various places, most of them at the Industrial School at Look-out Point. The mortuary, however, still serves its purpose at the present hospital, and the stone building, now converted into a shed, remains on the ground behind the City Chambers.

In 1865 the question of the disposal of the Industrial Exhibition Building in King street, which had served the purpose for which it was erected, and was then standing idle, engaged the attention of the Provincial Council, and on the 6th of May of that year the Council, on the motion of Mr. (now the Hon.) W. H. Reynolds, decided that the building should " be appropriated for the purpose of an Hospital, the annexes to be purchased from the Royal Commissioners, if obtainable at a reasonable rate, and that measures be taken to put the building into a proper condition for an Hospital." The absolutely necessary alterations having been made, the Hospital was transferred from the Octagon to its present position in 1866, and in the months of August and September the difficult task of removing the 124 inmates was successfully accomplished. Previous to this, the insane patients, who had increased to about 20, had been located in the Lunatic Asylum. With all the alterations, however, the King street building was ill adapted to the purposes of an Hospital; but in the course of years since then, it has, by the outlay of large sums of money, undergone great improvements, and as a curative establishment been brought to a high state of perfection, in spite of its architectural defects.

In 1887 a much-felt need was supplied by the formation of two children's wards, with twelve beds ; but to make way for them the removal of the maternity ward was necessitated. The latter is now in the Benevolent Institution at Caversham. In the same year another important addition was made by the erection of a large and fully-equipped operating theatre, at a cost of £1600 ; it is a substantial and handsome structure. As a medical school, Dunedin Hospital, with its operating theatre, is invaluable. Large numbers of students daily walk the wards, and receive from the honorary medical and surgical staff lectures based on the great variety of cases dealt with; and already several medical gentlemen trained in the University and in the Hospital are in practice in the colony, while a goodly number who elected to finish their course in the universities and hospitals in the Home Country were fitted by their well-grounded elementary training here to acquit themselves with marked success. Further advancement, in the shape of a gynecological ward and of a Nurses' Home, have for some time been under consideration, a considerable sum of money having been subscribed for these purposes; but in respect of these matters there seems to be a lack of unanimity, and, judging by newspaper reports, a disposition on the part of some of those concerned to make the money the nucleus of a fund for the erection of an entirely new Hospital on the most approved principles.

Since the Hospital was established in 1851 its management has undergone several changes. Dr. Williams, a city practitioner, was its first medical officer, by appointment of Sir George Grey ; but after a short period of service he was succeeded by Dr. Hulme in the capacity of Provincial Surgeon, which position the latter gentleman held up to his death in 1876. A visiting committee was also appointed in the first years, and that system of inspection was continued until the transference of the Hospital to King street; whilst independently of the visiting committee, the successive Superintendents of the Province ever took a direct and active interest in the institution's welfare. The control of the Hospital, however, was in the hands of Dr. Hulme. In 1863, owing to the tremendous increase in the number of patients, and with the view of relieving Dr. Hulme of the great responsibility attaching to the general affairs of the institution, the experiment was tried of entrusting the general management to a Superintendent; but it did not give satisfaction. In lieu of an independent Superintendent, therefore, a Secretary was appointed, and, with that officer resident in the Hospital, the control reverted to Dr. Hulme. Mr. Marcus Hume was the Secretary then placed in office; and in the year 1876 he was succeeded by Mr. Burns, now in charge, and under whom the principal improvements in the building and grounds have been carried out. Another change occurred in 1876, when the Hospital, with all other Provincial Government Institutions, passed into the hands of the General Government, who appointed a managing committee, of which Mr. A. C. Strode was for several years chairman ; and upon that gentleman's retirement and removal to England, he was succeeded by Mr. Henry Houghton, who, after devoting in the course of the years much of his time to the interests of the institution, still holds that honourable position. A further change took place in 1885, when the Hospitals and Charitable Aid Act was passed, and since then the Hospital has been in charge of Trustees, annually elected by voluntary subscribers to the institution, and by the contributing bodies within the Hospital district. Prior to the passing of the Act of 1885, patients from all parts of Otago were freely admitted ; but as the Act makes each district responsible for its own poor, payment for invalids received into the City Hospital from outside districts must now be guaranteed.

There has also from the first been great fluctuation in the number of inmates. While for over two years after the Hospital was opened not one sick person sought for admission, in the years 1862-3, when large additions were made to the building, the wards were filled to overflowing. In 1866, the year of removal from the Octagon to King street, the number fell to 124 ; but several years afterwards, when free immigration was in full swing, another enormous increase necessitated the addition of two large temporary wards in the annexe, and the conversion of small rooms in the main building into sick chambers, and even then every bed in the Hospital was occupied. Now, however, one hundred is the daily average. This reduction in the number of inmates is of great advantage to the Hospital, not only on the score of economy, but chiefly on sanitary grounds, as it enables the authorities to keep two wards in turn empty, which, while unoccupied, are throughout their length and breadth and height cleansed and disinfected and repainted. By this system the Hospital is kept in as thorough a state of purity as it possibly can be.

Until within recent years the Hospital was from force of circumstances made in part to serve the purpose of a home for incurables. As there was no place for the accommodation of such unfortunates, they had to be retained as patients, and in the course of the years their numbers increased considerably. This inconvenience, however, was obviated by the erection of the Old Men's Home at Caversham, to which the hopelessly infirm and disabled were gradually transferred, and the institution in King steeet is now wholly what it was intended to be—a curative establishment.

The Hospital stands in the centre of a block of five acres, and on each side are extensive, well-laid-out gardens, with gravelled walks and abundance of seats. The one on the south side is the exercise ground for such of the male patients as are not confined to the wards ; the other on the north side being reserved for female patients. A portion of the latter also forms the playground of the young people in the children's wards. Besides the comfortable seats under the shade of the trees, wheel-chairs are provided for those who are unable to walk, but whose condition permits them to go out into the open air and sunlight.

Among the Hospital facilities for the comfort of the physically
suffering is a covered-in ambulance, with bed on rollers and seat
accommodation for an attendant.   This vehicle is available in the
case of accidents or for prostrated invalids coming from distant parts
of the city or suburbs, or from the railway station ; a telephonic
or telegraphic message to the institution being the only notice
requisite to ensure its being sent where required.

A good many years ago, the opening of a public dispensary
in Dunedin was contemplated ; but the necessity for such an
institution was obviated by the establishment of the Out-door
Consulting Department as a branch of the Hospital work.   At
first the House Surgeon was the only out-door consulting doctor ;
but now cases of a general nature receive his attention, while as
experts, Dr. Batchelor attends to diseases peculiar to women,
Dr. John Macdonald to diseases of the skin, Dr. Lindo Ferguson
to eye, ear, and throat complaints, and Dr. de Zouche to the
ailments of children.   This charity is of great advantage to such
of the sick poor as can remain in their own homes ; but as it
was much abused by persons in fair-to-do circumstances availing
themselves of it, all applicants must now, to the satisfaction of
the authorities, certify to their inability to pay for medical
advice and medicine.

While in the aggregate those who in the course of the year
receive gratuitous out-door advice far exceed the in-patients in
number, the out-door branch of the Hospital work is, of course,
the least important.   The real work lies in the wards; all the
in-patients being under the care of an Honorary Medical and
Surgical Staff of nine gentlemen elected annually, with the
addition of the resident House Surgeon and his assistant.   This
system, which ensures careful consultation and all proper
treatment in serious and intricate cases, has with good results been in
operation since 1876.   The gentlemen constituting the present
Honorary Staff are: Drs. Batchelor, Lindo Ferguson, J. Macdonald,
Maunsell, Coughtrey, Gordon Macdonald, Jeffcoat, and Ogston.
Recently another honorary office was created by the election
of Dr. William Brown to the position of Honorary Consulting Surgeon in connection with the Hospital, he having,
when he retired in 1888, been senior member of the Honorary
Staff.

While in the early days the Hospital was placed under the control of Dr. Hulme as Provincial Surgeon, he had under him a House Surgeon, in the person of Dr. Yates (recently deceased), who held office until the year of Provincial abolition. Since Dr. Yates's retirement the House Surgeonship has been held successively by Drs. Tighe (who died while in the service), Roberts, Davis, again Roberts, Fleming, Barclay, and Copland. The last-named gentleman is now in office, in conjunction with Dr. Earnest E. Fooks. Dr. John Brown, recently retired, held the position of dispenser for over twenty years, and that duty is now discharged by Mr. Frederick Akhurst. Mrs. Jessie Reid was the first matron, she being succeeded in 1877 by Mrs. Burton, now in office. Mr. S. Smith, afterwards minister of Port Chalmers Congregational Church, was the first chaplain to the Hospital; and Mr. J. A. Torrance, after 21 years' services, now holds that office. Recently, the Anglican Church in Dunedin appointed the Rev. W. Ronaldson to visit patients connected with that persuasion. For several years Father Moreau, a gentleman universally respected, discharged the duties of Roman Catholic chaplain, and since his retirement the work has been carried on by the reverend gentlemen connected with that church in Dunedin.

THE LUNATIC ASYLUM.

Insanity too soon manifested itself in the young settlement of Otago, and it is a remarkable fact that this, the worst of all the ills that flesh is heir to, first appealed to the sympathies of the people and engaged the attention of the authorities. As stated in the previous sketch (that of the Hospital), when the Province was only two years old it was humanely determined to establish an Hospital, in anticipation of physical disease or injury, but it may be taken for granted that the possibility of mental disease appearing—or, at all events, so soon appearing— in their midst, was entirely foreign to the thoughts of the early settlers. The Hospital, as a place for the physically sick, however, was premature by two years, but it was fortunately in existence, and, in the first instance, it served the purpose of a Lunatic Asylum. Before two years elapsed after its erection it became the home of three insane persons, under the care of Mr. Barr.

This question of insanity has all along been a serious one to Otago, and indeed to the whole of New Zealand, not because this kind of malady has prevailed here more than in other places, but because of the shameful extent to which weak-minded and mentally impaired persons have been deported from the Home country by their relatives or others, and shunted on to the colony. Even now, notwithstanding the mortality that in the course of nature has taken place in the Asylum, there are friendless men and women who arrived long years ago, and who still bid fair to live for many years. As a matter of fact, the inmates of the Asylum live long. They are well housed, well fed, well clothed, are kept scrupulously clean, generally speaking they are free from care and worry, they are not subject to the risks connected with free life—the risks of accident or of disease by infection or exposure or excess, the work done by those of them who are capable of any service is of a healthful kind, and the careful nursing of the sick and really suffering is all that could be desired, and beyond what the outside world is aware of. In a word, all that makes up daily life in the asylum tends to long life, and, as a rule, death is the result of old age, or epilepsy, or other disease originating in the brain. All this is as it ought to be in the case of hapless beings who, from whatever cause, have been deprived of their reason; but it is nevertheless matter for regret that a prohibitive law was not from the first put in force that would have prevented heartless people in the Home country from freeing themselves of family burdens at the expense of the Province or of the colony—not to speak of the cruelty of ruthlessly sending the weak-minded or mentally afflicted away from all family connections and home associations to the extreme ends of the earth for the mere selfish purpose of getting rid of them. Taking into account the number of those who from time to time have been cast as helpless burdens upon our shores, and the cost of their maintenance throughout all the years, the expense so wrongfully imposed upon the colony must in the aggregate have been very great.

As time went by the three unfortunates located in the Hospital were added to, and in 1862 the number of insane men and women held in restraint was between twenty and thirty. A few were domiciled in the gaol, but most of them were in the

Hospital. There are citizens of that time still to the fore who will remember the entertainment given by a Frenchman, an insane inmate of the Hospital. He was an excellent vocalist and had a superb voice of great volume, and was wont daily to walk the grounds and ring out his melodies in his own language to the pleasure of passers by. The unsuitability of both the Hospital and the Gaol, however, and the impossibility of ensuring in these places the proper treatment of the mentally afflicted, forced the question of the establishment of a Lunatic Asylum upon the authorities, and it was decided to erect a temporary home on the ground now occupied by the Boys' High School, the intention being to build the Asylum proper on the site at Look-out Point, upon which the Industrial School now stands.

The first Asylum, or rather the nucleus of the first Asylum, was an unpretentious one-storied wooden building. Dr. Hulme, in his capacity of Provincial Surgeon, was its first medical attendant, and Mr. and Mrs. Robert Drysdale the first keeper and matron, but a year afterwards they were succeeded by Mr. and Mrs. James Hume, and to Mr. Hume was given the title of Superintendent. During his eighteen years' service the Asylum was extended to the right and to the left and far backward on to the Town Belt. The site chosen for the temporary Asylum consisted of eight or nine acres, minus the portion of the Belt encroached upon, and it was added to by the purchase of the adjoining property (one acre) of the late Mr. George Smith, with the building upon it called Park House. In the latter paying patients were located. With the exception of the Park House block, the ground was a wild and rough waste, and it was only by dint of eighteen years' steady, plodding labour that it was brought into the condition in which the Boys' High School authorities found it when they placed the school there.

Though a layman, Mr. Hume, who from his youth had acquired an extensive experience among the insane in the Home country, was well fitted for the work entrusted to him. He retired in 1882, when the Lunacy Act then passed made it imperative that large asylums should be under the control of Resident Medical Superintendents. Under his rule the institution grew piecemeal until it reached the dimensions it assumed at the

time of its removal to Seacliff, the great increase in the number
of patients to over 300 being unquestionably, in large part at
least, due to the free immigration system, or, rather, to
unscrupulous immigration agents, who, for the sake of the £1
per head, recklessly sent crowds of human beings out from the
Home country, without any regard to their fitness mentally,
physically, or morally.

The work accomplished by the patients while in the Asylum
in the city was considerable. Under the direction of competent
warders they levelled the very broken ground, for the
most part erected from time to time the additional buildings
required, and formed the large cricket and football park, now
partly used by the High School boys and partly by the public.
The formation of that flat necessitated the removal of a hill
fourteen feet high and the filling up of deep gullies. They also
formed a 2-acre garden and a large bowling-green, the first
ever made in Otago. By them the road leading past the old
cemetery to the top of the hill, which was in a very dangerous
condition, was put in order and strongly and securely fenced,
this work being suggested by the destruction of a horse and
vehicle, which rolled from the road into the great gully below.
That fence still remains. In addition to these and other works
of a public nature, the patients formed the road leading from
the Town Belt to Melrose, in connection with which there were
some heavy excavations, and in recognition of this service the
residents of that township generously imported from Melbourne
and presented to the Asylum a billiard-table costing £120. That
table is now in use at Seacliff.

In common with other Provincial institutions, the Lunatic
Asylum passed into the hands of the General Government in 1876,
when the Provinces were abolished; and just about that time
Dr. Hulme died, after twenty years' service. Dr. Hulme was
then succeeded by Dr. Alexander, and subsequently Dr.
Macgregor, now Inspector-General of asylums and hospitals,
was appointed to that office. After holding the position of
Matron for three years, Mrs Hume died while in the service, and
she was succeeded by Miss Ferguson, who retired in 1882 to
assume the matronship of Ashburn Private Asylum, established
by Mr Hume (in conjunction with Dr. Alexander), when he was

superseded by the appointment of a resident medical superintendent.

The reserve at Look-out Point, which, as already stated, was the first position determined upon for a permanent Lunatic Asylum, having been given over to the Industrial School, the Government had to cast about for some other suitable place. It was no doubt desired that the Asylum should be within easy reach of the city, but to that the high price to which land had attained was a bar. A better site for a home for the insane can scarcely be conceived of than the high table-land in the Waikari district overlooking the city, bay, and ocean beach. But the existence of the reserve at Seacliff settled the matter, and of that reserve 500 acres were allotted to the Asylum, and the remaining 400 set apart for the Industrial School and an intended Reformatory, the latter on the lines of the Redhill institution, near Birmingham, founded by the brothers George and Charles Sturge, of the Society of Friends. As, however, the removal of the Industrial School to a place so far distant from Dunedin has been strongly opposed by an influential section of the citizens, and as with the growth of the colony the inmates of the Asylum are bound to still further increase in number, it is not at all improbable that the whole of the 900 acres will eventually fall to the institution now on the ground.

When the Seacliff Reserve was decided upon as the site of the permanent Asylum, a working party of fourteen men was sent out in August, 1878, to prepare the way. They were located in a house quickly run up on a knoll at the south-east corner of the Reserve. Shortly after beginning operations they came upon the remains of a large Moa, which were handed over to Professor Hutton, then in charge of the Museum. The main trunk railway line running past Seacliff was not then opened, and the Reserve was a dense, trackless forest. In this connection mention may be made of an amusing incident. One day, before a break had been made in the bush, Mr. Hume and Mr. Alexander Cairns, who had been appointed Inspector of Works, visited Seacliff to examine the ground, with the view of forming a general idea as to suitable positions for the several buildings. The desirability of possessing themselves of a pocket compass, however, did not occur to them, and the day was close and sultry. They entered the bush at a spot nearly opposite the railway station, with the purpose of traversing it right through to the further end. For over three hours the two gentlemen, who were by no means of light build, forced their way through the prickly scrub and tangled lawyers, and over fallen trees, and across and through marshes, and then, exhausted and out of breath and drenched with perspiration, to their relief, but with a feeling the reverse of that of exquisite satisfaction, they emerged from the labyrinth, only to discover that they were not more than thirty yards from the spot at which they had entered!

Shortly after the first party began work in the bush, what is now known as the Upper Building, and which was intended to be the farm steading, was erected by Mr. Mills, contractor, then of Waikouaiti, under the inspectorship of Mr. Cairns, of Dunedin. Upon the completion of this building in 1879, it gave accommodation to a second party of 60 males and a number of females, with their attendants. The Seacliff section of the institution was then termed the Branch Asylum, and from the first it was placed in charge of Mr. John Macdonald as manager, and Mrs. Macdonald as deputy-matron. In the following year (1880) another building, to accommodate a third party of 60 men, and so constructed that it could be taken down in blocks and be put together again in the form of cottages for warders, was erected by the patients, under the direction of Mr. David Reid, carpenter, who is still in the service.

No one can form from the present appearance of the surroundings of Seacliff Asylum anything like a correct idea of the condition of the place when, and for a long time after, Mr. Macdonald took charge, and of the severe nature of the work that devolved upon him and his fellow pioneers. The Reserve, as already stated, was a dense, trackless forest, and the bush had to be felled, and the trees and scrub removed, roads made, water-courses formed, and the ground grubbed. As no road metal was available, in winter and in wet weather the grounds around the buildings were a veritable Slough of Despond, and, for about four years, in the rainy seasons the only means of access on the public road was a corduroy path formed of rough logs, and extending for about half-a-mile. All this is changed. Firm metalled and gravelled paths are now the rule, well-laid-out gardens have been formed, many acres have been brought under cultivation, and with all that is yet to be achieved, the work of the institution can be proceeded with with comfort. Mr. Macdonald, who with his co-labourers bore the heat and burden of the day, is, after the long period of 25 years' good service, still connected with the institution.

The main building, which can accommodate 500 patients and 50 of a staff, was commenced in 1879, and its erection occupied three years. Mr. R. A. Lawson was the architect, and Mr. J. Gore the builder. In architectural design it is said to partake somewhat of the form of Balmoral Castle, and its cost, all told, including the meat-house and laundry (separate buildings), attendants' cottages, the reservoir, &c., exceeded £100,000. It is 568 feet in length, by 228 in width at the broadest part, and the tower, in which there is sufficient space for a clock, and a large circular opening on each of the four sides for the dials, is 160 feet high. The spaces for the dials, 11 feet in diameter, are of course at present boarded up. In front the building rises three stories, and in the back part two stories. As seen from the Heads, or the Ocean, or the Waitati Cliffs, it is a very prominent land-mark. The Recreation Hall, which is also used for Divine service, and is capable of accommodating between 800 and 900 persons, has a large stage at one end, and a tastefully-formed gallery at the other end. The principal stage-drop is a fine view of Dumbarton Castle from the sea, the work of Mr. Willis, the well-known scenic artist. The dining hall, equal in size to and directly under the recreation hall, is a handsome room. The large day-rooms throughout the Asylum are carpeted or matted, as far as possible a homely appearance is given to them, the walls are profusely hung with pictures, and strong padlocked screens securely fixed in front of the fireplaces effectually protect the patients from fire. From the windows of the rooms on the second and third stories a magnificent view of the Heads and of the Ocean out to the horizon is obtainable. The airing courts are large, and each has a verandah running the whole length to shield from rain or from the sun's heat, while in the centre of each is a large, circular flower-plot. The Medical Superintendent's quarters are still in

DUNEDIN FROM THE JUNCTION.

the main building; but it was from the first intended that his residence should be on the knoll at the south-east corner of the estate, on which stood the small house erected by the first working party sent out.

For a time a good deal of anxiety was occasioned by the shifting of a portion of the northern end of the building, caused by the moveable nature of the ground. The faulty portion, however, has lately been taken down and re-erected of lighter material, and it is believed all danger of further damage is now at an end.

As already stated, the upper building first erected was intended to be the farm steading, while the second one put up by the patients was meant for temporary use. But they still serve as dormitories, the steading being now on another and more easily accessible part of the ground. Among other recent additions is a well-advanced handsome block of workshops, formed of bluestone, and which will do away with the frail shed-like structures that have for a number of years done duty.

While the institution at Seacliff is understood to be the asylum for the insane within the Otago and Southland districts, among its 500 inmates are patients from northern asylums, parties having on two or three occasions been sent south to relieve the over-crowded condition of these lesser asylums. In respect of their insane, Otago and Southland are no doubt on a par with other parts of New Zealand. But there seems to be an impression, at least among some of the public, that the number of the insane in the colony, as compared with the same unfortunate class in the Home Country, is unduly large. As a matter of fact, in proportion to the population, and as gauged by the number of inmates of our asylums, insanity in New Zealand is less prevalent than in the Home Country. While that in itself speaks well for the colony, the fact already alluded to must be borne in mind—viz., that many of our asylum inmates, though sane when they arrived in the colony, were, from their mental calibre, unfitted for colonial life—men and women who, if they had remained in their homes and with their friends, and continued in their easy-going mode of life, with all its old familiar surroundings, might (and in most instances at least would) have got on well enough in a way; but landing here among strangers

and placed in the midst of forceful conditions of life such as they
had never been accustomed to, and with the necessity laid upon
them to rely upon their own resources, they earlier or later broke
down under a pressure too great for them. Indulgence in
intoxicants is rightly said to be a large factor among the causes
of insanity, but it is not unreasonable to assume that in the first
instance the hard struggle for existence and the nomadic, com-
fortless life in which many homeless and friendless men in the
colony have been involved, leads to that intemperance which
completes the mental wreck. Even now, after the lapse of the
years that have intervened since free immigration ceased, the
number of men absolutely adrift in the colony is appalling, and
in many instances they find their way into asylums, where they
are cared for, or prematurely and as strangers end their lives in
the hospitals or benevolent institutions, with none of their kith or
kin present to cheer them in their last days and hours, and with
no one save the Chaplain or other minister to follow their remains
to the cemetery. If during the operation of the immigration
scheme something like a proper system of selection had been
adopted, many of the unsuitable persons brought to the colony
would have been allowed to remain at Home, to their own and
the colony's advantage. Still further, it has to be borne in
mind that many of our asylum inmates, such as epileptics and
silly, useless, but harmless creatures, would not in the Home
country be ranked as lunatics or be placed in asylums. To a
large extent they are retained in their homes, and when they
cannot be managed or maintained by their own relatives, the
poor-house becomes their home, and they consequently do not
appear on the lunacy list. Here, however, many such are committed to our asylums and rank as insane. All things considered,
therefore, in the matter of insanity New Zealand compares
favourably with the British Isles.

Reference has already been made to the change Seacliff
estate has undergone since the pick and the grub-hoe were first
brought to bear upon it. In addition to the extensive gardens,
and lawns, and paths, and water-courses that have been formed,
a very large portion of the forest has been cleared, and the many
acres under cultivation are steadily increasing in number.
Ornamental trees here and there dot the ground, and long belts

of such trees, which in time will be extended, line the south-easterly end. It is pleasant to see on Sundays groups of female patients, in their attire for the day, premenading the tastefully laid out plain in front of the main building, with the far-reaching landscape and seascape before them, or lolling enjoyably on the lawn, or, with book in hand, quietly seated on the rests. From the centre of this lawn a high flagstaff rises. In the general work of the institution and in the clearing and cultivation of the land, a large number of the patients are daily employed, not by compulsion, but by kindly inducement. Apart from the parties of males engaged in the fields, and the women serving in the laundry, kitchen, &c., all directly under the eye of male and female officers respectively, there are men who, in various kinds of asylum labour, and without any surveillance beyond that of the general superintendency, work to good purpose. Yet if they were out in the world on their own account, they would not only be aimless and useless members of society, but in some instances be dangerous to themselves and others. The regularity also, and the precision and efficiency, with which some of them attend to their respective charges are really amazing. While there are drawbacks unavoidably arising from the congregating of so many of the insane in one establishment, there is nothing connected with Seacliff Asylum to justify the common expression, " the horrors of a lunatic asylum." It is a home, as far as such a large institution of the kind can be made a home, where everything possible is done for the welfare and recovery of the unfortunate people on whose account it exists.

Dr. Neill was the first medical superintendent appointed. When he took office the asylum was in a divided condition—partly in Dunedin and partly at Seacliff, and under him the final transference took place. Upon his retirement he was succeeded by Dr. T. R. King; and upon that gentleman's removal to Auckland Dr. Truby King, the present superintendent, took charge. There have also at different periods been five assistant doctors: Drs. Elliott, Nelson, Macandrew, Money, and Jeffreys. There is no assistant now, and the charge wholly devolves upon Dr. Truby King. Mr. F. R. Chapman is the local inspector, and Mr. J. P. Maitland the official visitor. Mrs. Huston succeeded Miss Ferguson as matron, and that office is now held by Mrs. Grundy.

Mr. S. Smith was the first chaplain, and since 1868 that post has been filled by Mr. J. A. Torrance.

NOTE.—In the foregoing sketch reference is made (page 225) to the formation by the Asylum patients of the large Football and Cricket Park adjoining the Boy's High School, and which necessitated the removal of a hill 14 feet in height. As a matter of history, it deserves to be noted that on that hill were located the barracks of the soldiers, sent from Auckland on account of the rush of population into Otago, caused by the discovery of the goldfields. At that time Mr. St. John Branigan was engaged in the arduous work of organising the Police Force; but as his arrangements were not sufficiently advanced to ensure the preservation of peace and order, a detachment of the Imperial troops, stationed at Auckland, was sent to Dunedin by request of Sir John Richardson, the then Superintendent of the Province. So soon as Mr. Branigan's department reached the point of full working order, the military were withdrawn, and the buildings vacated by them were used in the additions made to the Asylum, but the house occupied by Major Ryan, who commanded the troops, still exists, and is now the residence of Mr. Weldon, Inspector of Police.

ASHBURN PRIVATE LUNATIC ASYLUM.

This useful Institution is the only one of the kind in New Zealand, and it is for the whole Colony. It is situated in the Waikari District, some two miles in a south-westerly direction from the outskirts of Dunedin. It is a lovely spot, and there is nothing in the cheery-looking block of buildings and picturesque surroundings to suggest the idea of a home for the insane. That it is the residence of some retired gentleman in very comfortable circumstances, is more likely to be the conclusion of any onlooker ignorant of its purpose. It was established in 1882 by Mr. James Hume and Dr. Alexander, upon the retirement of the former gentleman from the Superintendency of the Dunedin Lunatic Asylum. It is managed by Mr. Hume, who has had more than 43 years' experience of Asylum work in the Home Country and in the Colony, while Miss Ferguson, previously Matron of the Government Institution, presides over the female division, and Dr. Alexander is the medical attendant. It is licensed under the Lunacy Act, and is subject to the rigid inspection of the Inspector-General of Asylums, who visits when he thinks fit, and examines the patients, and also the buildings in all their parts, and the books, &c., and reports to the Government. It is also visited by Mr. F. R. Chapman, the local inspector, and Mr. J. P. Maitland, the official visitor, and, though a private undertaking, it is, in common with the general asylums of the country, subject to all the provisions of the Act.

Ashburn Hall has accommodation for 40 patients—22 on the male side, and 18 on the female side, and at present it has 33 inmates. Since it was opened, on October 23rd, 1882, there have been 122 admissions, and last year (1888) the discharges equalled the admissions. In important respects it differs from the Government Asylums. There are no airing courts, no high palisades, and no locked doors or gates, those who can be trusted being allowed freely to go out and in and to roam over the grounds, while patients who require surveillance are accompanied by attendants; and attached to the institution is a comfortable waggonette, in which on fine days the inmates are taken out for drives. Every endeavour is also made to interest the patients in some kind of healthful recreation or employment, in-door and out-door, instead of them being allowed to wander about in absolute idleness; and thereby their attention is drawn away from their own troubles, and their thoughts turned into rational channels, and sleep induced, and, it may be added, recovery facilitated. Altogether, the buildings, the arrangements, and the surroundings, are in a marked degree adapted to the mentally afflicted. In the nature of things, public asylums cannot provide such advantages as are ensured at this institution. With reference to this the Inspector-General, in his report to the Government, dated April 16, 1888, says:—" It is becoming more and more evident that at present the Government cannot undertake to provide separate wards, specially furnished, and having special attendants and other advantages, for such persons who are able to pay a sufficient price. In Seacliff the attempt had been made for some years to provide, by means of special attendants, for persons whose friends were willing to pay for them; but it was found impossible to make any real difference in their treatment and surroundings, and there were so many indirect evil results to the organisation of the staff, that the efforts had to be abandoned. Ashburn Hall is admirably adapted and managed with a view to provide for all such cases; and as long as the Government Asylums are compelled to over-crowd their wards with poor and helpless people, and cannot even find proper accommodation for them, persons who can afford it, ought, if they require exceptional treatment, to be sent to a Private Asylum."

Ashburn estate consists of 94 acres. With the exception of the level part immediately around the buildings, most of the property is slightly undulating, but the hilly part on the north side rises to a considerable height, and the natural bush on that slope has an exceedingly beautiful effect. A large proportion of the estate is under cultivation, the produce being consumed in the establishment. The pleasure grounds, with upper and lower garden and orchard, are extensive and tastefully planted with ornamental trees and shrubs; the paths and avenues are well gravelled and lined with flower-plots; comfortable seats are stationed in all directions; and the lawn-tennis court, bowling-green, and skittle alley (now in course of formation) are at the free use of the inmates. Facing the entrance to the grounds is an extensive up-raised lawn and terrace, with balustrade in old English style of the time of Queen Anne, and on the lawn a fountain is shortly to be placed. In the centre of a lower lawn fronting the terrace a high flagstaff has recently been erected, and arrangements are now being made to illumine the place by means of electric light placed at the cross-trees of the flagstaff, and in connection with the electric light a water-mill of 12 horse-power, used for cutting chaff, &c., is to be utilised. From the Asylum buildings an expansive view is obtainable, including the Peninsula and Ocean Beach and the ocean beyond.

The estate derives its name from the Ashburn stream, which runs through it. On the higher ground the stream flows into two ponds, in which the trout sport and leap, and then the water sweeps in cascade form down to the flat, the ever-rushing sound being far from unpleasant. The water is also led to the building in sufficient abundance to supply all the requirements of the establishment, and the force is sufficiently strong to bring the water to bear, by means of the hose, on to the highest parts of

the buildings in such an emergency as fire. In addition to a
plentiful supply of fire-hose, fixed fire-escapes are so placed that
the building can be emptied of their inmates in two or three
minutes.

Inside the buildings, as outside, there is really nothing, apart
from the eccentricities of the occupants of the rooms, to indicate
that Ashburn Hall is a home for the insane. As has already been
said, altogether it has the appearance of a country seat, of which
comfort and refinement are the chief characteristics, and
with a home farm attached to it. This Asylum, it should be
added, is also designed for the accommodation and treatment of
dipsomaniacs.

It deserves to be noted that the spiritual interests of the
inmates of Ashburn Hall are not overlooked. The Rev. R. R. M.
Sutherland, of Kaikorai, holds the office of chaplain, and by him
services are conducted and visits made.

THE FEMALE REFUGE.

From the nature of the work of this useful institution, and
the class of persons it befriends, all details connected with it
cannot well be minutely stated or enlarged upon. For that
reason its committee of ladies have from the first quietly and
unostentatiously, but steadily and nobly, laboured on "without
observation," not seeking the praise of men, but the good of
those for whose well-being they banded themselves together.
It was opened on the 3rd of June, 1873, and from that day to
the present time many young women and girls have for longer
or shorter periods, and with varying results, availed themselves
of its shelter; and now, after eighteen long years of such labour,
it is gratifying to find the chairman of the Charitable Aid Board
publicly saying, as late as November 21st of the present year
(1889), "that the Female Refuge is self-supporting; that he is
of opinion the endeavours of the ladies in connection with the
management are deserving of the highest praise; and that he
hopes they will be stimulated to still further efforts for the good
of the inmates." For twelve years the Refuge was maintained
by public subscriptions, a subsidy from the Government, and
the proceeds of the laundry work of the inmates, but since the
passing of the Charitable Aid Act in, 1885 it has been under the

wing of, and (as far as was requisite) been supported by, the Charitable Aid Board. The Home, capable of accommodating twenty inmates comfortably, is situated on the highest part of Forth street, has a half-acre of ground attached to it, and commands a fine view of the upper part of the bay, the Peninsula, and the Pacific Ocean beyond. The records of this institution form very sad and depressing reading. Notes of all who in the course of years have been inmates have been carefully kept—properly, short biographical sketches, faithfully noting failure when there is failure, and modestly noting success when there is success. Many of these sketches end disappointingly, some very sorrowfully, while here and there gratifying examples of recovery to a permanent better life are cited. The Hon. Mrs. Holmes, Mrs. Chapman (widow of the late judge), and other ladies, have from the first, or in the course of the years, been identified with this truly philanthropic and Christ-like agency, and in its noble work Miss McDougall (now laid aside by illness) and the late Miss Lambton took a very active part. There is good reason for the earnest hope that Miss Morrow, the present matron, will long hold office, as in her the young women and girls under her care have a wise and sympathising friend, who spares no effort to help them out of the sea of trouble into which indiscretion has led them.

THE DUNEDIN WOMEN'S CHRISTIAN TEMPERANCE UNION.

This institution was formed in May, 1885, and was the outcome of a visit from Mrs. Leavitt, the world's missionary from the American Women's Christian Temperance Union, and who was sent out to form unions and branch-unions wherever possible. Its object is the total suppression of the liquor traffic, and to that end its committee of ladies strive to influence Parliament by petitions, by helping at elections to return men favourable to the prohibition cause, and in all possible ways to arrest intemperance. Its place of meeting is a large building named Leavitt House, at the foot of Albany street. The building also serves the purpose of a boarding-house for females who desire privacy and quiet; but it is mainly, and to good purpose, used for gospel temperance work, and for juvenile free educational classes of various kinds. These comprise male and female night classes for instruction in special school subjects (see Dr. Hislop's article on "Education"), and industrial classes for both sexes—the boys being under the superintendence of Mrs. George MacKenzie, of Leith street, and the girls under the direction of Mrs. James Miller, of Athol Place. At the industrial classes the girls are taught plain and fancy sewing, the boys are exercised in carpentry and cabinet work, and both boys and girls are instructed in all sorts of useful ornamental work, such as leather, cork, and shell picture frames brackets, flower-baskets, &c., &c. In the course of the weeks and months the articles are stored up, and periodically a bazaar is held, at which they are displayed for inspection and sale, and a remarkably good and enchanting display they make. Not only do the lads and girls receive the money realised by their own labour, but prizes are also given to those who excel in the different branches of industry; and in connection with all the work engaged in, the minds of the young people are persistently, and in all interesting ways, imbued with religious and temperance principles. When it is stated that the great majority of the boys and girls thus taken in hand would otherwise spend their evenings in idleness or in horse-play on the streets, it will readily be understood that the ennobling influence brought to bear upon them, and the benefits conferred upon them, cannot be over-estimated. So far the ladies of the Christian Temperance Union, and especially Mesdames McKenzie and Miller and their assistants, have had their reward. Numbers of boys and girls possessing force of character and ability, and full of animal spirits, and who for want of friendly control and guidance were in danger of drifting into wild and dangerous courses, have had hoir interest onlisted in the work of the classes, and their better nature brought into active exercise, with gratifying results.

But there are other branches of the Union's work. The Sailors' Rest, at the wharf end of Rattray street, is one. It is a fine building, and in it good reading matter and refreshments are supplied—the former gratis, and the latter at moderate prices— and all seamen in port are free to spend their leisure hours and transact their business (such as letter-writing, &c.) in the comfortable rooms provided for them. The rooms are also used on the Sabbath evenings for religious services, and all the affairs of the "Rest" are under the direction of a sub-committee of ladies.

The Tahuna Park Temperance Refreshment Tent is another branch of the Union's work. Annually the Agricultural Show is held in this Park, and for the sake of exhibitors and visitors good temperance refreshments are provided—it is said with very satisfactory results.

The most recent development is that of the Young Women's branch, known as the "Ys" (an American term of abreviation) who have made themselves felt by their successful effort to establish a Cabmen's Shelter. It is situated on the eastern side of the Cargill Monument, in Custom House Square, and in it good refreshments are supplied at moderate terms.

The membership of the Union numbers (November, 1889) 150, and its chief officers are Mrs. J. Fulton, Hon. Mrs. T. Dick, and Miss Glasgow—President, Secretary, and Treasurer respectively. The "Ys" have a membership of about 50, and are presided over by Mrs. Sawell, junr.

DUNEDIN YOUNG WOMEN'S CHRISTIAN ASSOCIATION.

This institution is linked with the name of the late Rev. Dr. Sommerville, of Glasgow, and, like many other useful organisations, it had a small beginning in the shape of a suggestion casually thrown out by that gentleman on the occasion of his evangelistic visit to Dunedin in the year 1878. The suggestion was received with approval, and steps were promptly taken to carry it into effect. To avoid mistakes likely to arise from inexperience, and to ensure a sound basis, it was deemed advisable to obtain the services of a lady possessing a practical knowledge of the working of such societies, and to that end Miss Thomson, (now Mrs. W. Downie Stewart,) then resident in Melbourne, was invited to visit Dunedin, and give the promoters the benefit of her experience. The arrangements were soon brought to a successful ssue, and the Dunedin Young Women's Christian Association was established on the 2nd of August, 1878. The late Rev. Lindsay Mackie, minister of the First Church, manifested a deep interest in it from its formation, and to him it is indebted for much practical sympathy and counsel. The late Mrs. John Bathgate was its first President, and she continued an earnest supporter till her death. Upon its first Board of Management other influential ladies had a place—Mrs. (Rev.) Upton Davies, now in England; Mrs. (Rev.) Lorenzo Moore, now in Nelson; Miss Jarrett, now in America; Mrs. Coombes, now in another part of New Zealand; Miss Lambton, now deceased; and Mrs. Blackadder, who is still one of the Association's most earnest workers. Recently an effort was made to establish a "Lambton Library" in connection with the Association, in commemoration of Miss Lambton's long years of philanthropic labours in the city.

The Association was opened in Queen's Buildings, Princes street, but a month later it was removed to rooms in Rattray street, where for ten years it did good work, and towards the close of the year 1888 it took possession of the fine building in Moray Place formerly owned by the Young Men's Association. Its object is to benefit young women of all classes, and generally to engage in Christian effort. Its stated organisations comprise: the coffee, tea, and luncheon room for young women in business (last month, October, 1889, the number who availed themselves of it reached to 1,934—a goodly number for one month, certainly); the hospital weekly flower mission, much appreciated by the patients, and in connection with which, illustrated Scripture cards and leaflets are distributed, and words of cheer given; a Sunday Bible class; members' meeting for Bible study; mothers' meeting; a fortnightly social meeting for young women; and a fully equipped mission Sunday school, under the superintendence of Mr. D. R. Eunson. During the years of assisted immigration, a sub-committee was told off regularly to visit the Immigration Barracks to befriend the new arrivals generally, and to render all needed assistance by counsel and practical aid to friendless girls. In this department of its work the Association rendered service of the highest importance and value to many young strangers. It also during two periods employed female missionaries, or Bible women—Miss Nevison (now in Scotland) and Miss Campbell—but lack of funds necessitated the relinquishment of this branch of work. By its removal to the premises in Moray Place its work has been increased in every department, and its expenses proportionately. Still, with its membership of 267, financially it is in the satisfactory condition of being self-supporting; and when the efforts of the Board of Management to clear off its debt of £500 (already reduced from £600) are crowned with success, it will be free to extend its sphere of usefulness, and to resume the female missionary work in the city. As a society quietly and effectively, but unobtrusively, working for good, it deserves well of the people.

THE KINDERGARTEN ASSOCIATION.

This is the youngest of the Philanthropic Institutions of Dunedin, and its formation dates back only to the middle of the present year (1889.) There was room for it, as the children for whose welfare it operates were not embraced in the aims of the organisations already in existence. No doubt, the Kindergarten system of education, so successful in many other places, would sooner or later have been in operation here, but as a matter of fact its introduction into Dunedin is due to the accidental circumstance of Mr. Mark Cohen having, in the course of last year, received a communication on the subject from Mrs. Sarah Cooper, the foundress of the system in San Francisco. Mr. Cohen readily enlisted the sympathy of the Rev. Rutherford Waddell, and through that gentleman the warm interest of Mrs. W. H. Reynolds was secured. That lady, with her characteristic energy, perused the literature on the subject; and having satisfied herself as to the merits of the system, she accepted the responsibility of initiating the movement in Dunedin. She was joined in the effort by a number of ladies, several of whom had had large experience in teaching the young; and Sir R. Stout, Mr. James Allen, M.H.R., Dr. Wm. Brown, the Rev. A. C. Yorke, the Rev. James Gibb, and other gentlemen, gave earnest support. Advantage was then taken of the presence in the city of Sir W. Fox, who, by request, gave an address on the working of the Auckland Association; and in February of this year a public meeting was held in the Town Hall, at which, with other gentlemen, Bishop Suter, now the Anglican Primate, spoke favourably of the system as he had seen it in operation in America. Curiously enough, the Bishop, previous to his visit to the States, was strongly opposed to the system, but what he saw in the course of his travels converted him to it. Subsequently, Mr. W. S. Fitzgerald, Rector of the Normal School, also delivered a lecture on the subject to the Dunedin branch of the Schoolmasters' Association. The result was the establishment of the Dunedin Kindergarten Society on thoroughly unsectarian principles. After casting about for a suitable field in which to begin operations, the promoters decided upon the neighbourhood of Walker street; and the Rev. Mr. Waddell and Rev. Mr. Yorke having offered the free use of their school-rooms, Walker street Mission House (Mr Waddell's) was accepted. On the 10th of June the Kindergarten School was opened with 14 children, and now, after six months' quiet and steady working, about 60 are on the roll. The object is first to gather in children of six years and under, the offspring of poor parents, and whose mothers, in many instances, are out at work during the day to earn the necessaries of life for their families; and, secondly, to instruct the little ones in all interesting ways adapted to their tender age. The method adopted may be characterised as systematic play, and it comprises object lessons, marching, keeping time with feet, hands, and voice, singing, training of the memory without cramming, drawing, woolwork, &c. The discipline is, of course, strict, but kindly and winning. Samples of the work done by the young people are now on view in the Industrial Department of the Exhibition, and it is marvellously good, and said to be quite equal to that accomplished in the like schools of the northern cities, The value of this training, as compared with the baneful influence of days spent without restraint or guidance on the street, and as a preparation for ordinary school work when school age is reached, cannot be over-estimated. Admission is free, and the children are supplied with pinafores while in school. Miss Wienicke, who has had a large experience of Kindergarten Schools in Germany, is head teacher, and she has three assistants. The school, however, is managed by a Committee of ladies, who have the support of an influental Finance Committee of gentlemen. Mrs. W. H. Reynolds is President of the Association; the Vice-Presidents are Mrs. Belcher, Mrs. A. S. Paterson, and Miss Bathgate; Mrs Marsden Smith is Treasurer; and the offices of Secretary and Assistant-Secretary are held by Misses Kelsey and F. Wimperis respectively. Though the work is entirely dependent on voluntary contributions, the success which

has attended the Walker street School, and the generous support
given by friends, have determined the Committee to establish
similar schools in other parts of the city as soon as practicable.

A BRIEF REVIEW OF THE LEADING INDUSTRIES OF DUNEDIN.

By Westley Overton.

F the early settlers of Otago—the "Pilgrim Fathers" of Dunedin—who arrived at Port Chalmers in the "John Wickliff" and the "Philip Laing," could have taken a peep into futurity and viewed our fair city of Dunedin to-day, with her numerous white buildings glittering amongst her verdant hills, and girdled around by her magnificent emerald "Belt," they well might have exclaimed, "Can such things ever be?"

In those early days of the settlement every man, if he intended to become prosperous, required to make himself a kind of "Jack of all trades." He was compelled to understand a little of bush carpentering, be competent to build a sod chimney, and be able to manufacture his own furniture, before he could make himself even tolerably comfortable in his hut. He, or his wife, if he was blessed with one, would have to repair all the clothes, and also put a patch on a boot when necessary, or he would probably find himself bare-footed.

Many other little offices, which are so much more conveniently arranged in the Dunedin of the present day had all to be performed as "home industries" in those early days, when a pig-hunter's hut was the only building where High street now runs, and the waves of the Bay washed over the present site of the Colonial Bank. And yet that time is less than fifty years ago. A man need not have arrived at the threescore and ten years of the Psalmist to have a recollection of that period.

Since then the various industries of Dunedin have advanced not only by strides but by leaps and bounds. In some of the large industrial centres of the mother country they profess to manufacture everything, "from a needle to an anchor." Dunedin cannot yet go quite so far as that. She can, however, produce most necessary domestic articles, and a great number of what may be considered luxuries.

To the discovery of gold Dunedin owes in a great measure its rapid growth. Although gold-mining is not an actual city industry, still it has had a great effect on Dunedin, and has given a great stimulus to its commercial life. Not only are large quantities of mining plant manufactured here, but numbers of the miners visit the city at regular intervals, more especially in winter, when the mining is suspended, which tends to cause a circulation of cash, and is of great benefit to the citizens.

In order that the majority of the manufacturing industries may thrive, it is absolutely necessary, so long as steam is the motive power, that a good supply of fuel should be available. In this matter Dunedin is exceptionally favoured. Within a reasonable distance of the city there are numerous mines from which the requisite quantity of coal and lignite can be obtained. These mines are situated at Green Island, Kaitangata, Shag Point, and other places. They are generally worked by drives into the sides of the hills, and not by sinking a perpendicular shaft, as is usual in the coal-pits of Great Britain.

An excellent bituminous coal is also brought round from the West Coast by the Union Steam Shipping Company's regular line of vessels. To the use of this first-class steam-coal the engineer of the "Calliope" attributed the splendid work of the engines of that vessel, when she made her memorable escape from destruction off the coast of Samoa, whilst the American and German vessels were wrecked. A still further supply of coal is obtained regularly from Newcastle, N. S. Wales. Dunedin has therefore an ample supply of fuel.

In addition to quite a small fleet of coasting vessels owned in Dunedin, the city has the advantage of being the head quarters of the Union Steam Shipping Company, and by this means has convenient water communication with the whole habitable globe.

It is impossible in a brief review like the present to do little more than mention the names of the principal makers and one or two articles of their manufacture. An alphabetical order of trades and names will be adhered to as much as possible.

AERATED WATERS, ETC.

During the hot and dusty weather a refreshing draught of some cool non-intoxicant is very welcome, and to meet this requirement the manufacture of aërated waters and cordials is one of Dunedin's industries. During the summer months the demand for these articles is very great. All descriptions of cordials, &c., are manufactured. Messrs Thomson & Co. (Police street), Messrs Lane & Co. (Maclaggan street), Messrs Bennett & Son (Great King street), and Mr J. D. Feraud (Maclaggan street), are all engaged in this industry.

BREWERIES.

A country labourer on being told that the beer at the village inn was bad, replied: "Noa, noa, there be no bad beer: some on it be better than t'other, but there beant none on it bad!" So far as Dunedin beer is concerned, the foregoing opinion might be correctly applied. Whether the water of Dunedin is specially adapted for brewing—as is supposed to be the case at famous beery Burton—or whether the manipulation of the ingredients is better understood, there is at all events something about Dunedin beer which makes it a favourite tipple from the Bay of Islands to the Bluff. Among the breweries of Dunedin the City Brewery, owned by Messrs Speight & Co., has of late years taken the leading place. From comparatively small beginnings they have gradually crept up to the front rank, and their new premises lately erected in Rattray street contain one of the most complete and extensive plants in the colony. Mr Maurice Joel, Messrs McGavin & Co., The Dunedin Brewery Co., Mrs Strachan's Trustees, and Mr S. R. Briggs (of Caversham), also carry on an extensive brewing and malting business.

BONE MILLS, ETC.

A very useful industry is that carried on by Mr J. Durston at his Bone, Oil, and Tallow Mills at the Kaikoria, where what would otherwise be waste material is converted into valuable articles of commerce. The whole establishment being kept in such a state of cleanliness that the slightest offence possible is given to the sense of smell.

The Chemical Works of the New Zealand Drug Company (Messrs Kempthorne, Prosser & Co., Limited) at Burnside are an extensive block of buildings with large yards, and are provided with the most approved appliances for the manufacture of the various products. These consist of sulphuric acid, bone manures, tallow, oil, acetic acid, and other articles of a kindred nature. The works have been established for some years, and are continually being enlarged to meet the requirements of the increasing demand for the manufactures.

BRUSHES.

The manufacture of the various kinds of brushes is a very interesting and important industry, carried on by Mr A. C. Broad in his factory in St. Andrew street. The whole process is completed on the premises; a portion of the labour, which is of a light nature, being performed by females.

BASKET-MAKING.

One of the useful minor industries is basket-making and other kinds of wicker-working. There are three establishments for producing articles of this description. Two of these in Princes street south, and the other in George street.

BEE-HIVES, ETC.

In a country where flowers of some description are in bloom the whole year round, keeping bees will always prove profitable. The wants of bee-keepers for necessary shelter for the insects are provided for by Mr T. G. Brickell of Bath street, who, in connection with his other business, is a manufacturer of bee-hives.

BISCUITS, CONFECTIONERY, PRESERVES, ETC., ETC.

When Mr George Augustus Sala, the veteran correspondent of the London *Daily Telegraph*, visited New Zealand some years ago, he mentioned in one of his letters something to the effect "that New Zealand was a land of jam, and that he never sat down to a meal without finding jam on the table." This was certainly as much a compliment to the country as the old-time Biblical expression of "a land flowing with milk and honey." One of our great "home industries" is the annual "fruit preserving." Every thrifty housewife lays in a good stock of the toothsome article for the winter season.

In addition to this we have biscuit factories which are also engaged in the manufacture of confectionery and the preparation and potting of preserved fruits, not only for sale in our own country, but also for exportation over the civilised globe. New

Zealand jam is well-known and appreciated in the British Islands, and in all places to which it finds its way.

The principal firms who carry on various branches of this "sweet and luscious" industry are Messrs. R. Hudson & Co. (Moray Place), The St. George Jam Factory (Messrs. Irvine and Stevenson, George street), Messrs. Peacock & Co. (Jam Factory, Moray Place), and the Phœnix Company (Maclaggan street).

The Phœnix Company are also manufacturers of all descriptions of biscuits and confectionery, whilst Messrs. R. Hudson and Co. in addition produce various kinds of chocolate, chocolate creams, and cocoa. This industry has made rapid strides during the last few years, the out-put of cocoa, chocolate, &c., promising to be shortly sufficient for the local requirements, and the quality of the articles manufactured being quite equal to those imported from Europe. Messrs R. Hudson & Co. have also a flour mill working on the same premises.

BLACKING.

Blacking for boots although a humble is a very useful domestic necessary. The manufacture of this article is carried on by Messrs R. Anderson & Co., Moray Place. Their brand the "Raven" being well known.

The Bellows Company, South Dunedin, are starch manufacturers, and combine with it also the preparation of blacking, ink, gold paint, &c.

BOAT-BUILDING.

The harbour of Dunedin being a fine sheet of water and well sheltered from stormy winds, renders a sail or row a very pleasant recreation during the summer months. A demand for boats and yachts has naturally induced several boat-builders to establish themselves in convenient localities. Their work-shops and yards are distributed at intervals along the shores of the bar, where boats can be hired by either the hour or day.

BOOT AND SHOE MANUFACTORIES.

The manufacture of boots and shoes is a very prosperous industry in Dunedin and suburbs. There are a number of boot factories of varying sizes, where every description of boots, shoes, and slippers for great and small, and old and young, are being continually manufactured. Hundreds of work-people—both male and female—are employed in this industry.

In the space available, it is only possible to give the names
of the principal firms, viz.—Messrs. W. H. Burrows and Co,
Stafford street ; Messrs. A. and T. Inglis, George street ; Messrs.
McKinley and Son, Hillside ; Mr. F. T. Roughton, Manse street ;
Messrs. Sargood, Son and Ewen on the reclaimed ground behind
the Railway station, where they have lately erected a new
building of great extent, with all modern improvements ; Messrs.
Simon Bros.' Beehive Factory, Bath street ; Mr. H. Shelton,
Great King street.

BRICKMAKING.

Since it is not permitted to erect any wooden buildings in
the principal business portion of the city, the manufacture of
bricks has naturally become an important industry. Brick-
making is carried on by Messrs. C. and A. Shiel, Caversham ; and
Messrs. Smith and Fotheringham have a brickyard at Hillside,
where however, work has been discontinued at present. There
are also several other brickyards in the district.

The bricks are usually made by machinery, which will turn
out many thousands of bricks daily, and require but little labour.

CARDBOARD BOX MANUFACTORIES.

This is essentially an industry suitable to female workers,
and is carried on by Mr. T. J. Treacy at the Dunedin Cardboard
Box Manufactory in Cumberland street. Great quantities of
boxes are made yearly. Mr. T. G. Brickell also combines this
industry with his other pursuits in Bath street.

CEMENT MANUFACTORIES.

Till within the last few years all cement required for use in
the colony had to be imported. Mr. James McDonald, of Vogel
street, however, after carefully experimenting, ascertained the
exact quantities of local material, which, when combined, would
produce an excellent quality of cement.

This manufacture is now carried on by Mr. McDonald himself, and also by the Milburn Lime and Cement Co.

COACH BUILDERS, ETC.

An exceedingly well represented industry in Dunedin is that
of coach and carriage building. The show rooms of the various
firms are a credit to the artistic taste of the proprietors. Every
description of vehicle may be obtained, from the magnificent
chariot to the humble but useful express, or from the four-horse

drag to the farmer's light cart or hay waggon. The show rooms are well worthy of a visit; the workmanship and brilliancy of finish being quite equal to anything to be met with in either the Old World or America.

The principal carriage builders are :—Mr. Mark Sinclair, Great King street ; Messrs. Hordern, Brayshaw, and White, Princes street south ; Mr. J. Mathews, Great King street ; Messrs. Robin and Co., Octagon ; Messrs. J. and W. Stewart, Great King street ; whilst considerable work in the heavy waggon and dray making is done by Mr. A. G. Watson, Princes street south.

CLOTHING.

Since the time that Adam prepared the first primitive garments for himself and Eve, clothing has taken up a great deal of attention amongst their descendants.

Dunedin and the neighbourhood are not behind in these civilised requirements.

In the first place there are two woollen mills.

The Roslyn Worsted and Woollen Mills are owned by Messrs Ross and Glendining, the well known firm whose city premises are a handsome block of buildings situated in Stafford street. The Mills at Roslyn are complete in every respect, provided with all modern appliances, are lighted by electricity, and the products will compare favourably with any manufactures that are placed on the market. A great variety of goods are produced here ; amongst others are tweeds, coatings, crimean shirtings, serges, flannels, blankets, shawls, travelling rugs, hosiery, &c., &c.

Messrs Ross and Glendining have also a clothing factory, the building for which was specially erected in Stafford street, where the various materials manufactured at the mills are made up into clothing. Altogether, the firm employ several hundreds of work-people, amongst whom are a large proportion of females.

Another mill is known as the Mosgiel Woollen Factory, and is situated in the town from which it derives its name. It is owned by a company ; the shareholders in which have found it a very remunerative investment. The building is both substantial and commodious. It is lighted by electricity, and everything about the premises is of the most modern and improved construction. The manufactures are well known all over the colony, and are always admitted to be unexcelled in quality. They comprise almost every kind of material, of which wool forms the component part. Between three hundred and four hundred people are employed in this industry, about half of whom are females.

Besides the clothing factory mentioned previously, there are several others in Dunedin. The largest is the New Zealand Clothing factory (Messrs. Hallenstein Bros., proprietors.) The factory is a large and substantial building situated in Dowling street. The whole establishment is excellently fitted up, not only for the due execution of the work, but also for the convenience and comfort of the workpeople. A special feature in the business of this firm, is that instead of supplying the general retailers, they have retail branches of their own in nearly every town of importance in the colony, and sell direct to the public at factory prices.

The clothing factory of Messrs. Morris and Seelye is situated in the recently erected building at the corner of Princes street and Dowling street. The premises are well adapted for the purpose, and employment is provided for a number of workpeople.

There are two other clothing factories, one owned by Messrs. Innes and Macfarlane in Dowling street, and the other by Messrs. Levy, Guthrie and Co. in Rattray street.

The goods manufactured at these factories are dispatched to all parts of the colony.

Some of the best hands among the female employees are enabled to earn higher wages than labouring men or even the majority of artisans in the British Islands.

There are also several Shirt and Hosiery Factories, which provide employment for a great number of the female population.

The remarks on clothing would be scarcely complete without mention being made of head-gear. The bulk of the hats are imported from Europe. There are, however, a few firms who manufacture this article, amongst whom may be mentioned Mr. Geo. Bertinshaw, George street, Messrs. A. Masters and Co., Princes street, and Mr. J. Muir, Princes street.

In order to show the great progress which has been made in manufacturing industries in Dunedin during the half century, it may be pointed out, that if it was desired, a man could be clothed from head to foot in colonial made garments and also factory made at that.

COFFEE AND SPICES.

The preparation of coffee and spices is also extensively carried on in the city by Messrs. W. Gregg and Co., Princes street ; Messrs. Kearns and Son, Maclaggan street ; and Messrs. W. Whyte and Co., George street.

Some of these preparations are packed in tin canisters for safe conveyance to the outlying districts, whilst quantities are supplied to retailers in bulk.

GAS.

The gas for the illumination of the city is manufactured by the Corporation, the works being under the charge of Mr. D. A. Graham, Gas Engineer. They are situated in Anderson Bay.

The City and Suburban Gas Company, Ld., whose works are situated at Caversham, supply gas to a considerable portion of the suburbs. Mr. William Daley is the Engineer and Manager.

IRON INDUSTRIES.

A great requisite for the promotion of the prosperity of manufacturing industries is machinery, and to make this, iron and steel are necessary. Until within the last few years all this raw material had to be imported. Messrs. Smellie Bros., have however, established iron and steel works at Burnside, fully supplied with modern appliances, where scrap iron is converted into bars. The works are lighted by electricity, so that the production can be continued by night as well as day, should the demand render it necessary.

Dunedin is therefore to a considerable extent independent of the imported article, although a large quantity of the various metals will have to be imported for many years to come until the mineral resources of the colony are thoroughly developed.

The iron industry is well represented in Dunedin. There are mechanical engineers, agricultural machine makers, founders of iron, brass and lead, and nearly every description of metal workers.

A fine building in Moray Place near the First Church, is the factory of Messrs. Anderson and Morrison, who combine with the brass, copper, and lead founding, and plumbing, the electro-plating and other ornamental work ; hydraulic sluicing plant is also amongst their productions, employment being provided for many hands.

Messrs. A. and T. Burt's establishment in Cumberland street is one of the largest in the city. In addition to the industries of founding in various metals, it embraces engineering, plumbing, electro-plating, and manufacture of various decscriptions of electrical apparatus, &c., &c. In fact, the manufactures of this firm are so numerous that it is impossible to give even a brief list of them in the present paper.

The premises of Messrs. Cossens and Black cover a large area in Crawford street, opposite the Exhibition building. This firm make a specialty of windmills for pumping water, draining, &c. They also manufacture various agricultural implements, mining plant, and every description of machinery. Mining plant of their manufacture has been recently supplied for a Hydraulic Sluicing Co. in New South Wales.

The fine coasting steamer "Invercargill" was built for Messrs Ramsay and Sunstrum by Messrs. Kincaid, McQueen and Co., Great King street, who have also turned out about half a dozen other various-sized steam vessels. The massive railway overbridge was erected by the same firm, whilst dredges, gold mining plant, and all descriptions of machinery and ironwork, are amongst their manufactures.

The New Zealand Engineering and Implement Co., Castle street, is well known for the various patent articles it manufactures, a specialty of late being a flax dressing-machine. Dredges, agricultural and other machinery, and all kinds of ironwork are amongst the productions of the company.

Messrs. Reid and Gray, whose extensive premises extend from Crawford into Princes street south, and who have several branches in the towns throughout the Island, in addition to the manufacture of agricultural implements of almost every description, produce a twine Reaper and Binder, which compares favourably with either the British or American manufactures, and is in great request not only in New Zealand, but also in Australia.

Messrs Schlaadt Bros., engineers, Great King street, make a specialty of the manufacture of all kinds of machinery and appliances for the boot trade. They also produce tips and toe plates ; in addition to which they carry on a general engineering trade, for which they have the necessary machinery and appliances.

The works of Mr Joseph Sparrow are situated in Rattray street near the wharf. They are fitted up with all the necessary machinery and appliances to carry on a general engineering and boiler making business, all descriptions of ironwork being manufactured.

The ironwork for the Wingatui Viaduct on the Otago Central Railway, which is one of the finest pieces of work of its kind in New Zealand, was manufactured by Messrs. R. S. Sparrow and Co. of Willis street, and the workmanship does them infinite credit. Dredges, mining plant, machinery, and ironwork of every description, are turned out from the works of this firm, who are also iron-shipbuilders.

Mr. James Mann carries on a general engineering business in compact and convenient premises in Stuart street, where some excellent work is performed.

At Port Chalmers there are also two firms of engineers and iron-shipbuilders, whose names should be included, viz., Messrs. Morgan and Cable and Messrs. Gardner and Young.

The list of engineering works would not be complete without including those of Mr. F. H. Asbury in Castle street, whose name is so well known as the manufacturer of warming and ventilating apparatus and other specialties.

The Victoria foundry of Messrs. Barningham and Co. is situated in George street. This firm is well known for the excellence of their ornamental ironwork and various patterns of ranges and grates. Their " Zealandia " range is a great favourite, and numbers of them are in use in Dunedin and other parts of New Zealand.

Mr. H. E. Shacklock's Range Foundry is a substantially erected building in Crawford street, admirably adapted in every way for the industry. Grates, ornamental railings, and castings of nearly every description are made here. The great specialty is, however, the patent " Orion " Range, which, under the name of the " Shacklock " is as familiar in our ears as household words.

Another foundry is that of Mr. R. Callon at Ravensbourne, whose specialty is malleable castings.

MEAT FREEZING COMPANY.

The New Zealand Refrigerating Coy., Limited have works on the Kaikorai, where large numbers of carcasses are prepared for exportation. This is a very valuable industry to the colony. The company has also works in Oamarn and the offices are in Liverpool street, Dunedin.

NEWSPAPERS.

There are three daily newspapers published in Dunedin, the Otago Daily Times in the morning, and the Evening Herald and Evening Star in the afternoon. The Otago Witness is published weekly in connection with the Daily Times, and the Public Opinion weekly in connection with the Herald.

PAPER MILLS, ETC.

One of the industries that it is surprising to find flourishing in such a comparatively young community, is that of paper making. There are two paper mills in the Otago district.

The Woodhaugh Paper Mill is owned by Messrs. Fergusson and Mitchell of Princes street, and has been rendered as perfect as possible. Here, old rags, ropes, tussocks, or old canvas, are converted into serviceable brown or grey paper, a great quantity of which is made up into paper bags on the premises by the nimble fingers of female workers. Blotting paper of an excellent quality is also produced. Printing paper has been manufactured, but although a capital article, it could not be produced at a saleable price, as against the same description imported.

The Mataura Falls Paper Mills are the property of Messrs Coulls. Culling and Co. of Dunedin. The whole of the machinery and plant is of modern type, and the mills are enabled to turn out paper of first class quality. Paper-bag making by machinery is carried out to a great extent at these mills. The firm's city premises are in Crawford street, Dunedin.

The New Zealand Paper Bag Manufacturing Co. have well-fitted-up premises in Moray Place, with machinery and every facility for turning out well finished paper bags in large quantities.

PIANO MANUFACTORY.

A real article of luxury which can be produced in Dunedin is a piano. Messrs. Oakden and Howell, Octagon, manufacture on their premises instruments, which for richness of tone and chaste, yet at the same time elaborate finish, will compare closely with the imported articles.

POTTERY.

Good drainage is an essential factor in ensuring a healthy locality. The manufacture of drain pipes is an industry of great importance in this direction. It is carried on in connection with other pottery manufactures by Mr. J. H. Lambert, at his Pipe Factory, Kensington.

Mr. G. Jones of Milton and Mr. J. Nelson of Benhar near Stirling are also manufacturers of drain pipes, &c., and both have agents in Dunedin.

There are also pottery works at Milton, owned by Messrs. Graham and Winter, where large quantities of ornamental and domestic ware are produced, which meet with a ready sale. The firm's city offices are in Bond street, Dunedin.

PRINTING AND STATIONERY, ETC.

The printing and manufacturing of stationery is a particularly important industry in Dunedin. Some of the establishments are of large size, and the employés in the trade are very numerous. All branches are represented, and any description of work, both ornamental and useful, can be executed within the limits of the city.

ROPE WORKS.

Messrs. Donaghy and Co.'s rope and twine works are situated in South Dunedin. This industry is of special value to the colony, as the articles that are manufactured are always in demand, more especially the twine for reapers and binders, of which an immense quantity is manufactured during the year. In addition to using the usual materials, viz., manilla, Russian and Italian hemp, a great quantity of the native flax of New Zealand is used for some descriptions of ropes and twines, thus assisting in the development of another local industry.

Mr. William Markham has also rope and twine works in the same locality.

SOAP, CANDLES, ETC.

There is an old saying that " cleanliness is next to godliness," so that the manufacture of soap should be a blessing to the community. This industry is generally combined with other

manufactures, such as candles, glycerine, &c. The principal
works in the neighbourhood are those of Kitchen and Sons,
Green Island; Messrs. McLeod Bros. Ltd., Cumberland street;
Mr. Wm. McLeod, Castle street; and the Queen's Soap Co.,
North-East Valley. There need therefore be no dearth of soap,
candles, &c., in Dunedin.

TANNERIES.

The business of tanning is one of the industries which is
absolutely necessary to provide for the wants of the population.

The tannery of Messrs. Michaelis, Hallenstein and Farquhar
is situated near the line of railway from Dunedin to Port
Chalmers, about 1½ miles from the latter town. It is excellently
fitted up, well provided with water, and gives employment to
from 30 to 40 hands.

Mr. J. W. Coombs is proprietor of a tannery in the North-
East Valley, and there is also one in the same neighbourhood,
owned by Mr. Wm. Parker.

TUB AND BUCKET FACTORY.

Although there are several dairy factories in the district,
none are situated in the immediate neighbourhood of the city
The necessary machinery and appliances are mainly supplied
from Dunedin. One branch of industry in this line, viz., the
manufacture of tubs and buckets, is carried on very extensively
by Messrs. Thomson, Bridger and Co. at their factory in Bond
street. There is also a general timber trade combined with the
factory. A great demand for tubs and buckets exists all the
year round, and the factory is always fully employed.

TIMBER AND WOODWARE.

Woodware factories on a large scale are established in the
city, where all kinds of building materials, such as doors, sashes,
mouldings, &c., are prepared by machinery, which, in addition to
providing employment for a great number of men and boys, is
very convenient for building contractors. They can obtain from
these mills all their requirements, ready prepared for erecting
buildings, and the hard labour thus saved is simply enormous,
not to mention the saving of time, and as the old proverb goes,
" time is always money."

The principal woodware factories are as follows, viz. :—
Messrs. Findlay and Co. Ltd., which comprises a large block of

buildings and yard area between Cumberland, Castle and Stuart streets ; Mr. James Gilmour's yard and factory, Gt. King street; Messrs. R. Greig and Co.'s factory, George street ; Messrs. McCallum and Co.'s, Anderson's Bay Road; and Messrs. A. Tapper and Co.'s, who have recently removed their headquarters from Invercargill to Dunedin, and erected a substantial woodware factory in Crawford street, and laid down plant of the latest type.

In further connection with the manufactures in wood must be mentioned the cabinet makers and large furniture establishments. The various woods of New Zealand give great scope for ornamental cabinet making, and this is taken full advantage of by those interested in the industry. The show-rooms of the various firms will repay a visit, as some of the better class of furniture is quite artistic in design, and finished with great care.

. Amongst other firms may be mentioned Mr. John Gillies, the show-room being in George street, whilst the manufactory is in Great King street ; Messrs. Hooper and Co., show-rooms in the Octagon; Messrs. Scoullar and Chisholm, who have a fine commodious show-room in Maclaggan street, and an extensive factory in Rattray street; Mr. Thomas Stonebridge, whose factory is in Stuart street; Messrs. Thomson and Williamson, in Great King street ; and last, but not least, the extensive cabinet works of Messrs. A. and T. Inglis, in George street.

WIREWORKING.

Wireworking is also one of the industries which thrive in Dunedin ; the manufacture of wire-wove mattresses being a specialty of Mr. Charles Bills, George street, whilst Mr. J. W. Faulkner has erected new works in Castle and Cumberland streets, where he produces all descriptions of wire and ornamental fencing, &c. (wire sheep netting being a specialty).

In addition to the various industries that have been enumerated, there are die sinkers, flock manufacturers, a furrier, fellmongers, monumental masons, sculptors, tinsmiths, engravers, and all the usual trades found in a business city.

This brief and necessarily imperfect review will help to show what a change has taken place in Dunedin during the half-century ; those flourishing industries being now carried on where in those early days referred to there was nothing but a wilderness, a flax swamp, or the placid waters on the bay.

WALKS AND DRIVES.

(The following poem, by Thomas Bracken, descriptive of a scene which no visitor to Dunedin should omit to view, is inserted here as a fitting introduction to the more prosaic description of Dunedin's picturesque surroundings).

DUNEDIN FROM THE BAY.

Go, trav'ler, unto others boast
    Of Venice and of Rome;
Of saintly Mark's majestic pile,
    And Peter's lofty dome;
Of Naples and her trellised bowers;
    Of Rhineland far away:—
These may be grand, but give to me
    Dunedin from the Bay.

A lovely maiden seated in
    A grotto by the shore;
With richest crown of purest green
    That virgin ever wore;
Her snowy breast bedecked with flowers
    And clustering ferns so gay,—
Go, picture this, and then you have
    Dunedin from the Bay.

A fairy, round whose brilliant throne
    Great towering giants stand,
As if impatient to obey
    The dictates of her wand;
Their helmets hidden in the clouds,
    Their sandals in the spray—
Go, picture this, and then you have
    Dunedin from the Bay.

A priestess of the olden time
  (Ere purer rites had birth)
On Nature's altar offering up
  The homage of the earth ;
Surrounded by grim Druids, robed
  In mantles green and grey—
Go, picture this, and then you have
  Dunedin from the Bay.

O never till this breast grows cold
  Can I forget that hour,
As standing on the vessel's deck
  I watched the golden shower
Of yellow beams, that darted
  From the sinking king of day,
And bathéd in a mellow flood
  Dunedin from the Bay.

I.—THE QUEEN'S DRIVE.

Although the civic rulers of Dunedin have not, as yet, done much to enhance the beauties of their city, they have earned the thanks of many an inhabitant and visitor, as they will continue to do so long as the city exists, by affording facilities for admiring the natural beauties with which it is so richly endowed by Nature. The wise forethought of the founders of the settlement in reserving a wide belt round the city as a public park has been supplemented by that of the City Council in forming a road throughout its entire length. This road, which was constructed during the mayoralty of Mr. H. J. Walter, and is known as the Queen's Drive, winds along the face of the hills above the town, and from this vantage ground many of the finest views of Dunedin are obtained. As the stranger first strolls or drives leisurely along its meandering course new beauties are continually displayed. There is a sameness in the prospect, and yet it is never the same. The town is always seen nestling below, with the lake-like harbour and the sunny slopes of the Peninsula beyond ; but each point of view presents these features in some new aspect. The character of the Belt itself is also varied, for while at the north end the road winds through shady groves of native bush, at the south end it leads along the grassy heights, so that the Queen's Drive may lay claim to many and diverse beauties.

II.—THE ROSS CREEK RESERVOIR.

This favourite resort lies to the northward of the town, being situated on a tributary stream to the Water of Leith. The approaches have lost much of the beauty they once possessed in the days gone by, when the valley of the Leith was filled with a forest of dense bush containing many a noble pine and stately tree which have long since disappeared to supply the inhabitants of Dunedin with building material or fuel, and the picturesque outline of the hills alone remains unchanged. Still, when Messrs. Fergusson and Mitchell's paper mill is passed, the visitor to the locality finds himself in a secluded glen which might be miles from "the busy haunts of men." A wide, well-made footpath (beneath which lie the water-pipes for the supply of the city), raised above the creek bed by a retaining wall, leads up this sequestered gully, whose steep sides are clothed with native bush, still the home of many a luxuriant fern, while the streamlet in its stony bed below murmurs on its downward way. Emerging from the narrow glen, which widens suddenly at the site of the reservoir, the visitor finds a pretty little sheet of water spread before him, and though here also the woodman's axe has been at work and denuded the surrounding slopes of their covering of bush, there is compensation in the fact that the sides of Flagstaff and other neighbouring hills are more exposed to view. If a longer walk be desired it can be obtained with much pleasing variety of scene by proceeding along the side of the reservoir, and after passing the head of the smaller upper basin a road is reached, and from this point the visitor may regain the Leith Valley by a longer way than that by which he came, or he may make his way home by crossing the upper end of the Kaikorai Valley and reaching town by way of the pleasant township of Maori Hill.

III.—FLAGSTAFF.

Anyone who can enjoy a mountain ramble, should, if he has not already done so, climb to the summit of Flagstaff Hill, which rises behind Dunedin to the height of 2192 feet, and from whose top an extensive view over the surrounding country can be

obtained. There are two routes by which this can be accomplished ; one by way of the Halfway Bush up the south-eastern
spur over the open ground, and the other by a steep path through
the bush from Ross Creek, which leads on to the open land on
the north-eastern shoulder, whence the top is most easily reached
by making a detour to the northward. To anyone unacquainted
with the country who desires to go one way and return by the
other, the ascent by the Ross Creek track is recommended, as the
way down by the other route is easily found, but it is not so easy
to discover the opening of the bush track ; indeed, persons who
have ascended by that path and who were not blessed with what
is known as a "good bump of locality," have often failed to find the
track again, and have in despair taken to the bush and made
the descent at the expense of great exertion and torn clothes in
scrambling downwards through the thick undergrowth, a process
not unattended by personal danger. Choosing then the route
by Ross Creek, and leaving roads and habitations below, the
climber enters the bush a little way beyond the furthest dwelling.
The ascent is steep, and after rainy weather somewhat muddy
and trampled into holes by the cattle, but a stick to assist in the
climb is easily procurable, and there is much to please and
attract the eye in the bush vegetation, which may afford an
excuse for frequent stoppages to admire these beauties of nature
more closely. Shortly after entering the bush, by turning aside
to the left a few yards, a glimpse may be had of a pretty little
waterfall, pretty in itself, but which derives its main beauty from
its surroundings, for the little stream comes tumbling down the
mountain side overshadowed by embowering trees, whilst ferns
of innumerable form and shade deck the banks with a mantle of
green. It is a temptation to linger in such a spot, but the goal
is afar. Returning to the track and climbing steadily upwards,
only stopping now and again ostensibly to admire some fairy moss,
lovely fern, or other sylvan beauty, but possibly really to gain a
few minutes breathing space, the climber at length emerges on
the open land beyond. After a short rest on some grassy knoll
the upward way is resumed, and keeping well to the right and
circling round the hill top to avoid encountering some rough
stony ground, the summit is reached by an easy climb. A
glorious prospect over hill, dale, and ocean is the reward. To

the northward the prospect is limited by Swampy Hill and Mount Cargill, but turning to the eastward an extensive view is obtained of the lower lying hills about Dunedin and over the Otago Peninsula, with the wide Pacific stretching away beyond. Turning further round, the Green Island uplands, the Chain Hills, and those of Otakia district meet the eye, with glimpses of the lowlands between, while the dark wood-crowned summit of Saddle Hill stands out conspicuously against the sea and sky beyond. Away in the south may be seen the distant coast-line and the hazy forms of the South Molyneux ranges. Looking over the Taieri the bulky form of Maungatua looms large, beyond which lies the rounded top of the Lammerlaw. Further round again to the westward the long range of the Rock and Pillar mountain appears, with possibly patches of snow in its hollows, and if the day be clear the summit of distant Mount St Bathans and the Old Man or Umbrella Ranges, may be descried, whilst some long-sighted mortals say they have even seen the far-off peaks of the rugged Remarkables. Leaving these distant mountains the eye completes the circuit by resting on the grey rocky pinnacles of the Silver Peaks, and the bush-clad gullies of the Silverstream and its tributaries. By proceeding a little way down the mountain a more extensive view of the Taieri Plain is obtained, which lies at the feet of the observer like a gigantic irregularly marked chess board with its squares of varied colours, and the gleam of the sunbeams on the Waihola and Waipori lakes may be seen in the distance. The lover of such fair scenes will linger long revelling in the grand panorama by which he is encircled. But the descent must be made, so choosing that by way of the Halfway Bush and keeping well to the right along the leading spur, he rapidly descends the grassy slopes till he joins the North Taieri road near Ashburn Hall, whence by the Halfway Bush and Roslyn he makes his way back to town, tired probably, but certainly pleased with his excursion.

IV.—MOUNT CARGILL.

Another pleasant mountain expedition, though not such a favourite with the people of Dunedin as the ascent of Flagstaff, is the climb to the top of Mount Cargill, which lies to the north of the town and rises to a slightly greater elevation than its

companion hill, it being 2292 feet high.   Formerly, this hill, with
its nearer buttress, known as Pine Hill were covered with dense,
unbroken forest, composed chiefly of large pines intermingled
with leafy trees of lowlier stature, beneath whose shade luxuriant
ferns of all sizes and many species, from the lofty, wide-spreading
tree fern to the tiniest of the filmy ferns, found a congenial
habitation. But now, alas, fire and the axe have wrought
havoc with sylvan beauty, and the slopes of Pine Hill and
Mount Cargill now furnish sites for the home of many an
industrious settler, which is doubtless some compensation for
the loss of beauty they have sustained.   Even the small patches
and clumps of bush which remain have suffered much from the
inroads of vagrant cattle, so that the side of the hill next to
Dunedin at least, which was once the happy hunting ground of
the fern collector, is now, in his eyes at least, a desecrated
paradise.   One mode of reaching the summit of Mount Cargill
is by the road to Blueskin, from which, after a steep climb
through the bush, the summit is gained ; but the more generally
adopted route is by way of Pine Hill.   Taking the road leading
up the hill which leaves the North-East Valley Road at the
junction of that valley with that of the Water of Leith, and
following it steadily upwards, the pedestrian eventually reaches
a point where an old survey line, now a cattle track, diverges to
the right along the face of the hill. After following this for
some way a sharp turn to the left is taken, and a stiff climb
through the now burnt bush brings the climber to the rocky
summit. The prospect is in some respects similar to that from
Flagstaff, though such features of the landscape as are visible
from both localities are now seen from a different point of view.
The main difference, however, is in the view northwards, which
from Flagstaff was shut out by the intervening hills.   From
this point a view of the coast stretching away to the north is
obtained, with the hills lying in the same direction, such as
Puketapu, the conical Hill, which rises above Palmerston, and the
more distant Horse Range, over which appear the peaks of the
Kakanui Mountains. The foreground is very different from
anything seen from Flagstaff, as at the feet of the spectator lies
a large tract of still comparatively unbroken forest which covers
the slope of the mountain down to the head waters of the Leith

and Waitati streams.   The pedestrian in returning may clamber down to the Blueskin Road, or, if more adventurous still, find his way into the Valley of the Leith; but the more prudent course would be to return by the way he came, enjoying as he does so the prospect of the fair city of Dunedin from the many favourable points of view passed in the descent.

V.—THE PENINSULA.

One of the pleasantest drives in the neighbourhood of Dunedin is that down the Peninsula.   Let us suppose we are off in a tip-top turn out from one of the best livery stables in Dunedin, spanking horses, a splendid drag, exhilarating atmosphere, roads first-class, spirits up to the highest pitch that health, choice company, glorious scenery, and a determination to be happy, could raise them to, for anyone would be a moody individual indeed, who refused to be satisfied in such circumstances. As we leave town and pass by Anderson's Bay Road, along the harbour side, the foreshore, if the tide be out, will indicate what a considerable portion of the site of Dunedin at one time was—a mud flat.   This unattractive waste is a part of the Harbour Board endowment, and in a few years hence it will be all reclaimed, let at big rents, and occupied by a busy population.

Stepping out briskly along the fine level Anderson's Bay Road, the gallant steeds bring their freight to the first rising ground, known in older days as Goat Hill, now studded with a number of residences, occupied by leading citizens, among whom may be noted Mr. Justice Williams and the Crown Solicitor, Mr. Haggitt; a little further on, the town residence of the Hon. Matthew Holmes is passed. Passing through the village or hamlet of the " Bay " the stiff pull up to Shiel Hill is accomplished, and here the grand panorama begins to open up to the ravished vision.   No pen can describe the infinite and varied beauties spread around.   They must be seen to be known and felt.   Poet Burns, in describing the gowan, fell considerably short of the reality when he said so exquisitely to the

> Wee modest, crimson-tipped flower,
>
> *   *   *   *   *
>
> There, in thy scanty mantle clad,
> Thy snowy bosom sunward spread,
> Thou lifts thy unassuming head
>   In humble guise.

And how much more difficult our task to describe the sempi-
ternal beauties of this favoured locality?

Immediately beneath on the left the placid waters of the
harbour lie sleeping in drowsiness, sinuously wending their
course along through and among sandbanks and rocky isles, bluff
headlands and receding bays, until absorbed in the great
Pacific they cease to be recognised. Away to the right the
majestic ocean spreads, its limitless bosom wide open to the gaze,
so that far as the eye can reach any object on its surface can be
descried.

Lot's wife was turned into a pillar of salt because she looked
behind her at the city which she had left, but no such risk is
incurred by looking back from the peninsula hills on the fair
city of Dunedin. And perhaps from this point of view she is
seen in her widest extent if not in her best display. Looked at
from almost any point, however, the remark of inhabitants of Old
Edinburgh regarding their fair city, that " she's a bonny toon,"
holds good.

The city itself with all its surroundings can hardly be
surpassed anywhere for exceeding beauty. Whilst halting to
look behind, the attention will be attracted by the coast-line to
the south, which can on a clear day be discerned as far as the
Nuggets, south of the Clutha, on which one of those beacon
lights has been erected to guide the mariner along the frowning
coastline.

And now in front of us the northern seaboard as far as
Oamaru can with a good field glass be traced. A curiously
indented coastline it is. Rounding Purehurehu and Hayward's
Points, the furthest out stretch of the land on the north
entrance to the harbour, lies Kaikai, or Murdering Beach, of
which a ghastly story, as the name indicates, could be told. The
coast here is hidden from our point of view by Mihiwaka and
other heights. The land recedes from old ocean's embrace,
again to project at Kaiweka, or in our less euphonious language,
Potato Point, again to enfold the old sea-king in her bosom as
far as Otokoroa and Parintaha, jostling him out again round the
shore of Purakanui Bay and at Mapotahi, fantastically exhibiting
itself at the erstwhile dreaded cliffs, around which the North
line of railway sweeps along, allowing of a passing glimpse of

the restless billows and foam in which Neptune delights to revel
—immediately afterwards giving way so that the shallow basin
named Blueskin Bay, receives the waters of the Orokonui,
Waitati, and Whatiripuku Creeks. We pass in rapid succession
Te Awakoa, Te Akaipaoa (Green Point), and Te Pahawea
(Yellow Bluff), until Waikouaiti Harbour is reached, which, if
justice had been done in the estimation of the residents, would
be the best harbour in the Province. To dilate on all the
points of interest which jut out before us from the point of vantage
which we occupy would, take too much space; suffice it then
that we briefly enumerate the headlands, receding bays,
outlying reefs, and other notabilia which the eye and through
the glass can be descried, looming away to the north. Passing
Tumai and Pleasant River, Bobby's Head is easily distinguished..
Nearest beyond is Shag Point, and then comes Moeraki with its
associate point and sands and reefs, on which the wash can easily
be seen. Otopopo, noted for its Waianakarua River, troublesome
in early days, a short distance ahead Aorere Point, indicating
under its lea a good boat harbour, and then the Kakanui, where
works were erected to supply one half the world with preserved
meats, till Cape Wanbrow with its light tells that the limits of our
vision and of the Province terminates in Oamaru, our fair
northern town.

Whilst the pen could long be occupied in faintly describing
the many attractions of the distant scene, the visitor's attention is
naturally attracted by places and objects nearer at hand. Well,
be it known that we are now at High Cliff, about half-way
on the road to Portobello, and that this name High Cliff has been
bestowed because on the right hand side, down towards the
ocean, a barrier to the roll of the waters of the modest height of
800 feet stands guard against further encroachment. A perpendicular wall eight hundred feet high is not to be met with every
day, but it is not visible from the road, so in our next journey
a little further information will be given concerning it.

Immediately in front stands the "camp" home of our
genial friend and representative of the district, the Hon. W. J..
M. Larnach, C.M.G., who has done more for the district than
any other hundred men in it. To visitors this commanding seat
has always been open, and so far as the laird himself is concerned

he neither regrets nor begrudges his hospitality. The camp, or as some folk persist in calling it, Larnach's Castle, against the owner's wish, is a little off the main road, but the well-used line to it would at once indicate the position even although no " Scotch neebours were near, frae whom you could speer."

Down past the first dairy factory started in the Province our steeds gallantly carry us along, just giving time for a peep to the right and to the left of picturesque scenes such as are rarely to be met with. There is the hill called Harbour Cove, or Sugar Loaf, standing sentry, with old Captain Leslie still steady on the look out, and inviting the digger to set in and exhume the precious treasures it possesses, and for the accomplishment of which considerable labour and money have already been profitlessly laid out. But enough of that, we are not gold but pleasure seekers, and arriving at Portobello, if the hampers with their contents of good cheer have been omitted, there is the hotel, where Mrs. Coneys will supply food and drink for man and beast at the most reasonable of costs.

And now sufficiently refreshed we strike across the narrow neck in the centre of the Peninsula and at an easy distance reach Hooper's Inlet, or it may be Papanui, according as the driver or driven may select, and going at an easy pace reach the Cape Saunders Lighthouse, where the intelligent and obliging keepers will describe the whole surroundings, not garnished with the fables old Pilot Driver was wont to relate. A few hours well spent on this detour, the ride is continued from the last starting point down from the Maori Kaik to Taiaroa Head. Let us, however, pause a moment or two on the nether side of the Kaik.

Not far distant lies the sepulture spot of the Native race, where rest the remains of many of the heroes of olden times, and over several of whom a grateful country has erected enduring mementoes, bearing suitable inscriptions. Transcribing a few, the fore front must be given the father of the present chief, G. G. Taiaroa, Esq., M.L.A.

In Memory of
TAIAROA,
Of the Ngaitahu tribe, and of the Katimohi Family,
A great Chief of the Southern Island of New
Zealand.

He died 2nd February, 1863, aged about 80 years.
His direction of his people was eminently good, and his attachment
to the Queen's rule was great.

———

In Memory of
NGATATA,
Who died in Otago in 1854.
A leading Chief of the Ngatiawa, who welcomed the
Pakeha to Cook's Strait.
He was the father of the Hon. Wi Tako Ngatata, M.L.C.
Erected by the New Zealand Government in honour
of his memory.

———

In Memory of
KARETAI,
A Chief of the Ngaitahu and Ngatimamoe Tribes in
the South Island,
Who died 30th May, 1860, aged 79 years.
Under the shelter of Queen Victoria his conduct to
the people of the Maori and European races
was kind and liberal.

Many others could be given, but the visitor should inspect for
himself, and read the records on the tombstones, whereon, in
highly poetic language, is recorded the devoted loyalty of some of
the old chieftains to the cause of the Queen and the Pakeha, and
which speak nothing but the truth.

Returning to Portobello, and again resting our horses and
refreshing ourselves, we return by the road up the harbour side
to Dunedin. Here the sinuosities of land and sea, while
protracting the journey, add immensely to the interest, as
features of the landscape are revealed from unexpected points,
which otherwise would be withheld. The artistic eye can best
appreciate these unfoldings of beauty which a slight bend or turn
displays, as we move along in contemplative silence. Each
object has its own peculiar attraction. Primitive nature, as
regards its forest clothing, has been destroyed, but in the contour
of the land it is permanent. Different minds will form diverse
opinions, but the original can never be restored.

Leaving Portobello Bay and crossing the narrow neck of land
which still remains, joining Ridley's Peninsula to the mainland,
and which, in some former day, was connected with the
Quarantine Island and Port Chalmers Peninsula, so that the

ancient traveller, if such a one existed, could walk dry-footed from one spot to another, we now swoop merrily along the level road up to Dunoon, thence round Broad Bay and Grassy Point, until reaching Macandrew's Bay, the vista of Dunedin becomes fairly opened up, developing at every sweep some new beauty to admire. A few choice residences only have been built on this the best side of the harbour. Of these, the names of Colinswood, the home where Otago's foremost man (Macandrew) resided ; Glenfalloch, the mansion of G. G. Russell, Esq., a citizen worthy of the highest honours ; and pressing onward, as our nearly forty mile journey is somewhat exhaustive, we pass Anderson's Bay with its many villas, where law-makers, administrators, merchants, and professionals enjoy solace and retirement, if not seclusion, after the busy toil of the day, preparing for the morrow ; and in good time for dinner we reach our hotel in the city.

VI.—THE PENINSULA.
(Continued.)

The Peninsula furnishes another very enjoyable ride or drive, not so long as the previous one and hardly one whit less interesting, as in the first portion new attractions are exposed to view, and in the latter half, sights which, on our former trip, could be seen only by turning round are now a fair prospect lying before us unfolding at every turn something new and impressive.

Starting from the city the line of tramway may be followed to St. Clair, the favourite and health-giving resort of Dunedin citizens when holidays present the opportunity. Not being a very warlike race, and little up in big guns—we are flattered by the high encomiums bestowed on the three fortifications erected along the beach to defend the city from any would-be blackmailer. The visitor can leisurely inspect the St Clair Thunderer, proceed quietly along the sands, provided the tide permits, and inhale the healthful ozone, which the not always balmy breezes waft in towards the passer by, and renew or revive fading energies. Or if old father ocean declines to permit the liberty, there is the road by the racecourse by which the central battery can be inspected, and passing the temporary residence of His Excellency the Governor, onward by Tahuna Park Show

Ground, and the silent spot within whose pale perfect equality
alone obtains, we reach Lawyer's Head, on which the third piece
of ordnance constituting our city defences is placed. The descent
is then made into the Tomahawk Valley with its small lagoon,
once a much more attractive object than now, when it lay
smiling sweetly amid its forest-clad surroundings. Abruptly
rising again over the Tomahawk ridge with its reefs lying half a
mile out in the ocean, the homes of a number of well-to-do old
settlers may be seen scattered on the hills and valleys around.
Then again dropping down gently to sea level in another
valley, an uphill pinch has to be tackled, which, on being
accomplished, we now reach the top of the cliff with a sheer face
of 800 feet, and at whose base the waters are perpetually
surging and lashing, slowly but gradually undermining the solid
wall which has resisted and will for centuries continue to resist
their attacks. From this point a splendid view of the southern coast
can be obtained, whilst immediately in our front lies Seal Point,
with its two digits defying the water sprite, the beach along
Sandy Bay, with the Gull Rocks standing as sentinels a few
yards off, and the Low Rock as outer guard, fully a mile out to
sea. Beyond this point the road along the coast is not yet
formed, so that the excursionest cannot get down to Hooper's
Inlet, but this is unimportant, as very little variety in scenery
here presents itself. We therefore take the road to the centre of
the Peninsula, and pass around groves and glens, where the fancy
can rove at its own sweet pleasure, and the eye be delighted with
glimpses of Nature in her most attractive garb, almost as she
existed when the Pakeha first intruded on her solitude. On
the return journey along the main road into town, many varied
and enchanting views of water, land, and city will be obtained.
The harbour, the hills, and the town show a different phase of
beauty at almost every bend of the very winding road which had
to be followed in order to secure an easy grade. The ardent
wish of every traveller is to renew the visit to the Peninsula
as frequently as opportunity will permit.

VII.—THE TAIERI WILDS.

A trip up the Otago Central Line is one which the visitor
should not omit. · This line has been a bone of contention for a

long period of time. To gain the interior of the Province and open up its vast resources for development, as well as to give the greatest facilities for bringing the products to market, has unquestionably been the aim of all interested. How best to attain this has been the question of difficulty. Several different routes were suggested, all of which had their ardent supporters, who were equally strong in their denunciations of the rival lines.

A Royal Commission decided on the present course, and what Royalty does cannot be wrong. So the traveller, in journeying along in the comfortable carriage must just give rein to his fancy, and in idea form an estimate of how valuable these disturbed hills, glens and chasms would have been for human occupation, had nature only put a sufficiently heavy steam roller over the surface, squeezing down here and filling up there, so that there would be space flat enough on which a man could place the soles of his feet. There are pretty glimpses of crag and river to be gotten which will in the days to come fascinate the artist, but fine views do not fill the purse nor captivate the majority of human kind. As far as opening up land for settlement goes, this line, so far as it has gone, is decidedly the worst of those proposed.

The train after leaving the Main South Railway carries the travellers over a larger extent of splendid agricultural country— across the heart of the Taieri Plain—than either the famed carses of Stirling or Gowrie in the old land contain; and then leaving the flat country and taking to the hills, a winding course is followed, and now and again darkness envelopes, whilst the engine with panting haste passes through four short tunnels, " heighs and howes" occupying the intervening space. Then the Wingatui Viaduct is reached, which holds the reputation of being one of the greatest triumphs of engineering skill in the Southern Hemisphere, and for which Mr. Blair, the Engineer, and his assistants have received every meed of praise.

A journey along this line is strongly recommended, showing as it does the contrast between fertile plains and barren hills.

The Viaduct is, however, an interesting work. It stretches between two ridges of the mountain, and was preferred by the engineer to filling in and embanking, both for durability and safety. The length of the Viaduct is 690 feet, divided into eight spans, the widest of which stretches 106 feet, the others 66 feet The height of the line in the centre from the bed of the creek is 154 feet, and the width of the platform or carriage way is 12 feet 8 inches. The pier at the base has a width of 33 feet. The structure, viewed from the ground around, looks slender indeed, and many timorous passengers would shudder at the thought of crossing it at an ordinary rate of speed, and would be very chary about committing themselves to the experiment of so doing. Strength and durability are not, however, to be estimated by bulk. The secret of success lies in the mathematical accuracy which Mr. Ussher, assistant engineer, has displayed in calculating the strength of the bearing points, the truthfulness and precision with which each part has been put together, and the trustworthiness of the material employed. The total cost of the Viaduct was about £22,500.

The Railway Commissioners now carry their patrons much further on between eminences which, in other countries, would be called mountains, but here, only ridges, along the banks of the river Taieri, once in its day a pellucid water, fit habitat for the trout or any other of the finny tribe, now, alas, a thick " drumlie " current, into which one would hesitate to dip lest he should emerge therefrom with the complexion of a Chinese. The gold diggings, away up in the distant Naseby and Kyeburn Districts, and others nearer hand, have caused this radical change.

Seated in a railway carriage, bearing us onward at 15 miles per hour, sometimes in the open air, at other times momentarily under ground, still wherever the eye can see, there is that accompanying Taieri sluggishly moving along with scarcely a ripple on its turbid surface to indicate that life or vitality existed at all within its bosom.

The railway has not yet reached Middlemarch, the first stopping place in the open strath that lies beyond the rocky gorge, but even had it done so we should not have proceeded further. So returning down the line again we now leave the train at Mullocky Gully, where horses having been previously arranged for, we take to the saddle, and follow the ideal road line (which is neither formed nor fenced in), along the top of the range, where the traveller may revel amid scenes which even Turner's wildest ideals could not surpass. If he has a gun, "the conies among the rocks," the rabbits, will give him sport; but the true lover of Nature in her wildest mood wo uld forget such sport amidst such a scene, wild and desolate in the extreme.

How turbulent must have been the forces which were in operation ages ago to produce such a scene as that on which we now look with calm complacence, and allow fancy to play in tracing verisimilitudes, as we compare these massive overhanging rocks in the words of Burns to "Ruins pendant in the air," or recall the lines in which Hogg, the Ettrick Shepherd, described a scene tame in comparison to what is now spread before us :—

> " What bard could sing the onward sight?
> The piles that frowned, the gulfs that yawned beneath,
> Downward a thousand fathoms from the height,
> Grim as the caverns in the land of death ;
> Like mountains shattered in the Eternal's wrath
> When fiends their banners 'gainst His reign unfurled,
> A grizzly wilderness, a land of scaith,
> Rocks upon rocks in dire confusion hurled,
> A rent and formless mass, the rubbish of a world."

The reach of the Taieri from the Deep Stream to Outram is far and away the bleakest and most desolate of any river stretch we know of on the eastern seaboard of the Province. It will never be fit for anything but the habitation of wild pigs and rabbits.

The Taieri River is the most tortuous and sluggish of streams. From its source to its mouth it wends a weary way over 150 miles, although the crow starting from its source and landing at its confluence with the sea, would not traverse much more than forty miles, provided it took its proverbial straight course.

It is perh aps unnecessary to state that on this journey it is absolutely necessary to dispense with wheels. To traverse this enchanting country perhaps even a horse might be found superfluous, and the individual be confined to his own powers of loco-motion. However, we come safely out on the Strath Taieri Road, and in less than an hour we reach Outram, where we rest and are thankful.

VIII.—OPOHO AND THE BREEDING-PONDS.

For a quiet walk, when time presses not, the visitor to Dunedin could not do better than take the tram-car down to Dundas street and there alighting wend his way across the Leith and up to the Northern Cemetery grounds. To a spot like this, the attractions are very varied in character. Some frequent it to show their lasting devotedness to those who have gone before, others simply to read the records of the past and admire the artistic skill displayed in the attempts to perpetuate the memories of very many who formerly acted their part on this busy stage. To the stranger, the view of the city and its surroundings which is obtained is unsurpassed. Many declare it to be the best to be had from any point. So far as that question is concerned, the answer must be relegated to the observer, whose every reply will be—Beautiful, most beautiful.

Leaving the sacred acre, a pleasant and very enjoyable walk can be had through the Town Belt at the present time, the native manuka being in full bloom, filling the air with delicious perfume, regaling the senses with a profusion of delights. Along this road there are many fine vistas. The elder Kean, on his retreat at Loch Fad, in Buteshire, inscribed the immortal quotation :—

> " Through this loop-hole of retreat
> I gaze upon the world."

And so can the traveller do here. To be appreciated, these peeps must be experienced, and when once beheld, the temptation will be to dwell on them longer than time will permit. So onward our course must be taken to Opoho, a very pleasant place to live in, and where the grounds of the Acclimatization Society are situated. The obliging Curator, Mr. Deans, will be ready, if at home, to show all the curious developments in fish life, from the egg or spawn onward to the matured trout, salmon, perch, or other representative of the finny tribe, and explain the different stages through which they pass, the methods of treatment, the distribution throughout the Province, and the results of all this artificial work. The Opoho grounds were also the source from which the introduced birds, at once the plague and the pleasure of the inhabitants, were liberated and spread over the country to delight the ear with their warbling, contribute to the gastronomic tastes of the wealthy, and make deadly havoc on the fruits in the garden and the grain on the field.

Signal Hill rises up beyond Opoho, and as the ascent is easy, and the road in fair condition, its summit can easily be reached, and a magnificent view of land and water, hill and dale, be obtained. But if the energies have been sufficiently taxed, turn to the left, and soon the North East Valley is reached, the spot in which most of the early settlers made their first suburban selection, and which is now constituted a borough of the same name. Here the tram-car will convey the passenger up the Valley to the old Port Chalmers road, and on the ride, both up and down, some nice scenic views will be obtained, the murmuring brook and the crested mount alike demanding a share of admiration.

Some of our prominent citizens have elected the Valley as the place of their abode, and have erected handsome mansions, with tastefully laid out gardens and orchards.

This Valley, forty years ago, was a dense forest. There was not a single acre of clear ground throughout its length and breadth, so that judging from this fact alone, the mighty change which has passed over the scene may, to some extent, be realized. The clearance has not been effected without great labour and considerable cost. Add to this the fact that a large number of the early settlers were as little acquainted with bush work and tree-felling as dwellers in town usually are, and the traveller may form some idea of the magnitude of the labour involved.

IX.—CORSTORPHINE TO TAIERI MOUTH.

As our purpose is to show our friends the best of everything we possess, our proposal is that starting from Dunedin, on horseback or in buggy, we pass through the village of Caversham, and half way up Look-out Point take the road leading by Corstorphine to upper Green Island. The approach cannot boast of much beauty, but when once the hill is fairly gained, the panorama is grand indeed.

The vast expanse of restless ocean, the capacious harbour, the long stretch of coastline from the far north to the Nuggets, the numerous indentations and promontories, half-covered reefs and sea-girt rocks, sandy beaches and beetling cliff, city and suburbs, seaport and shipping, hills, dales, and mountains, the varied foliage of the native bush and the contrasting hues of introduced plants, herds and flocks, imposing mansions and sod huts, and a hundred other objects which meet the eye, bestow an interest on the locality which very few other districts can excel. Nature's lap has been filled to overflowing with gems of rarest loveliness, and is it to be wondered at that amid scenes like these the goddess of poetry should have enwrapped so many of her favourites in the mantle of her genius? Even prosaic individuals could hardly fail to draw inspiration from such abundant resources. The fact has been somewhere recorded that the rhymester who first felt the afflatus was a resident here; at all events volumes of poetry have issued from the Dunedin press, indited by local celebrities. One of the earliest efforts was thus expressed to Otakau :—

> " Land of the laurel and pine-circled glade,
> Land of the fern and evergreen shade,
> Isle of mild beauty in midst of the sea,
> What island in sweetness is equal to thee ? "

We are passing through changeful country in name as well as in character. The first surveyors called it Ocean Beach District, then the largest proprietor, Mr. Sidey, whose residence we see on the hillside, named it Corstorphine, after his birth-place, near Edinburgh, which name it now bears. From the summit, looking towards the east, a splendid view of the Peninsula, the harbour, the mainland, and a portion of the city is obtained. In front is the mansion of Mr. Cargill, appropriately named The Cliffs, as it stands almost on the brink of a precipice, 320 feet in height, with White and Green Islands lying close in shore ; whilst the ocean, calm this morning as a mirror, displays its vast bosom to the rays of the heat-giving sun in all his unclouded splendour. The southern coast-line shows the course we propose to follow, and will then have special notice. Turning inland, the Kaikorai Valley lies before us, stretching up to Wakari, and having its surface dotted with numerous factories, the homes of divers thriving industries. At the head of the Valley, and in the Borough of Roslyn, are Bone, Flax, and Flock Mills, and most notable, the Roslyn Woollen Mills, well worthy

the inspection of the visitor, which the spirited owners, Messrs.
Ross and Glendining, will readily grant. Immediately opposite
another extensive Woollen Factory is at work, being a branch of
the Mosgiel establishment. Lower down the Valley, which has
all been surveyed into townships, are the chemical works of
Kempthorne and Prosser's Co'y., adjoining which are the Cattle
Sale Yards and the Refrigerating Company's premises. Then
further down the Valley, along the main road, lie numerous wool
scouring establishments, the iron bolling mills of Smellie
Bros., a large soap and candle factory, tanneries, and a couple
of flour and oatmeal mills. Coal mining, brick and cement
making, and several other industrial pursuits, find a habitation
along the line of this Valley, which has received and deserves the
name of the principal industrial centre in our Province.

Splendid views are had of the mountain scenery. Starting
from Saddle Hill, the grand faithful sentinel standing as outer-
guard, and passing along the Chain Hills, we rise to Flagstaff,
the inner-guard, flanked by the Silver Peaks, so named from their
colour; while in the distance rises the Lammerlaw, seemingly
running into the Rock and Pillar Range, with their slightly snow-
streaked peaks peering out as if part of the clouds, and nearer at
hand stands Maungatua himself, backed up by the Lammerlaw,
and its remarkable stone, surveying now smilingly and anon
frowningly everything above, around, and beneath him.

Even when this survey is taking place, the horses are moving
onwards, and after a sudden and somewhat rapid descent, for
which a good brake and steady cattle are indispensable, the sea
level may be regained; but to avoid unnecessary risk of being
bogged and stuck, although at the loss of the sight, "o' some
bonnie spots," the driver will take a little longer route and reach
the road from Green Island Borough, celebrated for its hams and
bacon, by an easier gradient, proceeding thence smoothly and
comfortably along, and crossing the bridge over the Kaikorai
stream, we are fairly on the high road to Boat Harbour, re-
christened Brighton. A well-sheltered little harbour it is, where
safe places for bathing can be selected, and in moderate weather
the pleasures of boating and fishing can be indulged in; and as
the country around has plenty attractions for riding, walking, or
collecting specimens, Brighton has many of the requirements of a

watering place, to which dignity it may some day attain in the distant future.

At Brighton there is a good country accommodation house, where a plain, substantial repast can be obtained, and the water is first-class. Here, too, a pre-arrangement can be made for a change of horses, as the journey going and coming is rather too severe a tax on the willing steeds.

The farthest away headland within the range of vision is the Nugget Point, south of the Clutha River, which is so prominent as to shut out everything beyond from view. Nearer at hand the Wangaloa stream empties itself into the sea, and still carrying the eye northward, Quoin Point and the Tokomairiro River, with its small island rock, can be descried, and passing Akatore we see the Taieri Mouth, which is the limit of our journey. Having arrived at the south bank of the river, whilst the horses are having a spell, the man in charge of the punt, who is one of the oldest residents in the Province, will convey us safely across to the opposite side for a trifle, and, if inclined to listen, will tell some reminiscences of the past, interesting in the extreme. We are now landed on the north side of the Taieri, where a few scattered houses can be seen. This is called the Township of Hull, at present, and likely long to remain, in embryo, although the discovery of a large deposit of the black oxide of manganese may add a few souls to its present limited population. Looking up the river and on its overhanging hills on both sides, new and distinct sources of enchantment will be opened up to view, whose attractions will be visited on our next excursion.

But we must retrace our steps, so coming back to Brighton the return journey to Dunedin should be varied by taking the main south road up the Kaikorai Valley instead of the way we came. By so doing an easier route is obtained, and we pass close to nearly the whole of the busy industrial hives which we saw from the top of the upper Green Island on the beginning of our journey.

Leaving Green Island Borough behind, we pass these various works in rapid succession till we reach the top of Look-out Point, and after a glimpse is obtained of the Industrial School, we descend quickly through the Caversham Valley, and passing the now unoccupied Immigration Barracks and the

Benevolent Institution, we reach town in good time, and ready to
do justice to a well-appointed dinner.

X.—THE TAIERI RIVER.

In order to see the beauties of the lower reaches of the Taieri
River the visitor must take time by the forelock and be up and
ready for a start at 8 a.m., for at that pleasant hour of the
morning the only train which suits this excursion leaves Dunedin.

Starting with the morning train, after passing scenes
already noticed, and rushing through the Chain Hills
Tunnel, we suddenly emerge on the great Taieri Plain on its
eastern margin, which is certainly its poorest side, although the
first occupied by settlers, and are whirled along past Owhiro,
Greytown, and Otakia, we are safely deposited at Henley Station,
whence, after a short walk, just enough to put the joints all right
after our two hours' confinement, we reach the unpretending but
comfortable hostelry of Mr. Amos McKegg, where comforts of
every sort are to be obtained, and where, perhaps, the largest
apiary in the colony can be seen, with all the newest processes
certainly not for making, but for extracting the honey and saving
the wax.

The inspection of this industry is not our object, so we
embark on board the little steam launch, and gliding gently down
with the stream we pass the old Maori Kaik, whose inhabitants
have sadly diminished in numbers, and at a sudden bend, where
the Waihola, Waipori, and Taieri streams are confluent, we pass
beneath the East Taieri bridge, and gain the wide basin of the
tidal reaches of the river.

The screw, however, is propelling us along, and ere we quit
this fine land-locked sheet of water, we take a good look of the
Kuri Hills to the left and on the Beauly or Ferry Hills to the right,
and the conclusion is at once arrived at, that this is not
country fit for settlement. Nor is it. Nor are we on the out-
look for flat and profitable country. We came for and we want
scenery. The strong arms of the second occupants have denuded
the hill sides of their bush, and the bare surface is exposed to
view, a comfortable homestead or cottage dotting the surface here
and there, everything indicating peace and comfort. Unless the
thought arises, How can people make a living out of such land as

this? But be satisfied, critical visitor, many have on this same seemingly and really wild spot thriven and become prosperous.

We need not linger on this theme, as our mission is to view the wild grandeur of this river, towards which the steamer steadily bears us. In front rises a bluff—a bold projecting rock, which seems to arrest the further progress of the river, as, in days long past, it doubtless did, but now, after a long struggle, it has had to succumb and allow the water to make its way over its hard breast, wearing it down, until now the river course is deep enough to float half a dozen of the largest ships in the world.

Onward the river glides, winding through a narrow gorge in the hills which rise on either hand, now well-nigh precipitously, anon more gently, from the water's edge, the grey and forbidding aspect of their weather-beaten cliffs contrasting well with the softer hues of the stunted native bush, which clothes many a steep slope with a mantle of green; while in the hollows and ravines the trees attain a larger growth, and from beneath their friendly shelter the tree-ferns look out upon the swiftly-flowing stream. So sinuous is the course of the river that reach after reach presents the appearance of some lovely lakelet, till we arrive at the turning point, when another hill-encircled sheet of water meets our view. Proceeding onward, we at length reach a point where the hills recede and sandy shores intervene, with a rocky island seemingly shutting out the sea. This is our destination, and we steam slowly alongside a jetty and moor the launch.

This river was once the highway for the early settlers in the Taieri and Tokomairiro, who, instead of having our easy means of locomotion, were obliged to take ship in an open whale-boat from Dunedin or Port Chalmers, and after a passage of sometimes twelve hours, at other times some days, they reached the Taieri Mouth, and camping for a night or two under a cabbage-tree, proceeded up the river with the tide, and ultimately reached their destination by this toilsome and round-about route.

But these reminiscences are out of place here, though they were evoked by a question as to the use of the jetty or platform near which we lie. It was erected by the Provincial Government, who attempted to make this a landing-place for goods consigned to the Tuapeka Diggings, when roads were not, and in those days a steamer used to trade between Dunedin and the river mouth.

After a short halt the ship is put about, and we now steam back again up the river, getting another, and perhaps a finer view than on the passage down. To the casual visitor the names of each particular hill or promontory are not of much interest; the general or prevailing features are all he cares for, and in sailing upwards new views are disclosed.

Facing us now is that beetle-browed precipitous point, whose back we saw in coming down stream, but which now openly asserts its pre-eminence against all assailants. And it has a tale to unfold. Where was there ever a weird spot like this, to which some incident was not attached? And the wilder the country, and the more rugged the inhabitants, the more romantic would be the tale.

The steamboat is brought to a standstill whilst the narrative is told by the captain.

It was a beautiful summer evening, and the declining sun, glancing through the tops of the trees, cast a golden reflection on the smooth waters of the Waihola Lake, and rested on the form of a young girl, who was reclining on its banks on a rude couch of dry grass, beneath a large fern-tree, whose noble fronds almost touched a small canoe which was made fast close to the shore.

A richly-coloured mat fell in graceful folds to her feet, and was fastened below her shoulder by a large knot of purple flax, while her splendid dark tresses were interwoven with the wild vine and convolvulus. Her dark eyes sparkled with pleasure as the branches were heard to rustle, and a tall, handsome young man approached her. He was deeply tattooed, and his spear, the axe in his girdle, and his massive earrings, proclaimed by their curious carving that he was a man of some importance in his tribe.

Sitting down beside her, they conversed familiarly; but alas! they knew not that from a tree close beside them a man—who from the fiendish hate displayed in his face might have been mistaken for a demon—was listening to all they said.

Every now and then he poised his spear, as if about to throw it; and at length, just as the lovers were about to step into the canoe, he threw it with such deadly aim and force that it completely transfixed the youth, then springing from his hiding-place, he laid hold of the girl, and with a peal of savage laughter, pointed to the bleeding corpse, and with one blow of his tomahawk cleft her head; and the flowers which at sunset had bound her hair, the first beams of the rising morn beheld steeped in her life's blood.

Pursued by the vengeance of the tribes, who were exasperated by the violation of the sacred *tapu* in the murder of their gallant chieftain and the loveliest maiden in the pa, the murderer was hunted from place to place, ultimately taking refuge in a hollow tree on the spur leading to that cliff on the river side. Discovered in this his last retreat, he was pursued to the top of yonder precipice. His enemies were close behind him; there were no means of escape. He knew that if he were taken, the most horrid tortures awaited him; he preferred risking the leap and trusting to the river. With a wild unearthly shriek, he sprang from the top, but striking the rock in his descent, he fell into the water a mangled corpse. From that circumstance the cliff derives its name of the Maori Leap.

This is the tradition handed down from generation to generation of the dusky race, and communicated, in the first years of the settlement, to one of the earliest settlers, who faithfully transcribed it, and so it has been handed down, probably with emendations, to our own times.

" Time and tide for no man bide," so having breathlessly listened, the engine gives a shriek and a puff, and we are away from these memories of the past, hurrying on to the hotel at Henley to obtain some refreshment, and wait for the Invercargill Express, by which in due time Dunedin is reached.

Note.—The origin of the name of the promontory known as " the Maori's Leap," here given, is that " with emendations " which has long been current in the district : but the Rev. J. W. Stack, in his " Traditional History of the South Island Maoris," tells a much more pleasing and romantic story. (Transactions N.Z. Institute, vol. x. pp. 83, 84.) The passage is as follows :— " Tukiauau, who escaped with his son and a few followers, separated from the main body of fugitives and went down to the Waihora (now Waihola) Lake, where he built a pa. While there his son, Koroki Whiti, made the acquaintance of Haki Te Kura, the daughter of a chief whose pa stood at the mouth of Taiari (Taieri.) This maiden, unknown to her friends, used to meet her lover on the sands when the tide was low, and these clandestine meetings continued up to the time of Tukiauau's departure further south ; for hearing rumours of Ngai Tahu's movements, he became alarmed and determined to place himself beyond pursuit. Accordingly he abandoned his pa at Waihora, and embarked with his followers in a large war canoe. As they were passing below her father's pa, Haki Te Kura, eager to join her lover, jumped off the cliff into the water, but in doing so either fell upon a rock or on the edge of the canoe and was killed. Tu Wiri Roa, overwhelmed with grief and rage, swore to destroy the man who was the cause of his daughter's death." This vow he some time afterwards fulfilled by slaughtering not only Koroki Whiti, but all his party whom he surprised at Rakiura, now Stewart Island.—Ed.

XI.—LEITH VALLEY AND WATERFALLS.

By most people, a journey up and down this sequestered dell is considered one of the most enjoyable around the city. It is not now so lovely a grove as it was in days of yore, when the dense bush was penetrable only to the more intrepid of the citizens, and even to them, for a good portion of the way, the margin or bed of the creek was the only traversable spot, shut in as it were on to the sides of wood-clad precipices and steeps, along which progress could, with the utmost difficulty, be made even with the aid of the branches of the overhanging trees. To walk, drive, or ride, is now at the option of the visitant. In many respects the natural beauties have been considerably marred by the encroachments of the settlers, who are studded thickly along almost the entire route ; in other respects, the prospect has been opened up by removal of the timber, so that a much more extensive range is exposed to the vision, still a sufficient number of the romantic attractions remain, and will continue to the end to exist, fully entitling this valley to a place in the front rank among our picturesque delights.

The traveller may leave Dunedin by the coach, which for a modest fare takes him close up to the Waterfall, which forms an interesting feature in the scenery of the valley. Before reaching this spot, however, he will pass through the Town Belt, on which will be presented to view the first saw and flour mill, erected in the Province in 1850 ; not exactly the identical building, for it has undergone many enlargements as well as mutations, but the present building occupies the same site, and the same motive-power is used.   The portion of the borough of Maori Hill, which we enter after crossing the Belt, where we escape from the jurisdiction of the city magnates, was called by its first purchaser Woodhaugh, and in the course of years a very extensive trade was done at the saw mills, which, as the remains will show, dotted the valley along the river course, but their occupation, if not in every case like Othello's—gone, is very nearly so.   The Woodhaugh Paper Mills, the first which were established in the Colony, are situated at the bend of the river crossing, where the road leads off from the main road by the side of the creek to the Dunedin original Waterworks.

From this point the road follows the centre of the valley, and here will be seen the effect produced by disturbance of the ground in removing the timber.   A few years ago, during a continuance of wet weather, the Leith stream became so great in its volume and impetuous in force as to tear down its shingly banks, spread over the narrow valley, and form for itself new channels where it had never flowed before. So great was the havoc committed to both the county and borough works, as well as to those of private individuals, as to cause the better filled purse of the Colonial Treasurer to be invoked to have the damages to bridges and roads repaired.

We soon pass an old totara tree, which has for centuries occupied its position, a grand specimen of the kind in its day, and now, even with its broken limbs and noble trunk, a picturesque object, though degraded to the condition of being the bearer of a municipal notice board, instead of being carefully and zealously protected.   If the visitor is an artist, it will be hard to drag him beyond this hallowed spot, and when the eye has taken in and recorded all the special points of beauty and interest here to be observed, it will not be long before the pencil of the admirer will be busy in recording his impressions in a more enduring form. But without such artificial aids to memory when our journey has been completed, contemplation and reflection will enable us to realise the truth of the words of the ploughman bard :—

> " Still o'er these scenes, my memory wakes
> And fondly broods with miser care ;
> Time, but the impression deeper makes,
> As streams their channels deeper wear."

NICOL'S CREEK WATERFALL.

If, however, we are to loiter, no not loiter, but dwell on points of marvellous beauty which ravish us at every turn of the road, it will be quite twelve months before we get back to our starting point. Just cast the eye downward for a moment to the gurgling brook, its crystal waters now dashing into foam over some rocky impediment, or with calm and sullen face o'er-covering some old obstruction, which at a long antecedent date made a powerful but futile effort to stop its current. A little bend may show some laughing children disporting themselves in the shallow stream, and not far from them a waiting, watchful angler plying his art over some pool, where he knows the speckled trout love to congregate, while, as a mantle of green overhanging them, the native bush spreads its curious limbs and varied foliage to shelter from the too piercing rays of the mid-day sun. The picture is completed by those almost sheer cliffs, wherein, not whereon, trees of mighty stature have obtained a holding by simply penetrating and wedging their at first tiny rootlets into any rent or crack which unseen to mortal eye existed, and from whence these trees have for ages drawn sustenance, from which the eye rises to the clear blue vault above.

Onwards and upwards we pass, through glades or along embankments, and the vista becomes more fascinating at every turn, until at length, after a four-mile drive, "too pleasant to have expired so soon," the confluence of Nicol's Creek is gained. It is so called because a gardener of that name had bought a section, on which to graze his stock, on the hillside above, through which the creek ran. Perhaps as on his ground the burn had its source, he claimed the parentage.

Be that as it may, the visitor alighting from the vehicle may, if in season, regale himself with strawberries and cream before essaying the climb which lies before him. Now refreshed with the momentary gratifications, up the creek is the word. Devastations, irreparable and uncalled for are noticed on every side.

Let it be borne in mind that thirty years ago human foot had scarcely trod this sacred spot, where, in its deep solitudes, those gems of beauty, ferns—the exquisite Hymenophillums, Adiantums, Lomarias, Cyatheas, Dicksonias, Alsophillas, and others—were scattered in great profusion. Time would fail to recount their graces, and to express the regrets that the habitats, of which they were the fit adornment, now bear but faint and few traces of their existence. Still the eye and hand of the diligent can discover and secure mementoes of the former glories.

The distance up to the first Waterfall is about half a mile, and on the road up, by way of the creek bed, a passage is made between precipitous rocks, rising on each side, leaving only a narrow way between, the sides of the cleft being decorated by the hand of nature with a covering of ferns and mosses. At length the fall is reached, and as the quantity of water in the summer after dry weather is comparatively small, it may, at first sight, be to many disappointing, but as it drops over a face about 30 feet in height, which is covered with mosses of the finest green, it possesses beauties of its own, and on a hot summer's day it conveys a suggestion of coolness, not afforded by a more turbulent stream. After a fresh, however, the volume of the stream is of considerable magnitude, rising, as it does, from a rift in the side of old Flagstaff itself, and gathering its waters from a considerable water-shed above. A little period of rest and dalliance is generally indulged in here, admitted by all to be extremely pleasant. This over, those so disposed can tackle the ascent, not very difficult, and reach the upper falls, four in number, one of which is considered by some finer than the lower, and all of them derive a charm from the fact that the bush above is still almost in possession of its virgin beauty.

On reaching the summit the explorer can either follow the creek up to its source, and from thence along the mountain side and reach Dunedin by way of Halfway Bush, or, if this route be too long, a shorter one can be taken across country, bringing him to the Reservoir, previously alluded to, whence, reaching Woodhaugh, he may join the coach for the return journey, or he may deviate at the Reservoir and come along a very pleasant line to Maori Hill, from thence descending through the Belt, down past Cosey Dell to George street.

But it will not do to leave those at the Waterfalls who desire to go further in country, so returning to the conveyance, if it be a specially hired one, the traveller may proceed along a road of easy grade and good condition still further up the valley. The vistas opened up at every turning in this the county of

Waikouaiti, (for we have left municipalities behind us), show something ever changing, ever new, both on the right hand and on the left, all of them tempting enough to induce a stoppage in the journey, with a view of going up some of those tempting purling brooks, hopeful that in some dark spot on the downward career some rare specimen may be obtained, to be treasured as a memory of one of the most delightful excursions which can be enjoyed. The horses are a little anxious, however, so onward is the order, and in due time the apex or saddle is reached, near the head waters of the Leith and the Waitati streams, each taking their several ways to the ocean.

We now propose to follow downward the Waitati, after having surveyed the mountains around, Flagstaff, Silver Peaks, and the Hummock. The road is very tortuous, and there are several points of divergence, so that it were well that the guide knew the locality. Many of the places indicated in the Peninsula drive are seen here closer at hand, but not more effectively, so need not be re-enumerated. A short run brings us down to Blueskin Bay, where at the Saratoga Hotel some refreshment can be had before commencing to re-ascend.

A very good view of the line of railway can be had from Waitati, standing at sea level, whence the gradients, both north and south, are stiff and the curves sharp, neither, however, so much so as to prevent the powerful engines dragging the heavy freight upwards, or to incur over ordinary risk in turning the corners. To the north stands Seacliff Asylum, which provides a home where those afflicted with the most terrible calamity which flesh is heir to, can and do receive the humanest treatment which the most modern experience can suggest. To those interested in the question of insanity, the best mode of visiting the Asylum is to proceed by train. On the line to the south the bluff at the edge of the bay shows when the cliffs up to Mapotaki begin, and which for a time were passed along with no slight degree of terror on the part of the more timid passengers. Experience has proved, however, that the roadway is as safe as the most level part of the line, and a tunnel has recently been formed, through which the travellers escape passing what was deemed the worst part by the timorous.

On our way homeward, by the main Dunedin road, the first objects of interest seen and passed are the buildings intended for ' Orakanui College," at the mouth of the creek of the same name, which was started as a private enterprise, but being too heavily handicapped by the opposing endowed institution, it soon ceased to exist as a school. Close by is the Reserve, conferred on the district for agricultural shows, and not far off is the inevitable cemetery, containing the remains of one of Dunedin's well-known and highly esteemed citizens, James Marshall, to perpetuate whose memory the Jockey Club have instituted the " Marshall Memorial Stakes." In this connection it may be mentioned that the Blueskin races are held on the sands within the area of the bay, but the course, said to be a fine one, is only visible when the tide goes out. This circumstance recalls to the mind of the guide that on the far off corner of the land to the north of the bay is the country residence of the Hon. George M'Lean, M.L.A. and President of the Dunedin Jockey Club, as well as Chairman of the Colonial Bank and Union Steam Ship Company, one of the most genial and truest-hearted citizens our colony possesses.

For a time the road traverses ordinary-looking country, skirting the outline of Mount Cargill on the right, which was a dense forest of splendid totara some years ago, but now thoroughly denuded, until the junction with the Port Chalmers road is reached, and coming down hill into the North East Valley some of the choicest views of Dunedin and its surroundings are to be obtained. In fact, so highly appreciated was this line in former days, that visitors of note were driven by it into town, so that its attractiveness might be fully displayed. Down the hill we come now at a brisk pace, and passing along through the main street or road of North East Valley Borough, which, practically speaking, is the only level street within its bounds. The city is soon entered by the Leith Bridge, the point of departure, and each wends nis homeward way after a delightful day's excursion, through scenes of rare beauty, of about thirty miles.

XII.—OUR PLAIN.

What dweller in the South Sea Colonies, and even much farther afield, has not heard of the Taieri Plain ? Agriculturists, in particular, and those interested in the industry, may have noted the extraordinary yield of cereals obtained, the weight and quality of its oxen and sheep, and the superior excellence of its cheese and butter.

That long, wide stretch of land, forty years ago reckoned an irreclaimable swamp, fit only to be gazed on and moaned over, is now one of the grandest sights, as an agricultural and pastoral district, anywhere to be witnessed. 'Tis a transformation indeed, not yet altogether completed, however, as owners, either impecunious or absentee, have left specimens of what was the original swamp in a modified degree, for improvements have been effected by the labour and expenditure of neighbours, of which the drones gain the benefit. The labour, skill, and cash expended, have been enormous, but the return has, in most instancs, justified the outlay.

A good view of the Plain can be easily had from the top of any of the surrounding hills, Saddle Hill or (Maori) Pikawara, by way of preference, from which a bird's-eye-view can be had from north to south and east to west. To those who want more than a superficial view, it will be necessary to descend into the Plain itself and traverse its different road and rail lines. Already, in going up to the Taieri wilds, we have skirted the North Taieri District and seen the splendid farms of Messrs. Andrew, Shaw, Gow, Gibson, Oughton, Thompson, Gawn, and many others ; and then on another journey to the river, along the east district, the celebrated farm of the Grange might have been observed, whose owner's name, Nimmo, stands prominent in more than one department, as well as those of Cullen, Allan, Dowrie, Callander, Stevenson Brown, and many more in close succession ; whilst on the other hand lie farms showing the results of the labours of Smith, Cooper, Todd, Kirkland, Law, McKay, Sutherland, Blackie, Prain, and Charters, some of whom are still to the fore, and in their quiet contemplative moments laugh at the difficulties which their youthful successors have to surmount in comparison with those of over a quarter of a century ago, which they themselves encountered and overcame.

There is undoubtedly a great contrast between the comfortable, yea elegant houses of these and other farmers basking in the sun, surrounded with arbours, gardens, and orchards, and the old time sod or clay whare or weather-board " but and ben," which constituted the whole family apartments ; between the comfortable and pleasant now, with the less comfortable, but not less happy then.

To get a fair and satisfactory view of the Plain, our route must be to the west side. The east is steep, broken, and thin in depth of soil; the north is, to a large extent, shingly; the west and centre are decidedly the cream of the country. So having left Dunedin with the first train, or perhaps better, the Outram train, at 9.20, we pass through the classic Mosgiel, now devoted to industries of various descriptions, most prominent of which are the woollen factories, well worthy a passing call, and where machinery is in operation for carding, spinning, weaving, and carrying out all other processes requisite to produce fabrics of different descriptions and in every variety of pattern and colour, unsurpassed by any other manufacturing locality in the world. These woollen and worsted goods are all produced from wools grown in the colony. No raw material from foreign parts is needed, everything is from our soil, by way of the sheep's back to the loom, and shoddy is not to be found.

Resuming our journey across the Plain, we pass through the farms of the Findlays, Reid, Boyd, Thomson. And here it may be asked why the name Duke's Road Station was bestowed? It arose from the circumstance that His Royal Highness the Duke of Edinburgh, who honoured the district with a visit in 1869, drove along this road four-in-hand and officially declared it open. To commemorate the event, the name of Duke's Road was bestowed. In connection with this little historical episode, another event connected with the district may be related. On the Silverstream course the first great New Zealand Champion Race was run, under the management of the Otago Jockey Club, for a prize of one thousand sovereigns, with sweepstakes, which was gained by the Victorian "Ladybird," the time being 5 min. 52½ sec., distance 3 miles.

We now enter the grand farm land of the Plain, owned or occupied by such familiar names as MacFarlane, Anderson, Carmichael, Buchanan, until the train stops at the celebrated estate of Abbotsford, carried on by its first owner with wonderful energy and enterprise, but with such a lack of prudence and discretion as to bring him to disaster. A large proportion of this estate was recently sold by auction at prices ranging up to £31 per acre.

Reaching the small township of Outram, where the railway terminates, before partaking of a slight repast a little time can be delightfully spent in a stroll to the West Taieri Bridge, where the river emerges from the gorge, little in bulk at present, but at times of great magnitude, overflowing its banks, covering the lower portions of the Plain, causing immense devastation and destruction. Councils and Boards have been created to do their best to keep the old river within bounds, and they have exerted their utmost skill in this direction, but a flood comes and the puny efforts are swept away by the raging element. It is to be hoped better results will be obtained in the future.

Maungatua shows his immensity, towering away above, 2,944 feet, and stretching miles away before us. For the purpose of getting a better view, instead of driving along its base by Woodside, we keep the road line further out on the Plain, and pass through lands of extraordinary fertility. We have the Grants of Gowrie, Granton, and Cray, Patrick, and Heenans, Hastie, Ford, Thompson, Gordon, McDiarmid, and all the rest of the numerous clansmen.

Laying aside all prejudice or preformed opinion, it may be safely asserted that in no part of the globe which we inhabit could the eye be regaled with the sight of finer crops of all descriptions than can here be seen. It could not indeed be otherwise. The soil is rich alluvium, of considerable depth, with excellent drainage. This season has been very favourable, and the general management of the various farms shows that the owners know their business and attend to it.

We are now at the border town, Berwick, and it has been well named, as at this point the level lands terminate, and to proceed further would take us into a hill country indeed. Not that the journey would be devoid of interest, contrariwise it is brim full thereof, but it is beyond our scope. We are also entering on a Lake District, as immediately in front lie Waihola and Waipori, with their swampy margins and fantastic outlines; and it should not be omitted that in this land of Scotchmen, where everything Scotch has been renewed, the only sheet of water bearing the name of " Loch " is here situated. Loch Ascog lies

quietly ensconced in a little hollow, and contrasted with its-
neighbours hardly deserves the name. The Waipori River has
its source away back among the mountains in the Traquhair
Hundred, and like its greater mate—the Taieri—causes the
settlers considerable anxiety at times. The road from Berwick
across the Plain is somewhat tortuous, caused by the creeks and
pools which are encountered. Water fowl of different species are
abundant, and in the close season are comparatively tame. On the
road the changeful scenes opened up at every few paces will
delight the eye and fancy of all observers. Hardly anything
could be suggested as lacking. Nature's handiwork and human
artifice are wonderously displayed, and on reaching Henley, on
the east side, where the train for town is taken, the feeling is-
experienced that the time has passed too speedily.

XIII.—THE SILVERSTREAM VALLEY.
(By G. H. Turton).

This lovely valley may be visited either by walking, riding,
or driving, although the last-mentioned cannot be recommended,
as the road is very steep and rough in some places.

Leaving the terminus of the Roslyn Extension Tramway, we
pass down to the left through the Kaikorai Valley, and on up the
steep slope on the other side to the Halfway Bush. After passing
the Halfway Bush Hotel, a very primitive road may be noticed
on the right side of the main road, leading towards Flagstaff.
About half a mile further on, the road, which has all this time
been ascending, reaches the top of the ridge and begins to descend
into the Taieri Plain. We need not dwell on the fair prospects
spread before us at various points along the route, as they have
probably been already visited in some other excursion; but
their beauty never palls, though reiterated attempts at description
would doubtless do so. As we continue our descent we notice
a large water-race, which comes winding round the face of the
hill, and diving underneath the road, stretches away in the
direction of Dunedin. This is the race which conveys water to
one of the Dunedin reservoirs from the Silverstream, a distance
of about twenty miles. Another half a mile on our road takes
us to the bridge over the Silverstream. We do not cross this,
however, but turn up to the right and follow a track which leads

along the left bank of the stream. Passing over some grassy flats we come to several clumps of kowhai or goai trees, which in early spring bear quantities of large yellow flowers, to sip the honey from which the tuis gather round from far and near, and make the air melodious with their music. The track we are following, which is nothing more than a dray track used for bringing firewood to the farms situated lower down the stream, now crosses the stream once or twice; but as the water is shallow, there is no difficulty in doing this. As we go on our way, the mountains on either hand become higher. On the left rises Chalky Hill, and on the right we see the back of Mount Flagstaff, over the shoulder of which we have to climb to reach town. After crossing the stream for the fourth time, the road branches. We take the right hand branch, and leaving the Silverstream behind us we pass up a pretty wooded gully, down which flows a small branch of the main stream. The left hand side of the gully is covered with dense bush, in which birds of various species disport themselves. About half a mile further on the road again branches, and this time we take the left hand branch, and begin to ascend. A little way up we again cross the reservoir water-race, and after a stiff pull up the hill we arrive at the highest point, whence we descend, in a short time arriving at the main road, close to Mr. Hume's asylum; thence we return to town as we came. For anyone who enjoys a good long walk, there is no more pleasurable excursion in the neighbourhood of Dunedin, for in the romantic valley of the Silverstream we find a fair wilderness where mountain, wood and stream combine to form picture after picture to delight the eye.

XIV.—THE HARBOUR.

Call it what you will—a river, harbour, a bay, an estuary, a firth, or by whatever name it may be known, the fact remains that up or down that basin of water there are gorgeous views to be obtained. A sheet of water, at first apparently circumscribed, but as we move on some new prospect opens up which tells the end is not yet. Turning that point, rounding this sandbank, between these islands, where it were hard to tell where the opening lies, the progress of the boat discloses bays and harbours,

each different in shape, with winding approaches, so that the
visitant wonderingly exclaims, Where is the pilot going to take
us next?

All is right, however, the man at the wheel knows his duty,
and is devoted to it, and so long as a hundred passengers, or
thereabout, do not speak to him at once, he will keep the good
vessel right. So along we spin, take the long or the short channel,
it only makes a difference in time, and if the steamer go by one
water-way and return by the other, all objects of interest will be
seen. The great advantage is to have a thoroughly well-posted-
up skipper or guide to tell the lore of ancient times : how on this
side Black Jack's Point got its name, how across the water Grant's
Braes came to be celebrated, and as the course outward is sped,
how Burke's brewery on the one side, was celebrated once for the
now exceeding excellence of its brews, and for the energy and
enterprise which the owner always manifested in developing the
resources of the Province ; and to point out on the other side
Macandrew's Bay ; as well as to guide us through the intricacies of
the channels, for, as the fates would have it, boats drawing two
feet of water could sail across the bay at high tide, whilst at ebb
the pedestrian could make seven-eighths of the journey almost
dry shod, to find at the end of his mile journey that his stature
must grow to 16 or 18 feet before he can cross the few yards
yet to be accomplished, unless he were a powerful swimmer,
and able to stem the current.

How can the steamer get through or between these
rocks and hills ahead ? Easily, it will be found, because there is
a deep water fair-way between the islands, which the pilot knows
well.

And now through the Narrows, Port Chalmers, with its not
very busy, but picturesque appearance, unfolds itself. Rounding
the point, on which the fishery establishment is situated, and
from which the best and purest cod liver oil in the world is
procured, we steam round Koputai Bay, formerly the rendezvous
of the natives on their journeys south or north.

Leaving this lovely spot, our propeller posts us on to the
Heads, past Carey's, Deborah, Hamilton's and Dowling Bays and
Otapelo Point. The remarkable thing about the latter name is

the presence of the letter " l," whilst Maori scholars tell us there is no such letter in the Maori language. Now, if the steamer is light enough in draught and the tide well up, we turn at Harrington Point, skirting the land past the Maori Kaik until we stretch into Portobello Bay, coming out again from this not very safe cove. Rounding the point, which, although the most prominent of the whole, has never had a name, and pass the Quarantine Island, we then sail along the coastline past Dunoon, round Broad Bay and Grassy Point, reaching the starting point in capital time.

Taking a retrospect of the pleasing scenes which in our voyage we have witnessed, different minds will call up different resemblances to scenes elsewhere, and contrasts and comparisons will be made, none of them to the disparagement of those we have contemplated. Scotchmen compare our harbour to the famed Kyles of Bute, Australians to some views in Sydney harbour, but the concurrent testimony is that a fairer view of nature's handi-work is rarely to be seen.

The change that has taken place, however, since the white man invaded the scene, must be considered. When the "Philip Laing," the ship, or rather barque, which bore the first settlers from the Clyde to this their distant and future home, cast anchor in Koputai Bay, there was only a whare or two at the Kaik, occupied by natives, some of them of high renown, as devoted friends to the Pakeha, who are elsewhere mentioned, and up at Koputai a few " Hielanmen " had settled down to traffic with the whaling visitors and with the natives. From shore to summit, on both sides, a dense carpet of foliage of varied and pleasing hue covered the whole face of the land, one or two spots alone being unclothed. The woods echoed with the notes of the native birds, and the water was dotted with the ungainly-looking shag, eager in its watch for its finny prey, and swift as a lightning dash to dive in pursuit. No smoke wreath issued from any spot indicative of human occupancy, silence reigned almost supreme, and the placid clear water, reflected as in a mirror its wooded surroundings. Viewed either at morn, noon, or eve, the scene was inexpressibly grand. It were a situation in which to realize the beautiful words of Young :—

> " Twilight I love thee, as thy shadows roll,
>   The calm of evening steals upon my soul!
>   Sublimely tender, solemnly serene,
>   Still as the moon, enchanting is the scene."

But how changed was it when aneath a sullen sky a fierce nor'-easter or sou'-wester disturbed the elements? The reader can realize that picture for himself.

CLIMATE AND METEOROLOGY.

In almost all parts of the world, especially in the temperate regions, the state of the weather is a matter of very considerable importance, and for certain reasons, which will possibly hereafter become apparent, it is rather remarkably so in Dunedin. Such being the case, any publication under the title of "Picturesque Dunedin" would seem to be incomplete without some reference, be it ever so slight, to the prevailing climatic influences of the locality.

Dunedin, as will be remembered, is situated in latitude 46° south (nearly), while London is in the latitude of 51½° N.; and it may therefore be expected that being more than five degrees nearer the equator than the latter city, a milder climate, favourable to out-door pursuits, and the growth of all kinds of produce, would be experienced. Nor is this expectation disappointed, for although the summer heat of Dunedin rarely rises above 80° Fah. in the shade, or 120° in the sun, the winter cold is also comparatively moderate, the thermometer seldom falling more than a degree or two below the freezing point; with the result, as given by the New Zealand Pilot for 1883, of a difference of three degrees in favour of Dunedin, on the average yearly temperature of 15 years.

The average rainfall in Dunedin is slightly less than that of London and the south of England, as given by the same authority, namely—about 33 inches per annum here to 36 inches in London; sufficient, but not too much for agricultural requirements.

The winds in Dunedin and environs are extremely regular and persistent, with only slight variations from either the north-east or south-west. In winter it is for the most part calm, with

an occasional gale from one or the other of those points of
the compass.

To learn what the soil and climate are capable of doing in
the way of garden produce, it is only needful to take a stroll into
the suburbs in any direction, when, behind the close-clipped
hedges—of hawthorn, laurel, macrocarpa, or holly—screening
many neat dwellings, trim, well-kept gardens will be seen to
present, from early spring to latest autumn, a bright display of
those flowering plants and shrubs proper to the season. Nor is the
fruit garden one whit behind : cherries, apples, pears, plums,
peaches, are successfully cultivated, and with somewhat less
success, nectarines and grapes ; and, of course, all kinds of currant
and gooseberry bushes, flourish and bear abundantly.

But notwithstanding the general mildness of our winter
season, there are occasional falls of snow—snowstorms they
cannot be called—which may lie on the ground in a thin layer of
one or two inches in thickness, on the shady side of unfrequented
streets, for a day, with probably one or two degrees of frost. This
being a Scotch colony, we have a Curling Club, the members of
which make frantic efforts on such occasions to enjoy their national
game. But they do so under difficulties, for, possibly with the
night's rain or the morrow's sun, the snow vanishes, the frost
breaks, and the sanguine curlers are disappointed.

There do not seem to have been any very authentic records
kept of the weather in Dunedin in the earlier years of the
colony—at all events they are not accessible ; but it is nearly
certain that for at least the last forty years no winter was more
severe than that of 1889, when the frost invaded many dwellings,
and icicles of considerable size formed in bath-rooms and elsewhere for several nights in succession. Neither is it recorded
that during any year so little rain fell and so much sunshine was
enjoyed, as was the case during the winter and spring months of
the same year. During the whole year only 17 inches of
rain were registered, evidently out of all proportion to the
average 33 inches.

It is not to be imagined that the climate has no weak points.
People are apt to complain that it is always raining in Dunedin.
This, of course, is a groundless complaint, seeing that the rain-

fall is so comparatively slight. It must be admitted, nevertheless, that rains are frequent, if for the most part light, and an umbrella is by no means a superfluous article; indeed some of our more careful citizens rarely venture abroad without either an umbrella or a mackintosh. July, August, and September have come to be recognised as the months during which the most continuous rains may be expected, but this is not without exceptions.

There are others, again, who, with more justice, complain of our frequent winds. These, no doubt, occasionally test the condition of our roofs to the utmost, and if coming in autumn, as they sometimes do, the fruit-trees suffer severely. November, December, March, and April are the months during which these unpleasant visitors perform their highest jinks and sing their loudest songs. But, after all, taking these disagreeables at their worst, they are only exceptional, while our usual light breezes are healthful and invigorating, driving away miasma and purifying the atmosphere.

To sum up: It was, perhaps, after all, not without some reason that Mr. Maccabe, when asked, after his first visit to our shores, what was his opinion of the climate, replied, "Climate! Dunedin has no climate—only mixed samples." But, at the same time, it will be seen on reference to the table on page 299 that even in the worst years there are considerably more than one-half of the days in almost every month in which no rain falls, and on many of the instances noted a fair proportion are probably only showers of brief duration.

To the admirer of cloudland scenery, the streets in the upper portions of Dunedin afford frequent opportunity for the gratification of his favourite hobby. The variable climate brings with it an almost continual recurrence of sunshine and shade. Comparatively few days are entirely clear. Now, a heavy cloud overarches almost the entire hemisphere, and threatens possibly an early rain. Anon, a slight breeze springs up; the cloud breaks into many portions; the sun shines out from a patch of blue nearly overhead. Now a long and narrow stretch of azure appears over the south-western horizon, and presently the dispersing clouds, assuming, meanwhile, the most fantastic shapes, which may be interpreted according to the drift of the beholder's imagination, as lions rampant, griffins, or eagles with wings outspread—as monstrous saurians or Milton's Apollyon, "lying many a rood," chase each other across the sky. Then the answering shadows flit past, as if in sportive humour, from the direction of the ocean, over the Peninsula, across the bay, and after showing themselves for a brief space on Signal Hill, vanish at length over the sloping sides of Mount Cargill.

The following table explains itself. It may be mentioned, however, that the thermometer used hangs in a passage, near the outer door (in the shade), and that the readings are taken at 9 a.m.

| | 1887. | | | 1888. | | | 1889. | | |
| | Rainfall. | | Thermometer average. | Rainfall. | | Thermometer average. | Rainfall. | | Thermometer average. |
	Days.	Inches.		Days.	Inches.		Days.	Inches.	
January	7	1·7	66	15	3·5	56	5	·7	66
February	5	2·3	66	6	2·1	55	1	·1	60
March	11	2·5	63	16	7·5	53	13	3	58
April	12	2·3	57	17	1·5	50	9	1·5	50
May	19	3·5	46	11	3·5	48	5	1·1	49
June	10	4·7	46	8	1·3	45	8	1·5	42
July	9	2·7	44	11	6	36	5	1·5	42
August	15	3	45	15	7·7	44	3	1.1	49
September	15	4·5	43	4	·7	41	8	1·5	42
October	12	4·5	52	7	2·7	50	6	1·5	42
November	10	2·5	53	15	3·5	52	9	1·5	50
December	10	2·5	57	10	2·5	55	5	1·5	58
Totals	135	36·7		135	42·5		77	17	
Average for year (fractions omitted)			53			48			51

BAROMETER. *

1887.

	Jan.	Feb.	Mar	Apl.	May	Jne.	July	Aug	Sep.	Oct.	Nov	Dec.
	In.	In.	In.	In.	In.	In.	In.	In.	In.	In.	In.	In.
Maximum ..	30·2	30·3	30·1	30·4	30·3	30·2	30·3	30·4	30·2	30·2	29·9	30·3
Minimum ..	29·6	29·2	29·6	29·5	29·2	29·2	29·1	29·4	28·7	28·9	29·3	29·2

1888.

	Jan.	Feb.	Mar	Apl.	May	Jne.	July	Aug	Sep.	Oct.	Nov	Dec.
Maximum ..	30·0	30·2	30·1	30·3	30·3	30·1	30·2	30·3	30·3	29·9	29·9	30·1
Minimum ..	29·0	29·3	28·7	29·2	29·3	29·2	29·0	29·2	29·6	29·1	29·1	29·1

1889.

	Jan.	Feb.	Mar	Apl.	May	Jne.	July	Aug	Sep.	Oct.	Nov	Dec.
Maximum ..	30·1	30·2	30·4	30·3	30·3	30·3	30·3	30·6	30·1	30·2	30·2	30·1
Minimum ..	29·4	29·4	29·2	29·5	29·4	28·8	29·5	29·1	29·3	29·1	23·6	29·3

* At 200 feet above sea-level.

HOTEL
THE LEVIATHAN
A. D. SILK
KERWITZ & NICHOLSON

THOMSON & CO.

►►►►FINE◄◄◄◄

Crystal Mineral Water,

——AND——

Cordial ‡ Manufacturer,

——DUNEDIN——

Wellington, Napier, Invercargill and Brunnerton.

MEDICAL TESTIMONY TO THE PURITY OF THOMSON & CO.'S SODA WATER.

Riverton, March 9, 1881.

GENTLEMEN,—I have on different occasions prescribed your Soda Water, and found it highly beneficial in some cases of stomach irritation.

W. NELSON, M.D.

———

White Hart Hotel,
Melbourne, 28th September, 1886.

MESSRS THOMSON & CO., Dunedin.

DEAR SIRS,—I have much pleasure in informing you that at your request I have placed your Ginger Ale alongside the best article made here, before competent judges, and that their opinion is decidedly in favour of your brand. I consider the quality superior to anything I have tasted, and I heartily wish you the success which so creditable a production merits.

WM. BIGNALL,
Lessee of the White Hart Hotel,
(Opposite Parliament Buildings, Melbourne.)

McLeod Brothers, Limited,

DUNEDIN.

Manufacturers of Soaps, Candles, Lubricating Oils, Glycerine, Essences, and Perfumery.

AND GOLD MEDAL CANDLES.

They are undoubtedly the best brands in the market, the Laundrine Soap being equally good for Toilet and Laundry purposes.

"LAUNDRINE" being our Registered Trade Mark the public are cautioned against imitations.

Our **PARAFFIN CANDLES** are equal in every respect to the imported brands.

Our Specially Prepared **SOFT SOAP** was used by Messrs Rowley and Hamilton, Avondale Station, Southland, for scouring their wool, which obtained a Gold Medal at the Paris Exhibition, 1889, and we have other numerous testimonials speaking in the highest terms of its superiority over that sold by other manufacturers.

Our **LUBRICATING OILS** give universal satisfaction for all kinds of Machinery, and are specially recommended by Messrs Reid and Gray and other large Manufacturers of Farming Implements.

We also manufacture **TOILET SOAPS AND ESSENCES** in great variety, which, by reason of their excellent quality and cheapness, are rapidly superseding the imported article.

McLEOD BROTHERS, LIMITED,

DUNEDIN.

THE GRAND HOTEL
PRINCES & HIGH STS., DUNEDIN, NEW ZEALAND

For Tourists, Family and Commercial Gentlemen, is situated in the most central and open position in the city. This Hotel, just erected, is built upon the most modern principles of hotel construction, and is probably the most elegant and substantial building of its kind in the Australasian Colonies. The Proprietors call special attention to the fact that at very great expense this building has been constructed of almost entirely fireproof material, thoroughly ensuring the safety of guests. Passenger Elevator, Rooms *en suite*, General Drawing Room, Sample Room, etc.

J. & J. WATSON, PROPRIETORS.

PROVIDENT & INDUSTRIAL
Insurance Co. of New Zealand.

(Registered under the "Companies' Act, 1882," in compliance with
the "Life Assurance Act, 1873," as a Company having
secured Assets in New Zealand.)

Head Office - High-st., Dunedin.

DIRECTORS:

A. BATHGATE, Esq. (Chairman).

C. F. GREENSLADE, Esq. | J. HORSBURGH, Esq.

Dr. W. S. W. ROBERTS.

Christchurch:

HENRY THOMSON, Esq. | S. MANNING, Esq.

INDUSTRIAL BRANCH.

Assures Persons of both sexes from 1 month to 60 years of Age.
Endowments payable during life.
Premiums collected at Assured's house weekly, fortnightly,
or monthly.
No medical examination for sums under £50.

PROVIDENT & MEDICAL BRANCH.

Assures Sick Pay, with Family Medical Attendance & Medicine.
Amounts payable on death of Husband or Wife.
Endowments payable during life.
Premiums collected at Assured's house Monthly or Quarterly.

No Entrance Fees.   No Charge for Policies.

❧KAITANGATA❧

Railway & Coal Company,

LIMITED.

KAITANGATA COAL.

The Special Qualities of the Kaitangata Coal are its

General Cleanliness

—AND—

ENTIRE ABSENCE OF DIRTY SMOKE,

Requiring no attention whatever once the fire is made, and house-holders who use it exclusively will no doubt recognise the

GREAT SAVING OF CONSTANT CLEANING & SWEEPING.

To mix it with other Coal scarcely gives it justice, and the Company recommend consumers to

USE IT ALONE,

when its full advantages can be realized.

Sold everywhere by all Coal Merchants
in Dunedin and Suburbs.

A FEW ADVANTAGES OF
THE DRESDEN
PIANOFORTE COMPANY'S
HIRE PURCHASE SYSTEM.

1st—No matter where you live, it enables you to become the owner of a thoroughly good and sound Pianoforte or American Organ by simply Paying the Hire for a stated period.

2nd—Possession is obtained on Payment of the First Monthly or Quarterly Instalment.

3rd—No Further Expense whatever is incurred beyond the instalments for the period agreed on.

4th—The Piano or American Organ can be exchanged for one of a Better Class at any time within the period of hiring.

5th—An excellent Piano or Organ (warranted for 10 years) can be obtained for a deposit of 30s and payment of 30s monthly.

6th—A First-class Guarantee is given with every Instrument purchased.

7th—Catalogues, Terms, &c., sent Post Free on Application.

►►►MUSICAL SUNDRIES.◄◄◄

Accordeons, Bagpipes, Chanter Reeds, Brass Instruments in great variety, Violins, Flutes, Piccolos, Concertinas, Metronomes, Insulators, Music Stools, Music Chairs, Music Canterburies, 'Cellos, Double Basses, &c.

SHEET MUSIC A SPECIALITY.

THE DRESDEN PIANO COMPANY'S DEPOT,
29 & 31 PRINCES STREET, DUNEDIN.

J. A. X. RIEDLE, Manager.

DONAGHY'S BINDER TWINES

We are making Three Classes of Twine this Season, viz:

1. Best Prize Medal Double Reeled Manilla

About 590 feet to the lb.

2. Second Quality Half Manilla and Half N. Z. Flax

About 530 feet to the lb.

About 460 feet to the lb; all of which have been passed through the CHECK NIPPER, tested to proper strength, and Double Reeled.

Having manufactured for the wholesale houses throughout the colony several hundred tons specially ticketed as required, there will be no uniform distinguishing brands to indicate our Twines, we therefore recommend farmers and others

When Asking for Donaghy's Twine

to be particular as to the **CLASS**, and in cases of supposed mistake send us a sample ball for inspection.

M. DONAGHY & CO.

OTAGO STEAM ROPE & TWINE WORKS,

DUNEDIN.

G. MUNRO & SONS,

—WHOLESALE AND RETAIL—

MONUMENTAL WORKS,

CORNER OF KING STREET & MORAY PLACE,

(Off George Street), DUNEDIN.

PLANS FURNISHED AND EXECUTED FOR ALL KINDS OF

Monuments, ‡ Tombstones, ‡ Tablets, ‡ &c.

IN GRANITE, MARBLE, OR STONE.

*MARBLE BATHS. BUSTS & MEDALLIONS CUT FROM PHOTOGRAPHS.
STATUARY IN GROUPS OR SINGLE FIGURES FOR HALLS
——OR PUBLIC BUILDINGS.——*

TOMB RAILINGS, ANY DESIGN.

The Best Quality of Oamaru Stone supplied in any quantity from their Quarries at
Kakanui on the Shortest Notice.   Large Stocks on Hand.

☞ INSPECTION INVITED.   THE TRADE SUPPLIED.

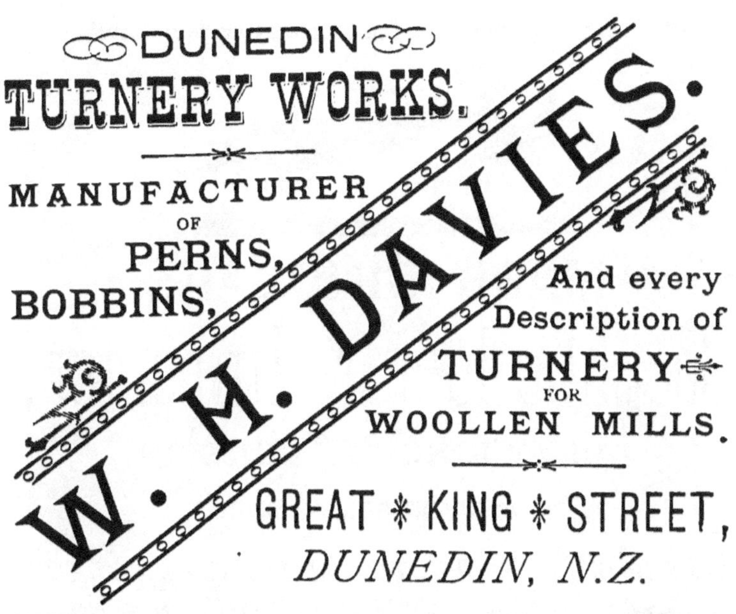

THE GENTLEMEN'S SHOP!

Outfitter and Gentleman's Mercer,

17 RATTRAY STREET, DUNEDIN.

DIRECT IMPORTER OF SHIRTS, HATS, BRACES, COLLARS,
TIES, GLOVES, SOCKS, HANDERCHIEFS, UMBRELLAS,
WATERPROOF COATS, GLADSTONE BAGS,
——PORTMANTEAUX, &c., &c.——

ALL GOODS MARKED IN PLAIN FIGURES AT LOWEST CASH PRICES.

Note the Address:

J. TAYLOR, 17 RATTRAY STREET, DUNEDIN.

ESTABLISHED 1869.

SPEIGHT & CO.,
CITY BREWERY,
DUNEDIN.

N. Z. & S. SEAS EXHIBITION.

AWARDS

Running Ales XXX	: First-Class Certificate.
Medium Ales XXXX	: First-Class Certificate.
Stout in Bulk	: First-Class Certificate.
Malt Bitter Ales	: Second Award.
Bottled Ales (bottled by J. Barron)	: Second Award.

FINEST SIGHT IN NEW ZEALAND.

BRAITHWAITE's BOOK ARCADE
50,000 BOOKS
TO CHOOSE FROM
PRINCES St. PRINCES St.
DUNEDIN

EVERYBODY

SHOULD

SEE IT.

IT

WILL REPAY

YOU.

EVERYBODY INVITED TO VISIT THIS WONDERFUL ESTABLISHMENT.

NO ONE ASKED TO BUY.

£15,000 to £20,000 worth of Novelties always on hand.

Mammoth Variety of Birthday and Marriage Presents.

As MR. BRAITHWITE buys from the Manufacturers and Publishers for cash, the Public get the benefit of all Home Discounts.

THIS IS WHY EVERYTHING IS CHEAPER AT B.B.A. THAN ELSEWHERE.

www.ingramcontent.com/pod-product-compliance
Lightning Source LLC
Chambersburg PA
CBHW021800110726
47902CB00006B/1597